FROZEN
SOULS

BOOKS BY RITA HERRON

FROZEN SOULS

RITA HERRON

bookouture

Published by Bookouture in 2021

An imprint of Storyfire Ltd.
Carmelite House
50 Victoria Embankment
London EC4Y 0DZ

www.bookouture.com

ISBN: 978-1-80019-873-9
eBook ISBN: 978-1-80019-872-2

To all the readers and fans who follow Ellie Reeves and ask for more of her story!

PROLOGUE

WILD HOG HOLLER

There was nothing more satisfying than watching a woman draw her last breath.

As he lay on the floor beside her, he stroked her soft blond hair from her face.

She was so beautiful.

Her plump pink lips were closed in blissful silence. Her body still in the peacefulness that had washed over her as she slipped into death, her eyes staring wide open at him, as if he was the only person in the world that mattered.

And in those last few seconds he had been.

He had held her life in his hands. And he'd taken it from her.

His blood burned hot with the exhilaration that followed the kill. Hunting was in his soul. The scent of her fear was an aphrodisiac. The touch of her skin so enticing that even as her body turned cold, he was tempted to make love to her.

But it was too late for that.

He wanted a warm, willing body.

The wind moaned outside his hut. The moon was nearly full tonight. A wolf's lone howl boomeranged off the mountain. He understood its loneliness. Wolves mated for life. Just as he would.

Soon it would be All Hallows' Eve, and then in a couple of months the blood moon.

He needed to find his mate before then. His daddy had told him. If he didn't, he would be alone forever.

He traced a finger over the leather heart-shaped necklace he'd made, then etched the words *Mine Forever* into the center. When he'd tied the cord around her neck, it had been his way of binding her to him.

But she hadn't wanted it—had rejected him.

That was her mistake.

Then he'd known what he had to do.

He stroked her arm, then her cheek, watching as her body grew stiff. Watching the dark red blood dry on her chest and her skin turn a mottled blue.

When he'd first seen her through the window of the bakery, she'd looked so perfect as she dotted cupcakes with pink icing and sprinkles.

His mouth had watered for those cakes. And for her.

Getting to his feet, he shuffled over to the underground cooler and opened it.

The other women looked back at him. Icicles clung to their eyelashes, frost coating ivory skin and cracked lips. Tangled strands of frozen hair looked like spiderwebs entwined in the ice. Crimson red swirled through the frost like snakes slithering through frozen blades of grass.

He had to make room for Cady.

Eeny meeny miny mo, which one of you has to go?

He knew the answer. Not the first one. She was special. He would keep her forever, just as he'd promised.

Number two. Nadine. Her blond hair was dyed. Nothing about her was natural. He wouldn't miss her at all.

Gripping an ice pick in his hand, he hummed to himself as he shattered the ice chunks encasing the woman. He laid plastic on the floor to wrap Nadine in, even though he knew that with the frigid temperature outside and this freak snowstorm, she wouldn't immediately start thawing.

The frozen state of her body made her as heavy as one of the dead boars in the holler, but he dragged her from the cooler and laid her on the floor. Then he returned to Cady.

He brushed his fingers through Cady's hair, memorizing her pale face as the memory of her screams taunted him. He'd fallen in love with her the moment he looked into her eyes.

Then she'd laughed and called him names and run from him.

He'd chased her through the forest, his bow and arrow over his shoulder, his hunting knife gripped in his hand, knowing she wasn't fast enough to escape him.

It hadn't taken long to catch her. She was already weak from the stun gun, her feet dragging in the snow.

Three miles in and she collapsed.

Lifting her into his arms now, he carried her to the cooler and laid her on top of the other bodies so he could see her eyes gazing up at him.

He dropped a kiss into her hair, then closed the lid. "I'll be back soon," he promised.

He wrapped the plastic around Nadine, then dragged her outside, shoved her onto his sled and hauled her away.

The frigid wind blasted him, and snow swirled through the air, blurring his vision as he hiked through the rows of pines, aspens and oaks toward Beaver Pond, far away from Wild Hog Holler. Snowflakes froze in his beard and tears flowed, stinging his cheeks.

When he finally reached the pond, he kissed her lips, then spread her out like a snow angel on top of the frozen surface and watched the falling flakes bury her.

ONE

TWO DAYS LATER

Monsters seem to lurk in every corner of the mountains. Detective Ellie Reeves had seen her share of them this last year. Devious, twisted predators who thrived on the weak and vulnerable.

People like her birth father.

She shivered, shaking intrusive thoughts from her head and knocking snow from her coat as she entered the Corner Café and slid onto a bar stool next to her friend, Deputy Shondra Eastwood.

"Drinks are on me tonight," Ellie said, snapping out of her gloomy mood and giving Shondra a hug. "Your transfer to CCPD came through, didn't it?"

Shondra's dark brown eyes glittered as she smiled. "Yes, it did."

Before they could order, Lola, the owner of the café, brought their usual drinks—Ellie a vodka and Shondra a bourbon. Then she set a basket of tortilla chips and salsa on the counter.

Ellie raised her glass and grinned. "Here's to the newest deputy at Crooked Creek Police Department."

Shondra clinked glasses with Ellie and they took sips of their drinks. "I can't tell you how relieved I am not to have to deal with Sheriff Waters on a daily basis anymore," Shondra said.

"I can imagine." Ellie had her own issues with Bryce Waters. "How did he take the news?"

Shondra gave her a wry look. "Frankly, I think he was glad to get rid of me."

Ellie chuckled. With his dark blond hair and green eyes, Bryce could be a charmer when he wanted to be. But he had a problem with strong women.

"I don't know what's going on with him," Ellie said. "But his drinking seems to be getting worse."

Shondra rolled her eyes. "He's probably just pissed that you got the credit for solving that last case. Angelica Gomez portrayed you as a hero."

"Ha. I'm just doing my job." And struggling to deal with the fallout. "Bryce has had it in for me ever since he was elected."

Shondra swirled the bourbon around in its glass. "You should have been the next sheriff."

Ellie shrugged. That was complicated. She had wanted the job, but her father, the former sheriff, had backed Bryce instead. She was still smarting over that.

The bell over the door jangled and local storyteller Tessa Tulane entered the café, her blood-red cape wafting around her, and conversation momentarily stopped. She wore crystal earrings that dangled to her shoulders, and her long, curly dark hair made her look like some kind of ethereal spirit or psychic. Unfazed by the whispers and stares following her, Tessa slipped past Ellie and Shondra, nodding hello as she passed, and seated herself at a small table facing the door. Tessa had been a couple of years behind Ellie in school and left town after graduation to pursue writing and acting. Her bestselling zombie apocalypse series had turned her into a celebrity.

Ellie took a sip of her drink and watched as Mandy Morely came in not far behind Tessa with two friends, all dressed as zombies. Mandy looked around and squealed when she spotted the author across the room, and the teenagers rushed over to her. "Miss Tulane, thanks so much for signing my book!" The girls circled the table like rabid dogs. "Tell us what the next book in the series is going to be about."

Tessa shrugged. "Sorry, but you'll have to wait for its release," she said, with a teasing glint in her green, cat-like eyes.

"Please, please..." Mandy begged.

Tessa laughed. "All I can say is that there is a new bloodsucker in town."

The girls laughed, and Lola approached the table with a smile. "Come on, girls, let the lady order." The girls thanked Tessa again, whispering excitedly as they went and found a booth.

Shondra plucked a chip from the basket on the bar. "Tessa sure made it big, didn't she?"

Ellie nodded. "Her grandmother was the school librarian at my grade school. I remember her telling stories. Maybe that's where Tessa got her talent."

"It's nice to see Mandy smiling," Shondra said.

"Yeah. Losing her mother was a real blow."

"I'm sorry," Shondra said softly. "I know you and Vanessa were friends."

"We were when we were young, but we'd drifted apart." Still, guilt dogged Ellie every day for not staying closer. While investigating Vanessa's murder, Ellie had discovered that she and Vanessa were actually half-sisters. Vanessa had died without knowing. Her daughter Mandy didn't know either, although Ellie had been checking in on her weekly to see how she was doing.

Shondra pushed her black braid over her shoulder. "By the way, I saw Special Agent Fox on the news at a press conference earlier. Have you talked to him lately?"

At the mention of Derrick Fox, an image of his dark black eyes and chiseled jaw taunted Ellie. "Just briefly. He called to tell me he was investigating threats against the governor."

"I kind of thought you two had a thing," Shondra said as she dipped a chip in the salsa.

Ellie took a chip herself. "It's complicated. Besides, he lives in Atlanta and I'm here."

She stared down into her drink. She couldn't shake the memory of the last evening before he'd left two months ago. She'd been distraught, shaken over finding her birth mother, and discovering she was psychotic. He'd wanted to help her. His soulful eyes had bored into her with a look of need, desire and shared pain. She'd been tempted to accept his comfort, but she'd felt vulnerable and needed time alone.

And he'd given it to her.

She had to move on.

The door opened again, and two scruffy-looking men entered the café, their woolly coats pulled up to ward off the snow. Ellie shivered.

"You okay, Ellie?" Shondra asked.

Ellie shrugged. "Sure. Just hungry." *Liar, liar, pants on fire.* Earlier, she'd paid another visit to her birth mother at the mental hospital where she was receiving intensive therapy, and the visit hadn't gone well. But tonight was about celebrating, not whining. She turned towards her friend, determined to focus. But just then Lola adjusted the TV above the bar, and she and Shondra both looked up, their attention drawn to the news.

Angelica Gomez appeared on camera in front of the town square. Fall wreaths, pumpkins, scarecrows, ghosts, spiders, goblins, witches and other Halloween decorations adorned the town. Twinkling black and orange lights on the storefronts and street posts flickered against the night sky. One empty building had been turned into a spooky haunted house.

"Angelica Gomez, Channel Five news. Due to inclement weather and for the safety of the community, Crooked Creek stores are closing early."

Angelica directed a smile at the camera, her glossy dark hair pulled into a knot at the base of her neck. The footage panned the sidewalks full of costume-clad children decorating the tree in the heart of the town square, adding their own ghosts and spiderwebs and glow-in-the-dark pumpkins to the limbs.

"But I'm pleased to say the snowstorm couldn't keep the

monsters off our streets today. Dozens of families gathered at Books and Bites to jumpstart the storytelling festival by joining local author Tessa Tulane for a reading of her popular zombie series," Angelica said, over footage from the event earlier that evening. *"Now let's hear from Cara with more on what the weather means for the rest of us."*

The view switched to Cara Soronto. *"Thanks, Angelica. I'm coming to you live from Crooked Creek's downtown where, as you can see from the images on your TV screen, it's snowing. Yes, folks, an early winter snowstorm is on us, this one predicted to drop at least five inches on the mountains over the next few days. Temperatures will drop dangerously low, and travel advisories are in effect. If you don't have to get out, don't."*

Ellie's stomach tightened again. For months now, crime had plagued Bluff County and the Appalachian Trail.

People were just starting to feel safe again.

But with another storm brewing and Halloween approaching, Ellie had a sinking feeling that was about to change.

TWO

BEAVER POND

He couldn't help himself. He had to go back and check on Nadine.

He hadn't thought he'd miss her, but he did. Somehow his home didn't feel complete with one of his prized possessions gone.

Coming back had been a mistake though.

He heard the damn dog barking as he crested the hill, then he peered around a boulder and spotted the black animal sniffing and pawing as if it had caught the scent of a carcass.

No... He couldn't let the dog dig her up.

"Roscoe!"

He jerked his head toward the voice and spotted a girl chasing after the dog. Her parka swallowed her thin body, strands of dark hair poking out from under her ski cap. She staggered against the force of the wind, clawing at a tree to stay on her feet.

The temptation to take her seized him.

"Roscoe, come here, boy! Mom and Dad are gonna freak out if we don't get back!"

He halted, hidden by the boulder. No, she wasn't right. She was too young. Just a teenager.

But her dog was heading straight toward where he'd buried Nadine.

Angry that she'd interrupted his visit, he pulled his ski mask on to shield his face, then jumped from the shadows of his cover. She screamed when she saw him and went still.

The dog snapped to attention at her scream, looked around, its senses honed, then loped over to guard her.

He raised his hunting knife with a growl, and panic flashed in her eyes. The dog barked and nudged her, and she turned and ran back the way she'd come. The dog growled at him before chasing after her.

He followed her, down a hill, around a bend, then he saw a ridge ahead. A minute later, he heard another scream and stopped to watch her flailing as she slipped and went over the edge.

THREE

CROOKED CREEK

After finishing their drinks, Shondra and Ellie devoured burgers loaded with the works.

"How are you dealing about your birth mother?" Shondra asked.

Ellie looked up warily. Her friend was definitely probing tonight. She just wanted to celebrate Shondra's news and forget about her own issues. She felt like she was at a counseling session and was ready to call it a night.

Then again, she'd tried to be there for Shondra when she'd had a hard time. That was what friends did. She had to get used to being on the receiving end of it, she guessed.

"Dealing," Ellie said, as she scooped up an onion ring and bit into it.

"Really?" Shondra looked intently at her, her eyes concerned.

Ellie took a swig of water. "I saw her today," she admitted. "It didn't go well. She got upset and accused me of lying about who I am." A deep sadness threatened to overcome her.

"It hasn't been that long since she started her new treatment. Give it time." Shondra reached across and squeezed her hand. "How are your folks handling it?"

Ellie nodded. "We're not really talking that much. They've been rebuilding their house."

The truth was Vera and Randall had both reached out multiple times since she'd discovered the truth about her birth mother, Mabel. But Ellie still had trouble forgiving her parents for lying to her. She might never have known she was adopted if Vera hadn't been forced to tell her.

Although it turned out Vera hadn't known the story behind Ellie's birth, or that Ellie had been taken from Mabel against her will. The news had upset Vera, which had softened Ellie toward her. After all, if Vera and Randall hadn't adopted her, there was no telling where she might have ended up.

The door to the café opened again, and a blast of cold air rushed in with it. Ellie turned and watched Ranger Cord McClain step inside, kicking snow from his boots and brushing it from his ski cap. She and the ranger, who worked for FEMA, had known each other for years and had worked together on numerous search and rescue missions. Cord had even risked his life more than once to save her.

Cord gave Ellie a wave, and she thought he was going to join her and Shondra. But as he crossed the room to the bar, Lola hurried to greet him, her face lighting up with a smile. Judging from her expression, Ellie guessed that Lola had a crush on Cord.

A spark of jealousy hit her, but she brushed it away. She had slept with Cord once after high school but that was a long time ago. Since then, they'd both decided to keep their relationship as friends.

"I'll have that order ready in a minute," Lola said.

"Thanks." Cord shifted, looking awkward as Lola disappeared into the kitchen. His gaze brooding, he approached Ellie and Shondra. "I just stopped by to pick up food for the search team."

"What's going on?" Ellie asked.

"Family went hiking before the snowstorm hit and got separated from their teenage daughter. With the temperature dropping, we need to find her ASAP."

"Let me know if I can help," Ellie offered.

His gaze met hers for a tension-filled moment, then his jaw tightened. "Thanks, but I've got it covered."

Lola appeared from the kitchen, carrying two large bags and a tray of coffees. "Sandwiches and hot coffee for everyone." Lola handed Cord the bags and tray, then squeezed his arm. "Be careful out there, Cord."

"Always." Cord blushed as Lola planted a big kiss on his cheek. Ellie glanced at Shondra, wondering how close Lola and Cord had gotten during his time off.

Not that it was any of her business.

After the hell Cord had been through growing up, she wanted him to be happy. And she and Derrick had a tentative relationship. Didn't they?

"Looks like those two are an item," Shondra said as she pushed her plate away.

"Yeah," Ellie said. "How about you? Are you still talking to Melissa?"

Shondra and her girlfriend had parted ways a while back.

"It's not going to work," Shondra said. "I think it's better I move on. Start fresh."

"I know what you mean." Trust was definitely an issue for both of them.

"Maybe we're just destined to be alone," Shondra murmured.

Ellie patted her badge. "Or married to the job."

As if on cue, Ellie's phone buzzed. She glanced at the screen. It was her captain.

Shondra waved to Lola to bring the bill while Ellie connected the call.

"Detective Reeves," Captain Hale said. "I need you in my office first thing in the morning."

His voice sounded odd. Was he irritated? Angry?

"What's up?"

"The sheriff requested we meet," the captain said. "He's making noises about the way you handled that last case."

"*Bryce* is making noises about *me*?" She raised her eyebrows at

Shondra, who understood exactly who the call was about. Shondra rolled her eyes in solidarity.

"Yes," Captain Hale said sharply. "I think it's best we discuss this in person."

Ellie's stomach churned as the captain abruptly ended the call. *Dammit.* Bryce Waters had run roughshod over her to be elected as sheriff when she'd wanted the job. And he'd dropped the ball so many times on the last three cases she wondered how or why he stayed in the game at all.

What the hell was he up to now?

FOUR

SOMEWHERE ON THE AT

Ranger Cord McClain and the two search teams he'd organized wolfed down the sandwiches and coffee then set off to meet the Owens family at the AT shelter where they'd sought cover. The temperature had dropped to the forties, the wind had picked up and was blowing the falling snow in a white haze.

Cord introduced himself and the other SAR members to the family and handed out blankets. The parents, Thelma and George, looked frantic. They'd managed to build a small fire and were huddled around it outside the shelter. Their ten-year-old daughter Maggie was hunched inside her pink puffer jacket, shivering.

Cord could tell from Mrs. Owen's red-rimmed eyes that she'd been crying. Mr. Owens was pacing the hut, his angular face streaked with worry.

"What happened?" Cord asked.

"We were getting ready to head back to our SUV when Roscoe ran off," Mrs. Owens said, her voice shaky.

"Roscoe?"

"Our black lab," Mr. Owens cut in. "Sally, she's fifteen, chased after him, but she hasn't come back." His voice cracked. "She must be lost out there. And in this weather..."

"That was two hours ago," Mrs. Owens said worriedly. "What if she fell and got hurt?"

"We've called and called, and I went looking for her, but saw no sign of her." Mr. Owens jammed his hands in the pockets of his parka. "Please find her."

"What was she wearing?" Cord asked.

"Black insulated pants, a University of Georgia sweatshirt and a black ski jacket," Mrs. Owens said. "Oh, and she had on a red ski cap – from UGA as well."

"Is she gonna be okay?" the little girl asked.

Cord offered her a small smile. "We'll find her. She couldn't have gone too far in two hours." Although with slick terrain and steep drop offs, she could have slipped and suffered an injury. "You guys stay here," Cord said. "My teams will start searching."

Mr. Owens bounced on his heels. The man was obviously antsy. "I can't just sit here and do nothing. I'm going to look, too."

Cord cleared his throat. "I understand your need to help, but it's dangerous out there and my team has the proper gear to deal with the elements. It's best if you stay with your family in case your daughter returns." Cord pulled a handheld radio from his backpack and gave it to the man. "Take cover in the shelter and radio me if Sally comes back. I'll do the same when we find her."

The man looked as if he wanted to argue, but his wife pulled at his arm. "He's right. Let them do their jobs, George."

The father nodded reluctantly, and Cord rejoined his teams, assigning quadrants before they set out on the trail. The wind was picking up speed, more snow was on its way, and the temperature was expected to drop to the low teens. With night setting in, they had to hurry.

If Sally was injured or left out in the elements, she could freeze to death.

FIVE

BEAVER POND

An hour later, the cold was biting into Cord through his coat as he trudged through the woods. He and Milo, another ranger he'd worked with multiple times, checked each AT shelter along the way in case Sally had ducked into one. His boots sank into the thickening snow coating the brush.

Flashlight beams slanted across the blanket of white in all directions, lighting the way, as each of the rangers led a team of volunteers, hacking away at the brush and climbing hill after hill, crossing the creek beds and examining the ground for footprints. But with every minute, Cord worried they might not find the girl.

"Sally! Roscoe!" Cord's voice echoed off the mountain, the sound blending with the shouts of Milo and his other team members as they called out for the girl, too.

The snow was covering their tracks fast, though, and reducing visibility. Cord navigated his way over fallen trees, up steep inclines, and through stands of trees that were so thick you couldn't see the other side.

"Sally! Roscoe! Where are you?"

Over and over, he shouted, brushing snow from his face with his gloved hand. Another mile then another. Milo heard a noise to the east and they split for him to check it while he stayed on the path, checking the ridges in case Sally had fallen over—but nothing.

Another mile and the sound of a dog barking echoed from the east. It seemed to be coming from near Beaver Pond.

"Roscoe!" He ran toward the barking, jumping over logs and brush, pushing branches out of his way. His boots skidded on the ice, and crystals clung to his eyelashes, but he blinked them away and picked up his pace.

Another half mile, and he spotted the black lab standing at the edge of a small ridge that dropped about ten feet. The lab barked, pawing at the ground, and Cord raced toward it.

"Sally!"

The dog's ears lifted, and he turned and barked furiously, his paws digging at the leaves poking through the snow. Cord held up a hand to the animal to reassure him that he meant no harm.

"It's okay, boy, it's okay." He rubbed the lab's back then eased toward the ledge and looked over. Relief filled him when he saw the girl was alive. "Sally, your parents called me for help."

The kid was crouched against the stone wall, shaking, her arms wrapped around her legs which she'd drawn up to her chest.

"Are you hurt?" Cord yelled.

Sally slowly pushed to her feet, holding onto a branch to keep from falling. "My ankle... maybe sprained. I couldn't climb. But I'm okay."

"Hang on, I'll get you up. Let me radio for backup and let your parents know we found you."

Cord quickly radioed the team to tell them that he'd found the girl and to inform the parents. He petted the dog again, murmuring he was a good boy to have stayed with the girl. Then he set his backpack on the ground and removed a heavy rope, ready to use when the others arrived. He talked to Sally to calm her while he waited on help to arrive. Ten minutes later, Milo and two other volunteers cleared the bushes. They tied the rope around a pine to secure it, then Cord lowered himself over the ridge edge to the ledge below.

Sally's cheeks were beet-red from the cold, her teeth chattering, her eyes swollen from crying. But she was lucky to have not broken any bones or hit her head.

Cord spoke to her calmly. "I'm going to tie the rope around you like a harness, and the guys up there will pull you up." He secured the rope around her waist, then patted her arm. "Have you ever done rock climbing?"

Sally nodded. "Yeah, there's a rock-climbing wall in Chattanooga where me and my friends go."

"Good. Just grip the rope and use your good foot as leverage while they drag you up."

Sally lifted her chin as in a show of courage. Five minutes later, she was up safely, and Cord climbed up behind her.

The kid hugged the dog, her body trembling. Her eyes wide with fright, she glanced around with a shiver. "There was a man out here. He had a knife and was chasing me."

Cord's heart hammered. "You're sure?"

She nodded, nuzzling her face against the animal's fur. "I was running to get away from him. I didn't even see the edge of the ridge until I went over it."

Cord jerked his head around, listening for signs someone else was around. "How long ago was that?"

"I don't know," the girl said, pulling her coat tighter around her. "A while ago."

"What did he look like?"

"He was big and broad shouldered and was wearing all black. I couldn't see his face because he wore a ski mask and a big scarf."

A white haze swirled around Cord, blurring everything in sight. The howling wind and shaking tree limbs blotted out even the sound of animals foraging through the woods. There were people who lived off the grid all along the trail. Hillbillies, recluses, survivalists, some mentally ill or running from the law.

Cord gestured to the volunteers. "Let's get her back. If someone was here, they're probably long gone." And it would be foolish for the volunteers to stay out in this weather. One of the volunteers slid an arm around Sally's waist to lend support, and they set off. But the dog ran the other way, back toward the pond.

Cord silently cursed. They should have put him on a leash. Then again, Roscoe might be protecting his owner by going after the man. "Start back with her. I'll get the lab and meet you at the shelter."

The men nodded, then headed down the path while Cord trudged through the snow after the dog. As he rounded the corner near Beaver Pond, he saw Roscoe digging in the ground.

"Come on, buddy," Cord called gently. "We need to get you back to your family."

The dog kept digging though, and Cord approached him. "What did you find, buddy?"

Roscoe angled his head to look up at him and Cord started.

The lab had a human finger in his mouth.

SIX

Ellie's head had just hit the pillow when the call from Cord came. He'd rescued the teenager on the trail but found a body at Beaver Pond half buried in the snow. Whether or not it was a hiker who'd fallen or there was foul play was the question.

The fact that the teenager had claimed she was chased by a man with a knife in the woods was disturbing.

Dear God, her earlier premonition that something bad was going to happen had come true. As she quickly dressed and set off to join Cord at the scene, self-doubt filled her. Was she ready to work another case?

Geared up, her compass in hand, she led the ME, Dr. Laney Whitefeather, and the Evidence Response Team through the woods, battling the wind, sleet and snow. The ground was slick, frozen, her boots crunching ice and digging into the thick slush as they climbed the steep inclines. Sleet stung her cheeks, and she pulled her scarf up to cover her mouth and nose.

Laney and the team followed silently, the wind rustling the trees as they wove through the woods. Finally, they broke through a clearing, and she spotted Cord standing against a pine, his hands in his pockets, head bent as if he was studying the scene.

He looked up as they approached, his expression grim, amber

eyes wary, brown shaggy hair blowing in the wind. "I didn't touch anything, except the finger."

Ellie's stomach somersaulted as he showed her the digit he'd stored in a baggie.

"Dog had it in his mouth," Cord said gruffly.

Ellie winced. The recovery team held back while she and Laney moved closer to where he stood. Her breath caught as she spotted the hand belonging to the missing finger sticking up through the weeds as if reaching for help. The rest of the body was completely covered in snow.

For a moment, the entire team paused as if to grieve for the woman, another victim of violence on the beloved Appalachian Trail. Ellie hoped this one was an isolated event. But her gut was churning.

"Let's get some pictures and search the area," Ellie told the forensic team. "For now, we're going to treat this as a crime scene. Look for a backpack or phone or anything that might help us identify her."

Laney examined the finger through the bag. "Looks like a woman's," she said. "Pink nail polish." She gestured at the signs of frostbite. "She's completely frozen. I'd say she's been dead for a while."

Ellie glanced at Cord. "Did you see or hear anyone when you got here?"

Cord shook his head. "No, I wouldn't have discovered the body if I hadn't been chasing the dog. He found it and started digging."

The ERT took close up photos of the finger and hand, then the surrounding area where the woman was buried.

Ellie stooped down and gently brushed snow away to expose the person beneath. The forearm came into view, then the face, dark brown eyes wide open, skin a sickly bluish white and covered in frost. Snow and ice clung to her eyelashes and her brittle blond hair.

Ellie's stomach clenched again. "Poor girl." Slowly, she exposed the woman's other arm and her torso.

Dried blood stained the body where a hole had been carved in the woman's chest.

Anger stirred inside Ellie at whoever had left her exposed in the elements like this. She looked up at her team. "This was no accident or stranded hiker," Ellie said. "She was murdered."

SEVEN

Ellie should be used to death now, at least after her last few cases, but her heart still ached for the woman. She looked young, maybe late twenties.

And the fact that she was naked definitely pointed to a predator. A sadistic one who had no regard for human life. Who'd discarded his victim as if she was nothing.

If Cord hadn't found her, the animals eventually would have ravaged her.

Reminding herself the girl needed her to focus, Ellie took a deep breath. Dark blond hair was frozen in a tangled mess around an oval face. No visible wounds on the face or neck, although her coloring was so distorted that Laney would have to determine other bruises or injuries that might have occurred.

A handmade leather heart hung on a cord around her neck above the gaping hole in her chest. Ellie read the words etched into the heart—*Mine Forever.*

Ellie looked closely, taking in every detail, and found herself talking to the girl in her thoughts. *What's your name, sweetie? Is there someone special in your life who gave you that necklace? Did you know your killer?* She looked up at Laney. "The kill was vicious," Ellie said. "She was stabbed in the heart."

Laney leaned closer to examine the knife wound. "Yes. We'll

have to let her body defrost slowly in a refrigeration unit at a steady thirty-eight degrees before I perform an autopsy. If we don't, the outside of the body will decompose, and the inner organs will stay frozen."

"How long will that take?" Ellie asked.

"Could take up to a week."

Damn. "There's not much I can do until we identify her." Frustrated, Ellie tried to piece together a place to start with the investigation. The poor girl's family, if she had any, would want her back, want to give her a proper burial. None of that could happen without a name and the completed autopsy.

If the family knew she was missing, every day without knowing what happened to her must be agonizing. She thought of Derrick. She'd heard the pain in his voice when he'd talked about his little sister, who disappeared when she was a child. They'd only found her a few months ago.

The wind was picking up, the skies darkening, and she knew she had to get to work.

First, she snapped a photograph of the woman's face, saying to Laney, "I'll run this through facial recognition software. Maybe we'll get a hit."

Cord joined them and cleared his throat. "Are you about ready to have her moved? The storm's gaining momentum and with the visibility, it's gonna be hell getting her off the mountain if we don't do it soon."

Ellie glanced at the trees that were now shaking more vigorously. Cord was right. The wind howled like a mountain lion, and the snow was falling harder. Even with her gloves on, her fingers were starting to numb and the bitter cold was cutting through her winter coat. "Yes. Let's get her out of here before we're all buried." Ellie turned to the ME. "Laney?"

Laney collected her kit. "Sure. There's not much I can do out here."

Ellie approached one of the crime techs. "Have you found anything?"

The big guy's breath blew out in a cloud. "Not really. Damn snow's covered any footprints. Although one of our guys found some drag marks a ways up. No blood though."

"I think she was killed somewhere else, then her body dumped here," Ellie told him.

"That fits," the crime tech said.

"She may have been here for hours or days," Ellie added. "Dr. Whitefeather will have to narrow down our timeline when she does the autopsy."

He gave a nod. "The guys will search a little while longer, then we'll have to call it a night. We can always come back once the snow melts and take a look."

Ellie released a weary sigh but couldn't argue. All around her the storm was intensifying. With six inches of snow on the ground already, it was a long shot that they'd find anything. Worse, if she'd been here for some time, the weather and animals could have already destroyed anything left behind.

EIGHT

PINE NEEDLE CROSSING

She was running away from home. From her life. And most of all from the men who were smothering her.

She pulled into the quick market at the turnoff to Pine Needle Crossing to fill up with gas, cursing the freak snowstorm. She'd hoped to reach her rental cabin on the creek before it struck but hit a snag with traffic coming out of Atlanta and had practically crawled her way here to the mountains. Cars were slipping and sliding all over the black ice, night making it difficult to see the dangerous spots. Three cars on I-85 had skidded into the ditch and the drivers had abandoned them for the night.

Tugging on her gloves and cap, she burrowed in her coat and climbed out of the car. Her hands shook as she inserted her credit card into the slot and lifted the pump handle. The scent of gasoline hit her as she began to fill her tank, icy crystals pelting her face.

The door to the store opened and a man in a thick dark coat lumbered out, his ski hat pulled low over his forehead. For a moment, she could feel his eyes piercing her, an intensity radiating off him that sent a shudder through her.

She was so jittery she dropped her keys in the snow and knelt to find them. A second later, she realized the man was stooped down beside her.

She tensed, then he began raking his big hands across the

ground, snagging her keys for her. A shudder coursed through her as he gave them to her, and their gloved hands touched. His breath puffed out, his eyes dark orbs in a gruff-looking face half covered by a black woolly scarf.

She stood, clutching the keys. "Thanks."

"Be careful out here, sweetheart."

Her heart stuttered. "I have to go." She took a step back, her unease mounting with every second as he stood there, watching her. All the warnings her parents had given her about traveling alone echoed in her head.

The gas was finished pumping, and she quickly replaced the nozzle in its holder and reached for her door handle. Thankfully, the door to the store opened and a couple exited. He glanced back at the couple and backed away from her, and she jumped in her car, slamming the door and locking it.

Anxious to reach the cabin and settle in before the storm got worse, she flipped on the defroster and wipers, then pulled back onto the mountain road, glancing in the rearview mirror to make sure the creep didn't follow her. She didn't see him getting into a car or truck. In fact, he'd disappeared in the haze of white fogging her vision.

Stop being paranoid. No one is after you.

She had been followed plenty lately. Sometimes she thought there was no way to escape.

NINE

He gripped his hunting knife in his gloved hands as he ducked into the shadows of the pines and watched the woman grab her suitcase and run through the snow to the cabin. She skidded on a patch of ice, and almost fell, and he took a step toward her, his hands reaching out as if to catch her, as if that were possible from this far away.

But she scrambled up the steps and he held back, dropping his hands to his sides and staying hidden.

He had known she was the one the moment he'd seen her at that gas station. A replacement for Cady.

He'd felt that instant connection he'd seen on TV when couples met and fell in love. His heart had soared, his pulse jumping, his blood racing through his veins.

Almost as exciting as the kill.

Tonight, he wanted her. Wanted to touch her soft-looking hair and taste her lips and offer her his heart in exchange for hers.

But he dug his heels into the thick sludge and held back. It was too soon. He had to wait. Watch her. Make sure she was alone, that someone hadn't followed her up here, or she wasn't meeting some guy who might interfere.

People thought he was stupid because of his work. Because of the way he lived. Because he didn't fit into society.

But he was smarter than they'd ever know.

He knew how to survive the elements and the dangers lurking on the trail. He'd been honing his hunting skills for years now. Years of searching for the perfect one to take her place beside him as his mother had with his father.

One night, when he was a boy, he'd woken up to the sound of grunting. He'd watched them rutting in bed together and later his daddy had told him that one day it would be time he found his own mate. Then when he was a teenager, he'd gone and left him, and his mother was all he'd had.

She was gone now, too.

But he didn't intend to spend his life alone.

He ran his fingers over his chest, remembering each name he'd carved into his skin. Tonight, he'd add another. Maybe it would be the last.

He dug his fingers into his pocket and felt the leather heart. Adrenaline shot through him as he pictured her ivory skin glowing in the candlelight as he fastened it around her neck.

TEN

CROOKED CREEK

The next morning, Ellie was dog-tired as she entered the police station. The image of the frozen body at Beaver Pond had haunted her all night, questions making her toss and turn.

Had the kill been personal, or was there another predator in the mountains?

Rolling her shoulders against fatigue, she grabbed a coffee from the coffee station and took a deep breath as she settled down at her desk, bracing herself for the meeting with the sheriff.

On the phone last night her captain had sounded upset.

She'd sensed something was going on with Bryce, and she realized she might be at the heart of the problem. Maybe Shondra was right, and Bryce was pissed about Angelica's report on the last case.

He wanted the accolades. There was no doubt about that.

But he was screwing with the wrong woman if he thought she'd cow down to his ego.

She rubbed her forehead where a major headache was starting to pulse. She dug two painkillers from her desk, downed them with a sip of water, then cradled her coffee in her hands. It was her lifeline.

After the last case, when she'd spent so many sleepless nights, she'd decided the coffee at the station tasted like mud. Dark and sludgy with a hint of burned coffee grounds. She'd gone out that day and bought a coffee system, one that brewed single cups, a pot and had an attachment for an espresso. She'd been experimenting with different flavors, too. Caramel macchiato was her favorite.

But this morning she needed the rich, pecan-strong caffeine to jumpstart her brain.

Voices at the front area of the police station echoed, then footsteps and Bryce's booming voice reached her. Closing her eyes, she took a long sip of her coffee. Then she got up and headed toward the captain's office. When she reached the doorway, she could see that Bryce was towering over the captain, who was seated at his desk, his expression agitated, his movements jerky.

Ellie frowned. What the hell was wrong?

"I don't think Detective Reeves should be back at work," the sheriff was saying. "After her ordeal on the last case, she should have taken off more time."

Ellie clenched her hands. Did Bryce actually care about the trauma she'd suffered or was he just trying to boot her out of her job?

"Where is this coming from?" Captain Hale asked.

Ellie cleared her throat and moved into the doorway. "Yes, where, Sheriff?"

Bryce spun toward her, eyes blazing with accusations. She stepped inside and closed the door.

"It's been three months since she closed the last case, Hale, and I've read and reread her final report. Something is not right there." Bryce aimed a suspicious look toward her. "There are missing pieces and I want to know why I'm being kept out of the loop."

The captain ran a hand over his balding head. Ellie clutched her coffee mug so tightly she thought it might shatter. "You aren't missing anything," she snapped.

"Both you and that damn reporter are hiding something," Bryce said. "Gomez is usually cutthroat, ready to rip through flesh to expose all the details. Yet this time she glossed over the summary of the case and the killer's motive."

For once, Bryce was right. Angelica had discovered that she was Ellie's half-sister, that they were both products of sexual assault years ago. Neither of them intended to share that with Bryce or the public. Not ever.

Ellie said, "You're seeing things that aren't there, Sheriff. We need to move on. We have another case to solve."

Bryce planted his hands on his hips and turned towards the captain. "Hale, don't you think Detective Reeves needs a break? Maybe some counseling? I can handle whatever's come up. She's too emotional—"

Ellie gritted her teeth in anger. Damn him for implying she was unstable.

"Enough, Sheriff. I will decide when my people take leave," Captain Hale said. "And I feel confident Detective Reeves is up for the task." His mouth tightened. "Deputy Eastwood has joined my team, so Detective Reeves will have even more manpower."

Bryce's green eyes narrowed to slits. He obviously didn't appreciate Hale's reminder that Shondra had transferred to Crooked Creek, the enemy side, as he saw it. Bryce had lost her respect with his loose tongue and lack of professionalism.

"Remember, I'm sheriff of the county," Bryce ground out.

Ellie straightened to her full five three. Bryce crossed his arms, but she refused to allow him to intimidate her. "Then you should be more concerned about the case I just mentioned than trying to sabotage my job."

"You are out of line," the sheriff barked.

"I said enough, both of you," Captain Hale said firmly. "If you want to know about the case, take a seat, Sheriff, and Detective Reeves will fill you in. It's time you two learned to work together."

ELEVEN

Ellie was fuming. She told them to meet her in the conference room and asked Shondra to join them. When they'd all taken their seats, she tacked photos of the crime scene on the whiteboard and explained how Cord had discovered the woman's body.

"At this point, we don't have an ID, but I'll run her picture through facial rec. Although with the state of her body, it may be difficult to get an accurate match." She pointed to the woman's chest. "It looks like she was brutally stabbed in the heart and probably bled out. We don't know how long she was out in the elements, if she was dumped immediately after death or held somewhere else. The snow made it difficult to find footprints or forensics, but there was no evidence of blood anywhere around where she was left, which indicates she was killed elsewhere." Ellie paused, imagining the violent slaying and how the murderer would have transported the body.

"Dr. Whitefeather did note signs of frostbite on the corpse. She was left naked, but she was wearing a leather heart necklace." Ellie gestured toward the photograph of the piece, pointing out the etching. "It's not clear if it belonged to the victim or if the killer gave it to her, but the fact that he didn't take it may be significant. The words *Mine Forever* could be a clue that he knew her personally, that they were lovers or even married. Although there is no wedding ring."

"He could have kept that as a souvenir," Shondra said.

Ellie nodded. "True. We won't know until we make an identification and can talk to her family and friends."

"You mentioned he might have killed her elsewhere," Bryce cut in. "Are there any cabins or AT shelters in close proximity where that could have happened?"

Ellie drummed her fingers on the board, then pulled down the map attached to the wall and stabbed a pushpin into the area called Beaver Pond. "Good point. I'll consult with Ranger McClain and see if he has any ideas."

Bryce's phone buzzed, and he glanced at it, his expression turning sullen. He stood abruptly, his chair scraping the floor as he backed away. "I have to go. Keep me posted."

Ellie frowned. A few minutes ago, he'd insisted on heading up the investigation. Now he was walking out. Something was definitely going on with him. But she didn't have time to dwell on it. She had bigger problems than Bryce. Her family relationships had been strained for months now. Nightmares of being held hostage and almost killed kept her awake at night. And her birth mother, who didn't even know who she was, was in a mental hospital. She sure as hell didn't intend to let the troublemaker sheriff use any of that against her.

As she turned back to the board, the captain got a call; a domestic situation that was escalating out of control. "I'll take it," Shondra offered.

Ellie stood. "I'll go with for backup."

Captain Hale shook his head. "Stay here and get to work on making that ID. Deputy Landrum can provide backup."

Ellie and Shondra exchanged a look, and Shondra gave a nod that it was fine with her. Ellie admired her friend for all she'd overcome. Shondra was best at defusing domestic violence. She'd grown up doing it with her own family.

"Copy that," Ellie said to her boss. "I'll run this picture through facial rec and start searching missing persons reports."

Ellie went to her office and shot Cord a text asking him about possible hideouts near Beaver Pond.

Then she plugged the grainy picture into the facial rec program and let it run while she accessed the missing persons database. Not knowing how long the woman had been dead or disposed of, she started with recent reports. She entered the basic information she'd gleaned so far—dark blond hair, petite build, approximately 120–140 pounds, age somewhere in her early to mid-twenties. Laney could narrow that down, but for now, it was the best she could do.

The task was laborious, the numbers staggering, her headache back and nagging at her as she studied photograph after photograph. Over half a million people went missing in the US yearly, including children, men and women. California, Texas and Arizona had the highest tally.

Just this year, around 250 people had disappeared in Georgia alone, 60 percent male, 40 percent female. Those also included runaways.

Two hours later, her eyes were blurring from studying the screen, and the faces were running together. She found a few missing women within a hundred-mile radius of Bluff County, but only three matched her victim's description, and two of them had been accounted for. The third had died in a car crash.

Frustrated, she stood and stretched, wishing she could go for a run to clear her head. But she looked through the window at the dismal gray skies and ice and snow and knew that wasn't an option.

Antsy and deciding she needed to expand her search, she went to the break room for more coffee, grabbed a protein bar and headed back to her desk.

She found Angelica waiting inside her office.

"Hey," she said, hesitating in order to gauge Angelica's mood. Both of them had had trouble reconciling to the truth, that they'd been conceived in violence by the same man, but Angelica was as tough as they came.

They'd been dealing in their own ways. Maybe she should have reached out.

"I heard you found a body in the woods," Angelica said. "Were you going to call me?"

Tension laced Angelica's voice, making Ellie stiffen. "I was up half the night, so yes, I was going to call and give you the exclusive. But I'm just beginning to figure out what happened myself."

Angelica's expression softened. "Sorry, I just don't want you to cut me out because of... you know."

"Because we're half-sisters?" Ellie said, deciding to be direct. "That's not what's happening. I figured you needed space and time to process what we learned, and so did I. I would've told you about the case as soon as we had enough to go public."

Angelica gave a little nod. "I've been doing a lot of thinking, Ellie. I'm sorry I didn't see who Max really was. I was an idiot. I'm supposed to be better than that."

Ellie released a strained breath, the image of Angelica's ex, who'd been exposed as a killer in Ellie's last big case, flashed into her head. "We're all human," she said. "For what it's worth, I was fooled by Max, too. I thought he was one of the good guys."

"Are there any left?" Angelica said sardonically.

Ellie thought of Cord and Derrick. "Maybe so. But for now, let's just focus on ourselves."

Angelica sighed, her expression troubled. "I wanted to talk to you about that. There may be more victims out there, children born of sexual assaults by our birth father, that we don't know about. We may have more half-siblings, Ellie."

Ellie's throat constricted. "Hoyt says there aren't."

"And you believe him?"

Believe the man who'd been complicit in their mothers' rapes? Who'd brainwashed a veteran into killing for him? Part of her said no, but then again, what did Hoyt gain by lying now? "I don't know, Angelica," Ellie said. "But what good could come of knowing? I figure if another rape victim saw the story of Hoyt's arrest, then she would come forward. If not, maybe she wants to keep her secret to protect her child or family."

"Don't you think the children have a right to know?" Angelica asked.

Ellie folded her arms. "I don't think we should go busting up anyone else's lives just because you're curious."

Angelica's expression hardened. "Is that all you think it is? For god's sake, Ellie, I have no family. I want to know."

I'm your family, Ellie wanted to point out. But she bit back the comment. Instead, she shrugged. "Then do what you have to do. But leave me out of it. I've got a case to work."

Irritated, Ellie turned and walked back to her computer. Behind her, she heard Angelica stalk out the door.

Five minutes later, Ellie's computer dinged that she had a partial facial rec match for the woman. The picture was blurry, and the woman's face was distorted by decomp, so it was only an 80 percent match, but it was a start.

Her name was Nadine Houser. She was twenty at the time she disappeared, eleven years ago.

A little more digging and Ellie learned that Nadine was from Helen, Georgia. The detective who had investigated her disappearance, Ben Emerson, was still on the job. Anxious for more information, she realized her headache had dulled. She was not going to focus on the past like Bryce and Angelica.

This dead woman needed her.

She found the number for the police department, called and asked to speak to Emerson.

"The Houser case has been bugging me for years," Detective Emerson said. "I'll clear my schedule if you want to come here and meet me."

"I'll be there ASAP." She hung up, snatched her keys and headed to the door, adrenaline energizing her at the possibility she was onto something. Knowing the victim's name and retracing her steps before she died might lead to her killer.

TWELVE

On Ellie's way out the door, Derrick phoned. She fastened her seatbelt and connected the call with her hands-free. "Derrick?"

"Yeah. I saw the police report that you found the body of a dead woman on the trail."

"We did," Ellie said, flipping on her wipers to clear the newly falling snow from her windshield. "Her body was frozen, but it looks like she was stabbed."

"Do you know who she is?"

"Not sure, but I ran her face through facial rec and may have an ID. I'm on my way to talk to the police in Helen. I think that's where she was from." Her snow tires ground over the icy asphalt as Ellie bypassed the park and turned onto the main highway leading out of town.

"What have you been up to?" she asked.

"Busy investigating threats against the governor, but if you need me to do anything, let me know."

"Thanks, but right now there's not much I can do until we determine time of death and how long she was in the woods. Laney has to let the body thaw before she can perform the autopsy."

A tense pause. "You think it's an isolated murder?"

"Like I said, I won't know until I ID her and find out if she was reported missing."

"Ellie," he said, his tone softening. "Are you okay? Do you think you should be working?"

She clenched the steering wheel tighter. She pictured him running his fingers through his coal-black hair, and remembered his calm analytical mind when dealing with the perps they'd encountered, and wished he was here now. But the governor needed him.

"I'm fine, but I just took shit from the sheriff. So don't start with me."

He growled a curse. "Waters is still being an ass?"

She grunted. "He tried to convince the captain that he should take over the case," she admitted.

"Bastard," Derrick muttered. "If I know you, hell will freeze over before that happens."

Ellie gave a wry laugh. "Thanks for the offer of help. I'll let you know if something turns up."

She hung up before she said more. Like that she missed him.

She didn't have time for a personal relationship. Neither did he. This woman's death was all that mattered.

THIRTEEN

HELEN, GEORGIA

Ellie parked at the police department, which was backed by woods and the mountains rising behind them. As a child, she remembered thinking the sharp peaks resembled arrowheads pointing to the heavens, as if trying to leave her some kind of message.

The quaint small town was one of the most visited cities in Georgia, a tourist attraction with its Bavarian-style buildings, restaurants, and shops. It was close to Unicoi State Park, which offered a lake and campsite, and trails that ran through the Chattahoochee National Forest, and visitors flocked to Anna Ruby and Raven Cliff waterfalls.

Ellie had been tubing here dozens of times and had fond memories of hiking and gorging on homemade fudge and pralines. Her mouth watered. Maybe she'd pick up some to take home before she left. Nothing like chocolate and caramel to soothe her on a sleepless night.

Tugging her coat around her, she hurried up to the front door, grateful the snow had eased off. The main streets in town had been plowed, and snow was piled on the banks and sidewalks. But the mountain roads had been treacherous, slowing her drive to a crawl as she watched for black ice.

She kicked snow from her boots before she entered the police station, then introduced herself to the officer at the front desk. A couple of minutes later, a stocky officer with a goatee appeared in tan slacks and a button-down collared shirt. He looked to be late forties, maybe early fifties, his light brown hair was thinning, his face square. He also smelled of cigarettes and some strong musky cologne that was probably meant to camouflage the smoke but only intensified the stench.

He extended his hand. "Detective Ben Emerson."

Ellie shook his hand. "It's nice to meet you. I'm Detective Ellie Reeves."

"I knew who you were before you called." His thick brows furrowed. "You're earning quite the reputation."

"Don't believe everything you hear," Ellie said wryly.

He chuckled. "Come on back to my office. I've already pulled the file you requested. Every time I hear about another female abduction, I look to see if there was a connection."

"Have you found any?"

He shook his head. "Nothing concrete."

She followed him through a set of double doors, then down a hall and into a small office with a window that overlooked the woods. Candy wrappers dotted the desk and a homemade clay ashtray that looked like a child's craft project served as weight for the papers scattered on his desk. The fact that he had his kid's artwork on his desk was endearing.

Emerson sank into his chair with a thud, and Ellie took the one facing his desk. Pulling her phone, she accessed the photograph of the woman at Beaver Pond and showed it to him. "This is the victim I mentioned when I called. I know it's difficult to tell for sure, but what do you think? Could this be Nadine Houser?"

A frown marred his forehead as he studied it. "Maybe." He opened the file and removed a picture of a young dark-blond girl with a bright smile, oval face and dark eyes. She cradled a fluffy yellow cat in her arms and looked so happy that Ellie's heart clenched. She compared the girl's features. Same pointed chin. Same pug nose. Same high forehead.

"It looks like her," Ellie said. "But let's keep this to ourselves until the ME verifies her identity."

"Agreed." He tapped his pocket where he kept his cigarettes, but thankfully he didn't take one out. "That family has been through hell. Father comes in every year on the anniversary of Nadine's disappearance asking if we've found anything or dropped the case completely. The mother was so depressed that she tried to take her own life. Survived but she's in a coma."

"That is awful." Ellie crossed her legs. "We definitely don't want to let the father know yet then. No need to put him through more suffering than necessary." Though he might feel better having closure, her death would hit him hard. The way she was murdered and left would be even more difficult to process.

"What can you tell me about the case?" she asked.

Detective Emerson drummed his short blunt fingernails on his desk. "Nadine was twenty, lived with a roommate named Zoe in an apartment complex outside town. She worked as a cashier at a local mini-market off the highway near the hunting preserve and was saving up to attend cosmetology school. Worked late one night and the roommate said she never came home. No one has seen or heard from her since."

"Were there security cameras at the mart?"

He shook his head, his brows furrowed. "Too far out in the country." He shuffled the papers around, though Ellie noticed he didn't look at them. He probably had the case notes memorized. A sign of a good cop. Some cases were impossible to let go of.

"Parents said she always came for Sunday dinner, and when she didn't show they called but got her voicemail." Emotions thickened his voice and he glanced at a photograph on his desk of a red-headed little boy. "My wife insists we have Sunday dinner every week, too. Busts my balls if I miss one."

Ellie smiled to herself. No wonder the case had hit him hard. He had a family.

He rolled a pen between his fingers as if jerking his mind back to the case. "When I finally reached Nadine's roommate, a week had passed. She'd been staying with her boyfriend, had left early the morning Nadine hadn't come home, and was devastated."

Ellie gave him a sympathetic look. "I assume you cleared the parents?"

"Yeah. They doted on Nadine. Were at an office party together the evening Nadine disappeared." He made a low sound in his throat. "Plenty of people at the party to verify it. And the couple's neighbors and coworkers all stated that the family was close. No problems there."

"How about Nadine's coworkers?" Ellie asked, her heart aching for the parents.

He shuffled the papers again. "Store owner's name was Hal Mitter. His alibi checked out. He was at the hospital with his mother who broke her hip that night and asked Nadine to close up. Other clerk who was getting off work when Nadine arrived said she liked Nadine, that she was friendly with the customers and was fine that last day, that she was excited about celebrating her mother's birthday that weekend." He patted his cigarettes again as if he needed one bad. "Parents and roommate confirmed that she didn't have a boyfriend and hadn't mentioned anyone bothering her or stalking her. Although the clerk did mention some regular who came in for beer, that he asked Nadine out. Said she turned him down."

Ellie leaned forward, her instincts sparking. "Did you find him?"

The detective nodded. "Name was James Dunce. Quiet, awkward truck driver who made runs from Atlanta all the way to Chattanooga, Tennessee."

Her mind raced with suspicion. "So he could have abducted her, then carried her somewhere and kept her until he killed her?"

The detective scrubbed a hand down his face. "That would fit. Frustrating part was that he had an alibi. A ride along that shift with a new trainee who vouched that he was with him all night."

Ellie shifted, understanding his agitation. "What about Nadine's car?"

"Drove an old Chevy. It was still in the parking lot of the mini-mart."

Ellie pursed her lips in thought for a second. "So he abducted her after she got off work. What time did they close?"

"Ten."

"Meaning it was dark and probably deserted." As the scenario played in her head, Ellie shuddered. "She locked up and probably headed out to her car. Where a predator was waiting to pounce."

FOURTEEN

"Do you mind if I take a copy of that file with me?" Ellie asked.

He stuffed the papers back into the folder. "Glad to have fresh eyes on it. I hate to think that the body you found is Nadine, but if it is, I'll do whatever I can to help catch her killer. After all this time, the Housers deserve answers."

"I know they do," Ellie said softly. "Did you obtain a DNA sample for Nadine?"

"Yes, the results are in here." He tapped the folder. "When we searched her apartment, we took a hairbrush and toothbrush. I also got a copy of her medical records. And before you ask, I notified all authorities across the state to look for her and circulated her photo. I've followed up periodically." His sigh echoed through the office. "This one's haunted me for over a decade."

"It sounds like you did everything you could. But eleven years," Ellie said, thinking out loud. "If he abducted her back then, where has she been all this time? And why dump her body now?"

"Maybe she no longer served her purpose?" he asked, his brows climbing his forehead.

Ellie's stomach roiled at the possibilities. "If he kept her alive for a while, what did he put her through before he killed her?"

The detective removed the pack of cigarettes and tapped them against his palm. "You have no idea how many nights that kept me awake."

No, but she could imagine. She'd nearly lost her mind with worry over previous cases.

"I hope I can help you solve this," she said. "Hopefully the ME can complete the autopsy soon and we'll know more. The DNA and medical records will expedite things."

"What was the victim's cause of death?" Detective Emerson asked.

"COD appears to be a stab wound to the heart." Ellie enlarged the photo of the victim on her phone. "Look at this necklace she's wearing. He left her naked except for this. It has to mean something."

Detective Emerson pulled on glasses and leaned closer to examine it. "*Mine Forever*," he murmured.

"I think it's significant. It's possible someone who knew her gave it to her. Or that the killer did." A heartbeat passed as he seemed to mull over her comment. "Did you get a description of what she was wearing when she disappeared?" Ellie asked.

He shuffled through the folder and peered at his notes. "Clerk said she was wearing Levi's and a blue T-shirt. No mention of jewelry."

"We need to know if she owned a heart-shaped necklace like this. If she didn't, the killer may have given it to her."

"I can call Mr. Houser and ask," he offered.

Ellie shook her head. "Hold off until we confirm the ID. If my victim is not Nadine, you won't have to bother that poor man." She mentally ticked off what her next steps should be. "Do you have an address for Dunce?"

"I did," Emerson said. "A rental house near the trucking company. But when I went to the house, he was gone." Another long sigh. "Owner of the place said Dunce would often disappear for days at a time into the woods. Liked to hunt. His place had been cleaned out. He never went back there."

Ellie's pulse jumped. "If he lied about his alibi and hurt

Nadine, he could have taken her into the woods and kept her some-where there." She stood and laid her business card on his desk. "If you think of anything else, please call me. I'll let you know as soon as we verify her ID one way or the other."

Meanwhile, she wanted to track down that truck driver and the ride-along. Killers had been known to work in pairs. Cover for each other.

Sometimes circumstances changed after years. Friendships or work relationships fell apart. Guilt set in.

And alibis were retracted.

FIFTEEN

TRENTON TRUCKING, OUTSIDE HELEN

Anxious for answers, Ellie drove straight to the trucking company listed as James Dunce's employer.

Getting out of her car, she surveyed the set-up. Several flatbeds were parked in a field by a large stone building boasting a giant sign advertising the trucking company's services. A smaller metal sign on the chain-link fence surrounding the yard read: *Hiring, Apply Within.* A couple of older pickups that looked as if they belonged in a junkyard sat on two wheels along with a rusted bus with shattered windows.

Ellie spotted a gray-haired man in overalls with a wad of tobacco in his mouth beside the entrance and introduced herself. He looked too old to be one of the drivers. His hands were battered, and oil stains darkened his clothes. He told her his name was Herman, the mechanic.

"I'm looking for a man named James Dunce. I was told he works here."

He spit tobacco juice onto the ground, his teeth were stained black. "James ain't worked here for years."

"Do you know where I can find him?"

The man shook his head. "Might have left an address with Bobbie Lynn inside. What you want to talk to James about?"

Ellie hedged. "I'm following up on a missing persons case from eleven years ago. A woman named Nadine Houser disappeared."

"Yeah, I remember that." He shifted his weight to one leg as if the other was bothering him. "Police came around asking about her back then. James said he didn't know the girl, but police acted like he did something to her just because he made deliveries to the store where she worked."

"According to the detective who ran the initial investigation," Ellie said, "James had a trainee ride-along with him the night the woman went missing. If it's possible, I'd like his contact information along with the forwarding address for James."

The old man's bushy brows furrowed. "Why you asking about all this now?"

Ellie shrugged. "Father comes in every year demanding we take another look. I feel for him, you know."

Sympathy filled the man's gray eyes. "Yeah, I reckon I'd do the same if it was my kid. Never had any, but Bessie's my baby." He gestured toward a hound dog curled up by a stack of tires at the side of the doorway.

Ellie smiled. "Tell me what you thought of James."

He clicked his teeth. "Guy was real quiet, kept to himself. Awkward around women. Think he'd been homeschooled and didn't know how to get along with people. Not sure if he had much education, acted like his folks were hillbillies."

"Did he have a girlfriend? Wife?"

"If he did, he never talked about it. And if he did talk, it was to brag about his latest kill."

Ellie arched a brow. "He a keen hunter?"

The man nodded. "Bragged about his venison stew. Said his mama taught him how to make it before she died."

Hunters were common in the area so that didn't make him guilty. But the victim's stab wound could have been made by a hunting knife. "Did he exhibit any odd behavior on the job? Or off?"

The man spat again, the dark brown juice landing a few feet away in the melting snow. "Boss fired him cause James stowed one of his kills in the refrigerated truck he drove to deliver groceries. Fresh blood all over the inside of the truck. Went against all kind of health codes."

Ellie pictured the bloody scene in her mind. "Strange thing to do."

"Yeah. Boss said blood was everywhere. Contaminated some of the produce. But James acted like it was nothing, didn't see why the boss got bent out of shape over it."

Ellie certainly saw the problem. "When was that in relation to Nadine's disappearance?"

"Must've been a few days after."

Ellie's skin prickled. The blood in the truck might not have been an animal's.

SIXTEEN

PINE NEEDLE CROSSING

More gray storm clouds gathered, rolling across the sky in a thunderous roar, raising her anxiety. All day she'd sensed someone was outside watching her.

She made a cup of hot lavender tea, walked to the window and stared through the sliding glass doors at the landscape and ridges draped in a canopy of white. It was majestic and beautiful and had inspired her artistic side today while she'd sketched designs.

But fatigue was threatening, the sounds and shadows in the woods a reminder that she was isolated. Last night she'd hardly slept. The encounter at the gas station with that strange man had unnerved her more than she wanted to admit.

Maybe she'd been watching too many scary movies on cable.

Her phone buzzed, and she tensed looking at the screen. Her ex again.

He wasn't taking the breakup well. But he'd been overbearing the last few weeks. Telling her what to do. How to act.

Her mother might be the docile kind, smiling and playing the woman behind the successful man. But she had her own ideas about what to do with her life. She wanted a man behind her to support her dreams.

The phone stopped ringing, then started again. He was nothing if not persistent. And narcissistic. He couldn't imagine her actually rejecting him. His first message this morning was a sweet plea to come back. The second and third, his tone had changed. With each call after that, it grew more edgy. "I can't believe you'd leave me. We can go places together, babe. Everyone will be looking at us."

The exact opposite of what she wanted.

Exasperated, she'd ignored the incessant calls all day and concentrated on sketching several jewelry pieces to feature on her website. She needed simple saleable earrings and necklaces, but she had to include a few splashy and unique items to grab the attention of buyers and bloggers. Pinterest and Etsy were her best friends. So was this area of the country, which was rich in gemstones and known for its gold nuggets mined from the mountains.

As soon as the snow melted and travel was safer, she'd visit some of the shops and add to her collection of stones.

A noise outside startled her, and the teacup rattled in her hand as she looked through the window and spotted a movement in the woods.

Was it an animal foraging through the forest? Had Stephen found her?

Or had that creep from last night followed her?

She narrowed her eyes, searching the darkness, but the figure had disappeared. Relief flitted through her, and she turned on the TV to relax. Her eyes were too tired and gritty to work anymore tonight.

Taking her tea to the oversized sofa in front of the fireplace, she realized the fire had died out, and the room had grown chilly. Outside, another noise sounded. She tensed and moved to the front window.

Fear darted through her when she looked out and saw the man from the night before. He was dressed in all dark clothing again, the ski hat and scarf covering his face, his big arms swinging an ax down as he chopped wood.

She ran for her phone, bringing it back to the window. He

seemed to sense she was watching and looked up at her, but she couldn't quite see his face. Then he lifted a stack of wood in his arms and walked toward the door.

Her breath stalled. Her hand shook and she dropped her phone. Terrified, she bent to retrieve it then heard footsteps on the front stoop. Snagging the phone, her heart hammered, then she saw the man retreating back into the woods.

Battling hysteria, she waited until he completely disappeared, then opened the door. He'd left a stack of wood on the landing.

She grabbed the wood, dropped it inside, then slammed the door and locked it, trembling.

SEVENTEEN

HELEN

Bobbie Lynn in Trenton Trucking's office hadn't found any forwarding information for James Dunce, but had confirmed the name of the ride-along as Dwight Pratt. Both men had been fired within a few months of each other. Armed with the name and contact number of the man who'd formerly run the trucking company, Roger Trenton, Ellie stopped for a mocha and peanut butter fudge at the local sweet shop, licking whipped cream from the top of her coffee and inhaling the delicious aroma of dark chocolate as she rang the number. He answered in a gravelly voice, coughing into the phone. "Hello."

She introduced herself and explained she was inquiring into the Nadine Houser disappearance. "Herman explained about the incident with James Dunce stowing the dead deer in one of your refrigerated trucks."

There was a pause. "I wish he hadn't done that."

"Listen, I'm not calling to get you in trouble or report this. I'm just concerned about the missing woman. Dunce was questioned in her disappearance. What are your thoughts on him?"

The man coughed again. "He always showed up for his shifts. But sometimes he veered off schedule and the route."

"Like that night with the deer?"

"Yeah. Didn't actually see the deer, but there was fresh blood in the truck, a lot of it. The stench 'bout near knocked my head off. Dunce said it was the buck he'd killed earlier, but there was something about how quiet and shifty he was that bothered me. Couldn't quite put my finger on it, but I thought he was lying." He wheezed a breath. "When I fired him, he started ranting and cussing. I got my shotgun and told him to get the hell away from me and my business. And not to ask for a reference."

"Did you think he was dangerous?"

"I did that day." The man whistled. "Glad to be rid of him."

"You never heard from him again?"

"Nope, and glad for it."

"Why didn't you report the blood in the truck at the time? It was right after Helen PD had talked to Dunce."

Trenton gave a deep sigh, which turned into a hacking cough. "I know I should have, but I didn't like to throw shit, you know? Plus, we'd already cleaned the truck up so it could get back on the road, and the cops had seemed happy with Dunce's alibi. I thought about calling up that detective after Dunce lost it, but by then I just wanted no more to do with him. Maybe it was the wrong thing, but I can't change it now."

Ellie stifled a sigh of her own. He was right—they couldn't change it now. "What about the guy who did the ride along with him? Dwight Pratt?"

"He seemed like a decent fellow at first," the man replied. "But couple months after I hired him, he got caught cooking meth. Bad batch killed some teenagers. Third offense. Last I heard he was serving time down at Hays State Prison."

"Thanks for the information. If you think of anything else, please give me a call." Ellie hung up, called Hays and learned that Pratt was still incarcerated. If he had had anything to do with Nadine's disappearance, he couldn't have dumped her body yesterday.

But if he'd lied about being with Dunce at the time of Nadine's disappearance, he might have helped a murderer go free. Or he could have been a conspirator.

Wanting answers, she carried the bag of fudge to her Jeep, hopped in and sped back toward Crooked Creek. Tomorrow she'd drive out to Hays. If Pratt had lied, maybe she could break his story.

EIGHTEEN

WILD HOG HOLLER

He hoped the woman appreciated the firewood he'd left her.

He'd wanted so bad to tell her how he felt about her. But earlier, while he'd dressed the deer and hung his latest kills up to bleed out, he'd listened to the cowboy in the old movie on TV talking about courting a woman.

The man said you had to be a gentleman. Show her you'd take care of her. Give her gifts. Protect her.

Kicking the wet sludge from his boots, he smiled to himself as he let himself inside the bunker his parents had built inside the mountain wall. The place he'd grown up, where they could protect themselves from the crazies out there. The ones who took your money. The spreaders of evil who lied about what they were doing. The people who conspired, listening in on your homes and families. The government that tried to take over your mind.

You had to be careful. Be prepared for the big war that was coming.

Growing up, he'd learned to live off the land and avoid other humans as much as possible. There were times as a kid when he'd wandered off and watched other families. Some of them laughed and played and sang songs and roasted marshmallows as if the world was safe.

His family had not been one of those.

Their voices haunted him. *Stay close to the bunker. Don't talk to strangers. People are out to get you. Spies from the government are trying to take control of all of us.*

We have to stockpile food and supplies. If a bomb strikes, we'll be ready.

Another memory of his daddy brought him a smile. The first time he'd let him shoot a gun. He'd barely been out of diapers. *Hunting is the only way you'll survive. You must focus. Be fast. Watch and strike without hesitation.*

His mama had made bread and cooked the meat he and his daddy brought home. Squirrel, rabbit, snake, hog, even possum. Venison was his favorite, although he did love some good pig's feet.

Last night he'd soaked the deer meat in a brine of salt water to remove the blood, then this morning he'd rinsed it and put it in the black cook pot over a low, slow-cooking fire. His daddy had first taught him how to dress a deer when he was seven, the same day he'd stalked and killed his first animal around Rattlesnake Ridge.

The aroma of the venison stew filled the kitchen area and made his mouth water. Gamey deer meat, potatoes, garlic onions and carrots—his mama's recipe.

For a moment, he saw her waving away smoke from her face as the stew simmered, and a hole opened up in his heart, the pain so intense it shot all the way to his bones. But then he remembered what happened the night she left, and anger made his blood burn.

He spread plastic at his feet to make clean-up easier, another tip he'd learned from his daddy, too, cause his mama bitched about how hard it was to get blood out of the floor. Firelight flickered off the walls and he climbed down below, went to the cooler and opened it. His body hardened at the sight of Cady's wide eyes staring up at him, as if she'd been shocked that he could hurt her when he'd said he loved her. Slowly he traced a finger over her stiff, cold cheek, then over her hair, which was frosted over and brittle.

"I would have given you a good life. Instead you made me take yours," he whispered. "But you're still mine forever."

He bent over and planted a kiss on her lips, which were purple and blue now in death.

"You should see my new love," he murmured. "This time things will be different."

Saying goodbye to Cady, he closed the freezer again, then hurried back up to the fire. He stoked the red and yellow embers until the flames sizzled, then settled beside the stone fireplace and tipped the edge of the blade into the flames to sterilize it. The woman's beautiful face flashed behind his eyes, and he removed his flannel shirt then his undershirt and ran his fingers over the names on his arms.

The names of all the women he'd loved.

He took a long hard swallow of the moonshine he'd traded some meat for, then another, then shoved a piece of bone from a wild boar he'd killed on the trail between his teeth.

"This is for you, darling."

Gritting the bone between his teeth, he welcomed the pain as he pierced the knife into his upper arm and dug away the flesh to blot out the name Cady.

How could he possibly bring a new woman into his life with Cady's name on his body?

The pain was raw and fresh as he carved an X over her name, crossing her out as he had the names of the other betrayers.

There couldn't be real love without pain. His daddy taught him that.

Blood dripped and spattered the plastic at his feet, the earthy aroma of the simmering venison stew around him blending with the scent of blood and dead animal.

NINETEEN

The next morning, as Ellie arrived at Hays State Prison, gray clouds hovered above the mountaintops, casting a dismal light over the majestic snowcapped trees, and promising more bad weather.

As directed by the warden when she'd scheduled an interview with Pratt, she left her weapon and phone locked securely in the dash of her Jeep. The razor wire and guards surrounding the maximum-security facility made her shiver. This place housed some of the most dangerous criminals in the state.

Prisoners were categorized according to levels of security, their accommodations based on the level of their violent tendencies and crimes. It could hold over 1,600 men.

It took almost twenty minutes for her to pass through security and for a guard to escort her to one of the visiting areas.

The dank dirty halls smelled of mold, urine and sweat.

According to the background the warden had given her on Dwight, he had a chip on his shoulder, claimed the cops set him up, and he'd been denied parole because of several incidents of violent behavior. Most recently he'd made a shiv out of a nail, attacked and killed another inmate, then assaulted the guard when he'd pulled him off the other man. He'd earned time in solitary for that, but he insisted he'd acted in self-defense, claiming the inmate was a gang member who'd raped him repeatedly because he'd refused to join the Brotherhood.

In the system, prisoners often allied with one gang to provide them with protection from another.

She'd seen a photograph of Dwight from eight years ago and was surprised that, with his slight stature, he hadn't succumbed. Violent offenders and sexual predators had probably targeted him because he looked too weak to fight back.

After multiple years inside a cell, the handcuffed man who shuffled into the room looked nothing like that frail kid who'd cooked meth. Pratt had beefed up, added muscle, and Ellie guessed he weighed around 190. Tattoos snaked down his arms and a scorpion tat wound around his neck. Beard stubble grazed a wide jaw with a jagged slash running from ear to chin, his mouth set in an intimidating *don't fuck with me* warning.

Ellie swallowed back a sliver of fear as he narrowed his beady eyes at her. "Mr. Pratt, my name is Detective Ellie Reeves."

He grunted in disgust as if he'd judged her and she didn't pass muster. "What do you want?" he asked in a deep baritone.

"I'm following up on a cold case from eleven years ago. Girl went missing, Nadine Houser. You were questioned about that?"

He raised one thick dark brow. "Yeah. Told the cops I didn't know anything. Why? You here to try to pin that on me?"

If he was guilty. "I'm just trying to find the truth. You did a ride-along with a man named James Dunce. He was questioned in the case, but you gave him an alibi for the night Nadine went missing."

He shifted. "Look, bitch, I got nothing to say to you pigs."

Ellie forced herself not to react. "Why not? You don't care that a young woman was murdered and that you might have covered for him?"

His eyes were flat. "Look, if Dunce killed someone, I don't know anything about it."

"But you gave him an alibi for the night Nadine Houser went missing. And now we found her dead." Granted, her ID wasn't confirmed, but Ellie's instincts said it was her. "And I know now that you were convicted of drug possession. Maybe that colored your story back then."

He stared down at his scarred hands. "Told you I got nothing to say."

Ellie crossed her arms. "What if I talk to the warden about getting you some privileges? Maybe some yard time? A little less time in the hole?"

He raked his gaze over her and then heaved a breath. "You're lying. You tell me that but you won't do a thing. You're just like the shitheads who put me in here. And you're not pinning a murder on me."

"I'm not trying to do that," Ellie said earnestly. "I care about this woman whose body I found frozen in the snow." She slapped the table. "I care that her family has mourned for her for years and they had no idea whether she was alive or dead."

A vein bulged in his chunky neck.

"Maybe you don't want privileges," Ellie said. "Maybe you like being someone's bitch."

This time he slapped the table with his hand, the metal cuffs rattling. The guard stepped forward, his hand over his Taser, but Ellie gestured for him to wait.

"That don't happen in the hole, lady," he said smugly. "Best place I can be."

Ellie forced her breathing to remain steady, her body still. Maybe he had been defending himself when he'd made that shiv. Maybe he'd wanted to be put in the hole.

That gave her an idea, and she pierced him with a challenging look. "Then I'll get you put back in general population." She stood. "Suit yourself."

His angry sigh punctuated the air and he hit the table again. "Wait just a goddamn minute then. You can't do that to me."

Ellie turned as she reached the door and met his gaze dead on. The guard shot forward and placed a beefy hand on Pratt's shoulder in warning.

"I can and I will," Ellie said, her eyes narrowed. "Because I intend to get justice for Nadine with or without your help."

She reached for the door handle when he snapped, "Wait."

Ellie angled her head toward him, shooting him a look that said she didn't intend to play games.

"I'll talk. Just don't put me back in general."

"All right. But the truth, no messing around with me."

His jaw hardened but he gave a short angry nod.

Ellie slowly exhaled as she reclaimed the chair across from him. She waited until she was seated, then crossed her arms again. "Let's start over then. You did a ride-along training session with Dunce that night?"

His handcuffs clinked as he spoke through gritted teeth, "All right, yeah, I rode with Dunce. But just that once."

Ellie nodded. That once was all that mattered. "You were with him all night?"

The man worked his mouth from side to side. Ellie watched him; he looked as if he was debating on how to respond. "Most of it."

This time Ellie raised her brows. "That's not what you told the detective back then. Why? Because you were on drugs?"

A rage-filled sigh escaped him. "Yeah. Dunce dropped me off at a warehouse for a little bit."

"So you could score some meth?"

He shrugged and looked away from her, confirming that he had.

Grim-faced, she laid Nadine's photo on the table. "This is Nadine. Did you and Dunce meet up with her?"

His breath wheezed out as he looked down at the grisly image of Nadine's face, then her corpse. "Jesus. I never talked to that chick, but Dunce had a thing for her. Told me he made it a point to stop there even when he didn't have a delivery to drop off."

"You stopped there the night she disappeared?"

"Yeah. But I didn't pay attention to what he was doing."

"But you saw her, then he came back to the truck, and later he dropped you at that warehouse?"

"That's right," Pratt said. "But I sure as hell wasn't gonna tell the cops I was buying meth. I never would have gotten that job driving." His fingers raked through his hair. "And I needed it back then. I... needed the money. Thought I could kick the habit and come clean. I just needed one more score."

"But your addiction caught up with you," Ellie said. "So you gave Dunce an alibi and he did the same for you." She couldn't disguise her disgust. "Do you know where he went while you were at the warehouse?"

He grunted. "He drove back to that little store and tried to hook up with Nadine."

Ellie waited a heartbeat. "And did he?"

He shook his head. "She wasn't with him when he picked me up a couple of hours later."

Ellie shifted in her seat. "Did he say what happened?"

Pratt cursed. "No, but he was in a foul mood. Refused to talk. Called her a cold-hearted bitch."

If she'd rejected him, he might have killed her out of rage, Ellie thought. "Did he say anything else?"

Pratt curled his fingers into fists then flexed them. "Said she was gonna pay."

Ellie bit her tongue to keep from showing a reaction. Dunce was looking more and more guilty. Emerson said he'd done everything back then, but maybe he should have worked harder to break Pratt's story and Dunce's alibi.

But she kept those thoughts to herself. "The owner of the trucking company said he found blood in the truck."

Pratt nodded. "I saw it. But Dunce told me he'd hit a deer and he picked it up and dropped it at a place to have it dressed. Said he'd clean the truck and not to tell anybody."

Ellie frowned. "And you believed him? When the police questioned you, you didn't suspect that he might have hurt Nadine? That it might have been her blood?"

Pratt closed his eyes on a grimace. When he opened them, his eyes were stone cold. "I was so high back then and afraid of getting caught that I kept my mouth shut."

Ellie folded her arms. "Do you think Dunce could have hurt Nadine? That he was dangerous?"

The man muttered a curse. "All men are when they're pushed. Learned that the hard way in here." He looked down at his scarred knuckles. "Dunce had a temper. Road rage. And that night Nadine blew him off... who knows?"

"You realize that if you'd told the truth, you could have saved her life?" she asked, her voice icy.

"I told you I didn't see or know anything. I was high. And boss believed the blood was a deer's, too." Although she could see the war in his eyes.

"That's not what Roger Trenton told me," Ellie said. "He said he suspected Dunce was lying."

The man clamped his lips together.

"You didn't totally believe him either, did you?" she said, not bothering to hide her disgust. "But you wanted to protect yourself and Trenton wanted to protect his business. If he'd reported Dunce, the health department might have shut him down or sanctioned him."

"Man gotta take care of himself," Pratt muttered. "Learned that the hard way, too."

Ellie clenched her hands around the edge of the chair to keep from slamming them on the table. "Cowards. You took care of yourself at the expense of an innocent woman."

And Nadine Houser had paid the price.

TWENTY

Ellie was still reeling as she left the prison.

Her interview with Pratt had only raised more questions. She called Detective Emerson on the drive back to Crooked Creek and filled him in.

"I talked to Nadine's father. As far as he knew, Nadine did not own a heart-shaped leather necklace," Emerson said.

"I thought you were going to wait until we had a firm ID," Ellie said.

"Sorry," Emerson said. "But this may be the first lead we've had in years. I didn't tell him about the body, only that I was doing a routine run through of the file to see if I missed something." He sighed. "He seemed relieved to know I haven't given up completely."

Sorrow for the man cut through Ellie like a knife. But she focused on the facts. "So the killer could have given the necklace to Nadine," Ellie said. "Pratt said Dunce threatened to make Nadine pay for rejecting him. I've already issued a bulletin for him."

"Dunce lied," Emerson said, his voice razor sharp. "That means he's guilty of something."

"We still need a firm ID. If it is Nadine, and we find Dunce, I'll let you know," Ellie said. "Meanwhile, why don't you call all the trucking companies in Georgia and see if Dunce was employed by one of them after he left Trenton's."

"I'm on it."

"I'll run a search for him when I get back to the station." Her phone buzzed with an incoming call. It was the facility where Mabel was undergoing treatment.

Her heart pounded as she hung up with Emerson and answered.

"This is Jeanie, Dr. Canton's assistant," the woman said. "She'd like you to stop by for a consultation about Mabel's care."

Ellie checked the clock. "I'm close by. Can we do it in about half an hour?"

"Sure. I'll tell her."

Worry gnawed at Ellie as she punched the accelerator and sped toward Oak Grove.

Her emotions were in a tailspin by the time she reached the property.

The facility consisted of a sprawling farmhouse-style building surrounded by oaks, nestled in the valley. It was a serene setting, yet inside were so many troubled people like her mother.

In-house therapists, social activities, physical and occupational therapists, meals, and a staff who provided comprehensive medical and psychological care helped treat residents on an individual basis according to their needs.

In spite of the scenery, as she drove into the parking lot Ellie's nerves were on edge. Her last visit hadn't gone well. Mabel had screamed at her to get out. She had thought Ellie was there to take her baby. Would Mabel ever be lucid and realize that Ellie *was* Mae, the baby who'd been taken from her years ago?

She parked, got out of the car and took a deep breath as she walked up to the door and entered the reception area. Five minutes later, Jeanie escorted her to the psychiatrist's office, a neat room with modern furniture that contrasted with the rustic mountain view through the woman's window. The slender doctor wore her raven hair in a chin-length bob and was dressed in a dark green pant suit. Her professional smile was meant to put Ellie at ease, but it failed miserably. Ellie knew her mother's condition was serious. She just prayed it wasn't hopeless.

Ellie settled into the wing chair facing the doctor's desk. "Did something happen? Is Mabel worse?"

Dr. Canton steepled her hands. "Not exactly. But she has been withdrawn since your last visit and isn't eating. She's also had nightmares and wakes up screaming. We've had to sedate her a couple of times to calm her." She paused and gave Ellie a compassionate look. "That's not uncommon for a patient with her history though."

The last thing Ellie wanted was for her to mother to constantly be in a drug-induced state. She'd lived that way for over three decades already.

"I understand this is difficult to hear," Dr. Canton said softly. "But please remember that therapy requires time and patience."

When Ellie had first decided to look for her birth mother, she hadn't known what to expect. But she hadn't been prepared for a mentally impaired woman who lived in her own world.

"I know you can't promise anything. But Mabel's been through so much, she deserves help."

"I agree wholeheartedly," Dr. Canton said. "And I didn't ask you to come because I'm giving up. In fact, I want to try something new."

Curious, Ellie leaned forward. "What?"

"Mabel's nightmares are based on experiences she has repressed," Dr. Canton said. "There's a therapeutic treatment called RMT, recovery memory therapy, that focuses on retrieving traumatic memories that are buried in the subconscious and affect current behavior."

"And you think this might help Mabel?"

Dr. Canton nodded. "I've done it successfully with many patients. But it has to be executed in a controlled environment. Although therapists believe that some memories return on their own when the patient is ready to recall them, the damage to

Mabel's psyche is extensive. I will warn you that some people find RMT controversial. Some patients have been known to form memories of events that never actually happened."

Ellie clenched her hands in her lap.

"That said, now we understand the specific event that triggered Mabel's psychotic break, I know where to focus and how to guide her on the journey."

"What does this treatment involve?" Ellie asked.

"A variety of techniques using group dynamics, hypnosis, visualization, relaxation therapy and dream interpretation. Also showing her photographs of her childhood and past and revisiting some places from her life might come into play." Dr. Canton offered her a sympathetic smile. "This therapy will encourage her to recall what happened to her. That can be painful, but I will monitor her, administer drug therapy and psychotherapy in conjunction with the techniques, to ease the way."

Ellie's stomach rolled. "Then she'll have to relive the sexual assault?"

Compassion softened the doctor's eyes. "I'm sorry, but most likely that will happen. The only way she can move past what happened is to face the catalyst for her break and deal with it."

Ellie shifted, worrying her lip with her teeth. "I hate to see her suffer any more than she already has."

"I understand. And I wouldn't suggest this if it wasn't a last resort."

"You think it will work?"

"I think it's the best chance she has of recovering emotionally so she can live a more normal life." The doctor gestured to a consent form on her desk. "But I need your permission before starting treatment."

Ellie gave a small nod. What other choice did she have?

TWENTY-ONE

WILD HOG HOLLER

His fingernails were stained a deep dark crimson from his latest kill, the scent of blood and death burned into his skin, just as it was his soul. He'd learned to enjoy that quiet stalking of his prey when he'd followed his father into the woods, knives and bows in hand, eyes piercing the darkness, tracking, searching, watching. The silence.

Waiting for the right second to attack.

They'd hunted birds, squirrels, rabbits, deer, turkeys, even the occasional wild boar. Sometimes he'd sit for hours, camouflaged by the thick trees and brush, ears straining for the sound of the animal scuttling through the weeds. Hours on end of wiping sweat from his brow and swatting mosquitoes, staying frozen and so silent that he could hear his heartbeat roaring in his ears.

Then the movement. Just as a falcon soared down to sink its sharp talons into the body of a bird or animal, he'd pounce. Sometimes with his hunting knife. Other times an arrow whizzing through the air at such speed that the animal didn't realize it'd been hit until the stinging pain ripped through its body and it collapsed into the dense foliage.

His appetite had deepened as he grew older. Hunting animals alone was not enough to fulfill him.

He wanted a partner.

Give her hearts and flowers, the cowboy on TV had said.

He'd give her his heart. But he had no flowers. The cold and snow had killed the wildlife right now. But he could leave her a gift.

He wrapped the skinned and dressed buck in plastic, laid it onto his sled, then hauled it through the foot-deep snow. Today the temperature had barely climbed above twenty-five, leaving the ground icy and covered in yesterday's downfall. The wind cut through his clothes, yet a smile tugged at his mouth as he crossed the creek to Pine Needle Crossing.

Although anxiety made him quicken his steps. What if she'd freaked out and left today? She hadn't exactly invited him in or thanked him. That roused his anger.

But he trudged on, the weight of his gift making him work hard to get it to her. She'd have to appreciate it. She would.

The anticipation of seeing her face light up drove him forward and he crested the hill then around a bend and his breath spilled out in relief. Her car was still there.

Excitement bubbled inside him. *Yes, yes, yes...*

Smiling to himself, he crossed the yard, passed the woodpile and shuffled to the front stoop. A light burned from inside and smoke curled from the chimney, telling him she was tucked inside by the fire. His blood sizzled. Maybe she'd been looking for him all day.

Had dressed in a sexy nightgown hoping he'd stop by.

Breath puffing out in the frigid air, he left the deer at the bottom of the steps and climbed to the stoop. He peeked through the window and saw boxes of whatever she'd brought inside, then gemstones spread out and a drawing pad on the table with sketches of necklaces and earrings she must have drawn. It looked like she was making jewelry. She wore a silky looking pink scarf around her neck that looked sexy.

His pulse clamored as he went down to haul the deer up onto

the stoop, imagining her face when she opened the door and saw his present.

His plan was working perfectly. Soon they'd be together, and he wouldn't be alone anymore. He'd have his wife.

Then they could start their own family. He smiled at the thought. If he had a son, he'd name him after his daddy.

TWENTY-TWO

PINE NEEDLE CROSSING

Ginger's phone buzzed for the dozenth time. She sighed, frustrated. When would Stephen get the message that they were through?

She finished adding the lobster clasp to the pendant with citrine features and a brass setting, laying it next to the display of pendants she'd crafted earlier. A sterling silver baguette pendant featuring a blue topaz, and the rose gold marble pendant necklace. One day she hoped to become an event style consultant with her designs, which showcased natural gemstones and an organic sculptural style.

Her family, her ex and even a couple of friends had laughed at her dream of running her own small business. They said it was just a hobby. She didn't need to work. She'd never make it.

What they didn't realize was their laughter, teasing and put-downs only strengthened her determination to follow her dreams and prove them wrong.

Yawning, she rolled her shoulders to alleviate the tension in her neck. Last night a tree branch had scraped the window, keeping her awake and jumpy. Icicles clung to the sharp pine needles and dangled from the awning like jagged knives. Just as she'd done as a child, she'd lain awake, searching the shadows on the wall and outside for monsters.

She thought of the big hulk-like guy who'd left wood on her stoop. After he'd gone, she'd called the owner of the cabins and asked if there was a caretaker for the property. He confirmed there was, which eased her nerves slightly. His name was Joey, although the owner hadn't realized Joey was coming by. He described Joey as gruff-looking and quiet, but safe. He had probably stopped by to check on her because of the storm.

Telling herself she was just jumpy, she poured herself a second glass of pinot noir, hoping for better sleep tonight. But outside a noise sounded. Another coyote?

Snow and twigs crunching. Footsteps.

She rushed to the window, pushed the curtain aside and looked out into the yard. Heavy gray clouds made the night even darker, and a limb snapped off in the woods.

The footsteps again. Someone was on her porch.

Had that creepy Joey come back?

She glanced at the woodpile, but it looked the same height as yesterday. And she hadn't heard chopping or seen the man all day.

Another noise as if something heavy had been dropped on the stoop. Hands trembling, she grabbed the fire poker then moved to the door.

"Who's out there?" she called.

The knock that came startled her. Surely if it was someone dangerous, he wouldn't knock. Maybe Stephen had found her. And if it was that caretaker, she'd tell him she was fine and not to bother coming back.

Still, she gripped the fire poker in her clammy hand as she unlocked the door.

The creepy man from the gas station who'd left the firewood stood there smiling down at her, his big imposing body looming over her. "A gift of love," he said in a deep voice. "You and I belong together."

She looked down and a cry lodged in her throat at the sight of a dead deer lying on the porch.

The animal had been skinned, organs removed, and it smelled of death and briny salt water.

Shaking all over, she screamed at him to leave her alone, then slammed the door and locked it, a sob tearing through her.

TWENTY-THREE

He banged on the door with his fist. How dare she scream at him?

He'd chopped wood for her and brought her one of his finest bucks. He'd skinned and dressed it, drained the blood and brined it then removed the organs so it would be ready for her to cook. He pictured it all in his mind—her at the stove, the hot stew bubbling, the intoxicating smell making the bunker feel all warm and cozy.

Just like the home they would have.

But she'd looked like she was going to faint when she'd seen the animal on her porch. Disbelief rolled through him. Would she freak out every time she saw the blood on his clothes or his hands? Wouldn't she cook the squirrels and rabbits and boar he brought home like his mama did?

Of course she would. That's what wives did.

He must have just caught her off guard. All he had to do was talk to her and show her the beautiful necklace he'd made for her. He'd seen her making jewelry through the window and knew she liked pretty things.

He knocked again. "Let me in so we can talk. I brought you another gift."

"Go away!" she screamed. "I'm calling the police now!"

His shoulders went rigid, anger taking root. She couldn't call the police. Couldn't tell them about him. They might find out about the other women. They were mistakes.

Maybe she was one, too.

He inched to the side of the house and looked through the window, saw her run toward her phone on the end table by the couch. She dropped the fire-poker as she reached for it.

No... He had to stop her.

He hurried down and snatched the ax from the woodpile, then ran back up the steps of the porch, raised the ax and hacked at the door. Wood splintered and cracked, and he hit the center again and again until he ripped a hole in it and the door crashed.

Her shrill scream filled the air as he lunged at her. He ripped the phone from her hand and threw it, sending it skidding across the wood floor under the kitchen table. "Be quiet," he growled. "You and I were meant to be together!"

She beat at him with her fists. "You're crazy! Leave me alone!"

He grabbed her around the neck and yanked her against him. She struggled and kicked and clawed at his arms then bit him on the hand. The pain shocked him. He bellowed and let go for a second, and she turned and ran past the fireplace. She grabbed the fire poker again and swung it at him, backing toward the door. Rage fired his blood and he chased her. She stumbled onto the porch and tripped over the deer. Her look of horror as her fingers plunged into the animal's sunken body cavity made him laugh.

She pulled her hands away and wiped them on the steps, then pushed up and scurried down the stairs, screaming.

He lifted his bow from his shoulder and moved toward her.

She thought she could outrun him. Escape.

But he was a seasoned hunter. She'd never get away.

She ran for her car, her boots digging deep in the snow and slowing her, then jerked at the door to open it. But it was locked. He shuffled toward her, his pulse hammering as she looked desperately around her, realizing she had no place to go.

Eyes full of fear, she frantically tried to open the car door. Icy sleet pelted him as he followed. Her shoes sank into the deep snow, and staggering against the wind, she grabbed at the car to stay on her feet.

He nocked an arrow, raised it and aimed it toward her chest. One step forward and he had the perfect shot. The ice below his feet crackled, alerting her, and she turned a pleading look toward him. "Please don't..." Then she spun around and pushed off from the car to run into the woods.

He released the arrow and sent it sailing toward her.

The sound of it spinning through the air blended with the wind, then the arrow pierced her back. She halted, her body jerking as she fell face forward into the snow.

TWENTY-FOUR

CROOKED CREEK

Night had set in as Ellie pulled into the local pizza joint, Pie in the Sky, to pick up dinner. She felt worn out; the day had taken it out of her.

She'd asked to see Mabel before she'd left, but the psychiatrist advised her to wait, saying that seeing Ellie might be more damaging to Mabel's already fragile psyche.

Ellie had gotten through worse things the past year and she would get through this. After all, how could she miss someone she hadn't known about until three months ago?

She had to drive around twice to find a parking spot as the place was full tonight, bustling with take-out orders and people probably going stir crazy with the weather. Having grown up in the South, one day of being snowed in was the Southerner's limit. But driving on the icy roads was dangerous and kept police and emergency workers busy. Shaded roads and side streets were slick with black ice and a challenge for those without snow chains or four-wheel drive.

She'd passed three accidents on her way and started to stop, but emergency workers were already present and thankfully they were just fender-benders.

Pop rock music blared through the speakers, the sound of

voices and laughter blending with the pulsing of the music, making her head hurt as she crossed to the bar to order.

Cord and Lola were sitting in a booth to the right, sharing a pitcher of beer and a pizza. Ellie tried to ignore the tiny stab of jealousy. She wanted Cord to be happy. He deserved it. And she really liked Lola.

She claimed a bar stool, and the bartender hurried over to her. "Hey, Ellie. Want a drink?"

She really did, but she didn't dare have even one cocktail and drive home on the roads tonight. "No thanks. Still on the job. But I do want a pizza to go." She knew the menu by heart. "The house special. No olives." She could already taste the spicy Italian sausage and the rich flavor of roasted onions, red pepper and earthy mushrooms.

"Be right back with it." One of the waitresses handed him another order, and he hustled to the kitchen.

Ellie turned in a wide arc and scanned the crowded room as she waited. She was surprised to spot Bryce in a corner booth, seated across from Trudy Morley, Mandy's aunt and now guardian.

She watched as Trudy set her water glass down, and Bryce lifted his mug of beer, his expression dead serious. Ellie couldn't help herself. She stood and walked over to them. Technically she was Mandy's aunt, though she hadn't explained their connection to the teenager yet. She felt the need to watch over Mandy, and she had no idea why Bryce would be arguing with Trudy. Trudy looked as if she was about to burst into tears.

Ellie cleared her throat to gain their attention, cutting off whatever Bryce was about to say. "Everything okay over here?" she asked.

Trudy startled and turned toward her, fidgeting then looking away.

Bryce licked the beer from his lips and clenched his jaw. "Fine."

"What's going on?" Ellie asked.

"Get lost, Ellie," he growled. "It's none of your business."

Trudy managed a small shrug. "It's fine, Ellie, just let it go."

Ellie searched Trudy's face, but she seemed to shut down before her eyes, and Ellie couldn't help herself. "If there's a problem—"

"It's fine, Ellie." Trudy stood, tossed her napkin on the table and snatched her purse. "I have to go."

She turned and rushed off, and Ellie glared down at Bryce. "What was that all about?"

Bryce lurched up, pushed away from the table and straightened. "Stay out of my business."

Then he stalked off, leaving her wondering what business he had with Trudy.

TWENTY-FIVE

ATLANTA, GEORGIA

Special Agent Derrick Fox seated himself in the governor's office in one of the plush wing chairs facing the desk, waiting until the man's chief of staff left before he spoke. He needed to focus but couldn't get his conversation with Ellie about the body she'd found out of his mind. There had been another murder on the AT. The crime wave there had been shocking the last few months. Ellie had her hands full.

But so had he here. And he went where his boss told him to go.

The gubernatorial election had been so close last month that it had been hard to call, and a group had challenged the results, claiming the election had been rigged, stirring anger, protests and riots.

"You have news for me?" Governor Weston asked.

Derrick nodded. "We made an arrest. A man named Jimmy Inez led that radical group who've been accusing you of stealing the election. He incited the protest that turned violent outside the Capitol." The crowd had gotten out of hand, storming businesses, crashing windows and looting. Some had even brought weapons and three people were shot. Several arrests had been made that day but putting the leader behind bars was the beginning of calming the situation.

"You can arrest him for inciting it?"

"Actually, we found evidence that he sent direct threats to you and proof that he was planning an assassination."

A muscle ticked in the governor's jaw. Derrick recognized a glint of concern in his deep gray eyes, the man's poker face slipping. He was an astute, well-spoken politician who'd made promises to improve the economy as well as to build programs to help feed those in need and fight the growing crime problem in Atlanta. Derrick wanted to see him complete those goals. The governor's wife was an educator who advocated for teachers and children.

"Do you think that threat was real?" Governor Weston asked.

"It was," Derrick said. "We're still monitoring the group, though, to make sure you and your family are safe."

Unease flickered on Weston's face, and he shifted, then cleared his throat. "I'm concerned about my family and have added an extra security detail. But I have a problem."

Derrick arched a brow. "What is it, sir?"

"My daughter, Ginger. She decided to leave town for a few days to get away from the media circus. But she's not answering my calls." The man blotted his sweating face with a handkerchief. "I know she wants space, but she said she was renting a cabin in that little mountain town that's been in the news so much lately."

Derrick raised a brow, his instincts going on full alert. "Crooked Creek?"

"That's the one," the governor said. "I saw the news that a woman's body was found on the Appalachian Trail, but they haven't released her name. I... God, with Ginger not answering, I've been out of my mind with worry all day."

Derrick went still, his conversation with Ellie echoing in his head. She hadn't identified the victim but thought she was from Helen. "Do you know where she's staying?"

He shook his head. "She wouldn't tell me. Said she didn't want to be bothered for a few days."

"She's probably doing just that," Derrick said in an effort to assuage his worries. "But if it'll make you feel better, I know a detective in the police department in Crooked Creek. I can make a call."

The governor relaxed slightly. "Yes, that would be reassuring. Considering the threats here..."

He let the sentence trail off, and Derrick nodded in understanding.

"Shoot me Ginger's phone number, too. I'll try to reach her."

"If you can't, track her phone. Also, she drives a black BMW sedan," Governor Weston said. "I know she'll be furious, but her safety is more important to me right now than having her angry at me for checking on her."

There was a knock at the door, then the governor's chief of staff poked her head in. "Sir, your meeting is in five."

Derrick stood. "I'll let you know what I find. If you hear from her, send me word."

Derrick left the office, a bad feeling in his gut. Hopefully he'd find Ginger Weston safe and sound. But with the climate surrounding the governor and the fact that a woman's body had just been found near Crooked Creek, he understood the man's concerns.

What better way to retaliate or hurt the governor than target the daughter he worshipped?

Ellie's face flashed before his eyes as he was escorted through the Capitol building to the exit.

He hadn't wanted to leave town after the last case. The fact that Ellie had almost died at the hands of a ruthless killer still tied his stomach into knots. He'd gotten too close to her. Started to care.

Caring was dangerous.

The cold air engulfed him as he stepped outside and hurried to his vehicle. As soon as he slid in the car, he texted his partner to set up the trace on Ginger's phone.

A spark of some emotion he didn't want to dwell on hit him. If he had to go to Crooked Creek to look for Ginger himself, at least he'd get to see Ellie.

TWENTY-SIX
ROSE HILL

Tessa Tulane had grown up in these parts and swore when she left that she'd never come back. But the stories of the South and the trail haunted her, and last year when she'd struck success with her zombie apocalypse story on the internet and gained half a million followers, a publisher had not only picked up the first story but had asked for a series.

Zelda, Zombie Slayer was born and so was her career.

The teenager's excited faces as she'd read from her work and then signed their books at the festival and returning to Crooked Creek had reminded her of her roots. How she'd lain awake at night, drowning out the sounds of her parents' fighting by using her imagination to travel to a different world.

"I'm gonna die tonight and you'll be sorry." Her father, doped up on whatever pills he could find, said those words every night. Yes, he was sick. But more mentally ill than physically. Her mama had never gotten over Tessa's older brother's death and become so frustrated with her father's whining and complaining that she'd started ignoring him. One night Tessa had realized her father really was having trouble breathing and begged her mother to call 911. But her mama refused and left him.

Her father died that night with Tessa in a cold sweat as she'd tried to revive him.

No wonder her thoughts went to dark scary places.

That young girl Mandy had asked her about her next book. Trouble was, she needed inspiration, so here she was climbing up to Rose Hill where old Miss Eula Ann Frampton lived.

As a teenager, she'd heard the rumors that the old woman talked to the dead. She'd also heard that she'd killed her husband and buried him in her rose garden. Except for her own grandmother, who'd befriended the woman, most of the other ladies in town stayed clear of her. The little children hid from her, while the teens claimed her house was haunted and every Halloween dared each other to prank her. Some left a dead animal, others painted scary messages and two boys in her class had drenched the porch in pig's blood.

Tessa thought she'd make a perfect character in her next story.

Snow dotted the foliage and rose bushes as she approached the tiny wooden house, and smoke curled from the chimney, drifting into the clouds. Hunched in her coat, she climbed the porch steps, but a brisk wind suddenly whipped through the trees and nearly blew her over. She staggered sideways to steady herself, then thought she heard a voice whispering to her in the wind.

Shaken, she raised her fist to knock, but the door screeched open, and Ms. Eula appeared, clutching a shawl around her bony shoulders. "Tessa?"

Tessa nodded. "You remember me?"

"Of course. I've been expecting you."

Tessa shivered.

Eula waved her gnarled hand. "Well, come on in, child, and get out of the cold."

Tessa followed the little woman into a small den where a fire blazed in the stone fireplace. The scent of herbs and garlic permeated the room and crystals sat everywhere. A dream catcher hung in the doorway and a silver-gray Siamese cat lay curled on the braided rug. As she approached, it lifted its head, ears pricking as its blue eyes tracked her.

"Let me get you some tea," Ms. Eula said.

Tessa agreed, although the rumors that Ms. Eula had no visitors because she poisoned them flitted through her mind.

"You knew I was coming?" Tessa asked as she seated herself on the dark purple velvet sofa.

Ms. Eula shrugged. "Just a feeling. And I saw your grandmother the other day. She was so happy you were coming to town." She fidgeted with the blanket. "Your mama brought you here when you were six," Ms. Eula said. "But I explained that I don't talk to the dead."

Tessa twisted her hands in her lap. "I remember. Mama thought you could tell her what happened to my brother. If he was pushed off that ridge or he just fell."

"I'm so sorry your family lost him, and I wish I could have helped explain what happened," Ms. Eula said. "I know what the folks in town say and think, but it's not true. I'm not a ghost whisperer or a psychic." She fluttered a hand to her shawl and pulled it tighter around her shoulders.

"You don't commune with the dead?" Tessa asked.

Ms. Eula shook her head. "I am haunted by spirits," she admitted. "I hear the cries of the dead sometimes, like those girls that were killed a while back on the trail. I feel their pain. And I've tried to talk to them, but that's not how it works."

Tessa took a sip of the tea. It was really tasty. Maybe chamomile with lavender.

"Is that why you're here?" Ms. Eula asked. "You want me to try and communicate with someone you've lost? With your brother?"

Maybe in the back of her mind, she had. But she shook her head. "I'm working on a new story about a child who talks to ghosts and helps their spirits cross over. Maybe she lives in the shadows and even helps solve mysteries."

Ms. Eula leaned forward and pressed her hand over Tessa's. A zing of something like electricity shot through Tessa, and Ms. Eula gasped and pulled her hand back.

"What is it?" Tessa asked.

"There's a dark aura around you, dear. You... need to be careful. Stirring up ghosts and messing with the Shadows could be dangerous."

TWENTY-SEVEN

CROOKED CREEK

Ellie had just lit the gas fireplace logs when her phone rang, and Derrick's name appeared on her screen again.

She picked up her phone ready to answer it and, glancing through the window at the sea of white-tipped trees, her chest squeezed as she remembered the one night they'd spent together. A blizzard had struck and they were trapped in a shelter on the trail while hunting a serial killer. On cold nights like these, she couldn't help but remember the feel of his warm body next to hers. His hands on her.

She answered the call. "Ellie, hey." His gruff voice focused her attention. "Any luck with that ID yet?"

So much for small talk.

"Not sure," she said, curious as to why he was interested. "The detective in Helen thinks she might be one of his missing persons cases. Why?"

"I just left Governor Weston's office. Apparently, his daughter came to the mountains to get away from the media, and he's worried because she's not returning his calls. He asked me to check on her."

Ellie ran her finger around the stem of her glass. "If you're asking if my victim is Ginger Weston, she's not. I've seen Ginger's photo all over the place." Ellie paused. "With facial rec, there's an eighty percent match to a girl named Nadine Houser who went missing eleven years ago."

"Sounds like you have a good start on the case," Derrick said.

Ellie sensed there was more. "About Ginger though. Did she and her father have a falling out or something?"

"I don't think so," Derrick said. "She said she wanted to get away from the media, so she may simply be hiding out somewhere."

Ellie understood about hiding out from the press. "Some of them can be vultures." She'd first thought that about Angelica. But she had slowly warmed to trusting her.

His voice sounded tired when he spoke. "What concerns me is these threats against the governor. I just made an arrest and stopped a possible assassination attempt. But we both know that someone might go after Ginger to hurt him."

"True." Ellie tugged at her ponytail. "If you know where she's staying, I'll drive over and do a well check."

"I'd appreciate that," Derrick said. "Governor Weston didn't know the name of the place, but I tracked Ginger's phone. I'll send you the GPS coordinates. Also sending you the make and model of her car."

Ellie hung up and went to get her coat and gloves, then checked the text from Derrick. Considering the fact that a dead woman had just been found in the mountains not too far from the address Derrick had sent, worry niggled at her.

If a predator was lurking in the mountains, Derrick might be onto something, and Ginger might be in danger.

TWENTY-EIGHT
PINE NEEDLE CROSSING

The GPS coordinates Derrick sent were for the cabins on the creek at Pine Needle Crossing.

Ellie phoned the property manager, but he had no record of Ginger Weston renting one. That didn't mean she wasn't there though. If Ginger had wanted to escape, she might have used a fake name to reserve a unit. There were only two, both rented by women. One by a mother of four and her husband. The second, a single woman.

Ellie knew exactly where the cabins were located. She'd snuck away and stayed there more than once during her time at the police academy when things had gotten rough. The natural beauty of the overhangs and the isolation had given her much needed R & R and time for soul searching. The dangers of the wilderness had not intimidated her. There she'd decided that the overbearing, male-dominated society of law enforcement wouldn't beat her down either.

Thinking about that time now, she still found it shocking that in the twenty-first century, she'd had to fight tooth and nail to make it through, fending off bullying, sexual harassment and superiors who thought her petite size would hinder her from taking down a dangerous felon.

So far, she'd proven them wrong, and she wasn't going to let Bryce's animosity against her change that.

Was Ginger Weston simply trying to find her own way in the paparazzi-scrutinized world of politics? Trying to break free from the limelight of her father's campaign to forge her own path?

If Ginger was safe, Ellie would assure her father she was fine and leave the girl to chase her own dreams. For all she knew, she might be holed up enjoying a romantic rendezvous with a secret lover she didn't want her parents or the world to know about.

She hoped that's what she'd find.

The thick slush spewed from her tires, but her four-wheel drive made it bearable to maneuver the switchbacks and her tires ground through the gravel and snow until she reached the cabin. She spotted the black BMW and parked beside it. A woodpile sat to the right of the BMW, an ax left jammed into a log. Ellie glanced at the front door and realized it was open.

Was Ginger here? Had she gone for a walk?

The hair on the back of her neck prickled as she got out and walked up to the front stoop. A blackish stain discolored the porch floor, and the stench of death wafted to her. And the door looked as if it had been busted in, maybe with an ax.

The hair on the nape of her neck prickled. Something was definitely wrong.

Senses on high alert, she pulled her weapon, stepped over the stain, then crept to the door and called out. "Ginger! Are you here?"

The air was still and silent as she entered the cabin. The living room and kitchen were one big room. The scent of burning wood greeted her, and although the fire had died down, a faint glow from the embers still remained.

Scattered across the pine table were various pieces of jewelry and supplies to make more. A sketchbook lay open; Ellie looked at it and saw a series of designs for stylish necklaces using different stones and arrangements.

"Ginger, are you here?" Slowly she eased her way down the

hall and found a bathroom and bedroom. Toiletries and a makeup bag sat neatly on the stone vanity.

She veered into the bedroom. "Ginger!" A Dresden plate quilt in blue and white covered the four-poster antique spindle bed, the bed neatly made. There was a plush velvet chair in one corner and an oak dresser the other. A suitcase sat open on the luggage stand.

Nothing seemed out of order. But that busted door told a different story.

Ellie saw snow boots and a heavy winter parka draped over the chair, indicating that Ginger hadn't gone for a hike. Returning to the living room, she searched for a purse and found it on the hall tree in the entry. The ID inside the wallet confirmed this was Ginger's cabin.

Gripping her weapon tightly, she walked back to the front door and examined the spot on the porch floor. Definitely looked like blood. Her gaze moved toward the forest and the stack of firewood and she spotted streaks of red staining the snow.

Her pulse hammered.

She headed down the steps and as she got closer, she could see that the blood looked fresh. Although the wind had blown snow across the ground, Ellie noticed drag marks, as if a sled had been pulled across the yard. Nerves bunched her shoulders. The deep grooves of the rungs had dug into the dirt and crushed weeds.

She followed the marks and found two sets. One leading from the woods to the house. Another leading from the house back into the forest. Both looked like a man's boot prints.

More blood, lots of it, dotted the snow along with the drag marks.

Ellie reached for her phone to call for a crime team. Then she'd call Cord. With the storm intensifying, she had to get search parties looking for Ginger before it was too late.

TWENTY-NINE

WILD HOG HOLLER

Pain screamed through Ginger's lower back and shoulders, and nausea climbed to her throat as she opened her eyes. She was surrounded by darkness, and the scent of something rancid filled her nostrils.

Her mind was fuzzy, but a fleeting memory of being chased taunted her. The knock on the door... the dead animal on the porch. The same creepy man in the big dark coat and black scarf. The ax splintering the wood.

Then snippets of screaming and falling and a stabbing pain.

Terror seized her.

She struggled to move, but realized her hands and feet were tied. The sound of something crinkling as she shifted made her go still. Plastic. She was lying on plastic. She peered around her and saw the walls were covered in it, too.

Dear God, where was she?

Low voices then laughter echoed from somewhere. She strained to hear. Maybe someone had come to help her.

But as she listened, she recognized the voices and canned laughter were from a TV show. An old western...

Panicking, she screamed for help, but her voice came out as a croak. Then a shadow moved in front of her, and she smelled sweat and a musky odor that intensified her nausea.

The black ski hat and scarf were gone now, and she could see a woolly beard covered the man's face. His beady gray-brown eyes bore into her. The coat was gone, too, a brown and orange flannel shirt that smelled metallic, like blood, strained the man's big bear-like body. The flicker of candlelight in the distance gave her just enough light to see sweat trickle down his broad jaw and forehead, where a scar trailed into his hairline.

Fear seized her. A bow and arrow were slung over his shoulder.

"Where am I?" she whispered. "Why are you doing this to me?"

"You ran from me," he said in an accusatory tone. "I brought you gifts. I was courting you." He dangled a crude leather necklace in front of her. "When I looked into your eyes at the gas station, I felt it. You wanted me like I wanted you."

Ginger's breath panted out as fear overcame her. She wished she'd answered the phone calls from Stephen and her father. Now no one knew where she was. Or how to find her. "I d-don't even know you."

"But I know you," he said, his voice husky and odd, as if he hadn't heard her. "When you looked at me that way, I knew we were meant to be together." He lifted the end of the cord and pointed to the center of a leather heart. "See. It says *Mine Forever*. I made this just for you."

Ginger's head swam with terror. He sounded delusional.

She struggled to remember stories where women were abducted and how they escaped. By talking... reasoning... playing along... "Please untie me and let me go," she said softly. "Then we can talk."

Even as she said the words, she knew it wasn't going to happen.

THIRTY

PINE NEEDLE CROSSING

Ellie phoned Derrick and filled him in on what she'd found at Ginger's rental cabin while the Evidence Response Team arrived and photographed the house and property, searching for forensics.

Worry reverberated in Derrick's voice. "I'm going to stall informing the governor until we know more. I'll be in Crooked Creek first thing in the morning."

Ellie closed her eyes for a moment, drawing comfort in the thought of seeing him again. Derrick had been a pillar of calm strength during the last cases they'd worked together.

But any semblance of calm faded as she pictured Ginger's pretty young face, and she imagined what might have happened at this house. None of the scenarios she imagined were good. "Maybe she escaped and is somewhere in town." Even as she said it, she didn't believe it.

According to Derrick, the family had received threats. Had someone abducted Ginger as a ploy to hurt the governor for his political agenda? Were they looking for a ransom?

Or... was this a personal crime against Ginger? Did she have enemies?

"What's around the cabins?" Derrick asked.

Ellie rubbed the back of her neck. "Not much. No neighbors to canvass. Cabins are pretty isolated and set far apart. If something happened here, it's unlikely anyone would have seen it."

"Dangerous for a young woman traveling alone. She made the perfect mark for a predator," Derrick muttered. "The governor said he warned her not to come up here alone."

"But she was probably sick of the press." Irritation tinged Ellie's voice. "It's not fair that women have to be on the defensive all the time. Governor Weston probably wouldn't have thought anything of it if he had a son who took a trip by himself."

"No one said it's fair," Derrick said. "But it is what it is."

Ellie silently cursed. "Do you think someone threatening the governor followed Ginger here?"

"I'll have my partner work on that theory," Derrick said. "But you know it could have been random. Someone who lived in the woods or a criminal hiding out, and Ginger was a crime of opportunity."

"Or another sick monster like Vera's son Hiram," Ellie muttered beneath her breath. At this point, they couldn't rule anything out. What if she'd been taken by the man who'd murdered her victim and buried her in the snow?

Worry knotted Ellie's stomach, and she prayed she was wrong.

One of the crime techs called out that he'd found a cell phone wedged in the snow by the woodpile. "I have to go," Ellie said to Derrick. "We found Ginger's phone."

"Good, that might be helpful. Keep me posted."

"I will." Ellie hung up, pulled on latex gloves and joined the crime tech. The shiny purple case looked like a woman's, and when she flipped it over, the initials GW shone in glitter. She tried to access Ginger's contacts, but it was password protected.

The investigator continued searching around the woodpile, and a minute later found a gold chain. Ellie's stomach sank deeper as she noted the gold letters that spelled out Ginger's name.

It had fallen—or been ripped off—and landed on the snowy ground near the phone. Examining it more closely, she spotted blood on the chain.

"Let's bag this and send the phone to the lab." Hopefully they'd get lucky and find that whoever had attacked Ginger had left some evidence behind. The heavy drag marks suggested the person was male. He had to be strong to haul her away, even if he used a sled.

That blood might even belong to him.

Cord arrived with a group of SAR volunteers and Ellie filled them in. "If Ginger is alive and escaped, she's hurt and can't have gotten too far. She could be lost or hiding out somewhere so be sure to identify yourself." She rubbed her hands together to stay warm and to settle her nerves. "Judging from those drag marks in the snow, her attacker may have had a sled or some way to transport her once he abducted her. Follow those marks as long as you can see them."

"I've alerted the central ranger station," Cord said. "If someone kidnapped her, he may have hauled her into the woods to hide or wait out the storm."

"True," Ellie agreed. "But if he had a car waiting, they could be long gone."

"We'll start with a ten-mile radius," Cord said. "Anything beyond that would have probably required a vehicle."

"Look for signs of an ATV," Ellie said, remembering that Hiram had used one to escape.

"The temperature's dropping again, supposed to be in the low teens," Cord said to the teams.

"If she is alive, she could freeze to death." The image tormented Ellie. So did the thought of a man wielding an ax against Ginger. And if he'd used it on her, what they might find.

Cord pulled the hood of his coat up, his amber eyes stone serious, strands of his shaggy brown hair whipping around his face in the strong wind. "Yeah, and more snow is on the way. My teams need to start searching."

"Set it up." Ellie shuddered at the thought of Ginger running from a predator while hurt and bleeding.

Her own breath quickened as if she was being chased herself. She had been stalked before, dragged into the woods, and had had to fight for her life.

She hoped Ginger had enough fight in her to survive until they found her.

THIRTY-ONE

Cord led one search team while the others fanned out to cover more territory, each team taking a SAR dog to aid in tracking Ginger.

Cord's team went north, hiking along the creek and checking AT shelters along the way. The first two were empty, but in the third they discovered two teenage boys who'd gotten lost in the storm. One member of his team parted ways to escort the boys back down the mountain safely.

The dark skies and foggy weather made visibility difficult as they maneuvered the sharp ridges, and as sleet began to fall, the paths turned more slippery. The icy pellets stung Cord's cheeks, but he trudged on, shouting Ginger's name and shining his flashlight through the precipitation.

The trees seemed to hug each other tighter at night, limbs heavy and bowing with the weight of the snow connecting them, like fingers laced together. Tangled vines, fallen boughs and tree stumps hidden by the downfall made every step treacherous.

The team's SAR dog, a beagle named Benji, trotted forward, sniffing at a boulder by the water, and Cord rushed over. Shining his flashlight on the area, he spotted a red stain in the white. Blood.

Not a good sign.

His heart rate picked up. *Dammit*, he hoped this didn't turn into a recovery mission instead of a rescue one.

Benji barked and howled, lifting his head and sniffing the air. Then he took off. Cord raced after him, boots digging in the snow, the wind hurling brittle twigs at him as he ran, the team following a distance behind.

He followed the dog, scanning the trees and brush for signs of Ginger, halting at a fork in the creek. In spite of the cold, perspiration trickled down the back of his neck. Benji pawed at the muddy, icy ground, emitting a long howl as he studied the water.

Cord stooped down to examine the area and noticed the brush was smashed, the mud marred as if someone had stepped in it. Using his flashlight to illuminate the area, he analyzed the mud for a solid footprint, but the water had washed over it, making it indistinguishable. To the right he saw more markings, disturbed brush and the imprint of the shell of the canoe that had been docked in the bushes.

Standing again, he studied the creek and how it wound through the forest. He'd run these waters himself plenty of times. Ahead, he knew there were deeper sections with rapids.

Fear for Ginger Weston bolted through him as he imagined a kidnapper dragging her through the storm, then shoving her in the canoe and paddling miles and miles away, to where they might never find her.

On the drive back to Crooked Creek, Ellie called Angelica and asked her to come to the station for a press conference. Next she phoned her boss to update him, and he insisted she talk to the sheriff. He said he'd had a firm talk with Bryce earlier.

She hung up and rang Bryce, forcing herself to keep a neutral tone. Captain Hale had been good to her so far, and she didn't want to risk pissing him off. Besides, he was right. They all needed to work together.

Ellie was surprised to find that Bryce sounded sober when he answered. She filled him in on her findings at the cabin.

"Ranger McClain is spearheading the SAR teams to comb the woods for her," Ellie told him.

"My father got a call from Governor Weston," Bryce said. "He's been updated and given his support to the media briefing."

Ellie winced. *Aha.* That was the reason he was being cordial.

"I understand his concerns," Ellie said, dreading having to talk to the Westons. "Deputy Landrum is still looking through Ginger's social media. I need your deputies to start searching abandoned cabins and properties in the county."

"I've already been doing that in the hunt for Dunce," he said tightly. "But I'll have my deputies expand the search."

"Thank you," Ellie said, grateful. Although she still wasn't sure she trusted him. "Deputy Eastwood can head up the search in Crooked Creek. If someone did escape with Ginger, he's probably looking for a place to hold up during the storm." Ellie's mind raced with the disturbing possibilities.

Bryce cleared his throat. "The fact that James Dunce is still in the wind and you just found a woman's body can't be coincidental."

"Agreed. We have no proof yet though. But the women are similar in appearance. If Dunce abducted Nadine Houser and killed her, he may have finally dumped her body and taken Ginger." Ellie ended the call as she drove through town and into the parking lot at the police station.

She couldn't shake the horrible feeling that something terrible had happened to Ginger.

That she might be too late to save her.

It had happened before. Victims dying on her watch. Their faces haunted her at night and sometimes appeared out of nowhere during the day when she was alone, eyes wide with terror and accusations. *How could you let this happen to us?*

She spotted the news van already there, parked, hurried inside and dropped her coat in her office. For a minute she stood and inhaled deeply to settle her emotions. If the town picked up on her concern for Ginger and her fear of failing, they would panic as well.

Her detective instincts finally helped rein in her nerves. The sooner she spread the word and circulated Ginger's photo on the news, the sooner they might get a tip that someone had seen her.

Taking another deep breath, she joined Angelica and her cameraman, Tom, in the conference room. Her gaze locked with the reporter's, silent questions passing between them.

A sympathetic smile lit Angelica's big eyes. "Ready?"

Ellie shook her head but stepped forward and cleared her throat. "No. But we have to get her face out there."

Angelica gestured toward Tom to roll on the count of three.

"This is Angelica Gomez, *Channel Five News*, coming to you from Crooked Creek's police department. I'm here with Detective Ellie Reeves and a late breaking story." She angled the mic toward Ellie. "Detective?"

"Yes," Ellie kept an even voice. "Most of you know or have seen photographs of Ginger Weston, Governor Richard Weston's daughter, on the news recently. Ginger came to the mountains for a retreat but hasn't been heard from since. We found evidence of foul play at the cabin where she was staying and suspect she's in danger." Ellie paused. "If you have heard from Ginger or know anything about her whereabouts, or if you know of someone who may have wanted to harm her, please call the police."

The number for both Bluff County's sheriff's office as well as Crooked Creek's police department would appear on screen.

Angelica pushed for more. "Do you think Ms. Weston's disappearance is connected to the homicide you're investigating?"

Ellie sucked in a breath, debating over how to respond. Did she want to imply that and stir up fear in town, or give the governor and his wife hope? "At this point I can't say, but we're considering every possibility. SAR teams are combing the woods for Ms. Weston now, and the sheriff and his deputies are searching all of Bluff County."

Angelica's brown eyes gleamed with the realization that she understood Ellie's hesitation to say too much. Still, she was a reporter who always pushed for her story. And for the truth.

"Do you have any information or an ID on the woman whose frozen body was found at Beaver Pond?" Angelica asked.

Ellie gritted her teeth but maintained a neutral expression. "Not at this time. However, we are looking for a man named James Dunce for questioning. If anyone knows him or his whereabouts, please call the police. I will keep you posted as the investigation progresses."

Angelica raised a brow as if suggesting she thought Ellie was holding back. But Ellie didn't take the bait. Instead, she reminded people the investigations were separate, asked them to call with any information, then ended the interview.

Angelica dismissed Tom and looked at Ellie. "What aren't you saying?"

"Nothing. We're at a dead end on the body until we confirm her ID."

"Is it possible Ms. Weston isn't in trouble?" Angelica said. "That she went into hiding or ran off with a lover?"

Ellie lowered her voice. "I thought of that. But all her things were still inside the cabin, including her computer, and her car was there. We found her cell phone outside by a wood stack. And the door had been busted in with an ax." Ellie rolled her shoulders. "This stays between us, understood?"

"Yes," Angelica said tightly.

Ellie lowered her voice. "We also found a trail of blood."

Angelica's brows rose. "That does sound suspicious."

Ellie clenched her jaw. "There were also drag marks in the snow outside the cabin, indicating she was abducted."

Angelica's eyes widened as she began to formulate her own theories. "You think this man named Dunce is connected, don't you? That Ginger Weston is already dead?"

"I pray she's still alive. But the timing seems too coincidental to ignore," Ellie replied. "Then again, if it is the same kidnapper or Dunce, we don't know how long he actually kept his victim before killing her. Ginger could be being held hostage and tortured as we speak."

Angelica shuddered and fear for Ginger made it hard for Ellie to breathe. There was no telling what this man was doing to her right now... if he was making her suffer...

And they were about to unleash a media circus. A governor's daughter would be a national, perhaps international, news story.

And Ellie was at the center of it now. It could also be the biggest story of Angelica's career.

Shondra was waiting for her at the door when she was ready to leave. "You want me to search around Crooked Creek for Ginger Weston?"

"Yes," Ellie said. "I just hope we're not too late to save her."

Shondra squeezed her arm. "You're doing everything you can, Ellie."

Ellie's gaze met Shondra's. "But what if it isn't enough?"

THIRTY-THREE

WILD HOG HOLLER

Tears streamed down Ginger's face as she felt the man's hands stroking her hair from her cheek. "You are so lovely. We're going to have a good life here together."

Ginger's sob caught in her throat. "Please let me go. My father has money. He'll pay you whatever you ask."

"I don't want money," he said gruffly.

"Then what do you want? My father is powerful. He'll—"

"I want you, silly." His rough fingers brushed her cheek. "Besides, it's too dangerous out there. There are bad things that could get you."

He was the bad thing. Except he was in here.

The pain in her lower back was so grating, nausea rose to her throat. Plastic crinkled as she struggled to move, and she felt a sticky wetness beneath her. Her own blood.

His fingers danced down her cheek then over her shoulder. "Let me help you, darling."

Every cell in her body tensed as he rolled her to her side so her back faced him. She screamed and ordered her body to move, to fight. She had to save herself. But her legs felt numb, and a heavy chain around her ankle weighed her down.

He stroked her arms as if to comfort her. "I know it hurts,

sweetheart, but you're mine now, and I'll take care of you. Just as a wolf mates for life, so will we."

His voice was coarse, low, sent chills up her spine. Then he pulled her sweatshirt up to expose her back and reached for the waist of her yoga pants.

Oh, God... What was he planning to do?

He slid her pants down her hips an inch, and she cried out and thrashed her arms.

One firm hand pressed her into the plastic, and he reached around her and stuffed a rag in her mouth. "Bite down on this. I'm going to clean your wound and stitch it up for you."

Her body shook with sobs and tears streamed down her cheeks as she felt a hot cloth press against the small of her back. He held it for a minute then lifted it. In the firelight, she saw that it was soaked in blood.

He dipped the cloth into hot water over and over, pressing it hard against her wound, then scrubbed her already tender skin until it felt raw, and her nerve cells cried out in agony. Terror seized her as he held a long needle over the flame, the orange and yellow glow illuminating his gruff face and the sinister hollowness of his eyes as he stared at it. Trembling, once again she tried to move away from him, but her body was too weak. The tears came faster and harder as she watched him thread the needle.

One hand brushed over her cheek again. "It'll be over soon and then you can heal, and we can start our life together just like my mama and daddy did."

The sharp sting of the needle puncturing her brought a wave of nausea. She prayed that he'd just kill her quickly.

Instead, he slowly threaded the needle through her skin over and over, crooning soft loving words, promising to build a home for them where they would be together forever.

THIRTY-FOUR

CROOKED CREEK POLICE STATION

The next morning, Ellie hurried to her office, hoping the day held better news than the night had. With every passing minute, the chances of finding Ginger alive grew slimmer.

She hoped that, given the threats against the governor, Derrick might have some answers when he arrived.

Shondra brought two coffees in, yawning as she entered.

"You have a late night?" Ellie asked.

Shondra tugged at her long black braid. "Yeah, searched several abandoned places. No luck. Then I couldn't sleep."

Ellie could sympathize. "The nightmares back?"

Shondra shrugged and handed Ellie her coffee. "Thought they were better, but I couldn't keep from thinking about Ginger Weston."

It made sense that the abduction would trigger bad memories for Shondra. "Do you need more time off?"

Shondra shook her head. "No, it's better when I'm busy. I want to help find her. What else can I do?"

Ellie gave her friend a quick smile in solidarity. "Well, because of the high winds and frigid temperatures, Cord had to call off the search in the woods at eleven last night. But other crews started at dawn this morning, expanding the search grid to focus on the forks at the creek and where a boater might have ended up." Ellie paused. "Extend your search to abandoned houses, cabins or properties north of Crooked Creek. They're building some news ones on Bear Mountain near the creek."

"Copy that. I know a couple of old farms I'll look at, too."

Ellie took a long sip of her coffee. "We'll have a briefing in a few minutes before you leave."

Shondra nodded. "I'll go to my desk, do some research and map out a plan."

She left the office and Ellie got to work at her computer, but a minute later, voices echoed from Captain Hale's office. As Ellie looked out into the corridor, she went still at the sight of Derrick Fox standing at the doorway of her boss's office. His deep eyes looked troubled, his jaw rigid. Instead of the suit he wore on the job, he was dressed in a button-down shirt and jeans that hugged his muscular body. She could see a hint of beard stubble grazing his wide jaw, adding to his rugged masculinity.

Ellie curled her fingers into her palms to stifle a reaction. She couldn't think about her attraction to him, not here. Not now. Not with two cases on her plate. And a high-profile one, the governor's daughter, no less...

He stepped to the side as she approached, and she realized he hadn't come alone.

Governor Weston was pacing the captain's office, his movements agitated. "You have to find Ginger," he said, his tone laced with fear. "I can't lose her."

Ellie's heart squeezed. She understood what it was like to worry about someone you cared about, to not know if they were dead or alive. She'd felt that way when Shondra had been taken. And then again with Angelica, and poor Vanessa Morely, her childhood friend.

This was every parent's worst nightmare, no matter the age of their child.

"I told him he didn't have to come, but he insisted," Derrick said gruffly.

Now Ellie realized who the dark sedan belonged to outside.

There had been two others parked across the street—the governor's security detail.

"I understand. I'd do the same if I were him," she said softly.

The captain glanced up at her from his desk and the governor stopped pacing, his breathing erratic. Ellie had watched him during the campaign and hadn't once seen him ruffled.

But this was different. Personal. Terrifying.

The governor's wife Gwyneth, an elegant woman in her late forties wearing a dark blue pantsuit, sat twisting a handkerchief between her fingers.

Captain Hale stood, as if he thought he might need to run interference, then made introductions. "This is Detective Reeves."

An eagerness for answers, for hope, lit the governor's eyes and tore at Ellie.

She offered him and his wife a compassionate look. "I'm so sorry we have to meet like this. I followed your campaign and am a supporter."

The governor's frown furrowed. "Thank you. My wife and I know who you are, of course."

Of course. Her face had been plastered all over the news the last year. She hadn't always been painted in a good light, and she and her parents had garnered enemies with a few of the locals over Hiram's crimes. She couldn't blame them. Several little girls had died during her father's terms of office. If Vera hadn't hidden the truth about Hiram for so long, they might have stopped him from taking so many precious lives.

Mrs. Weston perched on the edge of her seat, eyes pleading. "Please tell me you found Ginger and that this is some horrible misunderstanding."

Beside her, Ellie felt the tension in Derrick's body. She clenched her jaw to keep from reacting. "I wish I could do that," she said gently. "But I'm afraid I can't. Have you received a message from Ginger or anyone threatening or making demands regarding her?"

"You mean a ransom call?" the governor asked, his deep baritone cracking.

"Yes. Even if it's not money, she might have been abducted with the intent to trade her for some kind of political favor."

The governor's eyes blazed with emotion. "No. Nothing like that."

Derrick gestured to the Westons. "They've already given their permission to have their phones tapped and traced in case a kidnapper calls."

She figured the couple had. "Governor, Mrs. Weston, we had search parties looking for your daughter last night. They had to call off the search for a few hours due to the storm, but they're already out looking again this morning."

"Why is this happening?" Mrs. Weston cried.

"Gwen, shh." Governor Weston placed a tender hand on his wife's shoulder and rubbed her back. "We are going to get to the bottom of this. And we are going to find Ginger." He pinned Ellie and then Derrick with a steely gaze that begged for reassurances. "Aren't we, Agent Fox, Detective Reeves?"

"Yes, you have my word," Derrick said.

"And mine, too." Ellie squared her shoulders. "Now let's get down to business. I need to know anything and everything about your daughter and her life."

THIRTY-FIVE

Ellie took the Westons to the conference room while Derrick, Captain Hale, Deputy Eastwood and Deputy Heath Landrum joined them. She'd texted Bryce, but he was a no-show.

She'd already turned the murder board to face the wall so the couple wouldn't see the pictures of the alleged crime scene.

"Special Agent Fox said you found signs of foul play at Ginger's rental cabin," the governor began. "Do you think she's hurt?"

The blood indicated she was, but Ellie needed to get to that detail carefully. "We found her cell phone and a gold necklace with lettering that spelled Ginger's name in the snow outside the cabin. The door was busted open, and her car was still there, but there were drag marks in the snow outside indicating someone may have taken her into the woods."

Mrs. Weston paled and pressed her hands over her face. "Oh god, what is happening to my baby?"

Ellie hesitated, sympathy swelling inside her. She hated to be blunt, but neither could she lie. "I'm so sorry, but I'm afraid we also found blood outside in the snow near where her phone had been dropped. We're not certain that the blood belonged to Ginger but we're testing it. If someone abducted her, Ginger may have fought back and injured him so it's possible it could be his. We collected her toothbrush and hairbrush for DNA. They're at the lab now along with the phone and necklace. Her phone was password protected, but we hope to crack that and study her contacts, texts, calls and social media. Same with her laptop." She gestured toward Deputy Landrum. "He's our tech expert."

"I'll get right on it," Heath said, then he addressed the Westons. "If you know the password that would help."

"I'm afraid I don't," her mother said, her voice warbling. "Ginger was very private. She hated all the campaigning and media attention. That's one reason she came out here, to get away from it."

Ellie's pulse jumped. If she hadn't seen the blood, she might consider that Ginger faked a kidnapping to escape. But there *had* been blood...

Heath's voice was gruff. "It would help if you could compose a list, like her birthday, pet names, anything that you can think of she might have used to create a password."

Mrs. Weston worried her lower lip with her teeth. "Yes, I can do that."

"Governor," Ellie said. "We need a list of anyone you consider a threat."

He gestured to Derrick. "Special Agent Fox has already been digging into the threats against me, including correspondence I've received. He'll have that list."

Derrick filled everyone in on the arrest they'd just made regarding the possible assassination attempt. "There are other groups out there making noises," he said. "We have people monitoring online chatter. A survivalist group is spreading conspiracy theories, claiming the government has cameras spying on people in their homes. Some of them are pretty radical, have formed their own little communities. I'll have my partner dig deeper into them and see if there was talk of a plot that included Ginger."

Ellie's skin prickled. During her hikes with her father, he'd regaled her with stories about these people. Some were preppers, storing food and supplies in anticipation of an atomic bomb or government upheaval. Her father called the ones who hid in the woods the Shadows. The endless miles of wilderness along the trail were the perfect place to disappear from society.

Ellie placed Ginger's photo on a clean whiteboard, then beneath it drew a question mark. Below it she wrote *Threats against Governor* and listed the name of the man Derrick had arrested, then added a question mark noting survivalist camps.

She turned back to the room. "Now let's talk about Ginger's personal life. From your media coverage, I understand she has a boyfriend. Stephen DuPont."

"That's right. He worked on my campaign. He's a nice fellow," the governor said.

A frown flickered in Derrick's eyes. "We met during my investigation. I talked to him a while ago about Ginger and he said he hasn't heard from her either," Derrick said. "He was upset and is on his way."

Mrs. Weston knotted her hands in her lap, studying them. Ellie watched, her pulse quickening. There was something she wasn't saying.

"Mrs. Weston, did you feel the same way?"

The woman glanced nervously at her husband. "Yes, I mean he was competent at the job. And he cared about Ginger..."

Ellie tilted her head to the side. "But?"

The governor gave his wife a concerned look. "Honey, Stephen would never hurt Ginger."

"Maybe not," Ellie said gently. "But if you want me to find out what happened to your daughter, you have to be honest. About everything," she added. "Withholding details to protect someone you think you trust could be a mistake."

Mrs. Weston's breath fluttered out. "Ginger just broke up with Stephen. She found out he cheated on her, and she told him it was over."

Ellie glanced at Derrick and saw his jaw tighten. He hadn't known.

"How did he take the breakup?" Ellie asked.

"Not very well," Mrs. Weston said.

The governor shrugged. "He loved our daughter and thought they could have done great things together."

"Mrs. Weston, what do you mean, that he didn't take it very well?" Ellie asked.

She fidgeted. "Stephen is accustomed to getting what he wants, so he was angry. He kept calling and pushing her to come back. That's another reason she came here. To get away from him."

THIRTY-SIX

Governor Weston insisted he wanted to make a personal plea to the public about his daughter's disappearance, so they took a short break while Ellie called Angelica to set it up.

She, Derrick and the Westons were reconvening in the conference room when Stephen DuPont arrived, looking harried and upset. Ellie had seen the man on TV with Ginger and knew he was handsome. But there was something disingenuous about him.

She caught him at the door. "Mr. DuPont, I'm Detective Ellie Reeves." His light green eyes raked over her and seemed to disapprove. DuPont was handsome in a *GQ* sort of way. Neatly trimmed light-brown hair. Manicured nails. Fair skinned. Striking jawline. Always dressed impeccably. And he looked like he was wearing more makeup than Ellie ever did.

A perfect politician himself.

"I know who you are," he said, then brushed past her and walked over to where Derrick stood beside the governor, totally dismissing her. "Special Agent Fox, what the hell is going on?"

A muscle ticked in Derrick's cheek. "Like I explained on the phone, Governor Weston asked me to check on Ginger." He gestured toward Ellie. "This is Detective Reeves' town, so I asked her to drive out to the cabin to check on her. When she arrived, she discovered signs of foul play and that Ginger was gone."

Stephen gave Ellie another quick glance, emotions she couldn't quite define glittering in his eyes. Did he honestly care for Ginger? Or had he used her as a ticket to the governor and a way to boost his own career?

"What kind of signs?" he asked.

"Why don't you sit down, Stephen?" the governor suggested. "Agent Fox and the detective can fill you in, and maybe you can help."

DuPont's Italian loafers clicked on the floor as he crossed the room and seated himself by the governor.

Derrick claimed the chair opposite him, and Ellie sat by Derrick's side. He seemed stiff around DuPont, making her wonder what his opinion was of the man. He'd obviously gotten to know him during the time he'd spent with the governor.

DuPont clasped his hands together, and Ellie studied his body language searching for indications he was faking concern. That he knew where Ginger was.

"Mr. DuPont," Ellie said, forcing a neutral tone. "We found Ginger's phone, keys and her necklace in the snow outside the cabin by her car. We also discovered blood in the snow and other indications that she might have been abducted."

The man ran a hand through his hair, spiking the ends. "Jesus. I've been calling and calling her, but she hasn't answered or returned my calls. I told her it was a mistake to leave Atlanta and come here to the boonies."

Ellie ignored the jab at her hometown. "Where were you last night, Mr. DuPont?"

His angry gaze jerked to her. "Where was I? What are you implying, Detective? That I had something to do with this?"

"I'm simply gathering information," Ellie said bluntly.

"How dare you?" he hissed. "Are you going to let her talk to me like that, Agent Fox?"

Derrick squared his shoulders, irritation flashing on his face, and Ellie's fingers curled into her palms. She noticed the governor's wife startle. Even the governor shifted uncomfortably, his expression hinting that he needed to defuse the situation.

"I know you're worried, Stephen, but Detective Reeves is just doing her job. These are routine questions so we can eliminate you," Derrick said strategically.

Ellie cleared her throat. "You want to help us find Ginger, don't you?"

"Or course I do," he snapped.

"The first course of action in any investigation is to talk to the family and friends," Ellie said, determined not to let him intimidate her. "Any conversation between the two of you, anything you know about her friends, any problems she was having... any detail might help us find her and the person who abducted her."

DuPont flattened his hands on the table. "Well, I certainly would never hurt her," he said. "I loved Ginger."

Mrs. Weston shot him a disapproving look. "You cheated on her. Ginger came up here to get away from you."

Stephen's eyes narrowed to slits. "She came here to escape the limelight," he ground out.

"And because you were sleeping around," Ellie pointed out.

That earned her a mutinous look. "I told her we could work through that together. That she couldn't throw away what we had because of a misstep that meant nothing."

Ellie shook her head. No wonder Ginger had left them all for some time alone. They'd driven her away.

"Where were you yesterday and last night?" she asked.

The angry glint in his eye turned to one of snide victory. "In meetings with the committee discussing gun control. We've met the last three days and worked through dinner."

"We'll need names who can verify that."

"Of course." He pulled his phone. "I'll text them to Special Agent Fox."

He might have an alibi. But Ellie didn't like him. He was so cocky, he reminded her of Bryce.

"Mr. DuPont, Governor Weston and his wife have not

received a ransom call. Have you heard from Ginger or her kidnapper?" Derrick asked.

DuPont shook his head.

"We'll also need your phone," Ellie said with a saccharine smile. "Just to verify your calls and texts."

He handed it to Derrick. "Do what you have to do." He cut Ellie a menacing look. "But if you malign my name, I will sue you and the entire county. And then I'll have your job."

THIRTY-SEVEN

Ellie did not take threats well. If Derrick and the governor hadn't been present, she might have smacked Stephen DuPont on the side of his pompous head.

But if his alibi checked out, she would have to write him off and move on.

He didn't exactly fit the profile of a man with a hunting knife. Stephen was the type who'd hire someone to do his dirty work. But if he really loved Ginger, his reaction would have been more fear for Ginger than the need to protect himself.

A quick knock at the door and Deputy Landrum poked his head inside. "I got into Ms. Weston's phone and laptop."

Ellie wanted to know what he'd found but she wasn't going to ask in front of Stephen, so she stood. "Governor, Mrs. Weston, Angelica Gomez should be here any minute. Why don't you take a breather, speak with your chief of staff and think about what you want to say to the press?"

She ducked from the room and joined Heath at his desk. "What did you find so far?" she asked.

The deputy gestured toward the phone. "Nothing concrete. No threats, that is. She and her boyfriend had words. Apparently, she knew he cheated on her and she broke it off. He left a few pleading messages for her to come back, said they were perfect together. Each message he left sounded more and more agitated. But no specific threats."

"He's admitted to all that, but claims he has an alibi," Ellie said. "Agent Fox will verify it. Anything else?"

"Several calls from the governor saying he was worried about her. But he sounded sincerely concerned, not threatening."

"I don't think the parents had anything to do with it," Ellie said. "But someone who wants to get at them might."

"There's no evidence of that on her phone or social media. She had a few fans/friends/men who wanted to meet her in person. I'll see what I can dig up on them. Oh, and I found a number for her best friend. Name's Haley."

"Text me her number. I want to talk to her myself." Ellie paused. "Was Ginger on any dating apps?"

"No. Her social media consisted mostly of Etsy, Pinterest and she'd downloaded several podcasts on small business start-ups. She also collected dozens and dozens of pictures of handmade jewelry."

"That fits with the sketches and supplies I found at her cabin. She was going to start her own jewelry line." Ellie wrinkled her brow. From the pieces she'd seen on the table in the cabin, the young woman was talented. But her family wanted to steer her in another direction.

Ellie understood that kind of pressure. "The art and her social media posts don't fit with a motive for a kidnapping. It's looking more and more like this had to do with her father. Or like she was at the wrong place at the wrong time."

Which complicated the case. And meant she'd fallen into the hands of a predator who targeted women. One with nefarious motives.

They needed the results of that blood sample. Now. Ellie inhaled a deep breath and ran her hands through her hair, panic starting to claw at her.

Time might be running out for Ginger.

THIRTY-EIGHT

Derrick balled his hands into fists to keep his anger at Stephen DuPont at bay. He hadn't liked him when they'd first met, and his attitude toward Ellie today confirmed he was a jerk. He thought money bought everything and would use anyone to get what he wanted.

But he didn't peg him as a killer. Although if he'd been pissed about the breakup, maybe he followed Ginger, tried to convince her to come back with him, and they argued. The argument could have escalated out of control and turned ugly.

But the way the door had been smashed with that ax indicated a level of violence that didn't fit with DuPont's cool veneer.

Leaving the Westons to discuss how they wanted to handle the media with their press officer, and DuPont to stew and hopefully compose himself, Derrick went to Ellie's office and seated himself in the sitting area in the corner. DuPont had texted him the number for the chairman of the committee, a man Derrick had met when the governor introduced him to his staff, and he used the opportunity to call him now.

Leonard Johnson answered, his voice full of concern when Derrick explained the situation.

"I talked to the governor last night," Johnson said. "I know he's frantic."

"He is, and we're doing everything possible to find out what happened to his daughter. That's the reason I called."

"I don't understand how I can help."

"We're questioning all family and friends of the family. Stephen DuPont is here, and claims he was at a committee meeting with you yesterday, well into the evening. Is that true?"

A tense moment passed. "He was at the meetings, yes. We've been working late the last few days. Although..."

"Although what?" Derrick asked.

A tense second passed. "Yesterday he skipped out early and didn't make it to the dinner."

Derrick frowned. The bastard had lied to Ellie. "Did he say why he was leaving early?"

Another heartbeat passed. "No. I assumed he had plans with Ginger."

"Were you aware that they broke up?"

"I sensed there was trouble, but DuPont seemed confident they'd work it out." Johnson hesitated. "But it's hard for me to believe he'd hurt Ginger. He can't keep it in his pants, but he isn't violent, just self-absorbed."

"If you think of anything else, please give me a call."

Johnson agreed, and Derrick gripped his phone and strode back to the conference room. Angelica Gomez was setting up, so he motioned Stephen to join him.

"You lied to Detective Reeves, DuPont," Derrick said curtly. "Did you really think I wouldn't find out?"

The man leaned in toward him and spoke in a conspiratorial whisper. "You know me, Agent Fox. She doesn't. And I'm not going to let her pin some crime on me when I'm innocent."

I do know him, Derrick thought. DuPont saw himself as above reproach. And he was just the type that if he had done something to Ginger, he'd expect to get away with it. "Are you innocent?" Derrick asked, an edge to his tone. "Lying to the police certainly doesn't make you look that way."

DuPont adjusted his tie. "I wanted her back on my arm. Why would I hurt her?"

"Because she didn't want you." And DuPont didn't accept rejection in business or his personal life very well. Derrick had seen him run all over the governor's staff and practically order Ginger to smile for the camera. But she hadn't been able to fake it, and he'd heard them argue.

"She was just in a snit," DuPont said. "Once she took some time away and got this silly notion of designing jewelry out of her system, she would have come back. I know it."

Derrick doubted it. Ginger had more substance than DuPont. She might come from money, but she wanted to make it on her own where DuPont wanted to ride the governor's coat tails.

"Ginger may be in serious danger, and I'm going to find out what happened," Derrick said. He didn't have to pretend to like him. "I'm not in the mood for any more bullshit. Where were you last night?"

Perspiration beaded on the man's forehead, and he spoke through clenched teeth. "With another woman."

Disgust rolled through Derrick. "Her name and contact information," Derrick snapped. "Now."

DuPont accessed his contacts then sent Derrick the number for a woman named Pamela Woods. The man started toward the door to leave, but Derrick shook his head, his patience as thin as ice. "Sit your ass down."

There was no way he'd give DuPont the opportunity to give his lover a heads-up that he needed an alibi.

THIRTY-NINE

Ellie returned to the conference room from Heath's desk just as the governor and his wife stepped behind the podium. She'd spoken to Ginger's best friend Haley, but Haley hadn't added any new information. She had verified the picture Ellie had formed in her mind of Ginger—she was a talented, smart, independent, motivated woman who wanted to start her own business.

Ellie had a feeling they would have been friends. Maybe they still could be.

If you save her in time.

Déjà vu struck her though. How many times had she tried to beat the clock and lost? If she'd been a little later a few weeks ago, she wouldn't have saved Angelica. Even Shondra had suffered horribly at the hands of a mad killer because of her.

She inhaled sharply, struggling to control the guilt and panic as she watched Angelica begin the interview.

The governor clasped his wife's hand as they both faced the camera. His politician's persona was gone, and he looked like any other desperate parent. He'd opted to let the locals handle local coverage, although he had his own officer nearby and he was handling statewide coverage.

"We are at the police station in Crooked Creek," he began. "We have reason to believe our precious daughter Ginger has been abducted." He inhaled a slow breath. "I know that many of you supported my campaign, but others did not. It is a free country we live in, and one based on a democracy. Whatever your political beliefs or affiliations are, or how you feel about me and the election, please know that at heart I am a family man. My daughter and wife come first in my life and always will."

Mrs. Weston dabbed at the tears trickling down her cheeks, and the governor squeezed her hand, a silent heartfelt show of support.

"I'm appealing to you as a human being now, as a father, my wife as a mother. Like many of you who enjoy the beautiful mountains, scenic trails and waterfalls and peace of the area, Ginger came here for that serenity."

Mrs. Weston made a strangled sound. "Please help us bring her home. If it's money you want, tell us how much and we'll pay."

Ellie secretly winced. She understood their need to offer a reward. But instead of helping, doing so might bring out the crazies and false leads and impede the investigation.

FORTY

Frustration knotted Derrick's shoulders as he joined Ellie to watch the interview with the Westons. Ellie looked pained, and he realized she was probably thinking of the other cases she'd worked.

One of which involved his little sister.

The sight of Mrs. Weston breaking down sent him back years ago to when Kim disappeared and his parents faced the horrible unknown.

Rubbing salt into the wound, the police had treated them like suspects. The trauma, worry, and media scrutiny had torn his family apart.

Protocol insisted they question the parents and family. A necessary evil. But he didn't believe the Westons were guilty of anything except smothering Ginger. The emotions he saw on their faces couldn't be faked.

Captain Hale hurried to calm the Westons.

"I talked to Ginger's girlfriend, who confirmed the breakup," Ellie told Derrick. "According to Deputy Landrum, DuPont left several messages on her phone, some demanding her to come back. But they weren't actually threatening."

Derrick made a sound of disgust, half wishing DuPont was guilty and he could slap some handcuffs on the twit. "DuPont lied to you about his alibi. He was at the committee meetings but last night he went to dinner with his lover."

Ellie rolled her eyes. "Seriously," she said with a sardonic hint to her voice. "He claims to love Ginger but while she's in trouble and maybe fighting for her life, he's in bed with another woman."

"He is a dick," Derrick agreed. "But his alibi checks out. The woman said he was with her all night and didn't leave until this morning after they had breakfast in bed."

"You're sure she's not lying for him?"

Derrick shifted. "It's possible, although I didn't give him a chance to give her a heads up that we were questioning him."

Ellie seemed to mull that over. "He could have hurt Ginger, then stashed her somewhere and gone back and conducted business as usual in order to establish an alibi."

"I suppose," Derrick muttered. "But as much as I dislike the guy, for now, we have to keep looking at other alternatives."

"You're right." Ellie's phone dinged with a text from the medical examiner.

She read it out loud: *"Blood from the crime scene matches Ginger Weston's. Only that found near the car. No other human match found—blood on porch from a deer."*

That was odd. Why would deer blood be on the porch?

FORTY-ONE
WILD HOG HOLLER

Ginger lay on her side, tears slipping down her cheeks again as she searched the darkness.

The monster had left for a while. Said he had to go hunting. That he would be back. He'd promised.

Just as he'd promised to love her forever.

A sob clogged her throat. But her voice was so hoarse from screaming that her cries were only a whisper. Her back throbbed, but at least some feeling had returned to her legs.

Maybe she wasn't paralyzed after all. Although when she tried to push up to her hands and knees to crawl, they gave way beneath her.

Below her the ground was stone and dirt and it stunk of the sickly odor of the meat he was cooking. He'd moved her off the plastic and placed her on a blanket near the fire to keep her warm, then left her a cup of water from the pot of snow he'd melted.

The space felt small, but she knew there were steps that lead down to a cellar-like area where he bragged that he kept a freezer and supplies. He'd assured her that with the meat he brought home from his kills, he had enough that they could live here for months without him having to go into town for food.

Fear mingled with despair. Only a few weeks ago she'd been caught up in her father's campaign, smiling for the camera and listening to Stephen's dreams and his political agenda. As a little girl, she'd been close to her mother, but the last year she'd been so busy playing the supporting wife they'd argued.

Ginger had promised them she'd show up for the campaign until her father was elected. Then she would have her time. Time to start her business.

Her body shook with anguish.

This crazy weirdo was never going to let her go. She'd never see her parents again. Never get to have her jewelry business or her own baby.

Even if she got this chain off her ankle and made it outside, she had no idea how to get to a road.

He'd laughed when she'd screamed and told her to go ahead and cry, no one could hear her. Said that they were someplace deep in the mountains in a bunker where he'd lived with his parents all his life. That no one knew where they were.

And no one would ever find her.

She tried dragging herself across the stone floor, toward the doorway where he'd left, but the chain around her ankle dug into her skin and wasn't long enough for her to move more than a few inches.

She jerked at the heavy metal with her hand, fumbling in the dark for some way to release it. But it was secured tight, and she was so weak from her injury that she collapsed in exhaustion.

Curling into the dusty wool blanket, she closed her eyes and prayed that someone would find her. Although even as she prayed, she feared she'd die in this hellhole and be here forever just as he'd said.

FORTY-TWO

BLUFF COUNTY MEDICAL EXAMINER'S OFFICE

THREE DAYS LATER

As Ellie entered the ME's office with Derrick, she rubbed the back of her neck. Tension coiled through her entire body and her eyes felt gritty from lack of sleep. The nightmares had come again last night, dead bodies lying everywhere on the trail.

This time women frozen in chunks of ice.

She, Derrick, Shondra, Landrum, Cord and their teams had worked non-stop for the past three days searching for Ginger. The high-profile case commanded nationwide attention, with Ginger's photograph constantly looping on the news. Captain Hale was doing his part by attempting to keep the governor and his wife calm, but that was an impossible feat.

Already the media was in a frenzy statewide, with dozens of theories springing up each day.

Bryce had managed to stay sober, and he and his deputies were covering every abandoned cabin, property, empty warehouse and outbuilding they could find in the county. Train and bus stations had been alerted, and every police department in the neighboring counties had joined the hunt. Even those across state lines were keeping a lookout.

Derrick and his partner at the Bureau had worked a couple of leads regarding the threats and protestors making noise about the election, but so far, nothing had panned out.

The Westons' panic was escalating with each day that passed. Ellie understood that. The chances of finding Ginger, especially alive, diminished each day.

So far, the offer of a reward hadn't helped, but just as Ellie feared, it had hindered the investigation by inciting dozens and dozens of false sightings, leads and even two fake confessions. Some people had good intentions and thought they might have seen Ginger. But the attention-seeking crazies divided and exhausted manpower. Bryce had been handling most of them, thankfully taking that weight from Ellie. Although she had no doubt he was doing it in hope that he would solve the case and be the hero in the governor's eyes.

She tried to ignore the stab of nausea triggered by the acrid odors of the morgue as they met the ME. "Sorry this took so long," Laney said. "But it's impossible to rush the thawing of a frozen body. We wanted to be as accurate as possible."

"Understood," Ellie said. Besides, she'd been busy looking for a missing woman she hoped was still alive.

"We do have a solid ID," Laney said. "You were right. DNA and dental records confirm the woman is Nadine Houser. Cause of death was blood loss due to multiple stab wounds to the chest. He punctured the aorta and she bled out." She gestured toward the forensic anthropologist Dr. Lim Chi. "Dr. Chi can tell us more."

The petite woman adjusted her glasses. "Nadine suffered a fracture of her wrist during her childhood, as evidenced by the way the bone healed. However, her right ankle was also broken in adulthood. Judging from scoring on the bone, I believe she may have been restrained for some time."

Ellie's chest grew tight. "She was tied up."

The doctor pursed her lips. "Or chained with a heavy metal chain. The scarring indicates she'd probably tried to free herself by yanking against it, possibly with such force she'd broken her own ankle."

Ellie's hands suddenly felt clammy as that horrid image danced through her mind.

"Can you estimate time of death?" Derrick asked.

"Based on the date you said she disappeared, the injury, and the decomp I'd guess she died a few days or weeks after she was kidnapped."

Ellie's mind raced. "But we just found her body. She can't have been buried in the ice at Beaver Pond for that long."

Dr. Chi shook her head. "Signs indicate she was frozen before she was dumped."

Ellie tried to stifle a gasp but failed. In her mind, she saw Nadine screaming and fighting her attacker while he brutally stabbed her.

Then the killer stuffing her limp body inside a cooler or freezer where no one would ever find her.

FORTY-THREE

He'd had to go to his work hut for a while. Had to keep up his routine or else someone might miss him. He dragged the deer he'd shot with his bow to his field dressing stand, strung it up, then within five minutes, skinned and gutted it with his gut-hook tool, letting the blood drain.

His father had started the business and taught him everything he knew. Some hunters field-dressed their kills before hauling them to be processed, while others who didn't like to do the messy work depended on his services to do both.

His hut bordered the trail near the holler where the wild boars roamed, and his business was strictly word of mouth. He also made a few deliveries here and there to earn cash for supplies he needed.

All the time he was removing the animal entrails he was thinking about the woman waiting for him at home. The woman he loved.

Leaving her in his bunker alone couldn't be helped. There was no way she could escape. And no one had ever been to the bunker.

He'd make it up to her for leaving her when he went back. She was so beautiful that it made his body harden just thinking about her silky blond hair. The temptation to touch her all over and make her his was almost unbearable.

But Little Joe's daddy on *Bonanza* said to be a gentleman. To woo her. To take his time. To make her fall in love with him.

Besides, she needed time to heal from the arrow. Time to accept that she was his and that he would be her husband. Stitching her wound had been the first step in earning her trust.

Feeding her and letting her rest would show her that he was kind and would take care of her.

One of his regulars, a guy about his age who had a shack a few miles from the hut, stopped by with his latest kill.

Bill enjoyed the hunt, but he had a weak stomach when it came to the gutting. As he prepared the kill, Bill avoided watching and they chatted about the weather. Then Bill said, "Hey man, did you hear about that woman that went missing?" Bill scratched his big belly through his overalls. "Rangers and search teams been all over the mountain looking for her."

He went still, then shrugged, and pulled his knife from his belt.

"Turns out it's the governor's daughter, Ginger," Bill blathered on. "He's offering a hundred thou for anyone who helps find her."

Shit. Shit. Shit. Ginger said her father had money... But she never said her daddy was the goddamn governor.

"I'm gonna keep my eyes open." Bill whistled. "Sure could use that dough."

He grunted, wiping his knife on the side of his pants as he watched Bill. "Yeah. Me too."

The wind picked up, blowing snow and leaves around them. Bill pulled his coat up around his neck, then looked around the hut.

"You haven't seen anything, have you?" Bill asked.

He shook his head then gestured to the deer. "I better get this done before another storm hits."

Bill shifted, then glanced at the back room as if his mind was working.

Fuck. He saw what Bill was looking at. The pink scarf that had belonged to Ginger.

Suddenly the man moved toward the door. "I'll be back to get him tomorrow," Bill said, gesturing toward the deer.

He nodded, narrowing his eyes as he watched the man head back onto the trail, pulling his sled behind him.

Sweat beaded on his neck. What the hell was he going to do?

The coppers and search teams were looking for Ginger and probably wouldn't give up. And that scarf... he shouldn't have taken it. But he hadn't been able to help himself. The soft fabric smelled sweet, like wildflowers, like Ginger.

Don't panic, he told himself. His place was tucked away so deep in these mountains that his secrets had been safely hidden for years. Occasionally he'd seen or heard some hiker or other hunter nearby, but the bunker was so insulated that no one passing could hear what went on inside.

Still, a couple of times someone had gotten too close to the bunker. He'd feared they'd figure out what he was doing and he'd had to get rid of them.

His gut in knots, he made quick work of gutting the buck then dragged it to hang in the cooler room. Tossing his bloody gloves in the trash, he washed his hands then locked up and set off back toward the bunker to make sure no one ever found Ginger.

But Bill's curious eyes made him wonder if he'd just made his first mistake.

FORTY-FOUR

STONY GAP

Ellie parked at her parents' newly rebuilt home, her emotions in a tailspin. After everything that had happened, she'd thought her parents might move away from Bluff County. But they were adamant this was their home and they didn't intend to run.

It took courage for them to stay. She guessed she admired that. Their relationship was still tentatively recovering, and she'd kept her distance while they rebuilt their life. But Vera had left a message earlier pleading with her to stop by.

She finally relented just to get it over with.

On the drive over, she'd called Detective Emerson, the investigator who'd originally handled the Houser disappearance, and relayed the ME's findings. He agreed to notify the father so he could have closure and finally bring his daughter home.

Dunce was still nowhere to be found. That made him look guilty to Ellie, but they wouldn't know until he was located and brought in.

The house she'd grown up in had been nice, although a little stuffy and formal.

When her parents said they were rebuilding after the fire, she'd expected the new place to be a carbon copy of the first. After all, her mother had taken great pride in hosting the garden club and charity events there.

She paused to study the exterior before she went in. Oddly, this time they'd chosen a rambling farmhouse with wraparound porches that looked inviting and homey, not as formal as the one they'd lost. Ferns hung from the porch and flower boxes that would be filled with sunflowers in the spring added brightness to the front. A detached garage painted white with black shutters mirrored the exterior of the house.

Ellie knocked and opened the door, calling out to her parents.

Her father appeared, looking stronger and more rested than he had in a long time. It was hard to believe she'd almost lost him to a gunshot wound a few months ago.

"Thanks for coming, honey," he said, then reached out to hug her.

Ellie stiffened but accepted the hug. He breathed out as if relieved she'd come. He still felt thin though, his ribs poking at his shirt.

Then her mother appeared, her expression slightly wary, although Ellie could see an eagerness lit her eyes, too. Ellie knew Vera desperately wanted to make amends, but she couldn't forget. She was working on the forgiving part.

"It's good to see you, Ellie," Vera said. "You looked tired, though."

Ellie gritted her teeth. "We've all been working around the clock searching for the governor's daughter."

Her mother pressed a hand to her chest. "I feel so bad for that family. They must be going out of their minds."

Ellie nodded. Much the way Hiram's victims' families had felt. But she managed to refrain from reminding her mother of their suffering.

"Any leads?" her father asked.

"The offer of a reward triggered several calls, but nothing's panned out yet."

"Come into the family room," her mother said. "We want you to see the house."

A house tour was last on her list of priorities. But she followed her mother, surprised at the cozy feel in the room. Instead of formal, Vera had gone farmhouse chic with soft sage greens, creams, a sectional sofa in front of a white painted brick fireplace, and tons of throw pillows.

"It's nice," she said.

"I was hoping you'd like it," Vera said. "I thought it was time to freshen things up."

Ellie was not in the mood for chitchat. "It all looks good," she said. "But I really have a lot going on, Mother. I can't stay long."

Vera reached for her hand. "Just one more thing. I want you to see this."

Ellie glanced at her father and his look implored her to listen. Her mother led her to a long pine table and Ellie noticed dozens and dozens of photographs spread across the surface.

"We lost a lot of pictures in the fire," Vera said. "But thank goodness, I had copies of some of them stored in a fireproof safe."

Ellie's gaze settled on the pictures. The photos were family shots of holidays, her high school graduation, fishing and camping trips with her father, then in one corner, she saw pictures of her early childhood. She had come to live with the Reeves when she was three. The pictures started then and chronicled her years in elementary school and middle school.

"I've been thinking about Mabel and what she missed by having you taken away from her," Vera said. "I thought we might show her some of these pictures so she can see how you grew up, that you were safe and loved. Maybe it would comfort her and help her connect with you."

Unexpected emotions clogged Ellie's throat at the tender gesture. "I... don't know what to say, Mom," she murmured. "You want her to connect with me?"

Vera's eyes filled with tears. "I didn't know you were stolen, or anything about what happened to her," Vera said brokenly. "Selfishly, I am happy that we got to raise you. But..." She swallowed hard. "She gave birth to you. She loved you so much that it destroyed her when she lost you. She deserves to get to know you now."

Ellie swallowed hard too. "I'll talk with her therapist and see if she thinks it's a good idea," she said softly.

Vera nodded, and Ellie's anger toward her dissipated slightly. "Thank you." Then she pulled Vera into a hug.

Although doubts still plagued her, for the first time she wondered if Mabel did recover, was it possible the three of them could have a relationship?

FORTY-FIVE
WILD HOG HOLLER

Ginger's mouth was so dry she chugged the water he'd left for her. She needed her strength. Had to watch him. Wait until she had the chance.

Then she'd fight him and escape.

She peered around the interior of the space in search of the key to the stupid chain he'd fastened around her ankle, but she didn't see it anywhere. The fire was dying out, too, and the room had gotten so cold she couldn't stop shivering. But then she spotted an ax propped against the wall by the door.

If she could get to that ax, she could use it against him.

She flexed her fingers, rubbing her hands together to stay warm, and attempted to move her legs. They still felt weak and slightly numb. A cramp seized her calf as he she reached down to rub some feeling back into her legs, and a sharp pain shot through her back where the arrow had struck her.

A sob caught in her throat, and she rolled to her belly and crawled toward the door. She had to get hold of that ax. But she only made it a few inches and the chain cut into her leg, halting her progress.

The door to the bunker screeched open, and frigid air blasted the space, snow swirling inside. She curled on her side and pretended to be asleep, praying he'd leave her alone.

The metallic scent of blood and the acrid odor of something dead hit her as he shuffled over to her. Her chest ached with the need to cry, but she held her breath.

Then he picked up the ax and stood over her, the handle clenched in his hand. She swallowed back bile as the stench of a dead animal grew stronger.

"You didn't tell me you're the governor's daughter," he growled.

She finally exhaled. "I told you my father would pay you whatever you want," she said in a raw whisper. "Just let me go and I promise I won't tell anyone who you are."

He jerked her hair, pulling her head back, his sinister eyes boring into her. "Don't you get it?" he snarled. "I'm never going to let you go. You're mine forever."

Fear seized her, fueling her adrenaline. She'd rather die than have to be here with him. With a shout of rage, she reached for the ax. He grunted, shocked that she was fighting, then he shoved her down so hard the back of her head hit the floor.

"Do that again and you'll be sorry."

Terror seized her as he pressed the blade to her neck and mouthed the words *chop chop*.

FORTY-SIX

FIVE FORKS

Ellie's head had barely hit the pillow when a possible lead on the Ginger Weston investigation came in. An anonymous caller who claimed he'd seen a man who fit Dunce's description near Five Forks, an area known for the stretch of trail that forked in five directions.

According to the caller, the man liked the hunt, the kill. He was strange and lived alone deep in the woods. Captain Hale had tried to identify the caller, but he hadn't left his name and he'd used a burner phone, making it impossible to trace the call.

Ellie's adrenaline kicked in as she and Derrick met Cord at the entrance for the approach trail leading to the bend, about five miles from Beaver Pond, where Nadine Houser had been found.

A coincidence or not?

Ellie did not like coincidences.

More storm clouds had moved in, the night sky inky black. Their flashlights slanted beams through the spiny branches of the pines and helped lead them over fallen branches and debris that had blown to the ground from the latest storm.

Wind swirled snow from the trees, sending it fluttering down like white rain, ice crystals clinging to her cheeks.

Ellie tugged her scarf around her face to protect her skin from the biting air. The temperature was dropping again, the wind chill making it feel more like the teens than the low thirties. Cord used his compass to guide them, maneuvering the steep ridges and narrow paths with a precision that only a seasoned tracker was capable of.

Leaves and brush rustled ahead, and she spotted a white-tailed deer skitter around a bend.

Derrick hesitated, aiming his flashlight in a wide arc to the west. "What is that? It sounds like a child crying."

Ellie paused by a hemlock and listened. "Probably a bobcat. They can hiss, growl, snarl or sometimes sound like a crying baby."

"Will they attack?" Derrick asked.

Ellie shook her head. "Rarely, and then only if threatened or protecting their cubs. They're actually pretty shy around humans."

Derrick seemed to relax. "Are there mountain lions out here?"

"Once in a blue moon one might migrate here, but I haven't heard reports of any sightings recently," Ellie said.

Cord shouted to go east at the fork, and they followed the creek for another mile until they neared a small hut set on a hill. Overgrown brush and downed tree branches crowded the exterior of the wooden shack, and trees surrounded it. The exterior looked weathered, a stack of firewood was piled by the side, and an old sled sat by the wood stack. Kudzu had overtaken the side of the house and crawled along the rooftop, half burying the place in the weeds.

Ellie looked around, scouring the area for clues. No vehicles. But there were drag marks near the sled.

She motioned to Cord. "Stay back. Let us go first."

He caught her arm. "Be careful, El."

She nodded. Armed with his knife, he stepped behind a large oak and she and Derrick slowly approached the shack. As they neared, she spotted blood in the snow, then footprints imprinted in the icy sludge leading up to the door. Pulling her gun at the ready, she inched toward the window to peer inside while Derrick gripped his service Glock and knocked on the door. She held her breath as she waited.

"Police, open up," he shouted.

Ellie peeked through the small window, but it was dark inside and all she could make out was a firepit in the corner of the small room. She circled the hut in case there was a back door and the man tried to escape through it. But there was no door, so she crept back to the front and gestured to Derrick that the back was clear.

"Open up!" Derrick shouted.

Silence rippled with tension as they waited. The wind picked up, battering the dilapidated structure. Derrick jiggled the door, and it swung open. Ellie moved up behind him, gun drawn as he inched inside.

He stepped to the right, and she entered, sweeping her flashlight across the space. The hut was one room with a cot in the corner, and a camp stove for cooking.

The stench of blood and body waste hung heavy in the air, and she pulled her scarf over her nose and mouth as she spotted the source. On the floor a big guy in a flannel shirt and overalls lay face up, eyes wide in the shock of death. Ellie took a step closer. She'd seen Dunce's photo in Trenton's Trucking's personnel file.

It wasn't him.

A hunting knife was jammed into his chest, and blood had pooled beneath him on the floor, spreading around him as he'd bled out. A bow and arrow lay beside him, his fingers clenched around the bow, blood on the arrow. He still wore wet brown boots and a dark green ski hat, which roused her suspicions—it suggested he might have been caught off guard when he was stabbed.

Mentally cataloging the details of the scene, Ellie aimed the light around his frame and spotted more blood.

Blood that spelled the words, *Sorry, Ginger.*

FORTY-SEVEN

Ellie's suspicions mounted as she gestured toward the bloody wording. "Looks like some kind of a confession. But something feels wrong."

"I agree." A frown crinkled Derrick's face as he took in the scene. "If he killed Ginger, where's her body?"

Ellie surveyed the room. There was no closet, no extra room or bathroom. No furniture. No place to hide. "Not in here."

Derrick grunted. "I'll get McClain, start looking outside and call for a crime scene team."

He left and Ellie mentally pieced together a profile of the man who stayed here. He was primitive. A loner. Maybe a wanderer.

Definitely a hunter.

Was he the unsub?

Ellie frowned again, thinking things through. The shack was a short-term place to land. Although it was obvious someone was staying here now.

She looked around. A wooden crate served as a table. A tin coffee cup and bowl sat on top of it. The stone firepit was filled with burned embers, and the camp stove and a lantern sat on the floor beside it. A camping fry pan and pot along with a few tin utensils sat on the crate. A blanket and sleeping bag had been spread on the cot, along with a pillow. A rifle was propped up in the corner. The bow looked to be about a forty-pound draw-weight bow.

The howling wind outside shook the thin walls and startled her. She suddenly felt claustrophobic as the stench of human wastes and blood closed in on her. Pressing her hand across her forehead, she closed her eyes and breathed in and out as her therapist had taught her to when a panic attack threatened.

A moment later her stomach tightened when she opened her eyes. He fit the profile.

Sweat beaded on her skin, and she pulled on latex gloves, then gently eased her hand down inside the pocket of the man's overalls in search of an ID. She found a wallet, pulled it out and checked the inside. A few dollars in cash. A hunting license and driver's license.

The man's name was William Hubbard. His home address was in Rabun Gap.

Logic began to take over. This hut must be his getaway from home. At least with an address, she could track down his family and dig into the man's history and background. He could have abducted Ginger and taken her to his home then seen the news and realized just exactly who he'd abducted. Panicked, he might have murdered her, then guilt kicked in and he'd come here to kill himself.

Although if he was going to confess and commit suicide, why do it here where he might not be found? Why not kill himself in the same room as Ginger? And who had called in the tip?

Questions rattled through her mind as she snapped pictures of the man and his position on the floor. His eyes were wide open and glazed, his mouth also open, and judging from the way the blood had pooled beneath him, he was sitting up when he was stabbed—or stabbed himself—then fell backward onto the floor. There were no bruises on his face, though his hands looked scarred from knife wounds. Perhaps from field dressing his kills.

She stooped and examined his fingers and noted they were rough and scaly, callused from working the bow and arrow. The strong scent of sweat, the woods, and blood mingled with body decomp. She pressed two fingers to his skin. It felt cold and stiff, as if he was already in rigor, which meant he'd been dead one to six hours.

She stared at the bloody message again, pushing the horror of the scene to the back of her mind as her analytical skills kicked in. The words looked like they were scrawled using the man's own blood and were just to the left of his head. Ellie frowned as she studied the set-up. It was an outlandish thing to do, and something about it seemed odd from a purely logistical point of view.

If he'd stabbed himself, he would have had to twist sideways to write on the floor. He would have been in pain and bleeding, meaning the blood might have spilled or spattered the floor by his left side near the words, but the blood seemed to have trickled down his chest almost evenly on both sides. The lettering was also fairly straight, which was inconsistent with a man weak from blood loss.

At the angle he'd had to turn, the letters might have been smeared or crooked, as if crudely scribbled, the blood running together. But the name was carefully spelled out, as if he'd lifted his finger between each letter. That would have taken enormous control for a dying man.

She snapped close-up pictures of the man and the blood and letters, then went to examine the bow. Blood droplets had dried on the surface of the shaft and covered the sharp, pointed arrowhead.

If this man had killed Ginger, had he done it here? If so, there would be signs that she'd been in the hut. Ellie walked around the room again, looking for a hair, clothing fiber, button, more blood, signs of a struggle, ropes that might have been used to bind her hands and arms, any evidence she'd been in the space.

But she saw none of those things. A backpack lay on the floor by the makeshift bed. She crossed to it and stooped to look inside. Army green, dirty, stained on the outside.

She opened the bag, half expecting to find Ginger's clothing or ropes in the backpack, but found a hunting knife, twine and a gut-hook. She dug into another pocket and there found a bloody rag. Dried blood.

Her heart skipped a beat. Did that blood belong to Ginger?

FORTY-EIGHT

Derrick called for an Evidence Response Team and the ME, then searched the exterior of the shack, looking for another outbuilding, cellar, or storage box—a place where Ginger's body might have been hidden. Ranger McClain radioed for backup search teams, then hiked to the entrance to the trail to act as a guide for the ERT and ME.

A light snowfall had started, the air growing colder as Derrick moved the stack of wood in case the man had piled it in front of an opening to a fallout shelter. But his efforts proved futile. There was nothing, no outdoor storage shed, not even a box or cooler.

Next, he scoured the wooded area surrounding the hut for signs of a recently dug grave. Using his flashlight, he scanned the bushes and weeds for footprints, disturbed foliage, signs the snow that had accumulated hadn't been swept to cover a body. He looked for fresh blood, hair, Ginger's clothing, a fingernail, and broken branches that she might have grabbed while trying to escape an attacker. But he found no forensics. And no sign of Ginger.

Dammit.

Knowing the ERT and SAR workers would cover more ground, he dug his hands into his coat pockets, the wind beating at his face as he hurried back to the shack.

Ellie looked up at him expectantly, and his gut tightened at the worry in her eyes. She knew time was running out for Ginger. She'd battled the clock before and lost. He wanted to help her get through this and bring Ginger home to her family.

"Nothing outside. We'll widen the search once McClain's team and the ERT arrive."

Frustration lined her slender face. Ever since the last case, he'd wondered how she was coping, had wanted to come back sooner and see for himself. But the governor had needed him, and Ellie hadn't seemed to want him around.

They both needed him now though. He couldn't let them down.

"There's no sign of Ginger having been in here either," Ellie said, and explained her theory about the spatter and bloody lettering. "Blood pooled beneath him but there's no trail indicating he turned sideways to write Ginger's name."

"You have a point," he said. He trusted her instincts and attention to detail. "The angle and neatness of the writing doesn't fit with suicide."

"I found blood on the arrowhead and shaft, and a bloody cloth inside the man's backpack. Could be his or if he's a hunter, maybe from an animal. Or... it could be Ginger's."

Derrick heaved a wary breath. "Or Ginger was never here."

"But why leave her somewhere else and then come here to end his own life?" She pointed to the corner. "And why stab himself when he had a rifle right there? That would have been quicker and less painful than bleeding out."

Derrick studied the scene. "Good questions."

A tense second passed, then Ellie continued, "ID in his wallet says he's William Hubbard. His home address is Rabun Gap."

Derrick shifted. He could almost read her mind now. "I'll ask the local police to go to his house."

Ellie shook her head, sadness in her face. "The governor trusts you, Derrick. Let's do it ourselves. If we find her, you should be the one to break the news to him."

It would be difficult, but he knew she was right. For a moment their gazes locked, and something sparked between them. She was independent and feisty, but she trusted him now. Trusted them to be a team.

That meant more than anything.

Still, he prayed they found Ginger alive.

FORTY-NINE

RABUN GAP

Fear for Ginger tightened every muscle in Ellie's body as they drove to Rabun Gap. She kept imagining what might be happening to Ginger, and if they'd find her dead or alive.

Damn, she had to figure out what was going on. She kept coming back to the apology written in blood, which suggested Hubbard had killed her. But things weren't adding up.

It was nearly midnight by the time they arrived at William Hubbard's home. They'd left the ERT and Cord's SAR teams combing the woods and searching for forensics. Dr. Whitefeather had agreed with Ellie's assessment regarding the bloody writing. The stained rag, bow and arrow, and the man's clothing would be processed, and Ellie had asked a handwriting analyst to compare the sample to William Hubbard's handwriting, assuming they found a sample of that in his home.

Laney had agreed to start the autopsy the next day.

The place Hubbard rented was a small cabin about three miles from Lake Rabun, the third lake in a six-lake series that followed the course of the Tallulah River. The lakes were owned and operated by the Georgia Power Company to generate hydroelectric energy for Atlanta.

A distant memory floated through Ellie's mind as she passed the lake. One summer she'd camped here with her father. They'd been so close that she'd wanted to be just like him when she grew up.

She had no idea he wasn't her birth father.

It shouldn't matter, she reminded herself, thinking of how good it had felt to give him a hug when she'd visited. She'd been lucky to have him. But the lies still hurt...

Back then, they'd hiked to the falls and spent lazy days swimming, catching fish and cooking them over the fire for dinner. While they slept under the stars, he'd taught her the constellations and regaled her with the history of the area.

Derrick turned down the drive to the house, drawing her back to the present, and she glanced at her tablet where she'd been running a background check on Hubbard. The results were on screen.

"He was married but his wife divorced him, citing irreconcilable differences," she told Derrick. "He worked at a body shop in the town of Rabun Gap and had no record. His parents were deceased, and he had no children."

"The loner part fits the profile," Derrick said as he cut the engine.

"Yeah. So does the fact that he was a hunter. And that he had that secluded shack in the woods." Although that wasn't odd in itself, since people flocked to the area for peace and quiet and to enjoy nature.

She didn't see a car underneath the carport and darkness bathed the house. "According to the DMV, he owned a black Ford pickup." She texted her boss and asked him to put a BOLO out for it, then texted Cord and asked him to have his people search the parking lots of the entrance trails near Beaver Pond and Five Forks.

"We'll talk to his coworkers tomorrow." Ellie's stomach twisted as she climbed from the vehicle and they made their way to the front door together.

"Police!" Derrick shouted as he knocked.

A chill rippled through Ellie as the wind tossed her ponytail in her face. Or maybe the chill came from the dread coiling inside her. Ginger's face flashed in her mind, a beautiful, creative young woman who'd deserved to fulfill her dreams.

But predators didn't care about others' dreams. Their own madness drove them.

Derrick pounded the door again, and seconds ticked by. Hand shaky, she unlocked the door with the keys she'd found in Hubbard's pocket.

"Anyone here?" Ellie called.

Silence greeted her as she opened the door and stepped into the house. Derrick flipped on a light and she scanned the combined living room and kitchen. There was a basic rust-colored couch, green chair, a small fireplace, oak table. Muddy hiking boots had been tossed haphazardly on the floor and a thick fleece and heavy winter parka hung in the entry. A deer head was mounted above the fireplace and cheap prints of birds of prey hung on the wall above the sofa. Somewhere she heard the ticking of a clock, an eerie reminder that she might be too late.

She and Derrick exchanged a look as the scent of something rancid filled the air. While Ellie veered right, Derrick went to check a closed door to see where it led.

Down the hall, she found a bathroom that desperately needed cleaning and a shaving kit, which, judging from the heavy stubble on Hubbard's face at the crime scene, was rarely used. She opened the medicine cabinet and drawers but saw no signs of anything belonging to a woman, and no evidence that one had been here.

Senses alert, she moved on to check the bedroom. The decor looked primitive and masculine, not a place a man would bring a woman.

The room contained a simple oak bed, with a log cabin quilt in browns and oranges and a closet filled with work clothes. The name of the body shop where he worked was stamped on dark gray coveralls, and the name patch on the front said "Bill". Flannel shirts and T-shirts fit the picture of Hubbard Ellie was forming in her mind.

She knelt, ran her hands across the battered wood floor and

wall. No secret crawl space or piece of furniture that could hold a body.

Frowning, she searched the dresser and found boxers and whitey tighties.

When she returned to the living room. Derrick was coming back in from a room off the kitchen.

"Did you find anything?"

He shook his head. "No, just a freezer full of meat wrapped in butcher paper."

Ellie shuddered. "Nadine was likely stored in a freezer. You don't think..." She couldn't bring herself to voice the morbid possibility.

Derrick's dark-brown eyes flickered with the realization that he knew what she was going to ask. His jaw steely hard, he muttered, "Only one way to find out."

Stomach roiling, she followed him back to the freezer. The two of them exchanged grim looks as he opened it, and they each reached for a package.

FIFTY

Derrick laid a hand over Ellie's, his protective instincts kicking in. Granted, she'd seen Nadine Houser's body frozen in the woods, but if there were body parts here, he wanted to spare her. That would be the kind of image you could never erase from your mind. "You don't have to do this, Ellie. I can handle it."

Ellie's gaze met his, emotion burning in her eyes. "Don't baby me because I'm a woman. I know what I signed up for with this job."

"Being a small-town sheriff is not the same as dealing with the type of monsters you've come across. It could get to anyone."

Ellie lifted her chin in challenge. "I think I've proved my worth. Let's just get this over with."

"I know you're tough, Ellie, but you don't have to keep proving it to me."

"Who said I am?" Ellie said, her jaw clenched. "I wanted to be a detective, Derrick. And I'm not backing away now, not when Ginger needs me." She pulled her hand away and snatched one of the packages.

Derrick sighed. Her stubbornness knew no bounds. Of course, that stubbornness had saved her life a few times.

They both breathed out as they pulled the tape from the butcher paper and opened the first packages.

Derrick took one look and recognized the meat as a pork shoulder.

Relief flickered across Ellie's face as she found thick slabs of bacon inside hers.

"We have to check them all," Ellie said. "He could have mixed body parts in with the meat."

Derrick didn't like it, but she was right. The next ten minutes they tore into one package after another. Thankfully each one held parts of a butchered hog.

Ellie shoved the last piece of meat into the freezer. "I don't think I'll be able to eat pork for a while."

"Does make you lose your appetite. But at least we know Ginger isn't here," Derrick muttered.

Ellie rubbed her forehead with the back of her arm. "If Hubbard did kill her, where is her body?"

Derrick shook his head. "Somewhere in these woods. And you may be right—the bloody message beside Hubbard's body seems off. It could have been written by someone framing him. To give him time to get away with Ginger."

Possibly the person who'd called in the tip.

FIFTY-ONE

Body achy from lack of sleep, Ellie chugged her coffee as Derrick drove them back to Rabun Gap the next morning.

All night she'd tossed and turned, her nightmares filled with images of body parts cut up and jammed in a freezer. Then Nadine's naked body covered in frostbite and her sightless eyes had appeared in her mind. Each time she'd banished that image, Ginger's loving face appeared in its place.

As she watched the mountains and farmland fly past, she mentally composed a profile of the killer. He was a loner, perhaps uneducated, crude, a hunter, a man who'd coldly held Nadine Houser hostage for years then dumped her body in the snow.

He had to have holed up somewhere where no one would have seen him or heard Nadine scream for help. Hubbard's hut fit, except they hadn't found any sign that Nadine or Ginger had been there.

But if he'd abducted her, where had he kept her? Search teams had combed the woods near Beaver Pond, and another team was searching around Hubbard's now.

She couldn't shake the feeling that his death was a set-up. Derrick had suggested the anonymous caller who'd led them there might be the unsub and she was leaning in that direction herself. Was it James Dunce? So far they hadn't definitively linked

Ginger's abduction and Nadine's murder. If only they could find him...

Derrick swung the car into the parking lot for the Dollar Store where Hubbard's ex-wife worked.

"Hubbard doesn't have a record of violence," Derrick said. "No priors."

"Let's see what the ex has to say." Ellie opened the door and heard the sound of a toddler racing across the store squealing. Two registers were open with a lady in sweats checking out at the first. Ellie recognized Hubbard's wife Patricia from the photo she'd pulled up online when she'd dug into Hubbard's background. The woman was short and round with hair dyed a stark black. Costume bracelets jangled around her wrist and her earrings looked like feathers. She seemed friendly to the customer she was waiting on.

Derrick and Ellie waited until the woman in the checkout line finished paying, then they approached Patricia.

"Mrs. Hubbard?" Ellie said softly.

The woman's red lips pursed. "Used to be—I took back my maiden name after my divorce."

Ellie nodded. "I'm sorry to bother you at work, but this is important. Can you take a short break? We need to talk."

Patricia wiped her hands on her smock. "Who are you?"

Ellie identified them, and watched a myriad of emotions flicker in Patricia's eyes, her mind no doubt racing through possibilities. "All right." She called over to the other cashier, "I'll be back in a minute, Anita."

She grabbed her jacket from below the counter, then moved from behind the register and gestured for them to follow her outside. She led them around to the side of the building and leaned against the concrete wall. Tugging a pack of Camels from her jacket pocket, she tapped them on her hand, pulling one out and lighting it up.

Ellie gave her a minute, stifling a cough as Patricia blew a smoke ring into the frigid air. "What's this about?"

Ellie cleared her throat. "I'm sorry, but we have to inform you that your ex-husband is dead."

Patricia's eyes widened in shock, then she took another slow drag of her cigarette. "What happened?"

Ellie tried to soften the blow by lowering her voice. "He was stabbed to death with a hunting knife."

Surprise flared on Patricia's face. "You mean someone killed him?"

"We are looking into that possibility," Ellie said gently.

"Why would someone kill Bill?" Patricia asked. "It's not that he had money or anything nice to steal."

"We don't believe it was a robbery," Derrick filled in.

"When did you last talk to or see him?" Ellie asked.

Patricia tapped ashes onto the ground. "Not for a while. Three or four months."

"Did you stay in touch after the divorce?" Ellie asked.

"The first couple of months he called, wanting to get back together. To tell you the truth, I don't know why. He was never home, always hunting and staying in some shack out in the woods by himself. Primitive as all get out. He wanted me to go, but that wasn't my thing." She tossed the cigarette onto the ground and stomped it out. "I grew up poor, in a rotting house with no plumbing. Finally got away from that."

Derrick exhaled. "Can I ask why you divorced?"

"Wanted different things," she said. "Bill wasn't a bad man, but his idea of fun was a night in the woods. Wanted me to cook the meat he brought home, but I got tired of that. My idea of a good time was dinner out and a hotel."

"Was he ever violent?" Ellie asked softly.

Patricia chuckled. "Bill? No, heavens no."

"Even though he killed animals?" Derrick asked.

"He said that was sport," she said. "Grew up hunting with his daddy. But he had a weak stomach. Couldn't dress his kills himself. Got sick at the sight of blood."

Ellie and Derrick exchanged a curious look.

"Why are you asking about Bill being violent?" Patricia crossed her arms. "Did he do something wrong?"

Ellie chose her words carefully. At this point in the investigation, she didn't want to reveal too much. "We're trying to determine exactly what happened. Did you end the marriage or did he?"

"I asked for the divorce," she admitted. "But frankly, I think he was fine with the separation. It's not like he was interested in me anymore—in *any* way."

Ellie arched her brows. "So it was amicable?"

The woman patted her pocket where she'd stashed her cigarettes as if she wanted another.

A second later, she glanced at her watch and thought better of it. "Yeah, we cut our losses and parted ways."

"Was Bill depressed?" Ellie asked. "Would he have hurt himself?"

"Not Bill," the woman said. "Good lord, when the man cut his finger, he cried like a baby."

Which made it unlikely that he'd choose suicide by knife, Ellie thought. She shifted. "Did Bill have any enemies? Maybe someone at work he didn't get along with? Or a girlfriend?"

Patricia made a low sound in her throat. "No girlfriend that I know of. And I reckon he got along with the guys at the shop. You'll have to ask them if he pissed someone off."

The sound of cars pulling into the parking lot jarred Patricia, and she wheezed a breath.

"It's about to get busy. If I don't get back to work, I'll lose my job."

"If you think of anything else, please give us a call," Derrick said, handing her a card.

Ellie thanked her and Patricia hurried back around the side of the building.

"She certainly wasn't that broken up over her ex's death," Derrick muttered.

"No, she wasn't," Ellie said. "But that also means she didn't care enough to kill him."

"True. Let's talk to his coworkers."

Ellie followed him to the car, mentally processing what they'd learned about Hubbard.

"What are you thinking?" Derrick asked as they got into his sedan.

Ellie buckled her seatbelt. "The pieces don't add up. If Hubbard got sick at the sight of blood, how did he manage to stab himself and write Ginger's name without barfing?"

"Good point," Derrick said. "Without a body, we don't even know if Ginger is dead."

She tapped her fingers on her leg. "Right. Whoever took Nadine kept her for years. He could be hiding Ginger somewhere like he did her. The police gave up looking for Nadine. He may be biding his time until we give up on Ginger."

"And if Hubbard is not the unsub, the killer framed him, hoping we'd call off the search teams."

"Makes sense." She cleared her throat. "Serial killers want notoriety for their crimes," she continued. "As the governor's daughter, her story would be huge, just the kind of attention that would make national news and put him in the spotlight."

Derrick clenched his jaw. "If your profile is right and he grew up in isolation, he might not have known who Ginger was when he took her."

Ellie worried her bottom lip with her teeth. "But he may know now, and he's panicked."

Panicking might make him accelerate his timeline. That would be deadly for Ginger.

FIFTY-TWO

STANCIL'S BODY SHOP

Ellie couldn't help but watch the clock as they drove to Stancil's Body Shop, where Hubbard had been employed. Every second that ticked away meant Ginger might be suffering.

Her anxiety mounted as Derrick answered a phone call from the governor, and she heard his tormented voice demanding to know if they'd found his daughter.

God, she didn't want to fail him, or his wife and daughter.

If this sicko thought she'd give up on finding Ginger, he was damn wrong.

The vehicle wound up the drive, then they came to a stop at the shop. Ellie had always imagined junkyards as graveyards for abandoned vehicles. As a little girl, she roamed the junkyard near her house, climbing in different cars and pretending she was driving. She'd make up stories about where the vehicle would take her—or where it had already been.

This body shop and junkyard were no different. A fenced field housed broken-down and crashed vehicles that would be sold off or used for parts. Another area served as a parking lot for ones waiting to be repaired. A rusted pickup truck, sedan and VW bug sat in need of paint and dents to be hammered out.

The garage contained two lifts, one of which was occupied by a black SUV. The taillights and rear bumper were smashed, paint scratched off from the impact of a serious accident. Ellie wondered if the person or persons inside was okay.

A gray-haired man in a tattered T-shirt and baggy jeans stood inside the entrance to the garage rummaging through his tools, while a twenty-something man dressed in the body shop uniform seemed to be analyzing the damage to the SUV.

Ellie spotted a mutt sprawled by the entrance to the small office attached to the garage. A brisk wind blew snow across the rocky drive, icicles melting from the overhang and dripping steadily onto the cement walkway. The familiar scent of motor oil and gas wafted to her from the garage.

As they approached, Ellie introduced them. The older man turned out to be the owner of the shop and introduced himself as Walter Stancil. The young guy, his son Pete, watched warily.

"We need to talk to you about one of your employees. Bill Hubbard," Ellie said.

Walter scratched his white beard. "Bill ain't here. Didn't show up for work today."

"That's what we need to discuss," Derrick said. "When did you last see or hear from him?"

"About three days ago," Walter said. "He was taking a couple days off to go hunting. But was supposed to be back this morning to look at the SUV over yonder." Walter turned to his son. "You didn't hear from Bill, did you, Pete?"

The young man shook his head. "Naw, don't know where he is. Called him this morning cause the owner of this SUV wants this job done ASAP and Bill's our best man. But he didn't answer."

"Why? Did something happen to him?" Walter asked.

"I'm afraid so," Ellie said, her voice soft. "He was found dead last night on the AT."

Walter coughed, and Pete dug his hands into the pockets of his work coveralls. "Bill's dead?" the son said in a raspy voice.

Ellie nodded and let Derrick respond. "We found him stabbed with a hunting knife."

Walter staggered back and ran a hand through his thinning

hair while Pete looked down at the ground. "Was it some kind of freak hunting accident? Bill can be clumsy sometimes."

"It wasn't an accident," Derrick replied. "We think he may have been murdered."

Ellie studied the men's reactions—both seemed taken aback at the news.

"Who would want to kill old Bill?" Walter muttered.

"That's why we're here," Ellie said. "We were hoping you could tell us if he had any enemies. Someone who might want to hurt him?" *Or frame him for a murder.*

But she bit back the words.

"Far as I know, everyone liked Bill," Walter said, then tilted his head toward Pete. "You hear any complaints?"

Pete shook his head. "Bill was a loner, you know. Kept to himself. But he was the best at what he did and went out of his way to make sure the customers were happy. Took real pride in his job."

"Not everyone does that these days," Walter muttered. "But out here, people are more neighborly. And with vacationers coming in and the freak blizzard and tornado we had this year, we kept Bill busy."

"Was he seeing anyone?" Ellie asked.

"Naw," Pete said. "I asked him to go for a beer sometimes, but he didn't go. I'd joke that he must have a better offer but he always said he should be so lucky."

"Was he angry about his divorce?" Derrick asked.

Walter scratched his head. "Not really. More like relieved he didn't have to work at it anymore."

"Any odd things about him?" Derrick asked.

The men exchanged confused looks. "What do you mean, odd?" Pete asked.

Derrick shrugged. "Like a strange fantasy or obsession with women?"

Walter barked a laugh. "Hell no. Bill didn't even seem interested in women."

Ellie chalked up that detail, adding it to Patricia Hubbard's description. "Was he ever violent?"

This time Pete laughed. "Naw, he was a softie. He was a little different, but a good guy."

Ellie contemplated their comments. Judging from the picture they'd painted of Bill Hubbard, he did not fit their profile.

Which put them back to square one. If Hubbard hadn't killed Nadine or kidnapped Ginger, who had? They had to get back on the trail to Dunce.

FIFTY-THREE

SOMEWHERE ON THE AT

Tessa Tulane hiked deeper into the woods, reveling in the natural beauty of the sharp ridges, overlooks, white-tipped trees and ice crystals clinging to the branches and leaves. She knew it was dangerous to be out here alone, especially after Ms. Eula's warning, but photography had been her second passion since she'd enrolled in a workshop a few summers back, and she was hoping to get inspiration for her series from nature.

And maybe spot one of the Shadow people who lived out here.

Some said the woods were haunted. There had certainly been enough death on the trail this last year for her to believe it.

The dark ghost tales and stories of demons her grandmother had told her inspired her own interest in writing about the paranormal. All Hallows' Eve was less than two weeks away and supposedly the time when the veil between the world of the dead and the world of the living was so thin that it allowed the souls of the dead to come back and walk with the living. People used to leave candy out for the dead as an offering so the evil spirits would leave them alone.

Crooked Creek had always gone in big for the holiday and started decorating the first of October.

A shiver chased up her spine, and she sensed something—or

someone—in the woods nearby. She paused and turned in a wide arc, searching, and saw the brush move. An animal? Or a man?

The sound of the wind whistling gave her another chill. But rays of late-afternoon sunlight filtering through the branches created a vibrant cascade of shapes and colors. Raising her Nikon D3500, she looked through the lens, adjusted the settings, pointed and snapped the shot. The sound of a vulture's wings echoed in the wind, and she turned toward it, spotted the bird soaring above a boulder and caught it on camera.

In quick succession, she snatched shots of the icicles dripping from the pine needles, close-ups of a hemlock dusted in white powdery snow, and lichens.

Hiking further up the trail, she followed the sound of the creek and stopped to get shots of the snow melting on the rocks, of wild-flowers poking through the ground and a turtle hiding in the bushes.

She continued her trek for miles, up steep inclines and skating past the never-ending ridges. But she came to a halt when her foot caught on something and she nearly tripped. She expected a tree root when she looked down but noticed some kind of thick cable poking through the soil. How was there a cable out here?

It seemed totally out of place in the natural habitat and was mostly covered, but the melting snow had washed away some of the dirt obscuring it. Paw prints also marked the brush and ground, as if an animal had been digging around it.

Curious, she snapped pictures of it while she followed the cable, as if it were breadcrumbs left by Hansel and Gretel to lead her home. Or to a mysterious gingerbread house in the woods, to be lured inside by an old witch. Her imagination tended to go wild.

Although realistically, it had probably been placed by someone living in the woods who'd run it for power, although she hadn't seen any huts except for the AT shelters close by, and those had no electricity.

She pushed through thick weeds and brush, winding downhill

into what appeared to be a ravine. Ahead she heard a rustle, then spotted another movement. About twenty more feet, and the cable was almost completely buried. She saw teeth marks on a fallen log as if a beaver had been gnawing on it, then spied more paw prints.

For a moment she debated whether to continue. If someone did live out here, they might not want to be found.

Still, despite a moment of fear, her curiosity drove her, and she moved closer, sheltering between the trees as she climbed the hill, following where the dirt had been pawed away. The wind suddenly whipped the trees, and she maneuvered another few feet, then spotted an underground cave of some kind carved into the mountain.

She raised her camera and snapped a photograph, focusing on the brush covering what appeared to be a doorway.

She narrowed her eyes, remembering stories about the caves in the mountain when miners flocked to the area in search of gold and other precious gems. Maybe this was one of them and the cable had been used for some kind of machinery for the mine.

She snapped another photograph, moving closer and closer to peek inside, until she was not far from the opening, watching from the bushes. Her imagination took over and she decided this would be the perfect place to set part of her ghost series.

Her skin prickled as the brush moved and a big hulking figure in a bear-like coat emerged from the opening. He was at least six feet tall and bulky, his face half hidden by his jacket hood.

A frisson of fear needled her, but she realized he might be one of the Shadows. She focused the camera lens on his face. A thick woolly scarf hung around his neck below a bushy beard and thick tufts of unkempt hair poked below his ski cap.

She adjusted the lens to zoom in on his face and saw that a long, jagged scar snaked into his hair line. Just as she clicked the shot, he lifted his head and stared straight at her.

His menacing eyes pierced her.

Then sunlight glinted off the hunting knife gripped in his

gloved hand, and he bellowed like a wild animal as if he was coming after her.

Terror seized her and she went still, silently ordering herself to run.

FIFTY-FOUR

Every muscle in his body tensed at the sight of the woman in the woods.

What was she doing out here? How had she found him?

Already agitated from Ginger's unwillingness to say she loved him, he'd almost gone too far with that ax. It had taken every ounce of his restraint not to give up on her. But he had to be patient.

The wolf's cry had saved her.

But this woman... she didn't belong here.

He stood ramrod still, watching, waiting on her to make a movement. He could almost hear the click of that camera as she snapped his picture.

He couldn't let that happen.

What was she doing out here so far away from everything? What if she showed that picture to someone?

Balling his hands into fists, he slowly steadied his breathing. Watching. Waiting. Calculating her every movement.

She lowered the camera to just below her eyes. Then lower. Silently he assessed her.

She was small-framed, like a frail young deer. Dark brown hair hung to her waist below her ski cap. She wore a gray parka and gloves. And she was frozen still.

His breath puffed out in a white cloud in front of his face.

Damn. He wished he'd brought his bow and arrow outside with him.

He took a step toward her, gearing up for the chase. Her eyes widened in fear, then she turned and bolted down the hill away from him.

Part of him was tempted to let her go. She didn't know who he was. Or that he had Ginger. She couldn't.

Could she?

Bill had told him the cops were looking for Ginger. For him…

If she showed that picture to anyone, someone might find him.

Barreling through the brush, he broke into a run, shoving branches aside and jumping over broken limbs as he followed her. She was lithe and quick-footed, but he knew the woods and how to cut through the thickets and maneuver past the rocks in his path.

She was following the creek.

He veered onto a shortcut and came out a few feet ahead of her at one of the crossings, where he ducked behind an oak and waited silently. He heard her feet smashing the leaves and brush. Heard her choppy breathing as she raced past the hemlocks.

The biting wind stirred the frigid air, but heat spread through him as his excitement grew. The thrill of the hunt beat strong in his chest. She paused by a low rock, dropped her head forward to catch her breath.

Pulse jumping, he gripped his knife and pounced. Her scream rent the air, as shrill as the sound of a vulture. She clawed at his arms, digging sharp nails into his coat, but he put her in a choke-hold and raised his knife and stabbed her hard and sharp in the chest.

Her body shook and trembled as she choked out a cry, then blood gushed from her chest and spattered the white blanket of snow on the ground. His hands were drenched in her sticky blood, but he gripped her tightly until she began to convulse. Her sob lifted in the wind, then faded as her body gave into death and she sagged in his arms.

What to do now?

She meant nothing to him. Did not belong to his collection and certainly not in his life forever. Those places were reserved for his soul mates.

She'd just been a problem he had to solve. Someone nosing around in his business like the people his daddy warned him about. She might have even been a spy for the government.

He couldn't leave her here though. She was way too close to his bunker. Growling an obscenity, he dragged her away, her blood spilling out and creating a trail behind them as he hauled her deeper into the woods.

FIFTY-FIVE

ROSE HILL

Ms. Eula rubbed the worry beads around her neck, stroking the smooth bones with her callused fingertips as she prayed for serenity and peace. She'd made the beads as a protective measure and to calm her nerves when the killings had started this last year.

When she'd finally confessed that she'd murdered her vile husband and the truth had been exposed about his crimes, she'd thought the devil would leave her. That the voices in her head and the cries that drifted to her in the wind would quiet.

And they had for a few short weeks.

But they were back now. Ever since Ellie found that woman's body in the snow. And now Tessa Tulane had shown up asking questions.

Once she'd touched that young woman's hands, she'd sensed something awful was going to happen to her. That her questions and stories would get her in trouble and be the end of her.

The scream had come minutes ago. The darkness blinding her. Tessa's face taunting her, eyes wide open in terror and pain. And the shock that Eula's warning had come true.

Grief welled inside Eula. Another beautiful young girl had lost her life to the evil on the trail. And there was more of it to follow.

Tessa's stories told of zombies who rose from the dead to roam the earth and feed off others.

But there would be no rising from the dead for Tessa.

FIFTY-SIX

CROOKED CREEK

Ellie called a meeting at the police station to review the details of both investigations. Her captain, Sheriff Waters, Deputies Eastwood and Landrum were there, while Derrick spoke privately with the governor.

One whiteboard held the crime scene photos for Nadine Houser along with a list of everyone they'd questioned and the information they'd collected so far. "James Dunce still remains a primary person of interest. Where he is, though, is the question. Sheriff, any progress on finding him?"

"Not yet," he said. "Can't find any record of him being employed after he left Trenton's Trucking. No bank accounts or financial information on him."

Ellie bit her lip. "That's odd. He could have gone into hiding. Could have changed his name. Or he could have been arrested."

Bryce tensed, his tone irritated. "I've already looked into that angle but so far haven't found anything. Looked at various name combinations and every prison in the southern states."

Ellie rubbed her temple in frustration, then gestured to board number two, where they were chronicling the Ginger Weston case. "At this time, we're working on the basis that Ginger is still alive. Ginger's boyfriend has an alibi. Agent Fox's partner at the Bureau is still investigating threats against the governor. So far, no ransom call or demands of any kind. Which suggests that whoever abducted her doesn't intend to release her."

Ellie turned to Shondra. "Anything new on the leads from the tip line?"

Shondra tapped her notepad. "Nothing that panned out. False confession from a schizophrenic man who claimed he picked her up at a bar, killed her and buried her in his back yard."

"We know she was abducted from the cabin," Ellie said.

Shondra nodded. "There was a body in his backyard, but turned out it was a dead coyote."

"Waste of time," Bryce muttered.

"It was," Shondra agreed. "We had a few calls about a woman matching her description at the main bus terminal in Atlanta. The terminal has no record of her buying a ticket there and I reviewed security footage—Ginger was not in any of it. Another young woman with blond hair was, though, so I guess just a case of mistaken identity."

Bryce cleared his throat. "Actually, one ransom call did come in, asked a hundred k—a bit of a low ball considering that's the reward for information."

Ellie clenched her teeth in irritation. "Why am I just hearing this?"

"Because I handled it," Bryce said. "Got the money from the governor and staked out the drop point. Turned out to be a couple guys who just got out of the slammer. Saw the story on TV and decided to make some quick cash."

Ellie silently cursed at the cruelty of what they'd done. "I hope you locked them up."

Bryce gave a clipped nod, although he seemed distracted.

"Keep working the tips," Ellie said.

Shondra nodded, but the fact that Bryce didn't make a comeback suggested something else was on his mind.

"What about a link from Ginger Weston to this Dunce man?" Captain Hale asked.

"Only that the tip-off about Dunce led us to the Hubbard

scene, but that could just be someone who'd seen both stories too. I'll come back to that. So far nothing from the interviews with family and friends links Dunce to Ginger." Ellie nibbled on her lower lip and gestured to Deputy Landrum. "How about social media? Anyone stalking her?"

"Still nothing," Heath said.

"It's looking like she was a crime of opportunity, which could also be the case with Nadine Houser," Ellie said. "If Ginger was traveling alone on the highway and side roads, she might have stopped for supplies somewhere or gas and attracted the unsub's attention." She gestured to the deputy again. "Look at all the gas stations or convenience stores along the way from Atlanta to Pine Needle Crossing. Talk to the owners and have them pull security footage."

Heath frowned. "That'll take some time."

"Right now, it's all we've got," Ellie said. "So get on it." She moved to the next whiteboard. "Now, we have a male victim. As you know, a supposed sighting of a man matching Dunce's description actually led us to Bill Hubbard. Stabbed in the heart. 'Sorry, Ginger' was written in blood next to him, suggesting he was confessing to her murder." She pointed out the details regarding his body positioning and the lettering and her theory that he was murdered and framed.

"Why him, though?" Shondra asked.

Ellie shrugged. "Good question. It's possible he knows who took Ginger or he witnessed her abduction. His ex-wife claims he had a weak stomach, got sick at the sight of a lot of human blood. There's no way he stabbed himself then wrote the message. Forensics is analyzing the handwriting and comparing it to a sample of Hubbard's writing recovered from his home."

"Do you think Ginger's disappearance is connected to Nadine Houser's death?" Shondra asked.

"At this point, it's difficult to say, but the timing of us finding the body of a woman who's been missing for eleven years, and

Ginger being abducted in the same area shortly after that body was found definitely raises red flags."

There was a knock at the door and another deputy came in. "Detective Reeves, a Mandy Morely is here to see you. She's real upset and only wants to talk to you."

Ellie inhaled a deep breath, stood and told everyone they'd take a break.

FIFTY-SEVEN

Ellie ushered the teenager into her office. At Vanessa's funeral, she'd promised her old friend she'd be there for Mandy, and she intended to keep that promise.

She closed the door behind them. "Hey, Mandy. What's wrong?"

Mandy fidgeted, her ponytail swinging back and forth just as Ellie's did when she was running. Her breathing was erratic.

"Mandy, honey," Ellie said softly. "You seem upset. Tell me what's going on. Did something happen at school or with a friend?"

Mandy whirled on her, hands on hips, nostrils flaring with anger. "I know what happened to Mama. You and Aunt Trudy tried to sugarcoat it, but I know who killed her now and why. I heard Aunt Trudy talking this morning... and I made her tell me the truth."

Ellie's stomach sank as tears trickled down Mandy's face.

Ellie had had a hard time dealing with the facts herself. She couldn't imagine learning first-hand the kind of dark depravity that existed when she was still in high school.

She grabbed a bottle of water from the credenza in her office and handed it to Mandy. "Honey, please sit down and we'll talk."

Mandy shook her head, then paced the office, her movements jerky, the hurt in her eyes tearing at Ellie.

"What? So you can lie?" Mandy snapped. "I thought you were trying to be my friend. That you and Mama were friends and you were there for me. But now I find out that you're my aunt and you didn't tell me."

Sympathy and guilt swelled inside, and she wished more than anything that she could make everything right for the young girl. "I'm sorry I didn't tell you, but I knew you were grieving and didn't want to upset you more."

"You just didn't want me in your life," Mandy cried.

Ellie shook her head, her voice thickening, "That's not true, Mandy. I care about you. And I meant what I said about being there for you. I just thought it was too soon. That you needed time."

She stroked Mandy's arms gently. "I promise, I won't keep anything else from you. No matter what."

She knew how that felt with her own parents. She'd never do it to another kid.

Mandy's face crumpled and Ellie coaxed her to the corner into a chair. "Talk to me, honey…"

Tears filled the young girl's eyes. "What about my father? Do you know who he is?"

Ellie sucked in a breath. "What did your aunt tell you?"

"She said she didn't know who he was." Mandy stiffened but her voice cracked with pain. "*Do* you know?"

Ellie used a soothing tone, "No. Vanessa never told me. I was away at school when she had you and we didn't talk when I got back."

Mandy wiped at her damp eyes. "Would you tell me if you did know?"

"I promised you I wouldn't lie to you, and I meant it, Mandy. I really have no idea who he is."

Mandy wrung her hands together. "Why wouldn't she tell Aunt Trudy? Do you think the same thing happened to Mom? That she was assaulted, and she didn't tell me because she didn't want me to know?"

Ellie rubbed Mandy's back. "Listen to me, I have no reason to think that. There could be another explanation. Your mother was young when she had you. Maybe your father left or something happened to him."

Mandy covered a sob with her fist, took several shaky breaths then whispered, "But you're a detective and I know you're good at your job." She clenched Ellie's hand. "You'll investigate and find out for me, won't you?"

FIFTY-EIGHT

WILD HOG HOLLER

He wiped the woman's blood on a rag before he went back into his bunker. Didn't want Ginger to smell her body odor on him. She might get the wrong idea.

He dropped the bloody rag into the trash. It shouldn't have happened like that. He'd been so careful all his life. Had kept away from everyone except for the people who came by his work hut for his help. Occasionally he slipped into a market to pick up supplies and to make deliveries. But even then, he always kept a low profile. In and out, without drawing attention to himself.

Yet that damned woman had found his home.

The stories his daddy told him echoed in his head. The warning. *If you don't find a soul mate in the year of the blood moon and before you turn thirty-five, you'll die alone.*

A smile curved his lips. He had found her. He wouldn't die alone. She would be his forever.

Brushing snow from his coat, he ducked his head and hurried down the steps and inside. He secured and bolted the door, welcoming the darkness as he shuffled through the narrow hall and into his den. That's what his daddy had called the main living area. Like a bear hibernating for the winter.

The scent of the stew he'd made yesterday still lingered, but the fire had burned out and the room was cold. He crossed to where Ginger lay on the mattress on the floor, his pulse hammering at how still she was beneath the wool blanket. Anxious to see her, he hurried over and knelt down beside her. Her breathing rattled in the silence, and when he touched her cheek, her skin felt icy. He grabbed another blanket and covered her with it, then went to fetch firewood to rebuild the fire.

Minutes later, the blaze of the flames began to warm the room, the orange and red glow illuminating Ginger's beautiful face. His body hardened, and he crawled over and stretched out behind her, then wrapped his arms around her.

She stirred and pushed against him, but he pulled her closer and held her firmly in his arms, her butt tucked against his groin. She whimpered, and he felt tears dampen her cheeks, so he gently brushed them away.

"It's okay, darling," he whispered into her hair. "Sometimes I have to leave for a while, but I'll always come back to you."

FIFTY-NINE

Ginger had pretended sleep when the monster came in. That's what she called him in her head.

But he'd come to her anyway.

His breath bathed her neck, and his fingers stroked the tears from her cheek. She swallowed back bile.

He said he loved her. That she was his soul mate.

So far he hadn't forced himself on her. But she felt his hard-on pressing into her and knew it was only a matter of time. Revulsion flooded her.

She'd die before she let that happen.

Another sob caught in her throat, but she forced it down. Her skin crawled as he tightened his arms around her, and she lay perfectly still, terrified of stirring his arousal.

Seconds bled into minutes. The sound of the wind howling outside echoed through the cold cavern. Firelight flickered and shot jagged rays across the dirt interior.

Finally, his breathing grew steady, and she thought he'd fallen asleep. Opening one eye, she spied the ax again. It was almost within reach.

What about his knife? Was it on his body?

Holding her breath, she slid one hand around to feel his

pocket. But he caught her hand and squeezed it so hard she thought he was going to break her fingers.

"Not yet, darling," he whispered. "But soon."

Another sob welled in her throat. As she lay there, praying he would leave or fall asleep, panic and despair overcame her, and she formulated a plan. The next time he left, she had to get to that ax. She could use it to break the chain.

Stories of people surviving in the wilderness when they were trapped flitted through her mind. More than one person had cut off their own limb to escape.

What if she couldn't break the chain?

She pictured raising the ax and chopping off her foot and prayed she'd have the strength to do it when the time came.

SIXTY

CROOKED CREEK

Ellie hated to see Mandy so upset. The girl had been through hell lately. And now she wanted to find her father.

How could she blame her?

Just three months ago, she'd set the wheels in motion to locate her own birth parents. Not knowing had driven her crazy. She'd thought what she imagined about them couldn't be any worse than the truth.

She'd been mistaken.

Now she had to live with what she'd discovered.

"You will help me find him, won't you?" Mandy asked.

Ellie rubbed the teenager's arms again. "Honey, I don't know if I can. Your aunt said his name wasn't listed on your birth certificate."

"But you can investigate," Mandy cried. "That's what you do!"

Ellie breathed out. "Right now I'm in the middle of a homicide case, Mandy. And the governor's daughter is missing. I have to focus on finding her at the moment." She hesitated. "Maybe when the case is over…"

"You promise?" Mandy asked.

"We'll talk about it then," Ellie said.

"If you won't, I'll do it myself."

Before Ellie could respond, Mandy burst into tears, then ran from Ellie's office. When she looked up, Bryce was standing in the doorway watching.

"What was that about?" he asked.

Ellie shrugged. She sure as hell hadn't confided in Bryce about her birth mother or father. And she had no intention of talking about Mandy with him. "She's just having a hard time without her mother."

Bryce raised his brows. "Why come to you?"

"Vanessa and I used to be good friends when we were little," she said. "I reached out and promised to be there for her."

A second passed while Bryce studied her, then he cleared his throat. "I have to go. Another tip just came in about Dunce."

Ellie's pulse jumped. She was just about to ask what it was and offer to go with him when her phone buzzed. She looked at the display and saw it was Cord. Hoping he had good news about Ginger, she told Bryce to keep her posted, then connected the call.

"Ellie," Cord said, his tone grim. "One of the search teams just found a body buried in the snow at Hickory Flats Cemetery."

SIXTY-ONE

HICKORY FLATS CEMETERY

Ellie's breath stalled in her chest. She'd expected Cord to say the body belonged to Ginger Weston, but he said the woman's face was covered in snow and he knew better than to compromise a crime scene, so she had no idea what she was walking into.

Night was setting in as she, Derrick, Laney and the ERT hiked past Devil's Fork, a place named for the unique split in the trail that resembled a pitchfork. Some said in the summer when the sun was at its hottest, that the outline of the pitchfork could be seen sizzling on the ground as if it had been burned into the soil and brush by the devil himself.

The fork was about five miles from Long Creek Falls, where people hiked to the Hawk Mountain Shelter. Hickory Flats Cemetery was nearly 200 years old, and a draw for tourists.

Why had this woman's body been left here?

Dusk created shadows through the hemlocks and tall pines, but at least the snowfall had ceased. Temperatures hadn't yet risen above freezing though, turning the snow into sheets of ice that crunched beneath their boots.

The sound of the waterfalls echoed as they got closer, and the chill in the air intensified. Ellie broke through the clearing and found Cord by the creek. His SAR dog stood beside him, as if guarding the dead woman.

Cord crouched and stroked Benji's back, murmuring that it was okay for them to approach and giving him a command to sit. Then he stood and greeted Ellie and the others.

"After we found her and secured the area, I let the rest of the team go. They've been working around the clock looking for the Weston woman. If this isn't her, another team will go out."

"Tell them I appreciate everything they're doing," Ellie said. They all needed rest, but it was difficult to carve out time for that when Ginger's life hung in the balance.

Derrick, Laney and the ERT followed, each scanning the area, analytical minds already working. They made a good team, Ellie thought. She was glad to have them.

Looking around at their surroundings, Ellie noted the height of the falls and the overhang, her stomach knotting as she saw a woman's foot poking through the ice and snow. She and the team pulled on latex gloves as they approached the makeshift grave. The ERT began to scour the area for evidence, and Derrick began snapping pictures of the ground where the dog had uncovered part of the body.

Fear and anxiety tightened every nerve ending in Ellie's body. For a brief second, she closed her eyes, bracing herself for what might be beneath the ice. After a breath, Ellie gently raked snow away from the head, bringing a lock of dark hair into view.

Ginger had blond hair.

Her heart raced as she sifted more debris from the woman's face, revealing a high forehead, delicate nose and green eyes staring back at her in shock.

Relief that it wasn't Ginger bled into horror and then the kind of sorrow that nearly brought her to her knees.

The woman in the snow was Tessa Tulane.

SIXTY-TWO

"Do you know her, Ellie?" Derrick asked.

She nodded, a numbness setting in. Although she and Tessa hadn't been close, Ellie admired Tessa for her accomplishments. And she had fond memories of her as a quirky kid. She'd beat to her own drum, which Ellie had too, in a different way. "She's from Crooked Creek, a couple of years younger than me," she said. "Tessa Tulane. Her grandmother was the school librarian when I was little. She wore these big hats and had a bag of props she used when she read books to us."

"Oh, I read about her. She wrote that zombie series," Laney said. "All the teenagers are obsessed with it."

"Yes, she did a reading at the storytelling festival," Ellie said. "Her grandmother, Ms. Ivy, was so proud of her. She bragged about her every time I saw her in town."

Ellie gently traced a finger along Tessa's jaw then brushed more snow off her, revealing her neck then her torso. The sight of the hole in Tessa's chest made Ellie's stomach convulse. Dried blood mingled with the snow and stained her clothing.

A childhood memory teased at her mind. When she was in grade school and went trick or treating to Tessa's, Tessa and her grandmother had insisted the kids come in for a séance. The grandmother and Ms. Eula were friends, and Ms. Eula was always there. Some of the kids had been scared, but Ellie found it fascinating.

"You okay, El?" Cord asked.

She was plagued with self-doubts, but nodded anyway. "It looks like she was stabbed multiple times. This crime was vicious. Either personal or done in a fit of rage." Sucking in a breath, she stood and stepped aside to allow Laney access for her initial exam.

Grief for Tessa filled her, making her more determined than ever to find this sick creep. If the same unsub who killed Nadine murdered Tessa, he'd definitely escalated. And judging from the stab wounds and her body being left in the snow, Ellie was almost certain it was the same perp. Although Nadine had been naked and Tessa was dressed. But maybe the killer had been interrupted...

Laney squatted down and Derrick snapped close ups of Tessa's chest and the stab wounds. Shining a light onto the area, Laney tugged the fabric back and pointed out at least three entry points.

"He pulled the knife out and stabbed her repeatedly," Ellie said, regret eating at her. If she'd found this bastard sooner, Tessa would still be alive. *Maybe Ginger still is.*

A mental picture of the assault formed in Ellie's mind. "She tried to fight him off and get away, but he caught her again and drove the knife in deeper."

"Or he wanted to make her suffer," Derrick suggested, his tone grim.

"Do you think it's a different killer?" Laney asked.

Ellie rubbed her forehead with the back of her hand. "There are some differences, but similarities as well. The autopsy suggests Nadine was frozen for years before he dumped her body. But Tessa was at the bookstore every day the last week, so he left her almost immediately after she was murdered." Ellie leaned closer. "She's not wearing a leather necklace, is she?"

Laney shook her head.

"We'll have the crime techs look for one," Derrick said.

"Nadine was left naked, too," Ellie pointed out.

"Maybe someone was close by, and he didn't have time to undress her," Derrick suggested.

Ellie nodded, still thinking.

"If Ginger is still alive," Derrick said, "he's keeping her for some reason, like he did Nadine."

"He could have disposed of her somewhere and we just haven't found her yet," Ellie said.

A wave of sadness washed over Ellie. Tessa was so young, at the top of her career, had garnered fans who adored her. Mandy was one of them. It would be another blow for the struggling teenager.

"What was she doing out here?" Ellie wondered out loud.

"Have you read her books?" Laney asked.

Ellie shook her head. She had enough scary real things in her life. She didn't need zombie stories to keep her awake at night.

"She could have been looking for inspiration for story material, or places to set the next book," Laney suggested.

Derrick walked around the base of the falls as they were talking and yelled that he'd found something. As he approached, he held a camera in his hand.

"This may have belonged to her," Derrick said. "It's smashed, but there's a memory card inside."

"Hopefully it'll have something on it that will help us." In her mind, Ellie saw Tessa as a kid, standing beside her grandmother at the library using voices to portray the characters. She had so many more stories to tell.

But now those would die with her. Ellie's heart ached.

SIXTY-THREE
CROOKED CREEK

Dread knotted Ellie's stomach as she and Derrick knocked on Ivy Tulane's door. Tessa's grandmother lived in a gray Victorian house outside of town and was Tessa's only living relative. Her house was all decked out for Halloween.

While they waited on the woman to answer, Derrick turned to Ellie. "How well did you know Tessa?" Derrick asked.

"As a kid, she was quirky and funny. She and her grandmother always decorated their house up big for the holidays. In high school, she was a goth girl. Some of the kids thought she was weird. Rumors spread that her house was haunted, just like Ms. Eula's."

No wonder the two women had been friends. "Ms. Ivy seemed to enjoy the rumors and each Halloween decorates the yard with ghosts, goblins, spiderwebs and tombstones. Spooky music plays through porch speakers to the outside, and she dresses like a witch or psychic to hand out candy."

"Sounds like Tessa learned her love of storytelling from the woman," Derrick commented.

Ellie nodded. "Yeah, Ms. Ivy wore costumes and used props at school during her weekly storytelling hour for children. I remember being mesmerized by the folk tales and legends."

"Where are Tessa's parents?" Derrick asked.

"They passed a long time ago."

The door opened, and the seventy-year-old woman answered, her eyes narrowing with worry. Her hair was dyed stark black, an homage to the holiday, and a sharp contrast to her pale skin. Her nails were painted bright orange. Spider earrings dangled from her earlobes, and she wore a black velour jogging suit with a necklace glowing with neon orange beads.

"Ms. Ivy, this is Special Agent Fox," Ellie began.

"I know," Ms. Ivy said. "I've seen you both on the voodoo box." The woman pressed a hand to her chest, her breathing suddenly growing more labored. "It can't be good that you're here."

Ellie's heart squeezed and she exchanged a look with Derrick. "No, Ma'am. I'm afraid we have bad news." She gestured to the foyer. "May we come in?"

Ms. Ivy nodded, then stepped aside and they entered the foyer which was draped in fake spiderwebs and smelled of incense. A hall table held a collection of witches, and a fake tombstone sat on the floor with a paper-mâché Frankenstein beside it.

Other fall decorations filled the space as Ms. Ivy led them to the living room where a fire glowed in the antique brick fireplace. She sank into a rocking chair, and Ellie and Derrick seated themselves on a dark purple velvet sofa.

"It's Tessa?" Ms. Ivy said in a strangled voice.

Ellie nodded. "Yes, Ma'am, I'm afraid so."

Emotions strained the woman's thin face. "Wh-what's happened?"

Sympathy for the older woman softened Ellie's voice. "I'm so sorry, but she's gone, Ms. Ivy."

The older woman began to shake her head in denial. "No... no, not my sweet Tessa girl. She's all I've got..."

Ellie crossed to her and knelt at her feet, then cradled her hands between hers. When she looked up, Derrick's dark eyes glittered with turmoil.

"I'm so sorry," Ellie whispered. "I liked Tessa and admired her for following her dreams. She was so talented and reminded me of you."

Tears trickled down the woman's cheeks and she looked at Ellie with such deep pain that Ellie felt it in her own soul.

"Where... is she?" Ms. Ivy said in a raw whisper. "What happened?"

"We found her out on the trail," Ellie said. "I'm afraid she was stabbed to death."

"Oh, my word..." Ms. Ivy's voice choked on a sob.

Ellie swallowed hard to stem her own emotions. Derrick stood and walked to the kitchen then returned with a glass of water.

Ms. Ivy's hand shook as she accepted the glass, then she took a long sip and straightened, her eyes flickering as she put the pieces together. "You mean she was murdered? By the same person who killed that other woman you've been talking about on the news?"

"It looks that way," Ellie said softly. "But we can't be sure yet."

"I'm sorry to have to ask you questions at this time," Derrick said. "But if you're up to it, it might help."

Ms. Ivy clutched Ellie's hand so tightly she thought her bones might break.

"Of course. I want to help," she murmured. "And I trust you, Ellie."

Ellie inhaled a deep breath. Not everyone in town felt that way. With Bryce undermining her, she felt even more pressure to solve this case.

It touched her that Ms. Ivy did. Her kind words made her even more determined to find Tessa's killer. "Tessa was well known for her book series," Ellie began. "Did she have problems with anyone in particular? A boyfriend? A crazed fan or some kind of stalker?"

Ms. Ivy sipped the water again, then sniffed. "Not that she told me about. She seemed happy. Was excited about coming back here and letting all the kids who ignored her in high school see that she was a success."

Ellie could understand that. Yet coming back to Crooked Creek had gotten Tessa killed.

Some of the popular girls had been mean to her, Ellie thought sadly. They didn't understand that different could be good. She admired Tessa for ignoring them. And for using her creativity to build a career.

Derrick's voice interrupted her thoughts. "Ms. Ivy, was Tessa staying here with you?"

Ms. Ivy gave a little nod. "Yes, in her old room upstairs."

"Do you mind if I take a look up there?" he asked.

She gestured toward the steps. "First room on the right at the top of the steps."

Ellie and Derrick exchanged a look, and he disappeared into the hall. His footsteps sounded on the wooden steps as he went up them.

Ms. Ivy worried her bottom lip with her teeth. "Tell me where you found her."

"In the woods near Hickory Flats Cemetery," Ellie answered. "Would there be some reason she might have gone to that particular spot?"

Ms. Ivy tugged a hankie from her pocket and wiped at her eyes. "Tessa liked to explore the woods by herself. Look for the areas that had to do with the folklore. Said it inspired her stories. I guess she remembered me talking about that old cemetery." She set her water glass down with a trembling hand. "When she left here, she said she was going for a hike to look for the perfect setting for a ghost series she was pitching to her editor." Ms. Tessa's voice caught. "I warned her it was dangerous for a girl to go out there alone. Especially with what's been happening on the trail this last year. But she was so independent she wouldn't listen."

Another reminder of the crimes committed on Ellie's watch. Her gut wrenched with guilt and grief. The faces of the dead women who died in Bluff County the last year stayed with her all the time. Their souls might have already crossed into the light, but the memories of them would never fade from her mind.

Just as Tessa's wouldn't.

"It was so good to have Tessa back," Ms. Ivy murmured. "I was so stinking proud of that girl. And I missed her so much. But now..." Her voice trailed off and a keening sound came from her.

Ellie pulled Ms. Ivy into her arms and held her, rubbing her back and crooning to her while she cried. Tears burned Ellie's own eyes as the woman purged her anguish. She saw Tessa's long curly hair flowing around her shoulders, jewelry jangling from her ears and wrists the last time she'd seen her at the café. The glint of mischief in her eyes when Mandy and the girls had gone fan girl on her. Her excitement over the next book...

All those dreams snuffed out with violence.

Ms. Ivy's sobs were so heart-wrenching that Ellie rocked her back and forth. The poor lady had lost her son, daughter-in-law and grandson years ago. Now she was all alone.

"I promise I'll find who did this to her," she whispered. "I promise."

SIXTY-FOUR

Compassion for Ivy Tulane pushed Derrick to work the case.

The fact that Tessa was stabbed, left in the snow, and the timing of her death had his instincts believing it was connected to the frozen body of Nadine Houser. And possibly to Ginger Weston's disappearance and Bill Hubbard's murder.

But he had to cover all the bases and that meant looking at Tessa's case on an individual basis. It was possible that she'd had an enemy who'd killed her and wanted the police to think she'd been murdered by the same killer as Nadine Houser.

Except there were differences. Nadine's body had been stored for years. Tessa had been discarded as if he was in a hurry to leave her, as if she meant nothing to him.

Perhaps Nadine was the source of his infatuation, a personal connection.

Derrick stepped into Tessa's childhood room, noting that the room lacked frills. Instead, posters of storybook characters and supernatural creatures occupied a bulletin board. Another corkboard held handmade sketches of characters which were part of Tessa's zombie series.

He found a laptop on the white wicker desk along with a sketchpad and a folder of photographs of different areas of the country with unique landmarks, rock formations, and eerie names.

There were cuttings and notes about odd sightings of paranormal creatures, of haunted towns and supernatural beings. There were others of folklore about werewolves, vampires and demons. Another of the levels of hell described in Dante's *Inferno*.

He closed the folder and turned back to the room.

Forensics had not found Tessa's phone with her, so he searched her desk and bookshelves but didn't find it.

Inside the desk, he found a folder of fan mail, so he decided to take it and her laptop for lab analysis.

The closet held a box of her clothing from when she was younger, then a few jeans, shirts, warm winter wear and a pair of boots. Nothing out of the ordinary.

Ms. Ivy was wiping at her eyes with a tissue and Ellie was soothing her with soft words of comfort when he came down the stairs. They both looked up when he entered the room.

He gestured toward the items in his hand. "May I take Tessa's laptop and this folder with me? There might be something helpful here."

Ms. Ivy sniffled into her tissue. "Yes, of course."

He thanked her, and Ellie stood, saying, "Are you sure I can't call someone?"

Ms. Ivy squeezed Ellie's hand. "I'll call Emily with the Porch Sitters. She'll come and sit with me and pray a while." Her hand fluttered to her chest. "And I'm sure Eula will come, too."

Derrick had heard of the Porch Sitters, the local prayer group who gathered on porches to pray weekly and in times of need. He didn't know how much he believed, but he hoped their prayers helped them find this killer and give Ms. Ivy comfort.

Ellie said people thought Eula Frampton communed with the dead. That the two women were friends.

He thought about those pictures of the supernatural sightings. Did Ms. Ivy think Tessa could name her killer?

SIXTY-FIVE

By the time Derrick drove her home, a raging headache pulsed behind Ellie's eyes. She rubbed her temple, her vision blurring, yet the anguish in Ms. Ivy's tears bled through the fog.

Derrick cut the engine and turned to her. "Are you okay, Ellie?" He rubbed her arm. "I know it was rough back there. Making a death notification is always difficult, especially when you know the victim personally."

Ellie shrugged and opened the car door. "It's terribly sad for Ms. Ivy. I'm glad she has her faith to fall back on."

Derrick gently touched her arm. "Do you want me to come in and we can talk?"

"No, it's late. I just need some sleep." Sleep without the nightmares would be blissful, but she didn't expect that to happen anytime soon. Not with another killer loose. And every second that ticked by meant he could be getting further away. Or hunting again. "We'll talk to the press tomorrow. The last thing I want is to stir up panic this late at night."

"Understood. I'll start searching Tessa's computer when I get to the inn."

He toyed with a strand of her hair, and Ellie's gaze met his. His dark eyes were warm and made her yearn to lean into him. The past week had been filled with turmoil. Her visit with Mabel, finding Nadine Houser's frozen body, the governor's daughter's disappearance, Mandy's request to find her father. And now Tessa...

If she leaned on Derrick, she might get used to it. Then he would leave, and she'd have to learn to stand on her own all over again.

So she said good night, climbed from the car and hurried up to the door. As usual, she'd left the outside light on, and inside the kitchen light was burning. Although she hated the dark, tonight the brightness hurt her eyes. She stumbled inside, locked the door and went straight to her bedroom and stripped. A long shower would help her relax and wash the stench of death from her skin.

But even as the hot water sluiced over her body, when she closed her eyes, nothing could erase the brutal image of those stab wounds and Tessa lying dead in the snowy woods. She scrubbed her body and hair, then stood beneath the spray until the water turned cold. Heart heavy, she towel-dried her hair, pulled on pajama pants and a tank top, then shuffled to the kitchen, poured herself a vodka and fixed a plate of cheese and crackers. Inhaling the citrusy sweet smell of the Ketel One, she carried her glass and the plate to the living room and lit the gas logs, then curled up on the sofa.

She looked at her phone and saw she had two messages. The first one was from her father.

"Your mother wants you to come for dinner tomorrow night. She's invited the sheriff. Might be a good time for the two of you to make up."

Ellie rolled her eyes. The last dinner she'd had with the three of them was when Bryce announced he was running for sheriff and her father was backing him. She didn't want a repeat.

The second message was from the governor's wife. *"Detective Reeves, I'm going crazy with worry. Please don't give up. Find my daughter."*

Ellie pushed the cheese and crackers away, and poured a second glass of vodka, feeling overwhelmed. The demons and ghosts that haunted her flooded her, stirring her self-doubt. Ginger's life depended on her.

What if she failed?

SIXTY-SIX

RIVER'S EDGE

Cord paced his living room, his boots pounding the wood floor as a fire raged in his fireplace. He couldn't shake the image of Tessa Tulane's dead body from his mind. That and Nadine Houser's face.

Both were blonds. Both reminded him of Ellie.

Was there another serial killer in the area?

Ellie had nearly died on the last cases she'd worked. The thought of her in danger again made his gut churn. They'd been friends for years. And they'd slept together once a long time ago.

It had been the best and worst day of his life. The best because Ellie was the first person he'd ever really cared about. The first person he'd thought he could open his heart to.

The worst day because he harbored too many demons to be with her. He'd known he had to protect her, even if it was from himself.

Hell, he still felt that way.

So he had to keep his distance. Maintain a friendship. Nothing more.

He cursed, tossed more wood on the fire and watched it blaze. Then he picked up his knife and the wood carving he was working on and began to whittle the edges. He worked his anger out in the short fast strokes, nicking his fingers. Just more scars to go with the others. It didn't matter.

A knock sounded at the door, and his pulse jumped. For a minute he hoped it was Ellie. Then he could see for himself that she was safe. And maybe talk some sense into her, convince her to let that fed handle the case.

But even as he thought it, he knew she'd never listen to him.

Steeling himself to see her, he strode to the door and unlocked it. Instead of Ellie, Lola stood on the doorstep, a take-out bag in her hand. "I brought you some chicken fried steak and gravy," she said with a smile.

It was his favorite. And Lola was a sweet girl. Pretty and kind to everyone. She'd kept him fed while he'd recovered from his broken ankle. She didn't even seem to mind that he kept his house dark. A habit he had from his childhood where he'd hidden at night so his foster father would think he was asleep and not see him shaking with fear. That man liked to instill terror in anyone smaller and weaker than him.

The wind outside swirled Lola's hair around her face and sent a gust of cold air through the living room. "Can I come in?" she asked.

"Of course. Sorry." It was freezing and he should have insisted she come in from the cold. What the hell was wrong with him?

Lola was gorgeous and interested in him. Why couldn't he return those feelings?

She sashayed over to his breakfast bar, pulled out the food and then turned to him expectantly. "Are you all right, Cord? You look... upset."

"We found another body on the trail today. That local author."

Her hands began to shake. He felt guilty for being so blunt. Subtlety had never been his strong suit.

"That's awful," she said. "I know her from the café. She was just in after the book signing the other night." Fear streaked her eyes. "What happened?"

He shoved his hands into the pockets of his jeans. "She was

stabbed," he said, remembering the blood on her body, blood that tinged the snow. "I haven't been home long."

Lola's ivory skin paled. "It wasn't on the news tonight."

Cord shifted. "Ellie has to notify the family first, so don't say anything to anyone. She'll probably give a statement tomorrow."

Lola trembled, and he realized he'd frightened her. She was a single woman and vulnerable herself.

"Do you think her murder is connected to that other body?" she asked.

Cord wasn't a cop, but Ellie had hinted that it could be. "It's possible."

"Jesus," she muttered with a shiver. "This time last year I thought this was a safe little town."

Cord didn't know if any place was safe, but he refrained from saying that. Feeling like a heel, he crossed the room to her. "I'm sorry. I shouldn't have blurted that out. It's just I can't stop seeing her body in the snow."

Lola gave him a sympathetic look, then wrapped her arms around him and rubbed his back. He leaned into her and held her tight, the scent of her lilac shampoo clinging to her silky hair.

No one had ever comforted him as a child. He didn't know what to make of it now.

Suddenly uncomfortable, he eased away from her and went over to the food. "Thank you for dinner. It smells great."

"I thought you might stop by the café," she said softly.

He shrugged and reached inside the refrigerator for a beer. "I was too beat to go out."

"Sorry you had a rough night."

When he looked back at Lola, disappointment tinged her eyes as if she'd expected to stay and eat with him.

He was tempted to offer her a drink and to share dinner. She'd be a warm body to hold tonight. But when he closed his eyes, he'd probably see Ellie.

And Lola deserved better than that.

SIXTY-SEVEN

The media's coverage of Ginger Weston's disappearance had gone nationwide with constant coverage and a barrage of reporters hounding Ellie. The governor's own personal media consultant had taken over the calls though and security had been beefed up for him.

Dread clawed at Ellie.

She'd scheduled a press meeting with Angelica for 10 a.m. to discuss Tessa's death so she and Derrick met at the station at eight. The night before she'd reminded herself she'd made the right choice by not inviting him into her house, but in the late hours when she couldn't sleep, she'd almost changed her mind and called him. She'd phoned Shondra instead and they'd had a long conversation. It had felt good to talk things through with a friend.

But this morning Derrick kept watching her as if he thought she might break.

Dammit, she had to get a grip. Put her emotions aside and focus. She'd promised Mrs. Weston she wouldn't give up and she wouldn't. And now Tessa and her grandmother needed her to be strong.

She could see the strain on Derrick's face as he searched Tessa's computer and social media. The pressure was wearing on him just as it was her.

All the more reason to stick to the case and work every second. On the off chance the cases were not connected, she decided to scour Tessa's fan mail. She spent the next half hour skimming the individual pieces.

There were dozens and dozens of letters from teens raving over how obsessed they were with the series, wanting more stories, asking what would come next, when would she appear in their hometown, was the series going to be made into a movie or TV show.

There was also a handful of letters from budding writers requesting her advice and if she would mentor them. She found one piece from a man named Donnie Wiggins who accused her of ripping off his idea.

She phoned the publisher and, after explaining the reason she'd called, was finally connected to Tessa's editor.

"Oh, my goodness, we adore Tessa. Her fans are going to be crushed."

"I know," Ellie said. "We're investigating what happened. Did you know of anyone who had a grudge against Tessa? In her fan mail, I found a letter from a man named Donnie Wiggins who claimed Tessa stole his ideas."

A tense second passed. "Yes, that man called a few times, but our legal department handled it. Nothing he said was true or founded, and he finally just went away."

Had he?

Maybe she could get Shondra to dig deeper into him. Although even if he'd had a vendetta against Tessa, it was unlikely he was responsible for the other murders.

"If you think of anything else, please call me," Ellie said. "We haven't released news of her death to the public yet but will have to do it shortly."

"We'll need to work up something for a press release ourselves." The woman's voice sounded strained. "This is just so awful. Tessa was working on a new series idea. We were all on tenterhooks waiting for it."

And now Tessa would never get to see those stories published. The injustice ate at Ellie.

She hung up, and called Shondra, leaving a message explaining about the letter and asking her to follow up on Donnie Wiggins. "I think he's a long shot," she said. "But we can't leave any stone unturned."

Then she joined Derrick in the corner seating nook in her office. "I think the fan mail is a bust. I asked Deputy Eastwood to look into one guy who accused Tessa of stealing his idea, but that's it."

Derrick looked up from Tessa's computer, frustration etched on his face. "So far there's nothing on her social media indicating she was threatened or stalked. I can't find a boyfriend or girlfriend either. It looks like she was focused on her writing and promoting her zombie series. I found a calendar with dates she'd booked for speaking engagements and storytelling events."

"Did you find new content? According to her editor, she was working on a new series idea."

"Those files are encrypted," he said. "I'll have to ask one of our experts to decode them."

"Hopefully she had a will stating who inherited her intellectual property," Ellie said. "We don't want that to fall into the wrong hands."

"Exactly the reason I don't think she was killed for it," Derrick said. "If she was, the killer would have stolen her laptop."

"True," Ellie said. "Which takes us back to the theory that her death was connected to our other open cases."

Her nails dug into her skin as she curled her fingers into her palms. It felt like the answer was just out of grasp, like they were missing something.

But what the hell was it?

SIXTY-EIGHT

WILD HOG HOLLER

He didn't want to leave Ginger alone this morning. It had felt so good to sleep with her in his arms that he missed her the moment he got up. Anger at the way she'd pushed him away made his blood boil, but he reminded himself to be patient.

She was his. One day she would accept it and she'd love him the way a wife should.

He fried up some squirrel and made white lard gravy on his camp stove, then added a chunk of bread to the plate and carried it to her. She jerked her eyes open the minute he touched her and scooted back against the wall.

"I made you breakfast, sweetheart." He offered her the plate, but she simply stared at him with glassy eyes.

"What is that?" she said, her nose wrinkled in distaste.

"Squirrel and gravy. My mama taught me how to make it." He picked up the fork, stabbed the hunk of squirrel and dipped it in the thick white gravy then lifted it toward her. "Here, babe, take a bite. You have to eat."

She shook her head, shoving her tangled hair from her face. "You can't make me eat that slop."

His temper flared. "Your mama should have taught you manners, Ginger."

"And yours should have taught you that it's wrong to kidnap a woman and hold her hostage."

He saw red behind his eyes, the way he did when his mama had punished him by locking him in the cooler when she said he was bad. But he tempered his reaction. "You'll feel better if you eat. I can't have you withering away. A man likes a woman with a little meat on her bones."

"Please let me go," she begged.

He shoved the tin plate onto the ground at her feet, then touched the heart-shaped necklace he'd given her. "Don't you get it? You are mine. This is our home and we're going to raise our family here, safe from all the dangers out there."

"You're crazy," she cried. "I could never love a man like you."

Rage made him shake her. "Don't talk to me like that, Ginger. If you aren't nice to me, I'll have to teach you a lesson."

Her eyes widened in terror, bringing him a smile. Maybe he'd finally put her in her place. For now, that terror was enough.

Still thinking about those damn rangers out invading the trail with their sniffing dogs, he yanked on his coat, gloves and hat and headed outside. He'd leave Ginger to stew over what he'd said while he slipped into town.

He knew they were looking for her. Now, he needed to make sure they hadn't found Nadine or the girl who'd snuck up on his place yesterday.

Ellie and Derrick met Bryce in her office at nine thirty to discuss the case before they spoke to the public.

Bryce looked sullen this morning, deep grooves beneath his eyes, his blond hair rumpled as if he'd run his hands through it a dozen times. Ellie watched him, her guard up, and wondered if he was plotting a way to make her look unprofessional. Knowing the captain was watching both of them, she vowed to keep her cool if he did.

"I ran down a lead on Dunce last night," he said, skipping any semblance of small talk or pleasantries. "Neighbor who knew him years ago. Said he heard a commotion one day and went over to check it out. Said Dunce was all shifty and had a shitload of knives in his garage. Also had a field dressing stand and an old cooler he stored his meat in."

Ellie's pulse quickened. "What about the house?"

"House was about thirty miles from Cleveland. Burned down a few months after the Houser woman went missing."

Derrick looked up from his computer. "Was there an investigation into the fire?"

Bryce's jaw tightened. "Local police ruled it accidental. Found a bunch of paint thinner in the garage and a can of gasoline."

"How about the freezer?" Derrick asked.

"No mention of it in the police report."

"Dunce could have set the fire to destroy evidence," Ellie said.

"I know that," Bryce said tersely. "Neighbor said Dunce never came back though. He thought the man set the fire to collect insurance, but I checked and Dunce didn't have any."

Ellie offered him a small smile. "Thanks for following up, Bryce." Maybe she should go easy on him. He must be trying to work with them.

"It's my job," he said, his tone irritated. "I talked to the governor last night and swore to him I'd find Ginger."

Ellie sucked in a breath and glanced at Derrick, whose expression darkened. So Bryce was looking for points with the governor.

Bryce leaned against her desk, towering over her. An intimidating stance, she realized. "Where are you on the case, Detective?" he asked.

She ignored his tactic, sitting back in a relaxed posture to show she wasn't bothered, then filled him in on what they knew about Tessa Tulane's death. "We're waiting on the ME's report. But multiple stab wounds suggest blood loss caused her death."

Bryce arched his brows. "Any motive?"

Ellie shook her head. "Nothing in her personal things. Fans loved her. Grandmother said she often hiked in the woods looking for inspiration for her books. She was writing a ghost series so she could have gone to Hickory Flats Cemetery for ideas."

"Maybe she ran into someone who didn't want to be found," Derrick suggested.

Through the glass windows of her office, Ellie saw Angelica and her cameraman rush in, heading into the room they reserved for press conferences. Resigned, she stood, hands on her hips. "Time to meet the press. Let's get this over with."

Bryce went ahead of her, leading the way from her office to the briefing room, pasting on a half smile as he greeted Angelica. Ellie saw the reporter's look turn wary. Angelica had his number, too.

"Are you guys ready?" Angelica said, glancing at Ellie and Derrick.

They both nodded, but Bryce stepped up beside Angelica.

Annoyance flashed in Angelica's eyes, but once Tom began to roll, Angelica forced a camera-ready smile, "This is Angelica Gomez live from Bluff County where the news is exploding with reports of another murder."

Bryce addressed the public, "This morning we are still actively searching for the governor's daughter, Ginger Weston. It's vital that anyone with information regarding her whereabouts report it to the police."

Suddenly the door burst open, and the governor strode in, his body emanating tension, his face worried and angry. His media handler was right beside him. He started toward Ellie, but Derrick stepped toward him to intercede.

Angelica angled the mic toward Ellie, "Detective Reeves, is it true that another woman's body was found at Hickory Flats Cemetery yesterday?"

Ellie inhaled a deep breath. "I'm sorry to have to report that's true, yes. Local author and storyteller Tessa Tulane was discovered by a search team looking for Ginger Weston. Ms. Tulane was from Crooked Creek." She paused. "We know she was stabbed to death but at this time have no person of interest. If you have any information about her or her death, please contact the police ASAP."

Angelica gripped the mic. "Do you think Ms. Tulane's death is connected to that of Nadine Houser?"

"At this point, it's inconclusive, but we are considering the possibility that a single predator is out there hunting women. That said, I want to warn all females to be cautious and super vigilant about their surroundings and strangers."

"The *Hunter.*" Angelica's brown eyes widened. "Do you think Ginger Weston's disappearance is related to this predator?"

The million-dollar question. And one fear she hated to put in the governor's mind. But she could see in his eyes that he'd already made that leap himself.

And she'd promised his wife she couldn't give up and that

meant asking for any help she could get. Being honest with the public was a start. "Again, we're considering that possibility—"

The governor bolted forward, his tone shrill as he cut her off. "Just what do you know, Detective? It seems like you have made no progress in finding my daughter. The sheriff explained that you've suffered trauma at the hands of a serial killer a short time ago." He tugged at his tie. "I hope Ginger is not going to be another casualty of the violence taking place while you're in charge."

Ellie's throat closed and she felt her cheeks redden. She understood his frustration, but the gleam in Bryce's eyes made it clear he'd filled the governor with doubts about her.

Hands fisting by her sides, she tamped down her anger and, aware of the camera still rolling, injected sincerity into her voice. "I promise you, Governor Weston, and the people in Bluff County that we are doing everything within our power to solve these cases and to find your daughter. And we hope to find her alive."

"So far what you've done is not enough."

Weston's media consultant placed a hand on the governor's shoulder, then said something in a low voice that Ellie couldn't hear. But she had a feeling he wanted to handle the situation.

Weston shrugged it off with an angry look, then pulled the mic from Angelica. "At this time, I'm going to insist that a task force be created to investigate my daughter's disappearance and to track down this monster you're calling the *Hunter*." He gave Ellie a sharp look. "Special Agent Fox will be in charge. And he will be watching how you handle things, Detective, and reporting to me."

SEVENTY

Ellie summoned every ounce of restraint she possessed in order to maintain a professional mask. But at least the governor had put Derrick in charge and not Bryce.

The sheriff's expression indicated he didn't like the way that conversation had gone down either.

Derrick moved up beside her, but she gripped the mic instead of letting him take over.

Had *he* known about this?

"I understand your frustration," she said to the governor. "And of course, Special Agent Fox will lead the task force." Then she addressed the public, "While we continue to search for Ginger Weston, we're also looking for the man who killed Nadine Houser and Tessa Tulane."

There was also Bill Hubbard and the bloody writing. But she wanted to withhold that information for now in case another confession came in and they needed to weed out false ones.

"Both women were stabbed, the wounds indicating the killer used a hunting knife," she continued. "He held Nadine Houser for years before he disposed of her body, suggesting he kept her in a secluded place. The fact that he left these women in the woods indicates he lives off the grid. He may be a hunter himself."

She exhaled. "It's possible he's a survivalist, uneducated and awkward around people. He probably is not comfortable in society. We're imploring the public to inform us if you know of anyone who fits that description. Tessa Tulane was killed quickly, and he disposed of her body shortly afterwards, which makes it likely this was a crime of opportunity or that she possibly stumbled upon him or his location. We have organized search parties to comb the area near where Ms. Tulane was discovered and are extending that search to a twenty-mile radius. Now, I'll turn over to Special Agent Fox."

Without waiting for a response from him, she stepped aside, then brushed past the governor and Bryce, hurried into her office and shut the door. She was so angry she was shaking. She'd been blindsided by what had just happened, just as she was by this unsub who seemed intent on eluding her.

He was hiding in the shadows just as the ones from her nightmare were. Lurking, watching her and waiting for her to make a misstep.

She slammed her fist into her palm and bit back a scream.

Dammit. Maybe she was incompetent. *He* was hunting and planning to take more lives. And so far, she was helpless to stop him.

SEVENTY-ONE

He stared at the TV above the bar at the Corner Café, his blood pulsing hot at the way that detective described him.

Uneducated. Awkward. Couldn't fit into society.

He was damn well sitting in town right now, wasn't he? And no one knew who he was. With all the hype about Halloween and costumes being worn, he could walk through town dressed like Frankenstein or an ax murderer and no one would think anything of it.

The only thing the cop had right was that he was a hunter. Hell, hunters were crawling all over these hills.

He looked down at his worn coat and shoes, though, and wondered if he should have dressed in cleaner jeans and his best flannel shirt. There were some pretty women in here now. One caught his eye.

Silky blond hair, bright eyes the color of bluebonnets. A friendly smile.

Her ring finger was bare.

"You want anything else, sir?" the waitress asked.

Her voice sounded as sweet as honey. And she'd called him sir as if she knew how to respect a man. His mama always called his daddy sir. Yes, Sir. No, Sir. Just the way a wife was supposed to.

He smiled and ordered a piece of peach cobbler. She served it on a saucer then slid it in front of him. He'd tried to keep a low profile, didn't want anyone taking notice of him, but he couldn't help himself. He lifted his head and looked straight into her eyes.

Something clicked inside him, an electric zing that connected him to her. She stared at him for a long moment, and he could have sworn she felt the same.

Then she stepped back, breaking the spell and disappeared through a door into the kitchen.

Suddenly he felt alone, like he'd lost something special. And he wanted it back.

Ginger is your soul mate.

Except he'd been mistaken before. Maybe he was mistaken about Ginger.

You're crazy. I could never love a man like you.

Ginger's hateful words taunted him. Wolves were loyal to their mates.

Yet he wanted this woman with his heart and soul.

The pretty blond here was the devil, the forbidden fruit sent to tempt him. He couldn't betray Ginger for her.

He inhaled the pie, threw some cash on the bar, then hurried outside. Ginger was waiting on him. He'd make her his wife tonight.

SEVENTY-TWO

Derrick was pissed as hell at how the press conference had gone. He knew Ellie was upset and didn't blame her.

What was Bryce Waters' problem?

As Angelica and her crew left, Derrick pulled the governor aside and assured him that Ellie had been on top of the case and that he would head the task force.

"Thank you," Governor Weston said, his voice filled with fear and worry. "I'm grateful for your expertise and that you're on our side."

Bryce's body language spoke volumes as he stepped aside to take a phone call, shooting daggers at Derrick.

The man was a chameleon, and when he hung up, he turned to the governor. "I need to go, Governor. But I will make sure Detective Reeves stays in line. I thought she needed time off after that last case, and maybe this will force her to take it."

His smug smile made Derrick want to punch the asshole. Then Bryce said he had to follow a lead and rushed off.

Derrick struggled to control his temper. "Go home to your wife," he told Governor Weston. "I promise to call you the minute we have new information."

"Please find her," the governor said, his voice cracking. "My wife is falling apart."

So was the governor. "I understand," Derrick said, remembering the hell his own family had suffered when his sister had disappeared. The not knowing had shredded their family.

"The minute you learn something," the governor said firmly.

"Yes, sir," Derrick said.

The governor wiped a hand over his face, then nodded and left with his security detail and staff.

Derrick grabbed coffee on the way to Ellie's office, aware he needed to defuse the situation.

Ellie glared at him when he knocked on the door but waved him in. "Did you know he planned to do that?" She crossed her arms, anger flaring across her face. "Was that some kind of plan you devised because you think I'm falling down on the job?"

"I had no idea," he said emphatically. "It really has nothing to do with you, Ellie. He's frustrated and terrified. We both can understand that. And Waters has obviously got to him too."

Ellie heaved a breath, closed her eyes and waited a second before she spoke. "I know. But maybe I'm not doing everything I can."

"You are, and I assured him of that," Derrick said gruffly. God, he wanted to hold her. "But a task force is not a bad idea. I want Ranger McClain on it."

Surprise lit her eyes. "I thought you didn't like him."

Derrick shrugged. "It's not personal. This is a job, Ellie. His knowledge of the area and his SAR teams have been invaluable in the last few cases and so far this one, too."

Her expression softened. "That's true. I'm sorry I blew up."

"You're under a lot of stress and pressure, and Waters was out of line undermining you," he said. "Don't sweat it. Let's just get to work."

Her look of gratitude made his shoulders relax. Time to get their heads back in the case. All their careers were on the line. More importantly, so were lives. "I called forensics first thing this morning. They dusted the camera for prints already. The memory card was still inside so they pulled the photos and emailed them to us."

She gave a pained sigh. "Finally, maybe a lead." She carried her laptop to the corner seating area and set it on the table then opened the file.

Tension stretched between them as they scrolled through dozens of photographs of the town, of locals, the storytelling festival, costume-clad participants and even the house where Tessa had grown up with Ms. Ivy. Close-ups of nature and landmarks on the trail filled the screen, focusing on unique rock formations, clouds that formed shapes and animals, and the various waterfalls.

"There's none of the cemetery where she was found," Ellie said with a huff.

"Because the killer took her there," Derrick said, thinking out loud.

Ellie rolled her shoulders, then continued scrolling through several more shots until she suddenly paused on a close up of the ground. "Look at that."

Derrick leaned closer to study it. "It looks like some kind of cable running along the ground."

Another photo showed a different angle, as if Tessa had been following the cable to see where it went.

She paused, zeroing in on a close-up. "There, through those weeds and that brush, there's an opening like it leads into a cave."

Derrick's pulse pounded. "You suggested the unsub lives in these mountains. That he could be a survivalist. That could be his home."

"And Tessa found it." She clicked to the next shot and discovered a hulking figure of a man in a burly worn winter coat, hat and gloves. "His face is obscured by the shadows of the trees and brush. But that could be him."

Derrick tried to make out his features, but it was impossible, except the man had a scruffy beard.

"If this is the unsub, then Tessa captured a picture of him and where he lives," Ellie said. "That's what got her killed."

SEVENTY-THREE
WILD HOG HOLLER

Despair pulled at Ginger, but she shoved it away, summoning all her strength to fight the monster when he returned. She flexed her hands and feet, grateful the feeling had returned to her legs.

She'd strained her arms and clawed at the floor to grab the ax, but it was inches beyond her reach, so she finally gave up and rested. Seconds and minutes passed excruciatingly slowly. It was so dark inside that she had no idea what time it was, if it was day or night.

Or how long she'd been here.

It felt like months, but she thought it could only have been a few days.

The memory of his body pressed against hers the night before sickened her. She didn't know if she could bear it again.

The door squeaked open, then footsteps echoed as he shuffled through the space. Nausea climbed her throat and she blinked back more tears, shivering. The fire had burned out shortly after he'd left and the threadbare blanket he'd left her did nothing to warm her. The scent of his sweat and body odor permeated it, so she'd thrown it off.

"I'm home, darlin'," he called as he moved through the bunker. His hulking figure appeared, looming over her, his evil eyes piercing as he stooped down in front of her.

"I missed you," he growled.

Ginger choked back a cry.

"They gave up looking for you." His sinister smile revealed crooked teeth and indicated he probably hadn't seen a dentist in a long time, if ever.

"I don't believe you," she said, although her voice warbled. "My father would never do that."

"It's true," he said. "I saw the news in town. They called off the search."

Her throat tightened with emotion as total despair clawed at her.

"It's time for you and me to be together," he said. "For me to make you my wife."

She shook her head in denial. She couldn't give up.

"Yes." His rough calloused finger traced a line down her jaw.

She bit back a scream. Had to think. To stall. "All right, but I need to clean up first. Maybe wash up."

His eyes flickered with excitement. "Of course, darlin'. I'll heat some water."

He stood, went outside and came back with a bucket. He poured it into a big pot on the stove and she waited as he warmed it then poured some in a pan and brought it to her with a washcloth. She reached for the cloth, and he handed it to her.

She dipped the cloth into the water and realized how hot it was. Taking a deep breath for courage, she decided this was her chance. She grabbed the pan of steaming water and threw it at him. He bellowed and jumped back in shock. She lunged for the knife at his waist, caught the handle and tried to pull it from his belt. Screaming in rage, he recovered quickly, jerked it out and raised it toward her.

"You shouldn't have done that!" He grabbed her hair and yanked her toward him, and pain ricocheted up her skull.

She struggled, trying to wrestle the knife from him, but he raised his arm and struck her across the face. She fell sideways with the blow, then scrambled backward and lifted her feet to kick him when he came after her.

But he was so strong that he jerked her legs aside with one hand and jumped her. His heavy body slammed into her, and she shoved at his chest, then reached for the ax again.

But he grabbed her legs and dragged her towards him. She kicked and fought, clawed at his arms and face, but he slapped her face again so hard stars swam behind her eyes. With a feral bellow, he jammed the knife into her chest.

Sheer pain tore through her as he dug the knife deeper, and she screamed and gurgled up blood.

Her parents' faces flashed in her mind as the world began to spin and fade. The beautiful pieces of jewelry she'd created. Her hopes and dreams...

A tunnel of darkness. Then a light so bright that she felt it pulling her toward it.

And then there was nothing as she slipped into death.

SEVENTY-FOUR

He dragged Ginger into his arms and rocked her back and forth. Tears flowed down his face as he traced a finger over her cheek and wiped droplets of blood away. Her beautiful eyes stared up at him helplessly, blank, unforgiving.

He'd had such hopes for her.

But her words of hate resounded over and over in his head just like the statement that detective made. *He was uneducated. Awkward. Didn't fit into society.*

You're crazy. I could never love a man like you.

The rage inside him mounted. He'd thought she was so pretty, but her heart was as cold as ice.

Reeling with fury, he laid her on the sheet of plastic then went to his cooler.

Eeny meany miny mo. Which one of you has to go?

Not Brittany. She was his first love. Special.

Nadine was gone.

The other faces, their pleading eyes, their screams of terror as he'd taken their lives, taunted him. The fifth woman—he hadn't had her very long. She looked ugly now with the frost coating her body and her limbs all twisted and hard. It was too risky to dump her in the woods though. Especially now Nadine had been found and search teams had been out looking.

A memory of that ax coming down, blood flying, flashed behind his eyes. The screams. The fear. The... quickening of his pulse.

If he cut one of the others in pieces, he could make room for Ginger.

He went to get his ax.

For the first time since they'd found Nadine Houser's frozen body, Ellie allowed herself to feel a jolt of hope. If Tessa had seen the unsub, the *Hunter*, as she'd started calling him in her mind, this photograph might lead them to him.

And maybe they would be in time to save Ginger.

As she and Derrick entered the Corner Café, she saw Cord talking to Lola from a high-top table. Lola looked upset and Cord was squeezing her hand. She hated to interrupt them, but time was of the essence.

She said hi to Lola then addressed Cord. "Did you see the news about Tessa Tulane?"

He nodded and Lola's face paled. "It's awful," she said. "Do you have any idea who killed her?"

"Not yet," Ellie said.

Derrick turned to Lola. "Could you give us a moment, ma'am?"

Lola nodded. "I'll get you a refill, Cord."

"We found Tessa's camera, Cord," Ellie continued as Lola stepped away. "Her grandmother said she took photographs for inspiration for her books. On it, we discovered pictures of an area where it looks like a bunker was built in the ground." She showed Cord the photographs on her phone.

"That does look like a cable," Cord agreed.

"I can't imagine he left her body too close to the bunker, but it can't be too far either. Do you recognize any landmarks that might narrow down a location?"

Cord scrolled through the pictures, eyes narrowing as he studied them for details. A few photographs in and he paused. "See that mound there?"

Ellie nodded. "You recognize it?"

"Yeah," Cord said. "I think it's the grave of Hogzilla."

"Who's Hogzilla?" Derrick asked.

"It's a folk legend that originated in South Georgia about a giant wild hog that terrorized and attacked people," Cord said. "Some local finally killed it and buried it in a giant grave. One of the Shadows I ran into on the trail told me a similar tale about one in the mountains here."

"Are there really wild hogs in those woods?" Derrick asked.

"Some boar, wild pigs, yeah," Cord said.

Ellie found the picture of the man in the shadows. Lola appeared at Cord's shoulder, coffee pot in hand. Her forehead crinkled as she studied the image.

"Who is that?" Lola asked.

"A person of interest," Ellie said quickly, turning the phone away. "I'm sorry, Lola, but we can't discuss it."

The café owner looked abashed and backed away again.

Ellie turned back to Cord. "We think he might be the unsub, and that he's been holed up in that bunker. Have you seen him out in the woods?"

Cord shrugged. "Could be any hunter out there."

Dammit.

Derrick cleared his throat. "Maybe our tech team at the Bureau can pull it into focus and run it through facial rec."

"Can you take us to this place?" Ellie asked Cord.

"Sure. Let me grab my gear." He stood and glanced at Lola. "See you later."

Lola stood on tiptoe and kissed his cheek. "Be careful, Cord."

Her eyes flickered with some emotion Ellie couldn't quite define, and Cord looked uncomfortable but murmured he would.

But Ellie didn't have time to dwell on what was going on between them. She had to get to that bunker.

SEVENTY-SIX

Lola worried about Cord every time he went on the trail. But the minute Ellie asked, she knew he would go.

She'd been alone for so long. Had finally allowed herself to think she was safe. Finally allowed herself to trust and to love.

But Cord didn't want her. Sure, he was friendly and seemed to enjoy her company. But she knew she was just a fill-in for Ellie.

Ellie was the one he wanted.

Everyone knew it but Ellie.

She'd hoped she could break a chink in his feelings for the detective and win his love. But that was never going to happen. The moment Ellie called his name, he jumped and ran.

She had to run now, too.

That man in the picture... She couldn't be sure. But he reminded her of the man who'd come into the café earlier.

She'd had an eerie feeling about him when he'd looked into her eyes. Had tried to dismiss it as paranoia.

But... if he'd killed that woman Nadine, and abducted Tessa Tulane... if he was the one she'd seen in the woods years ago...

He might have recognized her.

She told her staff she had an emergency, threw off her apron, grabbed her coat, gloves and purse and hurried out back to her

Toyota. She hated the thought of leaving this town and the people she'd grown to love.

Hated to leave Cord, although he would barely miss her.

But if that was *the* man, and he remembered her, she might end up dead like the others.

SEVENTY-SEVEN
WILD HOG HOLLER

The snow was beginning to melt as the temperatures rose above freezing, making the ground slippery and turning it to mush. Ellie's boots sank into it like quicksand, the ice cracking and breaking like sheets of glass beneath her feet.

Ellie and Derrick followed Cord through the wilderness, the tall pines and oaks so thick in places they had to maneuver around them by wading in the edge of the creek. Mile after mile, her calves strained, yet she pushed on, hopeful they might finally catch this madman.

Though she'd compiled a profile, she still didn't quite know what made this unsub tick. But she sensed he was escalating.

The victims' faces haunted her as if their spirits were floating through the shadows. Nadine was just twenty when she'd gone missing. Ginger and Tessa were both late twenties, early thirties. They had different occupations—Nadine worked as a store clerk, Ginger was a celebrity of sorts and starting her own business, Tessa a writer. So their occupations had nothing to do with the Hunter's choice.

Nadine and Ginger were both blonds. Often serial killers chose a type. Maybe blonds were his.

Except Tessa had dark hair.

She didn't fit that profile. Maybe that was the reason he hadn't kept her.

They reached a grassy bald, stopped for a drink of water, then kept hiking, over the crest then down the incline toward the gorge.

She was so busy with her rambling thoughts that she tripped and stumbled over a tree root. Icy water sank into her shoes and soaked her hands and the sleeves of her jacket as she braced herself to avoid sinking into the creek.

A grunting sound broke the silence and she looked up to see a feral pig rooting in the ground. Knowing better than to make any sudden moves and spook the big animal, she remained perfectly still. Several heartbeats passed. Her body trembled.

A deer scampered through the woods to the west, and the pig startled, then turned and ran after it.

Ellie stood and jogged after the men. Their gruff voices drifted to her as she approached.

"So you're in charge of the case now instead of Ellie, Agent Fox?" Cord said. "Smooth move."

Ellie tensed.

"For your information, that was the governor's idea," Derrick said curtly.

Cord's voice was gruff, defensive. "Ellie can handle herself."

"Yes, I can," Ellie said, annoyed they were talking about her as if she wasn't there. "And I don't need either of you treating me like I can't."

"I wouldn't dream of it," Derrick said with a wry chuckle.

Cord clenched his jaw. "Sorry, El. I just didn't like the way things happened back at the station."

"You don't have to fight my battles for me," Ellie said firmly.

"The governor is just worried out of his mind," Derrick said. "He put me in charge because he knows me, because I was working with him before his daughter went missing."

They flattened themselves against a rocky ledge as they slowly navigated their way across.

"McClain, he wants me to put together a task force," Derrick said as they made it to the other side and halted to take a breath. "That includes Ellie. I want you to be part of it."

Surprise flared on Cord's face as he angled his head toward Derrick. "You do?"

"Yes," Derrick said. "We need someone who knows the area the way you do."

Cord mumbled that he'd help as he turned and continued. They pushed past a cluster of hemlocks and Cord led them down a path that appeared to be going nowhere. Silence fell between them as they hiked another mile, then Cord halted and pointed to the ground ahead.

"There's the cable," he said. "It's almost buried in the snow."

Ellie and Derrick immediately scanned the area, looking for signs someone was around. Except for the wind blowing and creatures scampering through the forest, everything seemed quiet. She pulled her weapon in case they were ambushed, and Derrick did the same, then she gestured to the men that they should follow the cable along the ground. After another half mile, pushing through the weeds and brush, they came to a door built into an underground cave.

Derrick pulled his flashlight and braced his gun at the ready, and Ellie gripped hers as he eased open the door. Cord stayed behind them, on the lookout in case someone was watching or guarding the place. Ellie went still for a moment as they entered the dark, cold interior, memories of being trapped in a cave as a child threatening to trigger her panic.

As she took deep breaths to calm herself, an earthy scent mingled with the odor of burning wood. Firelight flickered and danced across the big open room from a crude stone firepit, and she spotted a camp stove in one corner and a mattress in another. The metallic odor of fresh blood hit her as she and Derrick inched across the dirt. Along one wall, she saw canned and dried goods on wooden shelves.

Someone was living here. And judging from the dark crimson

stain she saw on the ground near the bed, someone was injured—or dead. But no one was there.

Heart hammering, she crossed to the mattress and found a heavy chain attached to a post. Blood dotted the thick metal and blanket, and strands of blond hair littered the mattress as if it had been pulled out. Her stomach convulsed as she imagined Nadine and then Ginger chained to the wall. Derrick passed the kitchen area and disappeared into a narrow tunnel that led deeper into the underground chamber.

Ellie shivered, claustrophobic again, but she forced herself to battle her way through it. She shined her light along the floor and wall, surveying the dark space once more. A large roll of heavy plastic leaned against the wall. An ax sat by the door, dirty, with wood splinters clinging to it.

For a moment, she imagined the unsub using it on a woman and cold sweat broke out on her face.

Footsteps sounded, and she looked up to see Derrick coming back up the tunnel. "Jesus, Ellie. You won't believe this. There's a cooler down there." His bronzed skin looked buttermilk pale as he motioned for her to follow him.

Cold dread knotted her insides, but she took a deep breath and followed him down the stairs. One step, two, three, four... with each step, her anxiety intensified. Somewhere a rat skittered. The smell of dank earth, musk, sweat, urine and... blood swirled around her.

"Brace yourself," Derrick murmured as she followed him to the right to a large cooler.

Every muscle in her body screamed with tension as he opened the door. *Dear God.* She staggered backward, gasping in horror at what was inside.

Bodies. Women's bodies piled and frozen, one on top of the other.

She gripped her stomach as bile rose to her throat. Ginger Weston's blank eyes stared back in death from where she lay on top.

SEVENTY-EIGHT

Ellie rocked back on her heels in shock. Suddenly she couldn't breathe.

A tremble rippled up her spine as she stared at the women's bodies contorted to fit together.

"This must be where he kept Nadine until he decided to dump her," Derrick said, in a voice thick with disgust. "He must have run out of room, so he decided to get rid of her."

Ellie swayed but caught herself before she touched the wall. She didn't want to contaminate the scene. They needed every bit of forensic evidence they could find so they could put this monster away.

Derrick stroked her back. "You look like you're going to pass out. Go up and call for the crime team and ME. I'll look around down here."

She hated to be weak, but she needed air. She couldn't throw up down here in front of Derrick and ruin evidence. And this place was secret, which meant they *would* find his DNA.

"Go, make the call, Ellie," Derrick said firmly. "The sooner we recover the bodies, the sooner we make IDs. Maybe one of these women's stories will lead us to his identity."

He was right. Exhaling to regain her balance, she straightened and pulled herself together, then turned and climbed the stairs.

The scene in the living area seemed even more terrifying now she realized what the bastard was doing. Images of the women fighting for their lives, begging for him not to kill them, raced through her mind like a bad horror movie.

She spotted the chain again and realized he'd kept the women like animals. Then he'd killed them and put them in the freezer like he would a kill in the wild.

She thought of the necklace carved with the words *Mine Forever*. Tessa had not been wearing one. Had she just stumbled upon his lair, as her photos suggested?

She checked her phone but had no cell service inside the cave, so she crossed to the door, careful not to touch anything. A noise outside startled her, and she froze, listening. The wind? Brush moving? A tree branch snapping off? Cord?

Or had the Hunter returned?

Heart hammering, she pulled her gun with clammy hands, plastered her body against the wall and waited.

SEVENTY-NINE

Derrick counted four corpses in the cooler, with Ginger's body on top. He looked deeper, his stomach churning as he discovered severed body parts of another. That meant five women in this freezer.

For a long minute, he had to look away from the grisly sight. But his mind was working to process the information. Why cut up one of the women and leave the other bodies intact? Because he'd run out of space?

Choking back his anger and disgust he did a mental tally.

Including Nadine and Tessa, who were not here in the cooler, this madman had murdered seven women.

Counting Hubbard, that added up to eight victims so far. Eight that they knew of.

There could be more hidden somewhere else or that he'd dumped in different locations, and no one had made the connection. Maybe he even had another freezer somewhere.

He scrubbed his hand over his face to pull himself together. A predator with this kind of psychological makeup didn't stop by himself. In his mind, he had a mission, some kind of logic, albeit terrifyingly skewed, that he followed. A motive behind his madness.

Ellie's profile had been spot on. The killer was a survivalist.

Most likely uneducated. Lived in the wilderness so he had no friends.

Derrick shifted. Many killers fed on revisiting their crime scenes and reliving the memory of taking a life. Did this unsub make the *Mine Forever* heart necklace for them because he couldn't let go? Did he have some sick perversion of visiting them each day?

Were the women his trophies?

He stepped into the storage room again and noted the dates on many of the canned goods were expired. There were extra blankets, flashlights and batteries, matches, a large tin of cooking oil, rags, and several buckets and tin pans. In a large trash can, he found long sheets of plastic wadded up, plastic covered in blood.

A sick knot clogged his throat, and he climbed the steps, scanning the room. This space had served as the living quarters yet there was only one mattress. Crates held jeans, flannel shirts, T-shirts, socks and underwear.

Questions ticked through Derrick's head. Although he brought the women here, he obviously lived alone. How long had he had this place? Did he live here year-round? Or did he have another place where he went?

He'd heard stories of people disappearing into the survivalist camps and raising their families in isolation, thinking they were protecting them from the outside world. Perhaps this man had been one of them?

The packaged meat in the second cooler downstairs was wrapped in butcher paper and looked as if it had been dressed and packaged by a professional. A thought struck him.

The man had to get money somewhere, have some kind of a job in order to purchase the canned goods and back-up supplies.

Maybe he worked at a local meat processing plant.

Adrenaline pumping through him, he rushed back up the stairs to tell Ellie.

EIGHTY

Ellie's pulse pounded as she flattened herself against the cave wall and strained to hear outside. Brush rustled and the wind created a draft as it blew wet snow inside.

They had closed the door when they'd come in.

Cord could have opened it to check on them. Or had the killer returned home? If so, where was Cord?

She was tempted to call out for Derrick, but if the unsub was outside, she didn't want to alert him to their presence. So she peered through the crack in the door where it hung on hinges. She didn't see Cord anywhere.

Holding her gun at the ready, she waited, but no one appeared. *Dammit*, was the Hunter waiting to ambush them? Or had he seen them and run?

Perspiration trickled down the back of her neck. Except for the leaves fluttering in the breeze and the sound of thawing snow slipping off the trees, everything seemed still and silent.

Cord emerged around the corner from the woods, his big body tense. "I was looking around out here. Didn't find anything except a woodpile."

"Radio for a crime team and the ME," Ellie told him. "The Hunter left more victims inside."

His eyes went bleak, then he nodded and snagged his radio.

"Did you see anyone out here?" Ellie asked.

"No. Thought I saw some movement in that direction." He pointed to the right. "I was about to check it out when I saw you."

"I'll go." Her gaze swept the forest, a sea of white-tipped pines, oaks, and hemlocks, and she spotted boot prints in the mushy ground a few feet away.

"I'm going to check out those prints," she said. "Tell the ERT to bring a recovery team and equipment. The bodies are frozen inside a cooler."

He frowned and cursed, snagging his radio from his belt and making the call.

Heart pounding, Ellie began to track the footprints, careful not to mar them or step into the indentations. The steps looked uneven and patchy, as if whoever had made them was dragging his foot.

Using her flashlight, she made her way toward a thicket of evergreens, then wove onto a narrow path that led deeper into the woods. Stepping over broken limbs and weeds mashed down and covered with the weight of the recent storm, she lost track of the prints a few feet in.

Suddenly she felt something—or someone—behind her and started to turn around. But a hard whack to the back of her head sent her vision into a spin and she collapsed into the snow face down.

For a moment, she was so disoriented she thought the man was standing above her. Was certain he'd kill her right there. She raked her hand in the snow in search of her gun but couldn't find it.

Nausea caught her in its clutches as she tried to get up. She heard footsteps crunching the ground and managed to lift her head just enough to see the heel of a hiking boot as it disappeared into the woods.

Dammit, Ellie, get up.

Determination fueled her strength, and she attempted to stand and push past the throbbing in her skull. She finally made it to her hands and knees, then heard Derrick.

"Ellie!" The sound of his voice yelling her name echoed in the wind again, and she blinked away tears, hoping to clear her vision as Derrick raced to her. "I think he was here. He ran into the woods."

He gripped her arm to help her up, but she yelled she was fine then gestured north. "Go after him," Ellie barked.

A tense second passed as he looked at her, then he pulled his gun and chased the prints into the woods. Ellie swallowed hard to tamp down the nausea, then braced her hands on a tree stump and managed to stand.

Battling dizziness, she staggered back toward the bunker, furious that the bastard had ambushed her and escaped.

EIGHTY-ONE

Cord's stomach knotted as he spotted Ellie staggering back to the bunker. "What the hell happened?"

"He jumped me and got away," Ellie grumbled as she wiped blood from the back of her matted hair. "Derrick went in pursuit."

"Let me take a look at your head."

She didn't argue but dropped her head forward, and he parted her hair and examined the wound.

"Good grief," he muttered as he noted a gash about four inches long. "The head bleeds a lot. You should get a CT scan for a concussion."

"I know the drill," Ellie said. "I'll be fine. I just want to catch this bastard."

He gritted his teeth. There was no point arguing with the infuriatingly stubborn woman. "Let me clean it up and we'll have a better idea of how bad it is."

"Did you call for the ERT and ME?"

"Yeah, they're on their way." He removed a first aid kit from his backpack, then opened it and took out antiseptic and gauze. "Milo, one of the rangers on my team, is going to meet them and lead them here. I told them to bring an ATV and equipment to transport the bodies."

Ellie winced as he dabbed at her head and cleaned the gash, wiping away blood with one piece then another.

"I'm sorry it stings," he said gruffly as he applied the antiseptic.

"I'm tougher than I look, Cord," Ellie said wryly.

He wanted to shake her. "You don't always have to put yourself in the line of fire to prove that."

"You sound like my mother."

Cord chuckled. "Maybe she's right."

Ellie lifted her head and stared at him. "Where is this coming from? You know I love my job."

Tension stretched between them. "I'm just worried about you."

Ellie's eyes flared with irritation. "I can take care of myself."

He laid the bloody gauze on the ground in front of her, the crimson stains macabre against the white snow, as if to mock her comment.

Then he applied a bandage and was about to say something else, but Derrick appeared at the edge of the woods walking toward them and shook his head indicating he'd lost the guy. They both fell silent, frustration like a live wire.

Better he kept his mouth shut. Ellie had a mind of her own and nothing he could say would change it.

But fear for her would dog him every day of his life.

EIGHTY-TWO

The next few hours were cold and grueling as the forensic team, recovery team and ME showed up to do their jobs. It took hours to process the bunker and the girls had to be loaded without disturbing the ice encasing them; they might lose precious evidence if the bodies warmed too quickly. Ellie knew that time of death could only be estimated based on decomp, the temperature in the cooler and the amount of space inside. Part of the ice had already been chipped away and disturbed, possibly by the killer when he removed Nadine.

IDs would also aid in establishing the timeline. They could use the dates the women disappeared to estimate how long they might have been dead. It wouldn't be exact, but hopefully the blood and DNA inside the bunker would lead them to the unsub.

Laney was just as horrified as Ellie at the sight of the naked female corpses piled one on top of the other. It was so inhumane.

Derrick insisted Laney examine Ellie even though Cord had tended her injury, which seemed to piss off Cord. He busied himself organizing another search team to comb the woods within a twenty-mile radius of the bunker, setting off on foot.

Exhaustion and frustration weighed on Ellie as she watched the bodies being loaded into the refrigerated truck. The sense that she'd failed to save Ginger made her want to double over and scream in frustration. She'd lost the race to find Ginger in time and catch this maniac. And now he was free to kill again. She choked back tears.

"The forensic team has it here," Derrick told her, his expression grim. "I should notify the governor and his wife tonight. I don't want the news that Ginger was found to be leaked to them before they hear it from us."

"I agree," Ellie said, feeling desperate sorrow and sympathy for the couple. "I trust Laney and Dr. Chi, the forensic specialist who will be working with her, but I'm not sure about Bryce. He has a big mouth when he drinks."

"He's an ass," Derrick said. "I can't believe he was elected sheriff."

Ellie smiled, glad he'd noticed. Then she rubbed her fingers together. "Money talks. And he had the backing of his father and mine."

Derrick's brows rose. "Why would Randall have backed him instead of you?"

"He said it was to protect me, keep me out of the limelight in case Hiram was looking for me."

His eyes flickered with emotion, and she felt guilty for reminding him of the painful memory of his sister's death.

"Let's just work this case," he said, his stony mask back in place.

She nodded, grateful to end the conversation, then went to tell the others they were leaving. Milo, Cord's friend and another SAR ranger, led them back toward the area where he'd parked an ATV to carry them down to their cars.

Night had set in, with clouds obliterating what few stars could be seen through the treetops, but the temperature had warmed, creating an oddly balmy feeling as the snow melted and dripped from the branches.

Once in her Jeep, an awkward silence fell between her and Derrick as they drove back to Crooked Creek.

EIGHTY-THREE

CROOKED CREEK

It was close to 11 p.m. when they parked at the inn and met Governor Weston and his wife in the sitting room off the lobby. Ellie had already called Captain Hale and filled him in, and he'd reported to the sheriff and the deputies so they would all be up to speed.

Once they'd seated themselves and faced the couple, Derrick took the lead. "I'm so sorry to have you tell you this," he began. "But we found Ginger."

Mrs. Weston's face turned ghostly as she realized the news wasn't good. The governor pinched the bridge of his nose and closed his eyes.

Derrick and Ellie both remained silent, allowing the couple time to accept the devastating news.

A few seconds later, the governor looked up at them. "Where is she?" he asked in his deep baritone voice.

"On the way to the morgue, sir," Derrick said quietly. "I'm so sorry we didn't find her in time."

Mrs. Weston gave a desperate sob as the governor turned toward Ellie, his expression furious. "The sheriff was right. You bungled this from the start."

Derrick noted the shudder that went through her, her only

reaction. He spoke up in her defense. "Governor, this killer is devious and knows exactly where to hide. Detective Reeves was on it from the beginning. No one could have done more."

"I'm so sorry, sir, Mrs. Weston. I truly am," Ellie said softly. "I... hoped we'd find her and bring her back alive."

"Sorry is not enough," the governor said, agony in his tone.

"Richard." His wife clutched his hand. "Stop it. Losing Ginger is hard enough, but I can't handle your anger towards the people who tried to help us." Then the woman burst into tears and buried her head into her hands. The governor pulled her into his arms, his face crumbling with anguish.

Ellie rose, went to the buffet area, poured two ice waters and brought them back to the couple, putting them on the table in front of them. She moved the box of tissues to the table too and offered it to Mrs. Weston.

They sat for several minutes, the couple holding onto each other, their grief spilling over in quiet heartbreaking sobs. Finally, they accepted the water, and the governor withdrew a handkerchief from his pocket and wiped at his eyes.

"Governor," Derrick said, "I'm afraid this case is bigger than just your daughter's disappearance. The AT is a large geographic area. It runs for over two thousand miles."

"What do you mean—it's bigger than my daughter?" Governor Weston asked. "What happened to my baby? Do you know who killed her?"

Derrick drew in a breath. "I'm not sure you want to know the details, sir."

"I damn well do," the governor said. "Was she killed by the same person who killed those other women?"

Derrick's throat ached as he swallowed. The cases shouldn't get to him. He could handle the gore. But it was the family's anguish that sent him into a tailspin. Violent deaths compounded the grief. No one wanted to think of their loved one suffering.

"Yes," Derrick said, certain now that they were dealing with a serial killer. He didn't add that the governor was right—if they'd caught this guy a day ago, Ginger might still be alive.

Now they had to figure out who the bastard would go after next.

If not, the cooler would keep filling up.

EIGHTY-FOUR

The governor's accusations echoed over and over in Ellie's head as she drove home. Derrick had insisted on following her in his car and had been watching her like a hawk at the inn, as if he expected her to fall apart at any minute.

She was not going to do that. She had to be strong. She'd borne the brunt of blame before and she'd survived, and she would this time, too.

Still, she felt sick to her stomach. Tomorrow they'd face the press and announce that another serial killer was stalking women in the area. That he'd gotten away with his crimes for years. That it would take time to identify the victims and notify the families.

Time that the Hunter would have to strike again.

She dodged puddles of melting snow as she hurried up to her front door. A strong gust of wind howled off the mountains behind her house, reminding her that the woods beyond held dangers and predators.

Derrick followed her, quiet and stoic, his body solidly behind her as she opened the door. He paused in the doorway and she turned to say good night.

"I know that was rough," he said gruffly. "The governor was out of line. He's reacting out of shock and grief."

"Maybe," she said. "Or maybe I did bungle the investigation."

Derrick shook his head. "If you had, I'd be the first to tell you. You went by the book."

"Yeah, and now we have another body."

Derrick touched her arm gently. "You uncovered several victims tonight, Ellie. Murdered women that no one even knew were out there. I'd count that as a win."

"It'll be a win when we catch this guy," Ellie said. "And even that won't bring Ginger or Tessa or any of the others back."

"No, but finding them may help us track down this lunatic. The women have to have been reported missing, just like Nadine was. Other investigators worked those cases, and the cases went cold." Derrick's low voice was firm. "You are responsible for finding them. That's more than they did."

Ellie sighed and ran her fingers over the back of her head where Cord had tended her wound. "Tomorrow we look at missing persons reports," she said, latching onto what he'd said. Or maybe if she could keep her eyes open, she'd start that tonight. "We also need to follow that cable the other way and see where it leads. The unsub must have connected to some place with power to keep the cooler working."

"The fact that he'd stockpiled supplies suggests he has a job," Derrick said. "Somewhere he can fit in."

"What are you thinking?"

Derrick shrugged. "Based on your profile, the butcher paper, and that he's skilled with a hunter's knife, he could work at a butcher shop or meat processing plant."

Hope kicked in as Ellie considered the possibility. She thought of the deer blood found on the porch where Ginger was taken. It could have been from a freshly butchered animal. "You're right."

Derrick's gaze raked over her. "How's your head?"

"I'm fine," Ellie said. "I just need some sleep."

"You may have a concussion," Derrick murmured. "I could sack out here and keep watch."

"Laney checked me out, and I'm fine." Ellie looked away from his intense gaze. He'd stayed on her couch before. And she'd been tempted to invite him into her bed again. Although technically the night they'd slept together they'd been trapped in the woods during a snowstorm, so there was no actual bed.

But they had a case to solve, and she couldn't get distracted from work. Already the governor thought she'd fallen down on the job. She had to stay focused.

She couldn't let anyone else die on her watch.

EIGHTY-FIVE

SOMEWHERE ON THE AT

He stalked back to his shack, slashing weeds and brush as he went, so furious that he thought he would explode.

No, no, no! They'd found his bunker. His home. His souvenirs in the freezer.

He couldn't go back there now.

Rage made him want to bellow, but he reminded himself they could be out looking for him now. He'd spotted the search parties a couple of times, that ranger and his teams combing the woods for Ginger. Had watched as they recovered Tessa.

Had wanted to kill them on the spot.

But he had to play it smart. Stay under their radar. Live in the shadows. Just like his father had taught him.

Memories of his family living in the bunker rolled through his mind, and he felt himself getting choked up. They'd all depended on each other. His daddy had taught him everything he knew about surviving. The animals were there to feed them, his daddy said. There was no need to feel guilty killing them.

Just like the women were there to take care of him. And if they refused, they deserved to die.

His fingers tightened around the handle of his hunting knife, his throat muscles working to hold back a scream of rage. What was he going to do now? He couldn't revisit the chosen ones. They'd be taken away and he'd be alone again.

And this time without the only place he'd ever called home.

Now they'd tear it apart. Invade his life. Plaster news of it all over the TV. Have people searching all around his bunker. Touching his things and violating his home, just like his daddy had warned him.

A thunder cloud boomed above, the melting snow dripping like rain from the trees onto his face. He pulled his hood up and started to run, weaving between the trees and bushes and through the creek. His boots sank into the muddy water which was turning from ice to slush.

No one was out here tonight though. They'd left the mountain to go home and rest. But they would be back.

He let himself into his work shack, the stench of the hanging meat enveloping him in a cloud. He inhaled the metallic odor of blood and wastes and checked his cooler where he had meat hanging from hooks. It was the familiar smell of home, the one he'd grown up with. The one he couldn't live without.

He closed the cooler door and walked to the tiny office in back, the one his daddy had built long ago. A jar of moonshine sat on the shelf. He pulled off his gloves, stuck them in his coat pocket and grabbed it. A turn of the lid, then he took a swig, the burn of alcohol sliding down his throat and warming his insides. Wound tight with outrage, he turned on the ancient TV to watch another episode of *Bonanza*. The women there liked rugged men. Little Joe had them eating out of the palm of his hand.

He stretched out with the moonshine, his eyes glued to the screen. Maybe if he watched enough, he'd learn what he'd done wrong. Why that bitch Ginger had spit at him and called him names.

How he could do things different next time.

The pretty girl from the café had been sweet to everyone in the place. He'd felt connected to her from the start. She reminded him of someone long ago. The first girl he'd loved.

Maybe she was the one, the last one he'd have to take. His forever girl.

EIGHTY-SIX

CROOKED CREEK

Ellie met Derrick, Captain Hale, Bryce, Deputy Landrum, Deputy Eastwood and Mayor Waters at the police station at nine.

First thing this morning, she'd seen the governor's press handler issue a statement that Ginger had been found dead and requesting that everyone respect the family's privacy. She'd barely been able to stand the sheer look of agony on the governor's face.

Shondra gave her a knowing look of encouragement as she entered. Last night after Derrick had left, she'd called her and they'd talked again for an hour.

Struggling to tamp down her emotions, she turned to her colleagues and began the briefing.

"Deputy Landrum, will you look up all the meat processing plants in the area and send a list with their GPS coordinates to me?" Ellie asked.

"On it," he agreed.

"Start sorting through missing persons reports from the past ten years, especially those who went missing in the area," she told Shondra. "Our killer appears to like blonds, so focus on those and send them to me."

Shondra gave a nod.

Sheriff Waters squared his shoulders as he faced her. He looked rough around the edges, and Ellie smelled the faint scent of whiskey on his breath. "Why was I not called to come to the crime scene?" he barked.

Ellie crossed her arms, still pissed as hell over what he'd said to the governor. "Captain Hale informed you what we found. There was no need for you to be on the scene. We called the forensic team to process it."

"I am sheriff, Detective," Bryce said, his tone cold.

"And I'm running this task force," Derrick said curtly. "Listen, we have multiple victims, we don't have time to stand around pissing and moaning. Did you make headway on locating James Dunce?"

Bryce shot Derrick a venomous look. "No, I talked to Mr. Houser though and asked if he recognized him."

"Did he?" Ellie asked.

"He remembered Dunce, said he saw him talking to Nadine once outside the convenience store when he went to pick her up. As soon as Mr. Houser approached Dunce, he headed for his truck without so much as a nod hello. Houser figured he was just taking a break during a long-haul delivery and didn't think much about it at the time."

"But we know he had a thing for Nadine," Ellie said. "We should run DNA found at the bunker to his and see if there's a match."

"What makes you think it's in the system?" Bryce asked.

"I checked when his name first came up, didn't you?" Ellie said. "The detective who worked the initial investigation got a sample for comparison in case they found Nadine. And he'd had an arrest charge for driving without a license."

"I'll follow up then," Bryce said. "But I don't want to be kept out of the loop again."

"Then stay sober," Ellie snapped.

His nostrils flared with anger, but Ellie was saved from an argument by Angelica rapping on the door and motioning that she and her cameraman were ready for the press conference. She, Derrick and Bryce all filed out together.

At the front of the room they used for press conferences, the governor had arrived with his security and press consultant. He looked as if he hadn't slept all night.

Derrick leaned over and spoke in a low voice to her. "I talked to the governor already. Mrs. Weston took a sleeping pill last night and stayed at the inn to rest this morning and to avoid the media. Reporters and paparazzi were hovering outside the inn and a couple followed him here."

"I'm so sorry for them." Ellie understood the need to hide from the press. Having one's personal life—and pain—splattered all over the news and being hounded by reporters only compounded the agony.

Mayor Waters joined the governor, and Ellie could hear him speaking in a low voice, reassuring him that his son, the sheriff, would find who did this.

Ellie's heart drummed. The Waters men both seemed out to sabotage her.

Beside her, Derrick gave her arm a gentle squeeze, but it did no good. The guilt was already crushing her.

Angelica took her position and spoke to camera. "We're here once again in the Crooked Creek Police Department with Special Agent Derrick Fox and Detective Ellie Reeves with an update on the investigation into the murders of Nadine Houser, Tessa Tulane and the latest victim—Governor Weston's daughter Ginger, whose body was found yesterday." Angelica tilted the mic toward Ellie and Derrick, and though Bryce moved up beside his father and the governor, she ignored him and let Derrick take the lead.

"Sadly, Ginger Weston's body was discovered last night," Derrick said, his tone somber. "Thanks to Tessa Tulane, who had photographs on her camera of an isolated area leading to a bunker, we located a cave where we believe the killer was living. After searching the bunker, we discovered several female bodies in an underground cooler." Derrick paused and out of the corner of her eye, she saw the governor pinch the bridge of his nose.

"This man is highly dangerous and is escalating," Derrick

continued. "We're asking all women to be hypervigilant and to travel in pairs. As Detective Reeves stated in her profile, the unidentified male is someone who grew up in these mountains, and is likely a hunter. He is also likely socially awkward and a loner. A grainy photograph from Ms. Tulane's camera captured an image of a man wearing a woolly coat. This man is approximately six feet tall, two hundred to two hundred twenty pounds, has dirty brown hair, a beard and a scar on his upper forehead. If you know of anyone who fits this description, please contact the police."

Angelica cleared her throat and Ellie caught her eye as they both clocked Bryce stepping up behind the podium and lean into the mic. "We are also still looking for James Dunce, who is a person of interest," the sheriff said. "If you've seen him or know his whereabouts, please call the sheriff's department immediately."

Ellie gritted her teeth. Bryce had to have his moment in the spotlight.

Emotions clogged Ellie's throat as the governor made a heartfelt statement pleading for help in finding the man they'd dubbed the *Hunter*.

Angelica listed the phone numbers for the tip line, then she wrapped up and motioned for Ellie to speak in private. They moved to the corner of the room and Angelica said, looking concerned, "You think he's going to strike again, don't you?"

"I do," Ellie said. "He won't quit until we stop him."

"Any links between the women?"

"This is off the record for now, until we ID some of the other victims, but we think all of them other than Tessa were blond."

"Why blonds?"

"I don't know, but it has to be significant. Some blond woman hurt him or abandoned him. A lover? Wife? His mother?"

"That makes sense. We both know how it feels to be abandoned," Angelica muttered.

"Yeah, but we don't go around killing innocent people because of it." Ellie arched a brow. "Have you been looking into the other matter we discussed?"

Angelica's mouth tightened. "I thought you weren't interested in knowing if we have more siblings out there."

"I just don't want to blow up anyone else's life." She thought of Mabel again and wondered if she was making progress in the therapy sessions.

Angelica worried her bottom lip with her teeth. "So far I haven't found anything. I'll let you know if I do. By the way, what's going on with the sheriff?"

Ellie bit her tongue to keep from going off about Bryce. There were too many ears in here for that. "What do you mean?"

"I saw him staggering out of Haints last night. And yesterday I saw him in a heated argument with Trudy Morely."

"I saw him arguing with her the other day, too." Ellie frowned. She couldn't imagine what it was about. Although... she couldn't help but remember Mandy's emotional state when she'd come to the station. When she put Mandy off, perhaps she went to the sheriff for help.

Her phone buzzed, and she checked the screen. Dr. White-feather.

"I have to take this. I'll keep you posted. Meanwhile, keep running that photograph of the man at the bunker. It's a long shot but maybe someone will recognize him."

Angelica nodded and left, and Ellie answered the phone call. "Laney, please tell me you have something."

"As with Nadine, we're going to have to wait for the bodies to thaw before we can perform an autopsy." A heartbeat passed. "But there is something I can tell you."

Ellie's pulse thumped. "Go on."

"The young woman found in the bottom of the cooler is younger than the others, maybe late teens. And unlike the other victims, I don't see stab wounds."

"The MO is different." Ellie tapped her fingers on her thigh. "She might have been special to him, someone he knew. Or her death was accidental?"

"Speculation," Laney said. "You know I can only work with the facts. And I won't know COD until I can get her on the table."

"So she was younger than the others?" Ellie said, thinking out loud. "Nadine has been dead eleven years. Maybe this younger victim was his first, not Nadine."

"It gets even more interesting, Ellie," Laney said. "Nadine, Ginger, Tessa and the other intact victim look around the same age: twenty to thirty. That also goes for the dismembered victim—I'm confident that's one set of remains, which I suppose is a small blessing. But from what I can tell straightaway, the other body intact is a little older woman, maybe mid-thirties at time of death.

Ellie blinked in surprise. She didn't fit the profile of his victims. Neither did Bill Hubbard, the male victim, but she'd theorized that he'd been framed to throw them off. Had this older woman figured out what he was doing and been murdered to keep her quiet?

Or did she mean something to the killer?

EIGHTY-SEVEN

Derrick attempted to calm the governor, who seemed intent on blaming Ellie for his daughter's death. He'd been on the receiving end of that kind of anger on other cases, and it sucked. No matter how hard a detective or agent worked, sometimes the killer was one step ahead of the police and the investigators chasing after the truth. In some instances, the investigator had so many avenues to explore that manpower was stretched to the limits and time ran out.

The mayor offered to coordinate with the governor and his family while Derrick, Ellie and the sheriff worked the case. While Derrick didn't fully trust Mayor Waters, he agreed, as his time would be best spent on investigative work.

Derrick headed to Ellie's office, where she relayed her conversation with the ME.

He folded his arms across his chest. "You're right. The first young girl and the older woman may be the key."

"The bodies have to thaw before Dr. Whitefeather can perform the autopsies," Ellie said. "Meanwhile, we need to see where that cable was connected."

Deputy Landrum knocked on the door and poked his head in. "I have a list of those meat processing plants, as you requested. There's a poultry processing plant and a local butcher shop."

Derrick and Ellie exchanged a look, then Ellie spoke. "We can cover more ground faster if we split up," Ellie suggested. "I'll get Cord to go with me to trace that cable while you check out the butcher shop and poultry plant."

She grabbed her jacket and phone, called Cord and arranged to meet him. Derrick took the list from the deputy and decided to start with the butcher shop.

The owner's name was Jim Bob Larson. Before driving there, Derrick pulled his laptop and ran a background check on Larson. According to what he found, the man had little education, had lived in the area all his life, and his parents were deceased. He'd also never been married.

Throwing on his jacket, Derrick headed out to his car.

The town's fall decorations looked macabre under the melting snow and gray skies. Halloween was only a week away and despite Tessa Tulane's murder, the storytelling festival was still carrying on as scheduled.

A group of teens dressed as zombies had gathered outside the police station. From what he could hear, they were planning a zombie parade to honor Tessa in hopes of raising her from the dead.

He didn't think the last part was serious—just part of the tribute, if a little misguided.

As he walked across the lot, he found himself wondering who he'd resurrect if people could be raised from the dead. As he started his engine, he decided he'd raise his father. Not because he was his hero: he'd ask him why he left him and his mother after his sister disappeared.

EIGHTY-EIGHT
BLUFF COUNTY

Fifteen minutes later, Derrick pulled up in front of the butcher shop, sitting at the corner of a turnoff for a road that led up the mountain. He guessed it served people planning barbecues up in the woods, and from hunters coming the other way who needed kills dressed. He got out of his car and surveyed the premises. The place was a crude cinder-block building with mud splattering the structure and fog-coated windows. With its distance from the bunker, if the unsub worked here, he'd need transportation.

Derrick stepped over puddles as he walked up to the door. A dark green pickup with jacked up wheels sat in front. The bell over the door jangled as he entered. On one side of the large square room were a refrigerator and freezer holding various packaged products. A glass-enclosed display case held precut meats along with larger cuts of meat for a family-sized meal. He spotted pork butts, steaks, roasts, venison, duck and chicken.

"Hello? Anyone here?" Derrick called.

The sound of a television echoed from the rear. Derrick imagined a processing room for butchering back there as well. Probably a walk-in refrigeration unit too.

A male voice responded, then he heard footsteps and a chubby bearded man wearing a bloodstained butcher's apron appeared. Scars crisscrossed his fingers, visible as he wiped his hands on a cloth. He pushed his ball cap back with the back of his hand, and Derrick noticed his right eyelid drooped.

"What can I get for you?" the man asked.

"Some answers." Derrick flashed his credentials. Could Larson possibly be the man in the photograph Tessa Tulane had taken? "Are you the owner?"

"Owner and butcher. Name's Jim Bob." He narrowed his bushy eyebrows. "What's this about?"

"I guess you've seen the news about the governor's daughter's death and the discovery of several bodies found in a bunker on the trail."

Jim Bob sucked his teeth. "Yeah, you were on the news earlier."

"That's right," Derrick said. "If you heard the profile of the man we're looking for, we think he's a hunter, that he lives somewhere in these mountains."

"Lot of hunters around these parts."

"That's why I'm here." Derrick wished he could search the place. But he had no warrant or anything incriminating on this guy for a judge to grant one. "Do you know anyone who fits this man's description? He had a bunker in the mountains stockpiled with supplies. There were packs of meat wrapped in butcher paper—labeled venison, duck and squirrel—similar to the meat packaged here."

"Lot of people buy from me," Jim Bob said.

"I'm sure you do good business. That's why I thought you might have seen this guy."

Jim Bob's eyes narrowed in suspicion. "Can't say as I have."

Derrick shrugged. "It's possible he learned about tracking and killing animals as a child."

"You're talking about half the men around these parts," Jim Bob muttered. "Their daddies teach them how to fish and hunt from the time they're knee-high."

"Did yours?" Derrick asked.

The man's beefy hands flattened on the counter. "Yeah. But that don't make me no woman killer."

Derrick shifted. "Then you won't mind showing me around. I'd like to see the back room where you store and butcher the meat."

Anger darted across the man's face. "I ain't stupid. You can't do that without a warrant."

Derrick gave him a steely look. "If you don't have anything to hide, then you won't mind."

The man huffed, but Derrick sensed his resolve wavering.

"I'll just take a quick look and then leave."

Jim Bob cursed but motioned for him to come around the counter then he led him through the double doors to the back. Derrick examined the refrigerators and found packaged meat sorted by type and ready to sell along with other slabs of meat on a block, waiting to be cut. Three large hogs hung in a cooler room.

"You practice whole animal butchery here?" Derrick asked.

Jim Bob shrugged. "Some. It's kind of expensive, but some hunters don't want to waste any of the parts. Couple of them do their own dressing then bring them for me to butcher."

Derrick scanned the room, searching for signs of fresh blood or any indication that a woman might have been kept in here, but could see no evidence of that.

"Do you have the names and contact information for those hunters?"

Jim Bob shook his head. "They pay cash. And I don't keep a list of their names. It's just word of mouth."

"How about surveillance cameras?"

The man grumbled a sound of disgust. "Ain't never needed 'em. If someone broke in to steal meat, I figure they're desperate, maybe hungry. Can't lock 'em up for that."

Derrick ground his molars. "You live above the shop?"

Jim Bob nodded.

"I'd like to see up there."

Another curse and Jim Bob led him out a back door then up a set of stairs. He opened the door, which hadn't been locked, and Derrick entered, his gaze scanning the small interior. One living space with a small rundown kitchen, bed in the corner and a dingy bathroom.

He walked through looking for signs a woman had been inside —or a captive had been here. But other than grime, dust and another refrigerator with beer and a few pieces of meat inside, there was nothing untoward.

He checked the bathtub for blood and found stains, but they looked more like mud than blood. In the closet, though, he found rolls of plastic. Plastic similar to the rolls found in that bunker.

"What are those for?" Derrick asked.

"Wrapping the full beast after bleeding it out. Makes easier clean up."

They also could be used to do the same for a stabbing victim.

EIGHTY-NINE
BONE RIDGE

Anxiety knotted Ellie's stomach as she and Cord followed the cable, raking dirt and digging around it to see where it led.

Her mind kept replaying the scene in Crooked Creek as she'd left town.

The chanting of Tessa's fans as they formed a zombie parade honoring the storyteller had been touching and disturbing at the same time. Another local lost to murder, while Ellie chased false leads. Although Tessa's own photograph might actually help them catch her killer. Still, Ellie's heart swelled with sadness. The talented storyteller had been too young to die.

The soles of her hiking boots dug into the mushy ground as she and Cord climbed the hills and wove through the tangled vines. Already the creek was rising to flood conditions as the snow melted. Wildflowers and mushrooms poked through the thinning blanket of white, frogs croaked along the water's edge, and a flock of birds flew in formation as they headed south for the winter.

They followed the cable for about five miles until they crested a hill then dipped downward.

"This place is called Bone Ridge," Cord said.

"I've heard of that," Ellie said. "The jagged edges of the ridge above look like a pulley bone."

Cord nodded, and they hiked the rest of the way to the lower valley. Ahead, she spotted a small shack built by the side of the creek.

The cable led to the little house where smoke curled up into the sky through a stone chimney. A woodpile sat beside the house covered in a tarp, but she didn't see a vehicle anywhere in sight. A gray cat lay on the front porch, which sagged on one side, and the shutters hung askew. The house had once been painted white, but the paint was chipped and peeling, the windowpanes coated with a thick layer of frost and grime.

Cord halted by a narrow pine that curved above the roofline. "I'd say no one is home but a fire is burning inside."

Ellie scanned the property and surrounding woods. Then a shiver rippled through her. "If this is his place, he could be out hunting."

She gripped her gun at the ready, peering in all directions as they crept closer.

NINETY

CROOKED CREEK

Lola stared at the photo of the man with the beard on the news, the familiar feeling of panic weaving its way through her. That scar on his forehead. The scraggly beard and hair. The menacing look that sent déjà vu streaking through her.

Was he the same man who'd come into the café the other day? The same man whose face had haunted her for years now? The man from her nightmares?

Pacing the kitchen, she felt an anxiety attack steal the air from her lungs. She couldn't breathe. Couldn't see straight for the images of the shadows in the woods.

A terrifying memory taunted her—the one that triggered those nightmares.

She'd been seventeen years old. She and her girlfriend had decided to camp in the woods one night and meet some boys. Only a deputy busted the boys for stealing liquor, took them to their parents and the boys hadn't shown.

Finally, she and her friend gave up on the boys coming and sacked out on the ground with their sleeping bags, although Lola had lain awake half the night afraid a snake or poisonous spider was going to bite her.

It had been near Halloween then, too, and her friend liked ghost stories. Each one she'd told had gotten scarier and scarier until Lola had imagined monsters in the trees, a psycho slipping up and chopping off their heads, a werewolf attacking.

A thunderstorm started brewing, the lightning zigzagging across the inky sky and cracking above the treetops in jagged lines. The bushes moved. Wind whistled. An animal growled.

A bear?

Terrified, she'd woken her friend and whispered they had to go back to her car. Little Red, she called her VW bug, would take them down the mountain where they'd be safe. If only they could reach it before the storm struck full force.

They'd snatched their sleeping bags and made a run for it, racing through the rows of trees and following the path. Suddenly the sky unleashed the clouds and rain began to pour, making the ground slippery. Lola lost her balance and went tumbling down a hill, her body hitting rocks in the patch. Briars clawed at her arms and legs and face. She landed in the creek and her head slammed into a rock. The world spun, her eyes grew cloudy.

Then her friend's scream pierced the night. Lola had tried to push herself up but couldn't see her.

Another scream, this one more terrified. "Help, Lola! Help me!"

Still dizzy from the fall, she'd swayed and wobbled but finally managed to push herself to her hands and knees.

She strained to see what was happening and spotted the undergrowth moving, her friend on the ground, and the outline of a hulking figure over her. She screamed and he turned then came toward her with a knife.

Terrified, she got up, staggering, and ran for her life.

NINETY-ONE

BONE RIDGE

The cat lifted its head as if might attack as Ellie stepped onto the porch, then dropped it back down as if it lacked the energy to move. Her gun at the ready, she knocked on the door. "Police, please open up."

She tapped her foot, finding the tension unbearable, as they waited. Cord motioned that he was going around the side of the house in case the unsub attempted to escape out back.

She knocked again and heard footsteps inside. The door opened slowly and a tiny hunched-over man with wiry gray hair appeared, his gnarled hands gripping the door. She guessed he was in his eighties. "What do you want?" he muttered grumpily.

"Just to ask you some questions," she said in a calm voice as she identified herself. This man seemed to pose no threat. But she kept her senses heightened in case the Hunter was hiding inside.

The man looked her up and down, then said, "Name's Henry." He motioned her to come in. Cord stepped up beside her and followed her inside.

The man adjusted his coke-bottle wire-rimmed glasses and leaned on his cane as he hobbled over to an ancient sofa covered in a threadbare blanket. He sat down with a grunt and waved them toward two straight ladder-back chairs next to the small oak table serving as his dining room. A single light burned from a chain dangling from the low ceiling, the only light other than the fire flickering in the stone fireplace.

"I don't get many visitors," the old man said. "What you two doing out here?"

Ellie introduced Cord. "We noticed that there's a cable running from your house through the woods to another place," Ellie said. "Did you run the cable?"

The man looked confused. "Naw. Another fellow asked a long time ago. Said he needed power to keep his cooler running, so I let him run off me. I was too damn crooked legged to hunt myself so he kept me in food."

"How long ago was that?"

Henry scratched his head. "Oh, I don't know. My memory's going on me. But I reckon twenty or thirty years ago."

Ellie laced her fingers together. If the killer had been in his twenties or thirties himself back then, that would put him in his fifties or even sixties now, which didn't fit the profile of the killer. Although he could have started younger. "Does the man still come around?"

Henry shook his head. "Ain't seen him in years. But his son comes by. Took over keeping me stocked with meat and corn liquor since I can't get out myself. He's a fine butcher himself. Guess his daddy taught him." A grin tugged at his mouth as he picked up a jar on the side table next to him. "Apple pie moonshine's pretty damn good. You two want some?"

"No, but thank you," Ellie said, deciding this old man was too kind to even harbor a killer.

Cord shook his head at the offer.

"What's this man's name?" Ellie asked.

Henry took a swig of the apple pie. "Don't reckon he ever said. His daddy used to just call him son."

Frustration tightened Ellie's shoulders, but she pulled the picture from Tessa's camera and angled it for the man to see. "Is this the man who stops by?"

Henry pinched the bridge of his nose as he squinted at the

picture. "Hard to say. Looks like half the mountain men that live in these parts."

Ellie put her phone back in her pocket. "Henry, when do you expect him to come back?"

"Don't know. He just shows up out of the blue and leaves me some meat. Chops some wood too so I don't freeze to death."

"When was he here last?"

"Few days ago. Probably be a while before he comes back. He left me pretty stocked up."

If this man was the Hunter, he obviously had a soft spot for Henry. "Have you ever felt like he was dangerous?"

Henry took another drink, then whistled as the alcohol went down. "Boy never said more than a couple of words. Just showed up, left my stuff on the porch and disappeared." He removed his glasses, rubbed at his eyes then put them back on. "Why you asking about him anyway? Something happen to him?"

Ellie sighed. "We aren't sure," she said. "But someone in these mountains is murdering women. And we found their bodies at the bunker where this cable had been run."

Henry's face paled and he choked on the moonshine.

NINETY-TWO

Ellie gave Henry time to process what she'd said. Judging from his reaction, he had no idea that the man he considered a good Samaritan was really a madman.

"Henry," she said, "does the man who brings you supplies come in on foot?"

He fiddled with his glasses and rubbed his eyes again. "No, it would be too much for him to carry. I can't hear too well, but I saw through the window he drives an ATV."

"That explains how he got from one place to the other quickly," Ellie said.

"I just can't believe that boy would do what you're saying," Henry said. "I mean, he seems strange, but if it wasn't for him, I probably wouldn't be alive now. All my family's gone and friends are all dead. No one bothers to come up here anymore. And I don't have any other place to go."

Ellie patted his hand. "I'm sorry, Henry. We can help find you a place to live in town. I'm sure one of the churches can help you with groceries and other things you need."

Tears blurred the old man's eyes. "This here's my home," he murmured. "Where me and Willie Jean set up our housekeeping."

"I know it's upsetting," Ellie said. "But until we catch him, I'm afraid it's not safe for you to stay here alone."

Cord leaned forward. "Ellie is right. We believe he saw us at his bunker, so he knows we've retrieved the bodies and exposed his home. He won't go back there. But if he thinks you might recognize him, he may come here."

Henry rubbed at his eyes. "I don't think he'd hurt me," Henry said, but his voice sounded weak, as if he was trying to convince himself.

Ellie clasped her hands together. "Maybe not. But he's thrown off his game and running scared now. We believe he murdered another hunter because he identified him."

Henry dropped his head into his hands, his frail body shaking. Then he picked up a photograph of an older woman who Ellie assumed was his wife. "I hate to leave here, Willie Jean, but I reckon it's time." He pushed up from the chair, his knobby knees cracking.

"Gather your things," Cord said, his expression grim. "My team will help you down the mountain."

Ellie breathed a sigh of relief that Henry agreed to go.

She couldn't bear it if this sweet man fell prey to the Hunter. And she couldn't live with another death on her conscience.

While Deputy Landrum and Deputy Eastwood checked out the chicken houses that populated the countryside in North Georgia, Derrick drove to the poultry processing plant north of Gainesville, Georgia, a town which had earned the title of the poultry capital of the world because of its numerous plants.

The main facility was housed in a large concrete building and employed almost 400 workers, Derrick knew from his research, but this one was smaller and employed around 200 hands who worked side by side with knives and heavy machinery to process the poultry. Liquid nitrogen was used in the refrigeration systems and could be dangerous if safety precautions weren't strictly adhered to. A leak in one of the Gainesville plants had caused the death of several employees a while back.

Derrick went straight to the main office and asked to speak to the manager, explaining the reason for his visit.

The manager, a rail-thin man, scratched his chin. "You think one of my employees is this killer you're looking for?"

Derrick shrugged. "Right now, we're exploring every possibility. We know he stabs his victims with a hunting knife and has stored the bodies in a cooler." Derrick was looking for similarities in the MO. He omitted the detail of the man chopping up one of the bodies. "Tell me the steps in the processing."

The man drummed his fingers on his metal desk. "We've recently updated so most of the work done here is automated. The birds are delivered to the plant and put in a dimly lit area to calm them. Then they're either given an electrical charge or gases are used to stun them and render them unconscious so they don't feel any pain when the heads are removed. After that, the feathers and internal organs are removed. The birds are quickly cooled and stored in refrigerated areas and inspected at various stages of the process to eliminate contamination."

Derrick nodded, listening carefully. If the killer worked here, it made sense that he might practice a similar regime, stunning or rendering the women unconscious before he killed them. But judging from the evidence of violent stabbings, he had been out of control and wanted to inflict pain.

"Can you think of any employee who might fit the description of the man we're looking for? Someone uneducated, a loner, one who has a temper or violent tendencies?"

The man plucked an antacid from his desk and popped it into his mouth. "Honestly, I don't know all of the employees personally."

"Do you run background checks?"

The man snorted. "No. In fact, many of our workers are migrants."

"You mean undocumented?"

"They need jobs," the man said defensively. "Not everyone is cut out for this kind of work. Takes a strong stomach."

Derrick knotted his hands by his sides. "Get me a list of everyone who works here. I'm not interested in deporting anyone, but I would like to question them. We're trying to stop a madman from murdering more women."

Ellie couldn't get Henry out of her mind as she returned to the police station. Cord had insisted on dropping him off at the men's shelter himself, a reminder to Ellie how caring and kind the ranger was beneath that gruff exterior.

The sheriff showed up ten minutes later, his foul mood evident in his scowl.

"Did you find anything in town or on Dunce?" Ellie asked.

Bryce shook his head. "My deputies are still looking."

She wondered what he'd been up to but didn't ask. Instead, she relayed her conversation with Henry. "We should still have records of funeral parlors and crematoriums we looked into before. They have cold rooms to store bodies."

"I thought that fed was in charge and would be giving orders, not you," Bryce growled.

"Special Agent Fox is working the case right now." She clicked her teeth. "I know you want to ruin me, Bryce, but I'm not leaving."

He made a rude noise. "I want that fed gone, so I can do my job. This is my territory, not his."

"That was the governor's doing."

He cursed, but Ellie cut him off before he could say anything else. "What's going on with you, Bryce? You seem intent on under-mining me, and Special Agent Fox too. I saw you arguing with

Trudy Morely the other day. Did Mandy ask you to find her father?"

He planted his fists on his hips. "What are you talking about?"

"When Vanessa died, Trudy said she didn't know who Mandy's father was, that Vanessa never told her. Mandy came in and asked me to look into finding him, but I told her I was busy with the case. I thought she might have asked you for help."

An odd look strained his face, and for once he clamped his mouth shut. But that lasted only a second. "No, she hasn't." He pulled his phone out and glanced at it. "I have to go."

Ellie frowned as he strode out the door. She didn't understand his attitude, or even the reason he'd stopped by, since he had no new information.

But she didn't have time to dwell on Bryce. As soon as he left, she phoned the ME. "Laney, any results on the bodies?"

"I'm afraid it's still too soon for the autopsies. I've photographed the victims though and will send the images to you."

"I've been thinking about the fact that our unsub keeps the bodies in a cooler. Can you think of anyone on your staff, maybe a part-timer, one of the body movers or employees who recovers bodies from crime scenes, someone who might fit the description of the Hunter?"

The sound of Laney clicking computer keys echoed in the background and Ellie wondered if she was shocked at her question. But Laney was a professional and did her job methodically. "Not off the top of my head, but I'll go through the employee files and look for complaints or instances where someone reported one of them to our office."

"Send me a list of anyone who could be considered suspicious," Ellie said.

"Okay. The victims' photos should be coming your way shortly."

Ellie thanked her and hung up, then sat down to start digging through the missing persons reports Shondra had emailed her.

Maybe she could match one of them to the photos Laney had of the victims.

Over sixty people had disappeared just in the last year in Georgia, forty-two of those women. There were dozens and dozens of runaways as well, but she focused on women between the ages of nineteen and thirty-five. Six of them had been found, four of those dead due to accidents or suicide. Two more had died at the hands of a spouse, their cases closed.

Laney's photos came through, the gruesome images almost surreal. Between frostbite, decomp and features distorted from the position the bodies had been left in, the women barely looked human.

One detail they had in common was that they were all Caucasian. That narrowed the missing persons' reports down, as she could dismiss women of other races or ethnicities. Except for Tessa, the victims had also all been blond. Another reason to believe he'd killed Tessa because she'd stumbled on his bunker.

She printed out the photographs, then pictures of missing women in their twenties and thirties with blond hair and tacked all of them on the whiteboard.

Laney had pointed out that one victim was older, mid- to late-thirties, and another younger, around seventeen or eighteen. Not knowing how long those two had been dead made it difficult to know when they'd been abducted. But if they were the first victims, they might be the key.

She made a list:

Victim one—mid- to late-thirties—date abducted? ID?

Victim two—late teens—date abducted? ID?

Victim three—first victim found: Nadine Houser; age 20 when abducted; taken eleven years ago

Victim four—twenties—ID?

Victim five (dismembered)—twenties—ID?

Victim six—28—Ginger Weston; Abducted Oct.—Death: Oct.

Victim seven—29—Tessa Tulane; No abduction—Death: Oct.

Working on the theory that the unsub had killed the women within a short time of their abduction and frozen them immediately after death, Ellie focused first on victim number four, as she fit the profile of the others age-wise.

She studied the faces of the eight blondes from the missing persons' reports and compared them to the photo of the fourth victim. Immediately she eliminated a woman with a scar on her cheek and another who had a small port wine stain birthmark. Next, she studied the features, the shape of the nose, chin, eye color and cheekbone structure.

A young woman named Leslie Kutchen appeared to be a match. She was twenty-eight when she disappeared from a campsite where she'd been staying with her church group.

Pulse quickening, she read the details of the report and learned she was from Dahlonega. She found the number of the Dahlonega Police Department and phoned them, asking to speak to the detective in charge of the case.

He had retired, but after explaining the situation, the man's partner came on the line.

"This is Detective Ellie Reeves from Crooked Creek. I'm investigating several murders in the area and trying to identify the victims we don't have names for yet."

"I've seen the news. What can I do to help?" Detective Sanchez asked.

"It's possible that one of the victims may be related to a missing persons' case you worked. Her name is Leslie Kutchen."

"Ahh, geesh, I never could figure that one out. She was raised by a single mother who was devastated when the case went cold. Are you sure it's her?"

"No, I'm not," Ellie said. "Her body was frozen and has to

thaw before the autopsy so I'm looking at a picture of her face taken by the ME. I assume you have samples of her DNA."

"We do," he said. "I can send them to your ME for comparison."

"Thanks. I appreciate it. And send me a copy of her file, too," Ellie said.

He agreed and they decided to refrain from talking to Mrs. Kutchen until they had a positive ID. No use upsetting the woman further by notifying her of her daughter's death until they knew for certain it was her.

Her phone buzzed with a text message, and she hung up and saw it was from the forensics lab:

Results from the bunker: Still checking forensics from the blanket, mattress, plastic, canned goods and other surfaces. One blood sample a positive match to Ginger Weston's. Another sample belongs to a male who is not in the system. Still working on comparisons.

Dammit. She needed something conclusive.

She sent a reply telling them that the detective in charge of Leslie Kutchen's case was sending over DNA for a comparison.

Adrenaline surged through her. Identifying these victims might be the lead they needed in solving the murders.

As soon as she got that file she'd see if there were any similarities between it and Nadine Houser's.

NINETY-FIVE

Before returning to Crooked Creek, Derrick searched a building that had once housed grocery store frozen goods but found it empty. On the way back to the station he picked up dinner from Soulfood Barbecue and met Ellie at her office. They quickly updated each other.

"So far Deputy Landrum and Eastwood haven't found anything at the chicken houses," Ellie said. "And the sheriff hasn't had any luck with locating Dunce. I asked him to check out local funeral homes and crematoriums."

"Good idea," Derrick said.

"I just got the file from the detective who worked the Leslie Kutchen case and was about to review it."

He set out the food, and while they inhaled smoky pulled pork sandwiches, southern coleslaw and collards, she studied the Kutchen file. Derrick opened his laptop and began running preliminary background checks on the list of employees at the poultry processing plant.

Employees who had been fired topped his list. But as he sifted through the information, with each hour he grew more disgruntled, as many employees had left the job with no forwarding address. He cross-checked names with the list of documented immigrants and found at least twenty men who were illegal. He didn't care about their immigration status.

"I'm going to need help locating the employees on this list," he said. "A lot of the employees gave fake addresses and no phone numbers. They're worried about being deported." He ran his hand through his hair.

"That makes it hard to track," Ellie said. "Let Deputy Eastwood go to the plant and talk to the workers," Ellie said. "They're more likely to open up to a local like her than a fed."

"True."

"Thanks for not questioning my ability," Ellie said with a tiny smile. "The sheriff and mayor want me gone."

"They're idiots." Derrick studied the shadows beneath her eyes. She looked exhausted and sounded it, too. "You know it's just anger and vindictiveness," he said. "The sheriff is jealous that you've garnered credit for solving three major cases. Even though he was elected, he doesn't like that you're showing him up. He should be proud to have you on his team."

"Maybe." Ellie frowned and seemed to be thinking carefully before she spoke again. "Although something else is bothering Bryce lately. Not that I care. But it's making him even more edgy."

Ellie rubbed her eyes and leaned her head into her hand. She was much more forgiving than him.

"We should call it a night," Derrick suggested. "I'll start tomorrow with this list."

"Just let me finish this file," she said, then read the details of the police report out loud. "Leslie Kutchen belonged to a church group of youth counselors and disappeared on the trail near Amicalola Falls. The night she went missing, the group turned in early after a long day of hiking. She disappeared sometime during the night. No one saw anyone suspicious watching her or approaching her during the trip, although a couple of her friends described her as adventurous and said she enjoyed swimming at night. At first, they thought she might have waded in the falls, but searched there and the creek nearby and didn't find her. About two miles from the campsite, one of the SAR team found a hairband that belonged to her along with her sneaker and a piece of the church T-shirt she'd been wearing. That's when they realized there was foul play, and that she'd been abducted."

She pressed two fingers to her temple, and Derrick wondered if she had a headache. *Stubborn woman should have had that CAT scan.*

"It looks like they did things by the book," she continued. "Organized search teams. Interviewed family and friends who all claim Leslie was happy and loved her job as a camp counselor. This retreat was a bonding experience for the counselors before they started summer camps."

He glanced at Ellie and saw the pained look in her eyes as she said, "But she never got the chance because of this bastard."

NINETY-SIX

Ellie's head was throbbing, but she wasn't ready to give up yet. While Derrick continued running background checks on the employees at the plant, she phoned Shondra about going to the processing plant the next day and Shondra agreed. She was about to close her computer when she received a second text from the lab:

> Found a DNA match to a woman named Cady North. Police had
> pulled DNA from her toothbrush when she was reported missing.
> Age twenty-five. Hers is the dismembered corpse.

Ellie's stomach roiled.

Fighting nausea, she struggled to put that image from her mind, then plugged the woman's name into the missing persons database and ran a background. Cady had worked at a small bakery in Adairsville and had disappeared just two weeks ago. Her sister had reported it.

Dread settled like a weight in her stomach as she called the police in Adairsville to ask about the investigation.

"I can send you what we have, but it's not much," a female detective said. "In fact, we were intending to contact you in the morning, after we heard about the bodies you found. I know you've been in contact with Ben Emerson regarding Nadine Houser. He was wondering if they were connected." She paused with a sigh. "I've dropped the ball on this one, Detective Reeves. I was convinced an ex-boyfriend had taken her, tracked him down in Charlotte where he'd moved, but the guy's alibi was rock solid."

Ellie heard the all-too-familiar self-reproach in the woman's voice. "Don't beat yourself up. We've all run a long way down a dead end more than once. Any background you can give me now could be a real help."

"Sure, well, Cady was a pastry chef. Everyone loved her specialty cupcakes and cookies. She and her sister owned the bakery together." A labored sigh. "Sister's going to be devastated."

"Any persons of interest other than the ex?" Ellie asked.

"No current boyfriend or lover. We looked at security footage, but there were dozens of people in and out all the time. Could have been one of them or a drifter."

A weariness overcame Ellie. How the hell did he take these women without someone seeing him? "Did the sister mention seeing anyone suspicious? Someone stalking Cady or showing special interest?" *Please, God, let there be a lead.*

"No. She said Cady was friendly to everyone. The customers all loved her."

"Where was she abducted from?"

"According to the sister, she left early for a doctor's appointment and left Cady to close up. Said Cady never made it home. Her car was still at the shop. We believe she was kidnapped in the alley out back when she went to put an order of birthday cupcakes in the food truck to be delivered. Cupcakes were still there, but no sign of Cady."

Ellie bit her lip to stifle a moan.

The detective paused. "You're sure it's her you found?"

She finally found her voice. "Yes, you can inform the sister, but please explain that the body won't be released for now. The autopsy has to wait until the bodies have been fully thawed, and, well, I'm afraid to say Cady's DNA was sampled from only one part of a corpse. The body we believe to be hers was not intact."

The officer's breath rattled out. "I hope you find this monster soon. I'd hate to tell Cady's sister that the man is still out there."

Ellie rubbed her aching head with a silent groan. Even worse would be telling the sister what the monster had done to Cady's body. She felt sick just thinking about that.

NINETY-SEVEN

SOMEWHERE ON THE AT

Anger churned through him as he hunkered down inside the back room at his work hut. The scent of raw meat and animal remains filled the room, a comforting familiar smell that reminded him that he was born for this life.

Dammit. Those cops had been at Henry's.

They'd destroyed everything. Taken his home now. Taken the loves of his life away. Plastered a picture of his face all over the news.

Now he couldn't go back into town or anywhere else. Although occasionally he ventured out. But ever since he'd seen that pretty girl at the café, he couldn't stop thinking about her. How her beautiful cornsilk-like hair would feel as he sifted his fingers through it. How soft her lips would feel if he kissed her.

He had never done that before. He'd tried but the others had pushed him away.

The laughter and ugly names they'd called him echoed in his head and he couldn't shut the voices up.

Son, you need to find your own soul mate, his daddy had said. *Just like I did.*

His daddy's voice was exactly what he needed to hear. But he would be disappointed that he'd failed with the others.

He wouldn't with the blond. He'd make her love him the way

his mama loved his daddy. As a little boy, he remembered seeing her over the woodstove, stirring the meat, the chain around her ankle clanging as she walked. He could see his daddy wiping the blood from his hands when he got home from work. Remembered the pig's squeal as he'd slaughtered it and the squawking of the chickens as he'd cut off their heads.

He could see his mama carrying a plate of food to his father and making sure he had his jar of moonshine to sip while she swept up the floor. Saw her kneeling in front of him and removing his shoes, then rubbing his feet.

Heard them as they rolled around in the bed at night and his father grunted and rammed himself inside her.

He stared at the spidery cracks in the ceiling, but the face of that lady cop swam behind his eyes. He imagined her finding the little present he'd left her and his body hardened.

She was ruining everything. Had sent him into hiding. Had called him backwards.

He balled his hands into fists. With his picture on the news, he had to lay low. But when the time came, he knew what he had to do. He had to get rid of her.

A smile curved his mouth. She'd squeal just like a pig being gutted when he killed her.

NINETY-EIGHT

CROOKED CREEK

Pain splintered Ellie's head and neck as she parked at her bungalow. Finally, she and Derrick had called it a night and planned to reconnect the next morning.

Plagued by the thought of the many violent offenders she'd dealt with, she always left the light on her front porch burning.

Tonight, it was dark on her porch; the light was out.

Instantly she knew something was wrong. She pulled her gun and flashlight as she climbed from her Jeep and scanned the porch. As she neared the steps, she saw that the light was smashed. Gripping her gun at the ready, she quickly scanned the front of her property then the sides, but at first glance saw nothing.

Had someone broken in? If so, her alarm company hadn't notified her.

She lowered the light to illuminate the door, but it was closed, not open. On the porch floor she spotted something dark. Her chest tightened as she climbed the steps, and she saw a stream of blood then a pile of black feathers.

Crow feathers.

Black crows were symbols of death coming. She'd seen them on power lines before and they always unnerved her.

But this was different.

A half dozen or more black crows had been beheaded and eviscerated, blood and guts spilled all across the floor. Then a message painted with the blood that sent a shudder up her spine:

You're next.

NINETY-NINE

Pure rage filled Derrick when Ellie called him about the dead birds. What a sick son of a bitch.

Ellie was sitting in her Jeep when he arrived with the door locked and had already called the security company about adding a camera outside her house. At least she'd been smart enough not to barge into the house looking for the man by herself. He could have been waiting in ambush, although Derrick suspected he'd simply intended to scare her.

The Hunter didn't know Ellie very well though. This kind of threat would only make her more determined to find him and lock him away.

She looked shaken when he tapped on the window, but she got out. He wanted to pull her into his arms and comfort her, but her body was rigid, her expression guarded, so he rubbed her arms instead. "You okay?"

She nodded, although he felt a tremble ripple through her.

"Did you see anything when you arrived? A car? The man?"

"No, dammit," she said irritably. "And I didn't go inside. I didn't want to risk contaminating any evidence out here."

He offered her an understanding smile. "Always thinking like a cop. It's okay if you're upset though. He violated your home." This wasn't the first time a perp had. But hopefully installing cameras would mean it was the last.

"I am shaken," she admitted. "But I'm also pissed."

"Good," he said. Better that than have her crumble.

"I already called the crime scene team," she told him, her voice growing stronger. "I didn't expect him to come into town, much less to my house, but that means he's scared now. He thinks we're onto him and maybe he made a mistake."

"I'll search the house in case he did go inside," Derrick said.

"I'll go, too," Ellie said. "I'll know if he disturbed anything."

True. "All right, let's go."

"Let's enter through the back door," Ellie said.

She led the way, gun drawn, and he shined the light on the ground to make certain they didn't step on evidence that could have been left behind. They climbed the steps to the back deck and she unlocked the door. The kitchen light was burning, but everything in the room and adjoining living room seemed untouched. No birds or blood or footprints to suggest the man had been inside.

She led him to her bedroom, and he hesitated at the doorway to give her time to look around. At first glance, the bed was made and nothing seemed amiss. She crossed the room and opened her dresser drawers to make certain he hadn't rummaged through her things.

"I don't think he was in here," she said with a sigh of relief.

He breathed out, grateful for that.

They heard the sound of an engine outside and left through the back door again. The crime scene van rolled up and parked.

"I'll look around out here in case he left footprints or tire prints," he said. "Are you okay to talk to the ERT?"

"Of course. Go find me something to nail this creep."

Derrick gave her arm a squeeze. The fight in Ellie was the thing he liked best about her.

He surveyed her property as she walked over to talk to the crime techs. Her bungalow was nestled on a wooded lot, private from the neighbors. He pulled his flashlight and shined it across the driveway and ground but didn't see tire marks or footprints in the drive. Slowly he walked up the path to her porch, searching, and finally found a partial boot print in the dirt by the step. It was set to the side though, suggesting the jerk might have come from around back through the woods.

He panned his flashlight on the ground. Areas with pine bark and pine straw created a back-to-nature feel but made it difficult to discern footprints. He looked for a stray button or jacket fibers but found nothing except for another partial near the edge of the woods. It looked as if the man had covered his tracks. He could have taken a canoe up the creek or parked an RV somewhere and hiked through the woods to Ellie's.

The fact that he'd found out where she lived meant he'd probably seen the news and knew her name. Then he'd done his research or slipped into town and followed her.

Tension coiled inside him as he walked back around to the front of the house. The team was already taking photographs, dusting the porch rail and door for fingerprints and one tech was making a cast of the partial footprint.

Ellie was on the phone with Shondra, relaying what had happened. He was glad she had the deputy for a friend.

The sight of the bloody birds made his protective instincts kick in. Now the man knew where she lived and had threatened her, Derrick didn't intend to leave her alone. If she refused to come to the inn, he'd park himself on her sofa.

That might be a better idea anyway. He'd love it if the bastard tried something. If he came back, Derrick would be ready.

If he touched one hair on Ellie's head, he'd kill him with his bare hands.

ONE HUNDRED

BLUFF COUNTY MEDICAL EXAMINER'S OFFICE

Ellie yawned as she drove her and Derrick to the ME's office the next morning. Laney had texted first thing asking them to meet her at the morgue to discuss the autopsies. And now Derrick was on the phone with the governor.

Last night, she'd urged Derrick to go back to the inn after the ERT left, but he refused and insisted that with the threat against her, she needed protection. Frankly she'd been too exhausted to argue with him. And she had slept better knowing he was on her couch.

As she pulled into the parking lot, she looked over her shoulder and all around in case the Hunter was watching her.

"We'll get him," Derrick told the governor. She could hear the distress in his voice, and although he would never burden her with talking about it, she knew the governor was pressuring him. The media coverage was relentless.

Mentally, she reviewed the details as he ended the call and they walked up to the morgue entrance. Shondra had talked to Mrs. Kutchen and the members of the church group Leslie had been with at the time of her abduction. Two of the girls thought they'd seen a man who resembled the one in Tessa's photograph, but it was years ago, and they couldn't be positive.

Now Shondra had gone to question employees at the poultry processing plant.

Ellie silently groaned as she entered the morgue, willing Laney to have something concrete today to move the investigation forward.

The pungent scent of death and cleaning chemicals permeated the autopsy room. Though she'd studied their photos endlessly, it was still a shock to her system to see so many young women laid out on their individual steel tables. Derrick drew his shoulders back, and she knew he was affected by the scene too, although he said nothing.

Laney greeted them and they joined her beside the body. "Most of the victims died from the stab wounds. Although with the dismembered body I'm still working on cause of death to determine if that was done postmortem."

A sickening, clammy feeling washed over Ellie.

Laney gestured to the oldest victim. She had ash-blond hair, brown eyes and looked about 130 pounds. Laney had already performed the Y incision and removed organs for weighing and examination.

"This woman's attack appears to be especially vicious," Laney said. "I counted seven stab wounds, each deeper and more forceful, as if he'd lost control in a rage and couldn't stop himself."

"It was personal," Ellie said.

"She also was not wearing the signature necklace like the other victims in the cooler."

Ellie tried to picture what might have happened. "He was furious at this woman for some reason. But he felt something different for the younger women he gave the necklaces to," Ellie said. "He was in love with them, or they reminded him of someone he cared about."

"Except there are no signs of sexual assault on any of the victims," Laney pointed out.

A muscle ticked in Derrick's jaw. "Perhaps he saw them as future wives," he suggested.

"And when they rejected him, he killed them." Ellie's mind

raced. "Can you narrow down a timeline for when this woman died?"

Laney nodded. "It's not exact, but I'd say she and the younger girl have been dead the longest. At least thirteen years."

"So they were the first victims," Ellie said.

"Unless he has another bunker or cooler where he's kept others," Derrick added.

"True," Ellie admitted. "But for now we focus on these victims."

"There's something else," Laney said. "The youngest woman, who was around eighteen years old, did not die from a stab wound."

Ellie wrinkled her brow. "What was cause of death?"

Laney stepped over to her computer and gestured toward an X-ray. "She had a congenital heart defect which led to heart failure. She also suffered from hypothermia."

Ellie's gut knotted. "She was alive when he put her in the cooler?"

Laney nodded and Derrick cursed.

Questions bombarded Ellie as she tried to piece it all together. "Why freeze her to death but stab the older woman and the others?"

"Maybe he didn't intend to kill her?" Derrick said.

"He left her in the cooler," Ellie said.

"There's more." Laney accessed the DNA, fingerprint comparisons and looked at dental records. "I have some IDs for you. The eighteen-year-old is Brittany Banning. You were right about Leslie Kutchen being one of the other stabbing victims."

"What about the oldest woman?"

"Her name was Millie Evans," Laney said. "This is where it gets even more interesting. Her DNA also was a familial match to the male DNA found in the bunker."

Ellie's pulse hammered. "You mean Millie is related to our killer?"

Laney nodded. "She's his mother."

Ellie's mind was still reeling when she and Derrick returned to the police station. Their unsub's mother had been in his freezer with the other women. The question was, who had put her there?

Derrick took a call from his partner about another possible threat against the governor while she went straight to the conference room with her laptop. The murder board stared back at her, the faces of the dead screaming for justice.

Ginger and Tessa were more personal, but the others needed her, too, and so did their families. Perspiration beaded on her forehead. She prayed she didn't let them down.

At least she had some names to work with now. She added Millie Evans, Brittany Banning and Leslie Kutchen to the board. Now she needed to find out all she could on them.

She decided to start with Millie, the unsub's mother. If Millie had other relatives, they might know her son's real name and where to find him.

She ran a search and found a missing report on Millie Evans, then accessed the file. Millie was born to a couple named Larry and Jan Evans from Jasper, Georgia. Millie's birthday would put her at age forty-seven now. But according to Dr. Whitefeather, she was mid-thirties at time of death.

She had disappeared when she was fourteen. The case had

gone cold ages ago. Noting the parents' names from the report, she ran a search for them but they were now deceased.

A wave of sadness caught her in its clutches. She couldn't imagine what it had been like to go to your grave without knowing what had happened to your only child.

She plugged in Brittany Banning's name and ran a search for her in the missing persons database. They didn't know how long the girl had been kept in the bunker before dying, but with Laney's opinion that she'd been dead thirteen years, and was eighteen at time of death, she extended the search going back twenty years.

After another ten minutes of scanning reports, she found Brittany. A young blond, aged eighteen when she disappeared, approximately five three, 110 pounds.

Ellie's heart squeezed. Brittany's mother was still alive and lived in Ellijay.

She grabbed her laptop and went to find Derrick. She had to talk to the detectives in both cases.

Dread and sorrow swept over her. Someone would have to notify Brittany's mother.

ONE HUNDRED TWO

JASPER, GEORGIA

Ellie battled nerves as she and Derrick parked at the police station in Pickens County. This case had just gotten a lot bigger and more complicated. Brittany had been so young when she'd died. And Millie... so young when she'd been abducted.

Pulling herself together, she glanced around the small town. It hadn't changed in years. She'd been to Jasper as a teen with her father and visited Eagle's Rest Park and Burnt Mountain Preserve Trail. While she and her father hiked, her mother had toured the local wineries and roved the antique shops.

On the drive, Derrick phoned the local police and requested the complete file for Millie Evan's case.

"Officer Regan died ten years ago," a young detective in plain clothes said as they entered his office. "It took some digging. Our system wasn't digitized then, but I finally found a hard copy in our records room." He handed them the file and they seated themselves across from his desk. "To tell you the truth, it's pretty thin. I don't think he had much to go on."

Or he hadn't done his job.

"Did another detective work on the case after Officer Regan?" Ellie asked.

He glanced down at the file. "Looks like it went cold."

"And with her parents' death, there was no one to keep it active," Ellie said sadly.

He shrugged. "I hate it, but it happens. New cases come along."

Ellie understood too but she didn't like it either. "Is there some place we can go to review these?"

"Sure. We have a work room you can use."

Ellie thanked him, and he showed them to a small room with a table and chairs. Antsy and hoping they were finally making headway, they divided the file up to read copies of the interviews.

Ellie read out loud, "The parents described Millie as a sweet girl who excelled in school. She was on a field trip from school for science class when she disappeared." Ellie looked at the girls' picture. At fourteen, she was petite, fair-skinned and blond.

Her chest ached as she formed a picture of the young teenager. "Derrick, this girl looks just like our victims. If she is the unsub's mother, it could explain his obsession with blonds."

Derrick nodded, frowning. "The victims are either a replacement for her or he had some deep-seated hatred for his mother and he's killing her over and over."

She skimmed the parents' statements and continued, "Millie was an only child. Mother said she'd just started liking boys, but she didn't have a boyfriend that she was aware of. Father said she talked about a career in nursing."

Derrick drummed his fingers on the table. "The parents both have alibis. They were at the wife's sister's wedding, so they were ruled out immediately."

Ellie sighed. "There were six other students on the trip along with the teacher, a Mrs. Gorlan. They claim that Millie was enjoying the trip and was infatuated with the foliage, especially plants with medicinal purposes."

Derrick grunted in disgust. "The officer scribbled a theory about the girl running away and seemed to stick with that theory."

Ellie skimmed statements made by the mother and the other girls on the trip. "Why?" Ellie asked. "The teacher and the girl's friends all insisted she wouldn't have run away. That she loved her parents and school."

"Maybe the cop was just lazy," Derrick said. "Or didn't find signs of foul play."

They exchanged questioning looks and Ellie turned back to work. Deeper in the file, Ellie discovered a photograph of a friendship bracelet that had been found by the creek along with the girls' notebook. "Except for these," she said then showed the pictures to Derrick.

Derrick leaned closer to study the photograph. "Definitely suspicious." Pulling a hand down his chin, he flipped through the notes again, then raised his brow. "One of the girls mentioned seeing an older teenager in the woods that morning. Said that she thought he looked creepy."

Ellie pictured Millie combing the woods to look at the wildlife, maybe wandering off from camp for a bit. "If another teenager approached her, she might not have been frightened. He could have struck up a conversation with her and then... he took her."

Derrick twisted his mouth in thought. "Most kidnappers and serial killers start in their twenties, but some have been known to start younger."

Ellie's mind spun with possibilities. "He didn't kill her right away. Maybe he was like Hiram—Hiram took the little girls because he wanted a playmate."

Derrick heaved a breath. "And to get back at Vera."

Ellie winced at the painful reminder. "Millie's abductor can't be our unsub though. The age doesn't fit."

Nausea flooded Ellie as her mind veered down a darker path. "She was abducted at fourteen and held hostage for years." The truth dawned in sickening clarity as she imagined Millie's first days of being held captive. Of her hopes and prayers that someone would find her. Of those same hopes dwindling each day as she realized no one was coming.

"Ellie?" Derrick squeezed her hand. "You need a break?"

The concern in his voice jarred her back to the file, and her shock turned to anger. She stared at their hands for a moment, her heart fluttering at his touch. Odd how his presence could ground her in the midst of a storm.

"No," she murmured. "Just thinking." Her gaze met his. Having him as her partner kept her focused. "Her abductor must have held Millie and raped her, then she gave birth to their son. And now the son is following in his father's footsteps."

As Ellie drove them the few miles from Jasper to the small town of Ellijay where Brittany Banning's mother lived, she was plagued by the mental image of a teenage girl trying desperately to claw her way out of the cooler.

"I wonder where the unsub's father is," Derrick said.

Ellie had wondered that herself. "He could have abandoned Millie and his son at some point, gotten ill or died. Or... he could have killed Brittany and the mother."

"True," Derrick said. "Hell, he could be in hiding out somewhere now, even—a conspirator in his son's crimes."

Ellie shuddered at that sinister possibility. "Abused children often become abusers," she said, more disturbing images pummeling her. "If our unsub grew up witnessing his father mistreating his mother or holding her hostage, his mental view of family is skewed. He could even be trying to recreate that family."

"We've disturbed his home now by finding his bunker," Derrick said. "He may escalate rapidly."

All the more reason to find the sick bastard.

She turned onto a long tree-lined gravel road that led to an old farmhouse on a hill amidst a field of apple trees. Fall was apple-picking season and people traveled from all over to Ellijay to pick their own apples or visit the apple houses which sold a variety of apples and other products like apple butter, jams and jellies, apple bread and homemade apple sauce. With this freak snowstorm, the trees were bare, tipped in white from the recent snow, the sun shimmering off the melting puddles.

It looked like a postcard with the mountains rising behind it, yet Ellie felt no joy or peace looking at it. The ugliness of the murders was preying on her mind. She wanted to stop this monster before he killed again.

Or she became his next target.

A black pickup was parked beneath a carport and dark-eyed juncos nibbled from the birdfeeder in the front yard. Another area housed a barn and building where the apples were sorted before being taken to market.

Her stomach clenched with dread as he knocked on the door and Derrick tapped his foot as they waited. She wished she had good news for Mrs. Banning, not the horrifying reality she was about to disclose.

Footsteps echoed from inside, and a minute later, a middle-aged woman appeared at the window beside the front door, dusting flour from her apron. When she saw them, her expression immediately wilted. Then she opened the door and her breath rattled out as she invited them inside to the kitchen. The scent of homemade bread filled the room along with apple jelly, a cozy feel.

Yet this woman's life had been filled with sadness for years.

Ellie spoke first. "I'm Detective Reeves—"

"I know who both of you are," Mrs. Banning said. "I've seen the news this last week and had a bad feeling."

Mrs. Banning sank into a kitchen chair and grabbed a napkin then twisted it in her hands.

Ellie and Derrick claimed seats at the table opposite her, both giving her a moment to breathe.

"You finally found Brittany, didn't you?" Mrs. Banning said in a raw whisper.

"I'm afraid we did," Ellie said. "I wish I had better news." Ellie spotted a picture of a blond teenager on a shelf by the kitchen table and her breath caught. "Your daughter was a beautiful girl."

Tears filled the woman's eyes, and Derrick shifted in his chair, his expression somber.

"She was," Mrs. Banning said. "She had so much energy it was infectious. She was looking forward to college and becoming a kindergarten teacher. She loved kids and wanted to have a big family one day."

But she'd been robbed of that. Ellie swallowed hard. She glanced at Derrick, his expression a mask. More than anyone, Derrick knew what it felt like to wait for news about a missing loved one for years and then to receive the dreaded news they were dead.

Mrs. Banning wiped at her eyes. "I knew she was gone," she choked out. "I didn't want to believe it, but somehow... a mother knows."

Ellie nodded sympathetically. "I'm so sorry for your loss."

Mrs. Banning dropped her head into her hands for a long moment and Ellie and Derrick simply waited.

Finally, she seemed to straighten and pull herself together. "What happened? Does this have to do with the other murders in Crooked Creek?"

"I'm afraid so," Ellie said softly. "Tessa Tulane, the local author, took photos of a man on the trail and an underground bunker where he lived. We located it and inside found the victims we mentioned on the news. I'm so sorry, Brittany was one of them."

The woman choked on a cry. "What... did he do to her? Did he—"

"There was no sign of sexual assault," Ellie said quickly. At least that was one horror she could erase from the woman's mind. "There were no signs of physical violence either," she said. "But Brittany had a heart condition, didn't she?"

Mrs. Banning twisted the napkin more furiously between her fingers, shredding it. "It was congenital. But she seemed healthy. I made her have a checkup before she went on that trip in the mountains with her friends."

Ellie gave her another second. "I'm so sorry. She died of heart failure," Ellie said gently. "Perhaps the stress of the abduction triggered her heart to give out."

Derrick shifted in his seat beside her. She intentionally omitted the fact that Brittany had been alive when she'd been put in the freezer. No mother needed that horrible image haunting her.

"Mrs. Banning, I know it was a long time ago, and we're going to review the initial investigation, but have you thought of anything else about that time? Maybe you remembered seeing someone watching your daughter? Or had Brittany mentioned anything strange that happened? Maybe a boy with a crush on her?"

Mrs. Banning shook her head. "I told the police everything I knew. Brittany was athletic, played volleyball at school. She had a nice boyfriend back then, but he was away visiting college and didn't attend the senior trip."

"The police verified that?" Ellie asked.

"They did." Mrs. Banning snatched another napkin and dabbed at her wet cheeks. "He was devastated. He came by to see me every day for months after she disappeared, asking if the police knew anything. I think that's the reason he became a cop. Because we never got any answers and didn't want the police to stop looking for her."

Ellie and Derrick exchanged a knowing look. Derrick had become an agent for similar reasons. "We'd like to talk to him," Ellie said.

"Of course. He'll want to know. To help." Mrs. Banning found his number on her cell phone. "Ethan Lansing is his name," she said. "He works at the Ellijay Department. I think he hoped one day to find Brittany."

Ellie allowed herself a small surge of hope. If Ethan Lansing had been working the case, maybe he'd uncovered something helpful.

Ellie patted Brittany's mother's hand while Derrick stepped out into the living room and phoned the Ellijay Police Department to set up a meeting with Lansing.

"I hate to leave you alone," Ellie told the woman. "Is there someone I can call for you?"

"I'll call my friend," Mrs. Banning said. "You two go talk to Ethan." She squeezed Ellie's hand. "Please find out who did this. I don't want another parent to go through what I have."

Several already had, Ellie thought sadly. "I promise you I will. I don't want that either."

She laid her business card on the table. "If you think of anything else, please call me. Anytime, day or night."

Mrs. Banning murmured thanks and took her cell phone from her pocket to call her friend. Ellie waved goodbye, then went to get Derrick and they made their own way out of the house to the car.

The ten-minute drive to the police station was steeped in the kind of grief that weighed on Ellie. She knew that Derrick felt it too, knew he was thinking about the fact that his own mother had suffered as Brittany's had, and had also received the devastating news that her daughter was dead.

Ethan Lansing, a dark-haired man in his early thirties wearing a white collared shirt and khakis, was waiting on them when they entered and directed them to his office. Ellie was struck by his blue eyes, which radiated a haunting sadness. She wondered if people saw the same in her own eyes.

The moment they introduced themselves Lansing's expression flickered with the same awareness that she'd seen on Brittany's mother's face. With the news running the story of the Hunter, everyone seemed to recognize her and Derrick. "You found Brittany?" he asked, his tone pained.

Ellie and Derrick nodded sympathetically. "I'm so sorry," Ellie said.

He sank into his desk chair and raked a hand through his thick black hair, then curled his hands into fists so tight his knuckles turned white. "Was she one of those girls in that bunker in the woods?"

"I'm afraid so," Ellie said softly. "We just came from notifying her mother."

Ethan dropped his head into his hands for a long moment, his breathing labored.

A long heartbeat passed while they allowed him time to gather himself, then Derrick spoke. "We believe she was abducted the day she went missing and kept hostage," Derrick said quietly.

The man swiped his hands across his face and looked up at them. His jaw hardened. "What did he do to her?"

"She wasn't stabbed like the other victims. She died of heart failure," Ellie said. "You knew she had a heart condition?"

He gave a nod.

As a cop, Ellie decided that he deserved to know the entire truth. "There's more though. She was put in a freezer alive and suffered hypothermia. That's what triggered her heart attack."

Shock and anguish flashed on his face. "Jesus Christ. What kind of monster is he?"

Ellie said, "We think he was raised in the wilderness by a man who abducted a young girl named Millie Evans. That woman gave birth to the unsub."

Lansing shook his head in denial. "Unbelievable."

Sympathy for him filled Ellie, and she gave him a minute to absorb the information.

He exhaled slowly. "What else can you tell me?"

Ellie cleared her throat. "Brittany was the youngest victim, so it's likely she was the unsub's first. Did she ever mention that someone was stalking her or following her?"

He shook his head. "If she had, I sure as hell would have told the police." Lansing moaned. "If I'd just gone on that trip, maybe she'd still be alive."

Ellie's heart ached for him.

"Mr. Lansing, this was not your fault," Derrick said.

Ellie glanced at him. She'd heard the underlying pain in his voice. Derrick had blamed himself for his sister's disappearance because he was supposed to be watching her when she was abducted.

Lansing straightened, wiped a hand down his face then faced them. "Do you have any idea who killed her?"

"We're getting closer," Ellie said. "We think Brittany was a crime of opportunity, but his other victims were more calculated. When Brittany died, he may have taken the others to replace her." She hesitated. "He has a type. Except for Tessa Tulane, all of the victims were blonds. Ms. Tulane was most likely killed because she stumbled upon his bunker and he feared she'd expose him. We also believe he murdered another local hunter who'd used his services, and assume he'd gotten too close to the truth as well."

"God, I can't imagine how frightened Brittany and those other women were." Lansing's voice cracked with emotion. "I... should have done something more."

Ellie gave him a sympathetic look. "You were just a kid back then, too. Brittany's mother spoke about how nice you were and how much you cared about her daughter. She knew you'd kept looking and that gave her some comfort."

He shrugged, and she knew for him it hadn't been enough.

"Go on," he murmured. "Tell me everything."

"This man may have grown up in the wilderness," she said.

"But he's evaded detection all these years. We think he saw Brittany on the trail that day and abducted her to be with him in his bunker." She paused. "When something went wrong and she died, he started a pattern that's continued for years."

Lansing heaved a breath. "I knew someone kidnapped her. But there were never any real leads."

"Because he was adept at hiding out." Ellie clasped her hands together. "He carried her far into the woods, where he's lived off the grid his entire life."

Lansing rubbed a hand over his chin. "What else?"

Ellie swallowed hard. "Brittany, and each of the other victims, were wearing a handmade leather necklace etched with the words *Mine Forever.*"

His gaze locked with hers. "Jesus. You're telling me he took them to be his partner?"

"That makes sense," Ellie said. "But when things fell apart and the girls fought him, he killed them and put them in the cooler instead of disposing of them."

"Because then he might have gotten caught," Lansing muttered.

Ellie nodded, and Derrick cleared his throat. "That and because after he killed them, he couldn't bear to part with them. The women actually became his trophies."

Disgust colored Lansing's face. "Who is this sick SOB?"

"I don't know, but we are going to find him," Ellie said, battling her own self-doubts. With every minute she was more and more determined to end all this suffering.

Derrick leaned forward, eyes intent. "Mrs. Banning said that you continued working the case over the years. Did you find anything? Someone who may have looked suspicious."

"No one specific," Lansing answered. "I re-interviewed everyone the police had first spoken to and the girls who attended the trip with Brittany. They said the woods were filled that day. A lot of the seniors gathered to camp and have a last get-together before college." He reached inside his desk drawer and removed a folder that looked worn, as if he'd read it hundreds of times. When he opened it, Ellie saw Brittany's smiling face staring back. It was her senior picture, a moment in time where she had her entire future ahead of her.

Emotions clouded Lansing's face as he stared at it, and Ellie's heart broke for both him and Brittany. They might have been married now, had the family Brittany wanted.

"None of the girls saw anything? A strange young man maybe?" Derrick asked.

Lansing thumbed through the notes, tapping his finger on the pages. "Wait, there was one girl from our class, Brittany's good friend Renee, who described a guy she thought was weird hanging around the edge of the camp. She met with a sketch artist and came up with this." He removed a sketch from the file and angled it for them to see. "But nothing came of it." His brows furrowed. "But now I'm looking at it, this could be the guy in that photograph you showed on the news. He was younger then, but it's possible."

He handed Ellie the sketch and she and Derrick studied it. The man was leaner than the man in Tessa's photograph, but he could have bulked up since then. But the dark hair and beady eyes could be the same.

"It could be him," Ellie agreed. "Did the police uncover any leads on his identity?"

Lansing shook his head. "They showed it around to hikers and campers for a few days, even on the news, but no one came forward. It was like the guy disappeared."

"To that bunker," Ellie said. "Where he had supplies stockpiled that lasted him long enough for the search teams to stop looking before he came out again."

"I should have kept that picture running on the news over the years," Lansing said.

"Stop beating yourself up," Derrick said gently. "Right now, let's just concentrate on finding him."

"I'd like to talk to Renee," Ellie said. "Can you give me her contact information?"

Lansing scratched his head. "I can, but it won't do any good. I tried to find her a while back to talk to her again, but she'd moved and left no forwarding address. I've searched databases and there's nothing on her anywhere."

Ellie twisted her mouth in thought. That sounded suspicious. "How about Renee's family?"

"A single dad. Alcoholic," Lansing said. "He claimed she ran off after high school and he hasn't heard from her since."

"He's sure she ran away?" Derrick asked.

Lansing made a low sound in his throat. "That's his story and he's stuck to it. I wondered myself if he hurt her or something but never could find any proof."

"There's another possibility," Ellie said. "If the unsub knew she could recognize him, he could have come after her."

"Then where is she?" Derrick asked. "She wasn't in the bunker."

Ellie had no answer to that.

ONE HUNDRED FIVE
CROOKED CREEK

He'd tried to stay out of town, but the draw to the blond at the café was too strong. He'd followed her a few times, so he knew where she lived. And he'd watched her through the window, but he'd been careful to stay in the shadows, his face hidden.

Since the photo had aired on television, he'd decided he needed a disguise, so he'd shaved his beard. Then he'd ditched his coat for a different one and picked up a Braves ball cap which helped him fit in with some of the locals.

His heart raced as he slipped onto a bar stool. It was chancy being here now. What if someone recognized him?

As he'd walked down Main Street, though, no one had even noticed him, as if he was invisible. The idea that he was hiding in plain sight made his blood hot. He smiled to himself, looking around, silently laughing that they thought he was ignorant, yet he'd watched as they'd run all over the mountain looking for him like dogs chasing their own tails.

His pulse quickened as he spotted her. She moved lithely across the room. *She* was worth whatever risk he was taking.

All around him families and locals chatted and laughed. Signs for a trunk-or-treat event in the parking lot of the local elementary school hung on the door and teenagers rushed in laughing and squealing about the haunted house.

All Hallows' Eve, the perfect time to find love, he thought, with another chuckle.

He watched her carry food to those squawking old women, then that ranger he'd seen in the woods with the detective. She smiled at the ranger and touched his arm, then the two of them walked outside together.

His blood boiled like rabbit stew did on the hot stove. What the hell was she doing? She was *his*.

And he would take her tonight. Even if he had to kill that bastard to get her.

ONE HUNDRED SIX

Cord glanced around the parking lot, feeling edgy. The most recent news about the case Ellie was working on taunted him. She'd almost gotten herself killed on the last case, and now she was in danger again, the latest sicko scattering dead crows on her porch. Of course, she hadn't told him. But he'd heard Waters talking about it at Haints last night, almost laughing like it was funny. He'd wanted to wipe the floor with that asshole.

"Cord, are you listening to me?" Lola said, her voice sharp.

She'd been acting jumpy and irritable all day, like something was wrong, and had called him a dozen times begging him to stop by. And now he was here, but all he could think about was Ellie and if she was all right.

Lola tugged his arm and half dragged him outside beneath the canopy of the live oak. She pulled his hand in hers and clung to him as if she didn't want to let go.

"Stay at my place tonight," she said with a pleading look.

Cord went still, then clasped her hand. "I can't, Lola. I want to run by and check on Ellie. Make sure she's all right."

"Ellie can take care of herself," Lola said. "She's a cop, Cord. She carries a gun."

"She's been through a lot and she's not as tough as she acts,"

Cord said, remembering her battered face after the last case. And the faces of the dead girls in that freezer.

Anger flared in Lola's eyes. "It's always about Ellie, isn't it?"

Cord clenched his jaw. "She's working a big case and this maniac is after her. Of course I'm concerned."

She released his hand, pain flaring in her eyes. "I knew you were friends, but I thought you and I had a chance at being together. That's never going to happen, is it?"

Her voice cracked, raw with hurt, and guilt cinched his stomach into a fist. Lola was a nice girl. She'd been good to him when he was recovering from his ankle injury. But... she wasn't Ellie.

"I'm sorry, Lola," he said then stepped back. "I really am. I like you, but Ellie and I have been friends for years. I don't think I can be what you want."

Her face crumpled and tears pooled in her eyes. Then she suddenly shoved him, turned and ran around the side of the café to her car.

Cord felt like the biggest heel. Lola's engine fired up and tires squealed as she peeled from the parking lot.

ONE HUNDRED SEVEN

Lola sobbed the entire way back to her house. She'd come here to Crooked Creek for a safe haven and with the hope of finding love and a family of her own. A real family. Not like the one she'd grown up with, where her father talked with his fists and her mother had flown the coop when she was two.

All she remembered about her was the sweet scent of lilacs on her skin. And sometimes she woke with the fleeting memory of her mother singing "Twinkle Twinkle Little Star" while she rocked her to sleep.

Then she'd think she'd made all that up, or she just wanted it to be real so bad that she'd invented the memory to have something pleasant to hold on to.

When she'd found out Cord grew up in the system, and sensed that he'd been abused, she'd felt like they were kindred spirits. Soul mates.

But Cord was too in love with Ellie to even realize they could be good together. And Ellie was too busy hunting killers to give him the love he deserved.

A slight rain began to drizzle, sprinkling the windshield and blurring her vision as she hurried into her house. A car engine roared as it raced past, then an SUV slowed, almost to a stop, and her skin prickled with unease.

Hand trembling, she jammed the keys in the door and unlocked it, then rushed inside and slammed it shut. Then she went to the window and looked out. The SUV flashed its lights then sped up and moved on.

Releasing a shaky breath, she flipped on the lights and hurried down the hall to her room. Nerves stretched thin, she dragged out her suitcase and began throwing things inside. Sweaters and jeans, underwear, her toiletries and the cash she kept in the box in her closet. Money for a rainy day.

Or an escape.

It would just be temporary. When the cops found this monster, she could come home.

For days now, she thought someone had been following her.

And tonight... good God, she thought she'd seen that weird guy again. Although this man had shaved and worn a ball cap. But there was something eerie about his eyes. They were different colors.

She should tell Ellie. But what could she say? That a man in the café gave her the creeps? She'd sound like a lunatic.

She flipped on the TV, hoping Ellie had good news, that she'd caught the Hunter, and the women in Bluff County would be safe.

Angelica's face appeared. *"Here with the latest in the Hunter case,"* Angelica said. *"Police have now identified all but one of the bodies found in the bunker on the AT in an area known as Wild Hog Holler. Police believe that eighteen-year-old Brittany Banning was the Hunter's first victim and that he kidnapped her thirteen years ago. Ms. Banning had a congenital heart condition and police cite heart failure as cause of death."* A sketch drawn by a police artist appeared. *"They believe that this is the abductor. He was late teens, perhaps twenty, at the time when he took Brittany, which puts the man in his early thirties now."*

Lola staggered sideways and grabbed the bed post to steady herself. She recognized that sketch. Remembered when Brittany Banning had disappeared...

The news displayed the sketch again alongside the more recent photo, and Lola began to tremble from the inside out.

She was certain it was him.

She had to talk to Ellie, tell her.

But first she had to get away from Crooked Creek.

ONE HUNDRED EIGHT

CHERRY BLOSSOM INN

An hour later, Lola checked over her shoulder as she entered the Cherry Blossom Inn fifty miles north of Crooked Creek. She'd stayed here once before when she'd been looking for a place to move. The rows and rows of blooming cherry trees had given her a sense of peace. The pink flowers were gorgeous in spring, but in fall the dark green glossy foliage turned a bright yellow and was just as stunning.

Tonight, the dark sky seemed ominous and etched with shadows, the sharp ridges of the mountains standing out like the turrets of a haunted castle. The wind wheezed through the trees, blowing the last lingering snowflakes across the ground. In a garden area to the side of the inn, a tent had been erected with white-tableclothed tables as if preparing for a special event. As she parked, Lola spotted a band setting up on the makeshift stage, fresh wildflowers on the table and heaters lit to warm the space.

Her first thought was that a wedding was about to take place.

The urge to cry clogged her throat. Foolishly, she'd let herself imagine tying the knot with Cord. The thought of never seeing him again or going back to the little house she'd bought in Crooked Creek—her very first home of her own—nearly brought her to her knees. The Corner Café had been a dream come true, too. She'd enjoyed meeting the locals there—they'd become a family to her, a family she'd never had.

She would go back one day, dammit.

She got out of the car and took her suitcase from the back seat. The scent of roses wafted around her as she entered the inn and the lobby had been decorated with paper hearts. A giant sign advertising a speed dating event sponsored by Hearts & Souls stood by the reservation desk. So it wasn't a wedding being held here, but a singles meet and greet.

It seemed odd to her that this event was being hosted so close to Halloween, instead of Valentine's Day, but inside the heart the words *Fall in Love* had been painted in cursive to link to the season. Another sign held a poster with a schedule of events, and Lola read that tonight there was a costume cocktail party.

She looked around; a room to the right of the lobby held several tables with seating for two, each table adorned with a single rose in a crystal vase to add to the ambience. Guests had started to gather inside the room and the adjacent bar area bustled with people mingling casually, chatting and laughing, the booze flowing. Costumes ranged the gambit from Cleopatra to Casanova to super-heroes, sex kittens and more risqué S & M.

The receptionist at the check-in desk greeted Lola with a big smile. "Welcome to Cherry Blossom Inn. My name is Myra. Are you here for the Hearts and Souls dating event?"

Lola shook her head. "No, just a night's getaway." The only man she wanted was in love with another woman. The last thing she was in the mood for was to meet a stranger, especially with a serial killer on the loose.

"You're in the Sunset Room, top of the stairs and on the left." The woman handed Lola her key. "If you change your mind about the dating, there's a sign-up sheet here in the lobby." The woman's eyes sparkled, and she waved her hand to showcase a glittering emerald-cut diamond. "I actually met my fiancé at one of these things. It does work."

"Congratulations." Lola took the key, anxious to escape and be alone. She wouldn't be changing her mind.

ONE HUNDRED NINE

He climbed from the trunk of Lola's car, quickly scanning the parking lot to make sure no one saw that he'd been hiding inside.

When he'd watched her drag her suitcase outside her house earlier, he'd had a stroke of genius and decided, instead of taking her at home, to sneak in her car and go with her. She'd run back in for her purse after putting her case in the car, and he'd opened the trunk and curled inside.

Shaking his limbs, which had grown stiff during the bumpy ride, he tugged his ball cap lower over his head and walked up to the door of the inn. The parking lot was filled with SUVs and fancy cars, suggesting the guests who stayed here had money.

From the porch, he looked through the window and saw Lola at the desk talking to a woman, so he waited until she headed up the stairs before going in.

The door opened, and a man in a pirate's costume walked out. The loud noise and crowd from inside suddenly made it feel like the world was closing around him. Or watching him. He was tempted to cover his ears and run. To get back to the quiet of the woods.

But running would only draw attention to himself.

Pulling his hat lower, he stepped inside and surveyed the room.

Too many people here. He had to wait until he got her alone before he took her.

The cloying scent of flowers and perfume nearly suffocated him. The laughter and voices made him duck into the shadows, then he spotted a big sign advertising a dating event called *Fall in Love*. If he hadn't already found Lola, he might have tried it.

There were a bunch of young women gathered like a brood of hens, drinking out of long-stemmed glasses and eying the men at the bar as if they were hunks of beef in a meat market. And they were all decked out in costumes. Three or four looked like princesses, one was a ballerina, one a French maid. He counted three women whose blouses were so low cut and skirts so short their tits fell out and you could almost see up their asses.

His heart thudded. He hardened.

Bunch of whores, that's what they were.

Surely Lola wasn't going to dress like one of them.

The men wore a variety of costumes; superheroes, a bull fighter, a doctor and one man sported a glittery one-piece suit with big sparkly jewelry.

He'd seen kids dress up in town for Halloween, but not grown-ups.

He shifted, debating what to do. He wanted to be home in his bunker, alone with his souvenirs, touching and looking at all the women he loved, his daddy's voice in his head.

But *they'd* stolen all that from him. He had to start over.

He needed Lola.

Reminding himself he needed to fit in, he wove past a couple of men ordering beers and brushed up against a pretty brunette.

She laughed. "What are you supposed to be? A hillbilly?"

Fury seized him as that detective's words echoed in his head, and his hand automatically slid to his jacket where he kept a pocketknife. *Fucking bitch.* He oughta slash her throat right now for talking to him like that.

But there were too many people watching.

In the corner at a small table, a dark-haired woman and a

redhead were watching him and smiling. One of them leaned over and whispered something and he realized they were talking about him. He started over to meet them, but the redhead shook her head and mouthed, "No way."

A guy with a shiny gold watch poked him. "You'd do better if you ditched the lumberjack costume."

He clenched his jaw, pushed past the asshole and headed outside. If Lola came down for the party, he'd find a way to get her alone. But he didn't intend on changing his damn clothes. His flannel shirt and jeans were his staples. No sense putting on fancy airs for a woman when most of them were fickle and heartless.

He smiled to himself as he stepped onto the front porch and inhaled the crisp mountain air.

His soul mate had to love him for who he was.

A hunter.

ONE HUNDRED TEN

A vase of flowers the color of cherry blossoms sat on the antique dresser in Lola's room. In the center of the four-poster bed, a white basket held bubble bath, lotions, scented candles, a bottle of champagne and a heart-shaped box of chocolates. A fluffy robe lay across the satin pillows with rose petals sprinkled on the plush white satin comforter.

A twinge of longing for Cord tugged at her. The room was set for romance, compliments of Hearts & Souls.

Loneliness set it, and she tore open the box of chocolates, grabbed a truffle and stuffed it in her mouth. Rich creamy caramel and dark chocolate were her weakness. Too antsy to think about sleeping yet, she gobbled down four more pieces, then set the basket on the dresser and sank onto the bed to call Ellie.

But she couldn't find her phone in her purse. Frantic, she dumped the contents on the bed and rummaged through it. It wasn't there.

Good grief. She must have left it in the car. Irritated, but knowing she needed it, she yanked on her jacket, snagged her keys and the room key then left the room and slipped down the stairs. The noise in the lobby had died down, and costume-clad guests were meandering outside toward the white tent where music flowed through the outdoor speakers.

She checked over her shoulder then scanned the male guests, but the costumes disguised the men, making her even more nervous. If the man she'd seen in the café was the one from the photograph and sketch on the news and he'd followed her, he could be hiding right here in clear sight, and she might not recognize him.

A man dressed as a Viking stepped aside politely as she neared the door. "I hope you're coming to the party," he said in a sexy drawl.

Lola gave a quick shake of her head, and rushed past him, bypassing the tent as she crossed to her car. As she reached it, out of the corner of her eye, for a terrified second she thought she saw the man from the café lurking by the birdfeeders, but when she turned, he was gone. Panicking, she pressed the key fob to unlock the car, then jumped inside and grabbed her phone from where it had fallen onto the floor.

Her fingers trembled as she called Ellie, and she got out of the car and scanned the group outside for the man again as she started back to the inn. She wanted to be inside. Safe in her room until help arrived.

Tension knotted her shoulders as the phone rang. Once. Twice. Three times.

She was nearing the tent when she thought she heard footsteps behind her. Just then Ellie answered.

She spun around to make sure no one was following her, talking as she walked toward the gardens. "Ellie, it's Lola. I... was with Brittany Banning when she disappeared. I saw the guy who took her—"

The whisper of someone's breathing suddenly bathed her neck. She jerked her head to the right, and the man from her nightmares grabbed her. Her phone hit the dirt and she struggled to scream, but he pressed a stun gun to her back then dragged her behind a tree.

She kicked and flailed but the electric shock zinged through her, and her body jerked and convulsed until the darkness pulled her down. She felt herself falling into a black vortex. Then the chatter and music around her faded to nothing.

ONE HUNDRED ELEVEN

CROOKED CREEK

Ellie clenched the phone with sweaty fingers. Lola's voice had faltered, the phone crackling as if they had a bad connection. Then she'd heard a scream. "Lola?"

Noise echoed over the line, sounding distant as if there were voices and music. "Lola, answer me! What's going on?"

But she didn't respond.

"Lola!" Ellie cried, her pulse racing. "Talk to me. Where are you?"

Nothing but noise again.

Derrick looked up from his laptop. "What's wrong?"

"Lola called, but we got cut off." She rubbed her temple, then rang the number again, but it went straight to voicemail. *Dammit.* "She said something about being with Brittany Banning when she disappeared."

Derrick's brows pinched together. "I don't remember a girl named Lola being interviewed in the report."

"Her last name is Parks," Ellie grabbed the Banning file and thumbed through it, skimming names. "You're right. There's no mention of a Lola Parks," she said.

"I'll check newspaper archives." While he did that, Ellie tried calling Lola again but got her voicemail.

She quickly phoned the café to see if Lola was there, but the hostess said she'd run out earlier in a rush and had left a message saying she needed a few days off.

Hoping she was with Cord, Ellie called him. He sounded out of breath when he answered.

"Is Lola with you?"

"No, why?"

"Do you know where she is?" she said, her pulse pounding with worry.

He made a low sound in his throat. "I saw her at the café earlier."

"She's not there now," Ellie said. "The hostess said she left in a rush and that she wouldn't be back for a few days. Do you have any idea where she'd go?"

A heartbeat passed. "No... I... uh... she was upset with me, I think." His breathing rattled over the line. "Why are you looking for her? Is something wrong?"

"I don't know, but there might be. She just called me and said she was with Brittany Banning when she disappeared. Did you know about that?"

"No. Hell no." There was a tense silence. "I had no idea."

Ellie heaved a sigh, a bad feeling knotting her stomach. "We were talking and suddenly we were cut off. But I heard voices and music in the background."

Cord cursed. "I'll drive to her house and see if she's there."

"Okay, keep me posted. I'll trace her phone and see if we can determine her location."

"Call you in a few."

They hung up and she set the wheels in motion to trace Lola's phone.

"Look at this." Derrick angled his laptop towards her. "This is a photo of Renee Parker. Who does she remind you of?"

Ellie's heart stuttered. "Oh, my god. That's Lola."

Derrick ran a hand through his hair. "We wondered what happened to her. Now we know."

"She ran away because she saw the man who took Brittany," Ellie said. "Which means he may have seen her."

"That sketch of him and Ms. Tulane's photograph have been all over the news," Derrick said.

Ellie nodded. "And if he's been in town or to the café, he might have recognized her."

Fear for Lola tightened Ellie's chest. She'd thought the unsub was coming after her. But what if Lola was next?

ONE HUNDRED TWELVE

Cord drove like a wild man to Lola's, guilt clawing at him as his truck ate the miles. She'd asked him to stay with her tonight, but he'd been so worried about Ellie that he'd blown her off. And now... was she in danger?

All because he hadn't realized how much she needed him.

The roads were still slick with sludge from the melting snow, but at least there was no rain. He cursed a blue streak, slamming his fist on the steering wheel and honking at cars to let him pass.

The image of the frozen dead women piled one on top of each other was imprinted in his brain. The brutality of the stabbings...

Lola was dark blond, just this maniac's type.

Why hadn't Lola come forward earlier?

Why should she have confided in you? You haven't exactly been up front with her.

His tires ground the wet gravel as he swung his truck into Lola's drive. Her car was not in the driveway and the lights were off, the house pitched in total darkness. He grabbed his flashlight, jumped out and jogged up the drive to the front door. The house seemed eerily quiet—no one was home. Lola usually had country music playing. Sometimes he'd heard it when he'd knocked on the door. She liked to sing and dance around the kitchen when she cooked.

A wave of emotion hit him hard and fast. She'd been so good to him during his recovery. She didn't deserve to be on the run from a mad killer.

He raked his hand under the welcome mat and then checked the flowerpot but didn't find a spare key. On the chance she'd hidden one around back, he hurried around the side of the house to the deck. No key anywhere there.

He shined his flashlight through the kitchen window, but the house was dark. Sweat beaded on his neck as he picked the lock on the back door and slipped inside. Raking his hand along the wall, he found the light switch and turned it on.

The kitchen looked neat and orderly, just the way Lola usually kept it. Her baking utensils were organized on the counter, the wall decorated with her collection of rolling pins.

Lola had been so kind. Always cooking for him. Bringing him meals from the café. How many times had she delivered home-made pies and cookies to his door?

He walked through the rest of the house, but nothing seemed amiss. No signs of a struggle suggesting Lola had been kidnapped from here.

But this madman had taken other women before, and no one had seen anything.

Fear choked him. He should have protected Lola.

ONE HUNDRED THIRTEEN

Ellie paced her office while Derrick waited on the trace to Lola's phone. Silently, she cursed herself for not warning every blond in the county that they might be targets.

Her phone buzzed, and she nearly jumped out of her skin, hoping Lola was calling back to say she was safe.

But it was Cord. She stabbed "Connect" and held her breath. Maybe Cord had found her.

"She's not at her house," Cord said. "Her car is not here either."

Ellie's mind raced. "I'll issue a BOLO for it. Do you see signs of foul play?"

"No," Cord said. "Although I'm inside now and it looks like her clothes have been thrown all over the place."

"Check the closet. Look for a suitcase," Ellie said. "She could have packed and run because she was scared."

More breathing, then Cord returned. "Her luggage is gone," he said. "The toiletries and her makeup are gone, too."

Ellie took a deep breath. "That could be a good sign that she left on her own. I'll get everyone looking for her car."

"Ellie," Cord said, his voice cracking. "Please find her. She... must have been afraid. She asked me to stay the night but I... didn't."

"This is not your fault," she said firmly. "For now, let's just focus on finding her."

"What can I do?"

Questions swirled in Ellie's head. "Is there any place you two went that might have been special? Some place she felt safe? Some place she mentioned going or where she was from?"

A tense second passed. "No... I should have listened better. Asked more questions."

Ellie thought of the file on Brittany Banning. That might lead them somewhere.

In spite of her fear that she'd fail Lola like she had Ginger and Tessa, she had to comfort Cord. "We'll find her, Cord. I promise."

Derrick's phone buzzed, and he answered, then motioned to her that he had news.

"I have to go. I'll keep you posted." She hung up and followed Derrick to the conference room, praying she could keep that promise.

"We traced Lola's phone to an address north of here." Derrick pointed out the GPS coordinates on the wall map. "Do you know what's in that area?"

Ellie studied the roads, then turned to a more detailed map of regional landmarks and locations. "Cord said Lola's suitcase was gone. There's an inn called Cherry Blossom off the highway in that area. She may have decided to stay there tonight."

She snagged her keys and rushed toward the door. Derrick followed and they headed to her car.

A pained silence stretched between them for the next hour as she drove out of town and climbed the hills north. Night set in, a few storm clouds lingering, blotting out the stars and the moonlight.

"If Lola is Renee and the Hunter came into the café, she must have recognized him," Ellie finally said. "And he may remember her. But why didn't she come forward sooner?" Ellie thought out loud.

"Lola was young when she witnessed Brittany Banning's abduction," Derrick said. "Maybe he came after her back then and she got away. So she gave the police a description then decided to run out of fear that he'd find her."

They fell into silence again as they drove, grinding over

potholes and graveled roads, the snow tires smoothing the way over the black ice.

Ellie felt mixed emotions as they approached the inn and parked. The place looked attractive and festive, a party clearly in full swing, but she and Derrick knew a sadistic serial killer might be lurking in their midst.

As they walked up to the inn, music blared from a stage in a large outdoor tent where guests in costumes danced as the classic song "Monster Mash" echoed through the speakers.

"Wow," Derrick muttered as they watched a couple dressed as the Munsters mingling with a werewolf and a witch. "Interesting."

It was like watching a spooky movie being filmed in real life.

They scanned the guests as they passed, searching for the suspect. As they entered the inn, Derrick gestured toward a large sign listing activities sponsored by the Hearts & Souls dating site. "Perhaps Lola just came here to meet a man," Derrick said.

"I hope that's all it is. But I have a bad feeling... she sounded scared when she called."

Ellie stopped at the desk while Derrick walked through the lobby and looked around.

She identified herself then flashed Lola's photograph to the desk clerk. "This is Lola Parks. Is she registered here?"

"Yes, she came in earlier," Myra said. "I told her about the dating event, but she wasn't interested. She went straight up to her room."

"Is she there now?"

"I don't know. I can call and check."

"Please do," Ellie said.

Ellie glanced at Derrick who'd returned to the bar area and was talking to the bartender while Myra made the call. When she hung up, she shook her head. "She's not answering. Maybe she turned in already."

Ellie curled her fingers around the edge of the counter. "This is urgent. May I have a key to her room?"

The young woman glanced around nervously. "I'm not supposed to do that unless the guest gives permission."

Ellie lowered her voice then flashed a photo of the suspect. "I think she may be in danger and need to check. Have you seen this man?"

"I don't think so." Myra shrugged. "But everyone is in costume tonight so he could be here."

Ellie gritted her teeth. That did make it harder to tell who was who.

Derrick joined her at the desk. "I noticed you have a security camera outside. Can I take a look at the feed?"

Myra's eyes narrowed with concern. "Of course." She made another call and a moment later a male employee named Frank appeared and escorted Derrick to the back.

"Show me to her room now," Ellie said, desperate to get in there.

Myra nodded, then pulled an old-fashioned key from the box on the wall behind the desk and led Ellie up the winding staircase.

When Myra unlocked the door, Ellie stepped inside, her heart pounding as her gaze swept the empty room. Lola's suitcase was still closed, as if she'd just dropped it off. Her purse had been dumped on the bed. The box of chocolates was open, wrappers tossed in the trash. The bathroom was beautiful with a soaking tub and marble counter, but it didn't appear to have been used. Ellie checked the room for Lola's phone, but it was not in the room.

Myra was still standing at the door, shifting her weight from one foot to the other. "Maybe she changed her mind and joined the activities outside."

Ellie didn't think Lola had come here looking for a man.

She'd come to escape one.

ONE HUNDRED FIFTEEN

While Derrick reviewed the security footage, Ellie began canvassing the guests outside. The party was in full swing, drinks loosening tongues and luring the crowd to the dance floor. She scrutinized the men, searching for the Hunter and Lola, and spotted a masked man wearing a hooded cape talking to a blond in a dominatrix costume.

She approached him cautiously, studying his features. He was about the right height and size, and he sported a beard. He saw her looking at him and his eyes glittered with interest. "Where's your costume?"

"I'm not here for a date. I'm looking for some people." She flashed the photographs of the unsub and Lola, but the man showed no reaction. She asked him to remove his mask and his expression turned uncomfortable, but he slipped it off.

It wasn't him, so Ellie continued canvassing the guests, showing them Lola's photograph and asking if they'd seen her.

"She was coming out of the inn at the same time I was," a man in a Viking outfit said. "She looked jumpy, though, and I haven't seen her here at the party."

A redhead dressed as a French maid glanced at Lola's picture. "I saw her walking to her car when I arrived."

The fireman next to her frowned, staring at the picture of the

Hunter. "A big guy like that came through the bar but didn't stay long. Didn't have a beard though."

A female in a witch's hat wrinkled her nose. "I saw him, too. Looked like a hillbilly, kind of scary." She shivered. "His hands were scarred, too, as if he'd been in a knife fight."

Two other women confirmed this man had been at the bar, and another said they saw Lola near the gardens. It seemed too much of a coincidence—a man of the same height and build roaming the hotel but not interacting. And the unsub could easily have changed his appearance after he found out they were tracking him. She texted Derrick to tell him to check for the guy on the tapes.

She headed back to reception and Derrick strode toward her, a grim expression on his face. "I saw Lola on the tapes, and the man we're looking for outside about the same time she called you."

"Some of the guests saw them both, but not together." As she said the words, her fear for Lola intensified. If he'd kidnapped Lola, he could be miles away by now.

Frantic, she motioned for Derrick to follow her towards the gardens. They searched the grounds and bushes and found boot prints—both a man's and a woman's, though the wind and other foot traffic from guests made them difficult to trace. Then Ellie noticed something shiny in the earth of a flowerbed. She pulled on gloves and retrieved a cell phone. It was definitely Lola's. She recognized the neon orange phone case.

Ellie brought up the call history, which confirmed that the last call had been to Ellie.

"There are drag marks over here," Derrick said. Ellie's pulse raced as they followed the marred brush and indentations in the mushy soil. The drag marks led a few feet away from the gardens, then stopped, and large boot prints led back toward the parking lot.

Sweat beaded on Ellie's neck. "He must have incapacitated her somehow, then carried her," she said. "Maybe a stun gun? And he was parked out here." Which meant they were long gone.

God help her. She didn't want to lose Lola to this monster.

"He may have taken her in her own car." Worry sent her

nerves into a tailspin. What was he doing to Lola? Where would he go now?

She had to follow the leads, and right now the only one she had was Lola's missing car. She called Angelica and asked her to run a photo of Lola on the news as a missing person, gave her the details of the car, then issued a bulletin for the vehicle.

Every second counted.

ONE HUNDRED SIXTEEN

SOMEWHERE ON THE AT

Lola's arms ached and pain throbbed down her spine as she slowly opened her eyes. Her vision was blurred, her head foggy and her mouth was so dry it felt like cotton balls. She blinked to clear her vision and see where she was, and a bright light nearly blinded her.

She tried to move and realized she was tied by her wrists to a metal hook hanging from the ceiling.

Terror shot through her.

She twisted her body sideways, and a scream caught in her throat. Animal carcasses hung from the ceiling, surrounding her. Two deer and a hog.

The stench of blood and animal guts made nausea clog her throat, and she had to swallow to keep from choking on it. Chill bumps skated all over her body from the cold.

"Hello, darlin'," he murmured.

The sinister sound of his voice sent a shudder through her, and she twisted sideways again and spotted the big mountain of a man sitting in a chair with a sheet of plastic below him. He took a sip of something that looked like moonshine from a jar, gripped a large hunting knife in one hand then stripped his shirt.

She gasped at the cuts he'd carved into his arms and chest. His skin was mottled and scarred, the hair patchy. She realized the cuts weren't random—they marked out names, the names of different women. She could just make out the names of his victims, crossed out with jagged x's. Brittany's name was there along with the women Ellie had mentioned on the news.

He dug the knife into his skin and made a slashing cross over the name Ginger, gritting his teeth as the blood dripped down his arm and spattered the plastic trap.

He placed one bloody finger over his chest, then smiled, his dirty teeth crooked and jagged. Then he began to carve her name in bloody letters.

ONE HUNDRED SEVENTEEN

CROOKED CREEK

Ellie felt bone weary as she returned to the police station. She and
Derrick had conducted a thorough search of the inn before leaving.
She'd called an ERT and two of their investigators had searched
the property.

But Lola was nowhere to be found.

They also interviewed every man at the inn in case the Hunter
had been in disguise and was biding his time to escape with Lola.
Each guest was accounted for, the names and IDs matching the
registry, indicating the unsub had not registered as a guest.

He'd disappeared.

Derrick's phone rang as they entered the station, and Ellie saw
his eyes sparking with concern as he stepped aside to answer. She
grabbed coffee and was on her way to her office, the air in her lungs
tightening when she saw Cord waiting in the corridor, frantic and
pacing.

"The butcher shop owner, Jim Bob, just rang," Derrick said
when he caught up with her outside her office. "He said he thinks
the man in the photo on the news sometimes delivers meat to his
shop."

"Does he come daily?"

Derrick shook his head. "It's sporadic."

Ellie sent a quick text to Shondra. "I'll have Deputy Eastwood stake it out."

"Good idea," Derrick said. "Owner also said the same guy sells to a food truck called All Things Deer. He works the local festivals and sometimes parks at the approach trail for the hike to Tallulah Falls."

Ellie's mind raced. "The Hunter may have a place near there where he stores the meat until delivery." She hesitated, thinking. "We should divide up to cover more ground. Why don't you talk to the food truck owner, and I'll have Cord look at the trail map? Maybe he can narrow down a location where the unsub might be hiding out."

"I don't want to leave you alone," Derrick said. "This creep threatened you, Ellie."

Her gaze met his, tension thrumming between them. "Don't worry. If Cord has an idea, I'll take him with me. Now let's hurry. Maybe we can save Lola."

He still looked hesitant, but he knew she was right so he turned and headed back to the door.

She tried to wrangle her emotions before she faced Cord. He'd stopped pacing, but his jaw was clenched as hard as steel. He'd been running his hand through his hair anxiously, sending the shaggy strands into a disheveled mess. Yet he looked at her hopefully when she entered, making her heart ache. She wished to hell she had good news.

"Where is she?" he said gruffly. "What is this crazy son of a bitch doing to her?"

Ellie struggled to tamp down her fears. She wanted to promise him she'd bring Lola back alive, but she'd already failed with Ginger and Tessa. "I don't know, Cord."

She walked back to the conference room to study the murder board and he followed. Adding Lola's picture to the list of victims made her feel sick inside with terror. She scribbled the name of the inn on the board, then the fact that they had a BOLO issued for Lola's car. That done, she stood back and began to study the map, struggling to get into the Hunter's mind and figure out where he might go.

"If she dies it's my fault," Cord said, his voice breaking. "She was upset with me."

Ellie gave him a sympathetic look. "She left because she recognized the photo of our suspect. She was with Brittany Banning when she was abducted thirteen years ago. We think she saw him and worked with a police sketch artist to make a composite drawing of him."

Cord scrubbed a hand down his chin, his breathing choppy. "Why didn't she tell me or you about him?"

"She may not have realized he was the man we were looking for until we released Brittany's name and circulated that sketch on the news."

"I still should have stayed with her," Cord said.

Ellie folded her arms. "Don't do that, Cord. Let's just figure out where he took her."

Fear darkened Cord's face, but he lifted his chin, his eyes somber. "He wouldn't go back to that bunker."

"I agree," Ellie said softly. "But he's lived in the woods all his life so he's bound to find another place where he can hole up somewhere off the trail. If anyone can help us work out where that might be, it's you."

Cord strode over to the maps of the AT Ellie kept on the wall. She had a topographical one and another she'd enlarged and pinpointed with location names that were not listed on the map of the cities along the trail.

"We checked out a chicken processing plant, and we know he sells meat to a butcher," Ellie said. "We know that he hunts wild game, deer, duck and wild boar. Hog blood was found by forensics in the bunker. It's possible he has a place where he dresses the animals."

Cord rubbed his chin then snapped his fingers. "I may know a place. There are some hunters who dress their deer in the field, but

I've heard there's a guy who keeps a work hut where he does it for other hunters."

Ellie raised a brow. "Do you know where it is?"

Cord studied the map. "It's not too far from Wild Hog Holler."

Hope flickered as Ellie's gaze met Cord's. That was near the bunker.

"Let's go."

ONE HUNDRED EIGHTEEN

WILD HOG HOLLER

Ellie raced around the mountain, grateful her four-wheel drive could handle the icy roads and that she was experienced in maneuvering the switchbacks.

She parked at the approach trail and hit the ground running. Using flashlights to illuminate the path, Cord led the way, the tension radiating from him, mirroring her own anxiety. But he was cool under pressure, and his innate sense of direction was uncanny. With the snow nearly gone, the ground was muddy, the moss and lichen slippery.

The temperature had warmed to fifty during the day but was dropping quickly, leaves shaking in the wind, branches rattling. Deer and squirrels skittered through the forest. An owl hooted in the distance and frogs croaked from the creekside.

A mile in and Ellie froze as she spotted a wild pig in a thicket, half hidden by bushes. She knew better than to spook it. "They won't attack, will they?" Ellie asked Cord.

"Feral hogs rarely attack humans and then only when they're wounded, cornered or threatened," Cord said. "Just move slowly."

They eased toward the west and Cord cleared the way, climbing another mile until they crested a hill, and she spotted a small shack nestled between a cluster of pines. She motioned to

Cord, and they darted along the tree line until they reached the hut.

A shrill scream came from inside, and Cord took off running before Ellie could stop him.

Ellie drew her gun and raced after him, but suddenly she heard the sound of pine cones and brush snapping behind her.

She spun around, raised her gun to fire, but before she got off a round, a man grabbed her around the throat. Then the sharp jolt of an electric current burned through her.

ONE HUNDRED NINETEEN

Fear for Lola drove Cord as he ran to the door of the hut. Gripping his hunting knife in one hand, he looked inside the small window of the shack and saw a long table and sink used for gutting and processing game. A large barrel to one side probably held waste and feathers he'd discarded, and he spotted a door leading to a back room where the man must hang and store the game in a cooler.

Not bothering to wait for Ellie, he charged inside, praying he was in time. He paused at the door leading to the back to listen. There was another scream, then a woman sobbing and yelling for help.

His lungs fought for air, and he clenched the handle of his knife in a white-knuckled grip and eased open the door. If the bastard had hurt Lola, he'd kill him. He slowly crept in, looking around at an area that must be used for prepping, then ahead he saw a closed door to the cooler. Sweat beaded his neck as he inched toward it and reached for the door handle.

The metal door screeched open as he yanked on it. Horror and rage filled him when he saw Lola dangling from a hook, strung up like an animal. Blood dripped down her chest and shirt, and her head was lolling forward.

He took one step toward her but suddenly felt the sharp whack of something against the back of his head, then a knife piercing his back. He choked on the pain and tried to turn to fight, but his vision faded, and he collapsed onto the hard floor.

ONE HUNDRED TWENTY

CROOKED CREEK

Derrick found the All Things Deer food truck parked near the Haunted House. The owner, Emmet Rogers, was a short, heavy-set man with jowls, and was just shutting up the hatch when Derrick approached.

"Sorry, man," Emmet said as he locked the counter window. "Ran out of food about ten minutes ago."

"I guess you cleaned up tonight with all those teenagers."

"Best night I've had in a long time." He grinned and jangled the keys in his hands.

"I'm not here to eat," Derrick said. "But I heard a hunter in the area supplies you with game he processes himself."

Emmet's expression turned defensive. "Who told you that?"

"It doesn't matter." Derrick flashed his credentials. "And before you go radio silent, I'm not interested in your health standards. I think that man is the killer we've been looking for."

"Aww, crap, I thought I'd seen you before," Emmet muttered. "Are you sure he's the one you want? Guy's a hunter all right, but that don't mean he kills women."

"We have good reason to suspect he does, and I need to find him. Another woman has gone missing, and her life may depend on it," Derrick said. "I need to know his name and how to reach him."

Emmet scratched his belly. "Don't think he has a phone. Lives somewhere in the mountains near Wild Hog Holler."

"How do you do business with him?"

"He drops by once a week. Got a little place where he does his own dressing and processing."

"Have you ever been there?"

Emmet shifted, jiggling his keys again. "Am I in trouble?"

"Not unless you helped him murder those women or you're covering for him," Derrick said, losing his patience.

Panic flared on the man's craggy face. "I ain't never killed anything. Well, except for some deer here and there. That's how I met him."

"What's his name?"

"I don't know," Emmet said. "He called himself Blade."

Blade? "You said you met him hunting. Do you know where his hut is?"

Emmet grunted. "Yeah. But you have to know those parts to find it. And I got no sense of direction out there on the trail."

"Hang on. One of my colleagues is out looking for it," Derrick said. "Let me see if she found it."

Emmet shifted back and forth on the balls of his feet as Derrick called Ellie. The phone rang four times then went to voicemail. He hung up and dialed Cord, but his phone did the same thing. Frustrated, he tried again and left a message for them to check in.

His stomach knotted with worry. What if they were in trouble?

ONE HUNDRED TWENTY-ONE

WILD HOG HOLLER

Ellie woke, her body tingling with ice-cold air swirling around her, her arms aching as if they were being wrenched from the sockets. The acrid odor of blood and death made her want to vomit. She tried to pull her arms free, but terror seized her as she realized her wrists were tied together; she was hanging from the ceiling.

Forcing her eyes open, she gasped as she saw Cord hanging beside her, strung up among the animal carcasses. His eyes were closed, and blood dripped onto the plastic below him. She narrowed her eyes to determine where he'd been cut, but the light was too dim. She fought not to cry out with fear. Was he still breathing?

Slowly she angled her head to study the layout of the room and then she saw Lola. Just like Cord and Ellie, Lola was dangling from the ceiling, her hands tied above her head. The floor below her was spattered in blood, her skin bluish, blood drying on her clothing. Frost had already started to gather on the strands of her dark blond hair.

A sob of horror rose in Ellie's throat, and her gut wrenched. Dear God, she was too late again.

Furious at this monster and at herself for letting him get the better of her, she yanked at the ties. "Cord?" Ellie hissed. "Cord, wake up."

The sound of breathing echoed from behind her, then she heard footsteps shuffling. She went totally still, battling panic as the killer moved around in front of her. She gasped at the sinister evil in his beady eyes. Gone was the beard, but a black ski cap still covered his head, although he must have cut his hair because the long shaggy strands were gone. Wearing all dark clothing, he looked like something out of a horror movie with his big brawny body and hands the size of ham hocks.

"You ruined it all," he growled in a menacing voice. "You stole my home and all the women I loved."

Ellie gritted her teeth, her voice warbling with the pain in her shoulders and neck. "You murdered them," she hissed. "That's not love."

He whipped a knife up in front of her face, his eyes flashing with wild rage. "I did love them, but their hearts were as cold as a block of ice. That's why they had to die." He traced the blade of the knife along her jaw, his rancid breath bathing her face as he leaned closer. "And now you're going to join them."

Fear gripped her. But she didn't intend to die without answers. "Tell me about Brittany. She was the first girl you kidnapped, right?"

A far away gleam flickered in his eyes. "She was. I saw her with her friends on the trail and I knew immediately she was the one."

"The one?" she scoffed.

He snarled in her face. "Yes, the *one*. She was so sweet and beautiful and when she looked at me, I knew she felt the connection, too."

His voice sounded childlike and grated on her like nails on a chalkboard. But now she had him talking, she had to keep it up. Stall. Give Derrick time to find them. "If she liked you, why didn't you just talk to her? Why did you have to take her against her will?"

He waved the knife in front of her face again. "Because she tried to run." His eyes flickered with a wild, crazed looking. "At first I thought it was a game. So I chased her just like I did when I saw the perfect doe in the woods."

"She was a person, not an animal," Ellie said. "And she had family. Family who loved her and missed her and were sick with worry when she disappeared."

Rage sharpened his voice. "It was time for her to have her own family." He pounded his chest with his fist. "Time for us to be together and make a life together."

Ellie's breathing stuttered in her chest as she struggled to understand the workings of his mind. Doing so might enable her to talk him down. "You were what, eighteen at the time?"

He took a minute to answer, as if he had to think about it. "Nineteen," he said, his voice low, eyes glazed, as if lost in the memory.

"Old enough to know the difference between right and wrong," Ellie said.

The floor creaked as his boots moved across it. Like an animal, the crazy man was circling his prey. "And it *was* right," he stammered. "We were right for each other." He paced by Lola, barely giving her body a glance as he patted one of the dead deer's flanks. "Eventually she would have loved me, just the way Mama loved Daddy."

A shiver rippled through her. He was clearly delusional. She reminded herself that his role model was a man who'd abducted his mother, that he'd been taught to be afraid of the world and not to trust. But that didn't excuse his behavior.

"Your mother didn't love him," Ellie finally said. "Your father kidnapped her and forced her into seclusion so no one could find her."

He shook his head in denial, ruddy face reddening. "No, she *loved* him. She stayed with us all the time and never left the bunker."

"Because he didn't allow her to leave," Ellie said, a picture forming in her mind. "Did he chain her inside to keep her from leaving? Is that the reason you chained Brittany and Nadine and the others? To keep them your prisoner?"

He spat his next words. "She wasn't a prisoner. He chained her to keep her safe. From wandering off and getting hurt." The knife came within an inch of her cheek as he swung it down. "Don't you understand? We *had* to live in that bunker. The world was going mad. The government was out to get people, they were tapping into our minds and trying to control us."

"Your father brainwashed you and your mother to keep you under his thumb," Ellie said. "He chained your mother so she couldn't escape. Just like Brittany tried to escape you."

He shook his head back and forth in denial. "No, no, no... that's not how it happened—"

Ellie cut him off. "That's why you killed her, isn't it?"

Fury hardened his voice as he paced and ranted, "I didn't kill her! I loved her. But when I was out hunting for dinner, cause that's what a man does, he provides food for his family, Brittany tried to get away." He shoved one of the deer and sent it swinging back and forth, the metal hooks screeching.

"It was *her* fault she died," he bellowed. "She was going to help Brittany get away," he shouted. "So, I put Brittany in the cooler like Mama did me when I was bad. I just wanted to teach her a lesson." He dropped to his knees, sobbing. "After I talked some sense into Mama, I... was going to get her out so we could be together."

The picture in Ellie's mind sickened her. She stole a look at Cord, praying he'd come to, that he was still alive. Lola hadn't moved, and she didn't think she was breathing.

But she'd gotten this far and wanted answers. "Then what happened?"

Sweat dripped down his face. "Mama and I fought, and she fell down. Then I pulled Brittany out of the cooler, but... b-but she was dead."

Ellie closed her eyes, tormented by the image of Brittany being closed in that cooler alive. Terrified and screaming for help, losing hope with every second that passed.

"Brittany had a heart condition," she said, choking out the words. "She died of heart failure and hypothermia because you locked her in that cooler."

"I didn't mean to hurt her," he cried. "I didn't... She was supposed to be with me forever..."

"But you killed her." And once she'd died, he'd had to replace her.

Derrick raced back to the station, his anxiety mounting. The fact that he hadn't heard from Ellie was not a good sign. He called her number again and again, but the voicemail picked up each time. *Dammit.*

He tried Cord's number next and got the same results.

He rubbed a clammy hand on his chin. They were probably on the trail where cell service was spotty, but if they'd found the unsub, they could be in trouble. He hurried to Captain Hale's office and knocked, then poked his head in. The man was on the phone but ended the call quickly.

"Have you seen or heard from Ellie?" Derrick asked.

Ellie's boss shook his head. "I thought she was with you."

Derrick filled him in on their plan to divide up and told him what he'd learned from the food truck owner. He'd tried to draw a map to the location of the hut, but it was crude and he couldn't make heads or tails out of it. "She took Cord to look for another place where the Hunter might be holed up."

Captain Hale gestured to his phone. "I'll see if the sheriff's heard from her."

Derrick's jaw tightened. Waters would probably be the last person she'd call. "I'm going to trace her phone and call the ranger station. Maybe someone there has heard from them."

The captain muttered agreement, then gestured to his phone and Derrick left his office. But his gut was churning with a bad feeling as he rushed to Ellie's office and arranged the trace. Perspiration beaded the back of his neck as he called the ranger station and explained he was looking for Cord and Ellie.

"The last time he checked in he told us he was tracking a location near Wild Hog Holler," the ranger said.

"Is there another ranger who can guide me there?"

"Of course. Milo knows that area almost as well as McClain. I'll text you where to meet him."

Derrick hurried out to his car. He'd come to Crooked Creek because of the governor's daughter. He wouldn't leave until he stopped the man who'd killed her and the others.

He sure as hell didn't intend to lose Ellie to him.

Ellie bit her lip to keep from screaming as he bellowed and made slashes in the air with the knife, stalking from the room to the back.

As loud as she dared, she hissed Cord's name again. "Cord, please... you have to be alive."

But his eyes remained closed, his body limp, blood spattered on the plastic beneath him. Too much blood. She was running out of time. She wrestled with the ties, swinging her body to release the hook from the ceiling. Her arms throbbed and her hands were going numb, but the metal hook refused to give way. Her legs felt weak with terror.

What was he doing back there? She heard footsteps. He was muttering and howling in rage. Barely a sliver of light seeped through the cracks in the hut, but she felt the wind rattling the wood walls and heard a rat skitter across the floor scrambling into a hole in the corner. She shuddered as the dark dank walls closed around her.

If only she could get down, reach her phone. Let Derrick know where they were.

Footsteps pounded again. His boots shuffling. A crashing sound echoed as if he'd knocked something over or had thrown something. She held her breath, praying he'd leave for a while. That would give her time to free herself.

Closing her eyes, she willed herself to be strong. Maybe she could convince him to cut her loose...

The door squeaked open. A streak of light illuminated his big body. The sound of plastic rustling echoed from the door, then she watched in sheer terror as he dragged it across the room and spread it beneath her.

Oh, god...

"Tell me more about your mother," Ellie said.

"You sure as hell ask a lot of questions," he growled as he stretched the plastic on the floor beneath her. "Why you wanna know? It's not like you're gonna leave here and go on the news again and talk about me like you did before."

"I'm just curious if she was good to you," Ellie said, searching for a connection to get into his head. "See, my real mother is in a hospital and my adopted one lied to me. Did your mother ever tell you how she came to live with your father?"

He shot her a look of rage, nostrils flaring. "No, she didn't talk much. Daddy liked it that way."

She just bet he did. "That night with Brittany. Did she tell you the truth then? That your father took her when she was fourteen and held her hostage?"

"Shut up," he bellowed.

"You were angry with her because she was going to help Brittany leave, weren't you?" she pushed.

"I loved her and Mama," he shouted. "But Brittany was mine, and... and I got so mad..."

"You got so mad you stabbed her," Ellie said, realizing she'd been mistaken about his father killing his mother.

"Mama tried to reach the ax, then said awful things about my daddy and I raised the knife. I had to shut her up, so yeah, I stabbed her over and over and over." His voice choked, and he kicked at the floor, his arm mimicking the stabbing motion as if he was reliving the moment.

Then he went still and looked at her again. "That was the first time I took a life," he said with a sinister smile. "I'd killed deer and rabbit and squirrel and hog, but watching her eyes widen in shock, watching the blood flow from her..." Metal jangled as he set a folded cloth on the floor and opened it. A hunting knife, carving knife and a small pocketknife lay in the center, gleaming in the darkness.

Ellie gasped for a breath, trying to control her rising terror. "I understand why you killed your mother," she said. "But you don't have to kill me. The police, the FBI, they're looking for me," she whispered.

His chest rose and fell with his erratic breathing as he picked up the hunting knife and gripped it in his beefy hand. He seemed lost in the memory again, in the thrill of the kill. Then he came at her with the knife. "You're one of the bad people Daddy told me about. One of the heartless bitches. Your soul belongs to the devil."

He placed the tip of the knife at the top of her shirt and popped a button off.

Summoning all her energy, she swung her body backward, raised her legs and kicked him in the chest, knocking him as hard as she could. He bellowed, lost his balance and hit the floor.

She braced herself to fight again, but he pushed himself up, stalked over to Cord and put the knife to his neck.

"He's still breathing, you know. Fight me again and I'll gut him right in front of you."

ONE HUNDRED TWENTY-FOUR

"No!" Ellie cried. "Don't hurt him. Untie me and I'll go with you and do anything you want."

He went still, his eyes glittering with distrust as he studied her. A growl erupted from deep in his throat as he raked his gaze up and down her body. Then he slowly stepped away from Cord. Standing in front of her, his breath brushed her face. He leaned toward her and pinned her with the most evil look she'd ever seen in anyone's eyes.

"I'm blond just like the girls you like," she said, her throat thick with emotions. "You kept the others so you wouldn't be alone. If you keep me with you, I can learn to love you like your mama learned to love your daddy."

A smile slowly curved his mouth as if he was considering her offer. His rage made sense now. Once he tasted the euphoria of the kill, he couldn't stop himself. Just like he wouldn't be able to stop himself now.

But she could at least stall.

Then he lifted the knife, ripped her shirt open with it, exposing her bra. His dark chuckle made her stomach churn as he traced the knife over her chest in a heart shaped pattern.

"Untie me and let me show you how a woman can love a man," she murmured.

She sucked in a breath as his look turned as feral as a wild animal. Then he dug the tip of the knife into her chest and made a slash, drawing blood. A sharp pain ripped through her, but she bit her lip to keep from crying out.

"Please cut me down," she whispered.

"Oh, I'm going to cut you all right." He grinned then made another slash and another. Blood dripped down her chest as he carved her skin. A sob caught in her throat, tears blurring her eyes as she fought a scream.

He dug deeper, angling the knife to cause the most pain, and she bit her tongue. Then, chuckling, he lifted the blade and wiped her blood off with his finger, smearing it across her cheek.

She cried out, then spit in his face. A laugh boomed from him, and he pierced her skin again, drawing out the agony. She gritted her teeth as he continued, sucking in a breath to keep from crying. When he finally completed his handiwork, she looked down and realized he'd carved a word into her body. She could just make it out: *Blade*. He hadn't done that with the other victims.

"Why Blade?" Ellie asked, gasping to keep from sobbing.

"That's what Daddy called me, cause I was so handy with the knife." A muscle ticked in his jaw. "Now you'll never forget me."

A noise sounded, and a glance sideways revealed that Cord was opening his eyes. He groaned and wrestled with his ties, and her attacker looked over at him.

"She's mine now," he told Cord then gestured to Lola. "Both of them are."

Then he brought the knife up and angled it over Ellie's stomach.

"No!" Cord shouted. "Don't hurt her!"

Ellie threw her body back again, lifted her legs and kicked Blade as hard as she could. He came at her, and she kicked again, hoping Cord could somehow get free and help her. The man shoved her body, and blood dripped onto the floor as she slammed into one of the animal carcasses.

ONE HUNDRED TWENTY-FIVE

"Leave her alone!" Cord shouted. He looked over and saw Lola, and terror seized him. She wasn't moving. Her eyes were closed. She was so pale.

The killer jerked around towards him. "I'm saving you for last so you can enjoy the show." He laughed. "You just might learn to like watching them suffer."

Cord's body churned with fury. The two women he cared most about were in this room, both tortured by this evil bastard. He twisted his wrists, then fisted his hands and jerked as hard as he could. The ropes cut into his skin, and he did it again, using all his force, but still they didn't break.

Ellie was trying to wrestle the ropes free, her body swinging back and forth, the chain creaking.

"You won't get away!" Ellie hissed, her face wracked with pain as the psycho lunged at her and slashed her arm with the knife. She screamed, and Cord threw his body back then used all his force to jerk the metal hook and yank it from the ceiling.

But it refused to loosen. He tried again and again while the killer toyed with Ellie, taunting her. The son of a bitch took the end of her hair and cut a strand of it with his knife, then stuck it in his pocket as if he wanted to remember her by it.

Cord saw red. He hated the man with every fiber of his being.

Roaring in fury, he swung his feet up to the ceiling and kicked at the thin wood, cracking plaster and sending it raining down.

He lunged at Ellie again, and Ellie wrapped her legs around his neck and head, squeezing him into a chokehold.

Cord roared again, every muscle in his body screaming at her to fight, fight, fight.

ONE HUNDRED TWENTY-SIX

Derrick met Milo at the approach trail, his gut instinct urging him to hurry.

Images of all those women's stab wounds, of their bodies piled and frozen together, haunted him as Milo led him onto the trail.

"Cord isn't answering his radio," Milo said as they hiked through the massive trees and briar patches. "That's not like him."

"It isn't like Detective Reeves not to pick up either." The bad feeling he had intensified. The creek gurgled in the night, the night sounds of the forest cutting into the tense silence. He heard wild pigs rutting and snorting close by and hoped they didn't run upon them.

He was so damn scared he'd find Ellie dead that his heartbeat roared in his ears, and he was shaking as they climbed a grassy bald. With the ground slick, they carefully maneuvered along the sharp ridges, followed the creek past Wild Hog Holler, then Milo motioned east.

The seconds turned into minutes then an hour, every moment that passed another one that Ellie might be one step closer to death. Derrick could hardly bear it. Darkness bathed the woods, their flashlights illuminating the path as Milo whacked through weeds. Finally, Milo gestured ahead, and Derrick spotted a small hut with a dim light burning inside.

He flipped off his flashlight, and Milo followed his cue, then they crept along the bushes until they reached the hut.

"Stay outside," he mouthed. "If you hear gunshots, call it in."

Milo gave a nod of understanding and Derrick inched up to the stoop.

He'd reached the door when he heard a scream. *Ellie.*

Clenching his gun in a white-knuckled grip, he pushed open the door and scanned the front room. A table sat inside, but there was nobody there. Crossing the space, he found a second door and eased through it, then heard a man's strangled cry and a banging sound.

Adrenaline spiked his blood, and he yanked open the door and looked into the cooler room. Animals strung up. Lola. Cord tied and shoving his feet against the ceiling.

Beyond them Ellie was bleeding, the Hunter wrestling with her, stabbing at her thigh as she tried to choke him with her legs. The man was flailing wildly, gasping for her to let him go.

Derrick rushed forward, gun drawn, and raised it, aiming it at the man as he crossed the room. Ellie had him gripped with her thighs, her eyes crazed-looking, blood spatter on the floor beneath them.

"Ellie, let him go," he said as he approached. "I've got him."

But she was lost in the throes of the fight and didn't seem to hear him. He inched closer, gun aimed as he continued to talk to her. "Ellie, let's take him in. Make him face the families he hurt."

Finally, she registered that he was there and looked down at him. Tears streaked her cheek mingling with the blood smearing her skin. Cold fury engulfed him.

Her choppy breathing shuddered in the air as she slowly eased her grip. The unsub staggered, gasping, and Derrick aimed the gun at his head.

"Put the knife down or I'll blow your head off."

But the man came at him. Derrick fired a round, hitting him in the stomach. The bastard's body bounced backward so hard he collapsed in the blood on the floor.

Ellie's blood.

Derrick rushed to cuff him, but he recovered and tried to kick the gun from his hand.

Derrick dodged the blow, then the man slashed at him with the knife again while grabbing the wall to stand up. He was shaky and bleeding though, and Derrick took advantage, flung his hand up and sent the knife flying from his hand. He dove for it, but Derrick slammed the butt of his Glock against the son of a bitch's head, and he fell forward. Derrick wasted no time in handcuffing his arms behind his back.

When he turned, Cord kicked the ceiling again until the metal hook gave away and he crashed to the floor.

"Get Lola," Derrick shouted to Cord. "I'll get Ellie."

Ellie heaved for a breath, her face pale as he ran to her and cut her down. Cord rushed to Lola, pulled her down and carried her from the room. Ellie slumped onto Derrick, her blood soaking his shirt as he ran outside.

Milo raced to them. "Medics and backup on the way," he called, then hurried to help Cord and Lola.

Derrick lowered Ellie to the ground, jerked his coat off and covered her with it. He ripped the sleeves of his shirt off, folded them, then lifted the jacket and pressed the makeshift blood stoppers to her wounds.

The sight of the man's carving on her chest tore him in knots. He wanted to go back inside and kill the monster.

She opened her eyes and looked up at him weakly. He knew what she was thinking and said, "Cord has her."

"Is she alive?"

"I don't know yet," he murmured as he glanced at Cord, who was already performing CPR on the pale, limp woman.

Hours later, Derrick paced the hospital waiting room, worried about Ellie, Lola and Cord. The aftermath had been hectic but disciplined. It had taken a while for the medics to get to the scene. The ERT team had arrived soon afterwards, and Milo had stayed behind to lead them back when they finished.

Derrick hadn't wanted to leave Ellie. But the medics assured him she'd survive, so he'd ridden with the unsub in the ambulance to make certain he didn't escape.

That monster was going to pay for the rest of his life.

Sheriff Waters had shown up at the hospital to watch the prisoner, and he and the jerk had had words. Derrick warned him if the man escaped, he'd have his badge and see that he never worked in law enforcement again. Bryce had done nothing to help find the killer and had undermined Ellie at every turn. Now she was desperately hurt.

Derrick's admiration for Cord was rising. The stab wound to his back wasn't serious and he'd been stitched up. He was tough, not the kind of man who complained, and his only concern was the women.

The medics had finally detected that she had a slight pulse. Derrick was amazed that she was alive. But she wasn't out of the woods yet. Although it seemed the cold temperature in the cooler might have actually saved her.

Cord had parked himself by her bed to watch over her.

The doctor appeared in the waiting room and Derrick stood and hurried to him. "How's Ellie?"

"Bruised, sore, and she has stiches in her thigh and arm," the doctor replied. "She'll need plastic surgery for the carving on the chest. Other wounds are superficial. But she's dehydrated and sedated and needs rest."

"I understand. Can I see her now?"

"Yes, but she's sleeping so I wouldn't disturb her."

"I won't."

He slipped into her room and approached the bed, his heart in his throat. He should have gone with her instead of sending her there with Cord. It was his job, not the ranger's, to track down the most wanted.

Ellie looked ghostly white as he brushed her hair from her face. Gently he took her hand and pressed it to his cheek. "I'm sorry, Ellie. I let you down. I should have been there for you."

"Just get him," she murmured, her eye lids fluttering. "He calls himself Blade."

Blade? God, the sicko had carved his name into Ellie's chest. "He's in custody now. I promise he won't get away." He kissed her hand then stroked her cheek until she settled back into sleep.

He pulled up a chair and sat watching her for an hour or longer, but as time ticked by, some innate sense in his gut urged him to go check on the prisoner.

ONE HUNDRED TWENTY-EIGHT

The darkness in Cord took root as rage festered inside him. The sight of Lola struggling for her life made him want to kill the maniac who'd hurt her. If only he'd agreed to go to her house with her, she wouldn't have left in a rush. She wouldn't have been abducted.

She wouldn't be lying here in a hospital bed fighting for her life.

Dammit... he lowered his head and kissed her hand, wishing he was a better man. Wishing he'd loved her the way she wanted. Wishing if he prayed the big man upstairs would listen.

But why would he listen to him after the things he'd done?

If he cared, he wouldn't have let Ellie be carved up by that sadistic maniac.

And Lola... she'd been nothing but good to him. She hadn't deserved what this sicko had done to her.

His jaw ached from clenching it and his hands itched to get revenge. Too wired and infuriated to sleep, he kissed Lola's cheek then ducked from her hospital room and made his way to find the Hunter.

ONE HUNDRED TWENTY-NINE

Derrick stepped out to call the sheriff and make certain the prisoner was still guarded. But Waters didn't answer.

Irritated, he went back in and whispered to Ellie that he'd be back, then left the room and took the elevator to the wing where the man was being held. He still didn't have an official ID for him —just the name Blade.

The night shift was working, most of the rooms dark as patients were sleeping, and there was an eerie quietness and odor of sickness permeating the halls that set him on edge.

Instead of visitors and staff bustling around, nurses gathered at their stations and were conducting routine vital checks.

He darted down the hall towards the room where the unsub had been taken, virtually unseen, and saw the chair outside the room where he'd expected to find the sheriff. But the chair was empty.

Dammit, where is Waters?

Body wound tight, he glanced up and down the hallway, then checked the waiting room and coffee machine as he passed, but no sheriff. His footsteps echoed in the hall as he picked up his pace, and when he reached the Hunter's room, he peeked through the crack of the closed door, expecting Bryce to have moved inside to stand watch.

Instead of Bryce, Cord stood by the bed, his body rigid, the tube to the man's ventilator in his hand.

Derrick froze, heart hammering. Was Cord about to pull the plug?

Maybe. He could see the need for vengeance in the man's rigid posture. Felt the tension radiating from him. The same thirst for revenge Derrick shared.

Cord had feelings for Ellie. They had a past. And he seemed to be involved with Lola.

Watching the two women he cared about being tortured and nearly murdered would have done things to the man's mind. Any man's.

It sure as hell had screwed with his.

He couldn't forget how Cord had grown up either. Abused and alone, raised by a psycho who played with dead bodies.

Cold sweat trickled down Derrick's back, and for a moment, he took a step back and gripped the door jamb, debating on whether to walk away. To turn a blind eye and ignore what was happening. He wouldn't mind seeing the man dead either.

He breathed in and out, and rubbed his head in his hands. His mother's loving face taunted him. His little sister Kim's.

Ellie. She'd been through so much. Yet she still kept fighting for justice.

Death would be too easy for that rotten to the core sicko. He deserved to face his victims' families and rot in prison.

Squaring his shoulders, he pushed through the door, watching Cord as he hesitated. Cord turned, the tube in his hand, a vein pulsing in his jaw. Derrick recognized the hatred in Cord's eyes— he felt the same fury. But he'd always stayed on the right side of law.

He shook his head. Mouthed the word *no.*

Cord seemed to shake with emotion, and he didn't move for a long tension-filled moment.

"Go back to Lola. Or... Ellie," Derrick said quietly. "Wherever you think you need to be."

Indecision streaked Cord's eyes for another heartbeat, then he finally dropped the tube and left the room.

Derrick sank into the seat by the prisoner's bed, watching his chest rise and fall. When his hands had stopped shaking, he texted the sheriff and asked him where the hell he was. Then he phoned Deputy Eastwood and asked her to come and guard the killer.

Shondra showed up twenty minutes later and after peeking in on Ellie, eagerly took over. Derrick knew her concern for Ellie and Lola and her need for justice was as strong as Ellie's. "I swear this monster won't get away," she promised. "He needs to suffer for what he's done."

Derrick nodded and left her with the unconscious Hunter. As he headed down the hall to Ellie's room he ran into Bryce. Derrick smelled alcohol on his breath.

It was such a shitfest that he had been elected sheriff.

"I thought you were guarding the prisoner," Derrick said.

"Had to go to the john." Waters looked away.

Derrick shot him a look of disgust. "Go home and sober up. Deputy Eastwood is taking over."

"What the hell?" Waters snarled.

"You heard me," Derrick hissed.

Bryce glared at him, nostrils flaring, but he spun around and strode down the hall, cursing as he went.

ONE HUNDRED THIRTY

Ellie stirred awake. She was sore and hurting all over. The damn drugs were making her dizzy and the drone of the hospital machines was driving her almost as crazy as the memories of what had happened. It was like a horror movie she couldn't stop watching.

Footsteps sounded, and she glanced at the door, ready to run, although pain ricocheted through her abdomen with every movement.

Cord stood in the doorway, looking tortured, his brown eyes intense. She tried to put on a brave smile but didn't know if she'd succeeded. A second later, he walked over to her bed, stopped and looked down at her.

"How do you feel?" he asked gruffly.

She licked her dry lips and clenched the sheet. Thankfully the hospital staff had washed the blood from her hands. "Like I was in a fight," she admitted. "But I'm okay."

He reached down and squeezed her hand, then opened his mouth to speak, but closed it as if he didn't know what to say.

"How do you feel? You were bleeding," she said, remembering the way he'd been strung up and unconscious.

"I'm fine. Got a few stitches but it'll heal." He made a low sound in his throat. "I'm more worried about you. And Lola."

"How is she?"

"I'm going there next," he said. "El... I'm sorry."

She squeezed his hand in return. "You were there for both of us. You helped save her."

He lingered another minute as if he was lost, and she sighed. "Go to her, Cord. She needs you."

"I know," he said, his voice cracking.

She heard a sound from the doorway and saw Derrick there. The men exchanged a silent look, then Cord's boots clicked on the floor as he strode to the door.

"Take care of Ellie," he said quietly.

Derrick gave a nod. Then Cord closed the door behind him.

ONE HUNDRED THIRTY-ONE
BLUFF COUNTY MEDICAL EXAMINER'S OFFICE

Five Days Later

Five days later, Ellie was struggling to recover but at least she was out of the hospital. Shondra had brought ice cream and spent the night with her the night she'd been released, hovering over her like a mother hen.

Derrick had updated the governor and Angelica and after the press revealed that the killer had been caught, he'd attended Ginger's funeral. He'd also visited Ellie at the hospital every day, smothering her with his attention. Cord was doing the same with Lola.

The two of them clearly needed to let these men know they were survivors.

At least she hoped Lola was. They'd managed to see each other once they were allowed out of their beds, and Lola had been quiet and distant. Ellie had no idea what was going on in her head.

The ERT had found plenty of forensics at the Hunter's shack to put him away for life. His DNA matched the DNA in the bunker, and confirmed he was Millie's son.

They had also discovered human bones in another cooler at the shack.

Laney met them in her office with the autopsy report on the bones, her expression grim. "How are you holding up, Ellie?"

"Good," Ellie lied. She was sore as hell and haunted by that blasted carving. But she had an appointment with a plastic surgeon to have it repaired and removed. "What do you have?"

"A few things. I've been able to confirm all the dismembered body parts belonged to Cady North."

Another wave of sorrow washed over Ellie at the thought of having to explain the body's condition to the family.

"He became more and more vile toward the end."

"When you hear the rest of the report, you'll see he always had a cruel streak," Laney said. "The bones found at that shack belong to a male, a man named Wayne Dunsmore. His DNA is a familial match to the Hunter's."

"So he was the killer's father," Ellie said. "He attacked me before I got the chance to ask him what happened to him."

"Chances are he killed him, too," Derrick said.

"I'm not so sure about that," Ellie said. "He looked up to him. He was his role model and imitated his behavior by taking girls to be his mate."

"There's more," Laney said. "The ERT found bones of another man there. I identified him as James Dunce."

Ellie absentmindedly rubbed her thigh. "That's the reason we couldn't find him. Maybe he somehow discovered that our unsub killed Nadine. What was COD?"

Laney gestured toward the autopsy report. "He was slaughtered and eviscerated like an animal."

Ellie stood with a shudder as the image played through her mind. "I can't stand to have loose ends. I'm going to confront his ass and make him tell me what happened with his father and Dunce."

Ellie heard a commotion outside, then through the window of her office saw Bryce storming toward them.

Temper flaring, she stepped outside the office. He pierced her with an angry look and strode toward her. "We need to talk. Alone."

Ellie was so not in the mood for his attitude today. "What's this about?" she asked quietly.

He shoved a file toward her. "You knew about this and didn't tell me. What kind of damn game are you playing?"

Confused by his reaction, Ellie frowned. "What are you talking about?"

"Mandy." Accusations glittered in his eyes. "You knew she was my daughter, and you didn't tell me. I knew you hated me but not enough to keep something like that from me."

For a moment Ellie reeled from the news. Derrick appeared beside her, his stance intimidating. "Do not make one move toward her."

She raised a warning hand. "I can handle this, Derrick."

His dark gaze met hers, anger simmering. "I mean it, Waters. Touch her and I'll handcuff your ass. I've already filed a complaint against you for leaving the unsub unguarded at the hospital."

"The man was unconscious and clearly not going anywhere," Bryce snarled.

"Let me deal with him," Ellie told Derrick. A vein throbbed in his neck, but he gave a little nod and stepped back into Laney's office.

Ellie lowered her voice. "Talk to me, Bryce."

"Mandy," he hissed. "She and Vanessa and Trudy kept it from me all these years."

Hurt underscored the anger in his tone and she softened. "Listen to me, Bryce. I did not know that you were Mandy's father. Vanessa never told me, and Trudy said she didn't know."

He stared at her for a long minute, the tension rippling between them as thick as fog after a summer storm. His breath puffed out, then he cleared his throat. "You really didn't know?"

She shook her head. "I really didn't. Are you sure it's true?"

His rigid posture deflated. "Yes. When you saw me and Trudy arguing that day, she was asking about my relationship with Vanessa. I didn't know what that had to do with anything, and I told her that."

Ellie tried to follow along. "Then what happened?"

"Apparently Mandy found her mother's diary, where she talked about me. It was the summer after high school."

The summer Ellie had left.

"You two were together?"

"Briefly." He shoved his hands through his hair. "But after me, she dated someone else and when I heard she was pregnant, I figured it was his." His voice thickened. "And she never said anything."

Ellie's pulse quickened.

"But after Trudy talked to me and then you mentioned Mandy asked you about her father, I started thinking." He ran a hand over his jaw, his beard stubble bristling. "I had to know... So I asked Trudy for Mandy's toothbrush, and had my DNA run for a paternity test."

Ellie folded her arms. Now she understood why Bryce had been so agitated and distracted during the investigation.

"Mandy knows?"

He shook his head. "Not yet."

Lifting her chin, Ellie gave him a challenging look. "The question is, now that you know, what are you going to do about it?"

Ellie and Derrick wanted answers and the Hunter was the only one who could give them the truth. Soon they could have him transported to a maximum-security prison where he'd spend the rest of his sorry life, but for now he was being held in the county jail.

They were escorted through security to a visiting room for interrogation purposes. A guard went to retrieve the prisoner, and seconds later, Blade shuffled in, looking angry and sinister. The guard secured the man's shackles and cuffs to bolts to keep him from escaping, then stepped from the room.

The Hunter ignored Derrick and looked at Ellie, then his lips curled into a menacing smile. "I knew you couldn't stay away from me."

Instinctively, Ellie's finger touched her chest where he'd engraved his name. She jerked it away when a laugh rumbled from him.

Damn him.

"Told you you'd never forget me," he murmured.

Ellie felt Derrick tense beside her.

"The plastic surgeon will take care of that," she said, although she didn't need it as a reminder. "Tell me your real name."

His eyes narrowed to slits. "Daddy called me Blade."

"Your *real* name," Ellie said sharply.

He cut his eyes sideways. "Luther." He lifted his chin, a proud gleam in his eyes. "It means 'army of people'. Cause Daddy was always ready for us to fight to survive if we had to."

Like father, like son. "Our people found some interesting things at your hut."

He went still, big body rigid.

"See, all along we'd been looking for this man named James Dunce," Ellie continued. "We knew he was infatuated with Nadine Houser."

Luther's eyes gleamed with a sickening kind of pleasure as if he was reliving his time with Nadine in his twisted mind.

Ellie removed a photo of the bones the forensic team had discovered at his hut and laid it on the table.

A tiny smile sparked in his eyes. Derrick shifted beside her, his posture braced in case Luther turned violent.

"You thought we wouldn't find them, but our people were thorough." She tapped the first photograph. "We know these bones belong to James Dunce. Now tell me about him."

He worked his mouth from side to side. "That prick was obsessed with Nadine. It was his fault he died."

"Why do you say that?" Ellie asked.

"He was following her, but I wanted her, and I waited outside for her. But the stupid jerk was hanging around in his car and he had the nerve to follow me," he screeched. "I *had* to kill him."

"You didn't just kill him," Ellie said, her voice laced with disgust. "You eviscerated him like he was an animal."

He gave a little shrug, as if he was proud of his handiwork. Derrick remained silent, but she sensed he was ready to jump the guy at any minute.

She crossed her arms, feeling dirty all over. Keeping a cool face, she laid the second picture on the table, this one just as gruesome as the first. You could see striations on the bones where the limbs had been severed. "You acted like you loved your daddy. But these bones belong to your father."

Shock and pain flared on Luther's face, and his breathing turned choppy. "I did love him," he bellowed. "I did."

Ellie pinned him with a sharp look. "Then why did you chop him into pieces?"

ONE HUNDRED THIRTY-THREE

Luther stared at Ellie Reeves, the bitterness and pain eating at him as memories flooded his mind. That night... his father... his mother...

He angled his head toward the fed... The man just kept staring at him, letting the bitch do all the talking. "What kind of man are you? You let the woman talk to me like that."

The fed's eyes were black. Flat. Emotionless. Maybe he was a psychopath himself.

"Tell us what happened," the bitch said. "How you hacked him into pieces."

He had pushed the truth so far back in his mind, but now it was all coming back to him in horrible flashes.

"You cut off his hands," Ellie said. "With the same ax you chopped your wood for the fire."

He shook his head, rolling his neck from side to side to blot out the images.

"You cut off his hands and feet, his arms and legs, and stuffed him in something and carried him to the shack—"

"I didn't do that. I would never hurt Daddy!" He tried to get up and come after her, but the chains clanked and held him in place just like he'd chained his victims.

"I didn't kill him," he muttered again. "*She* did that."

The fed stood, arms folded, a warning in his eyes. The detective jerked her head back, and he smiled at the fear on her face. But when she spoke, her voice was calm, matter of fact, as if she knew what had happened already and was just baiting him. "*She?* You mean your mother killed your father?"

"Yes, she did it," he spat. "I left Brittany there with her while I went hunting, and when I got back, I found her standing over Daddy with the ax. Blood was everywhere and she was screaming and ranting and saying she was going to take Brittany and leave us there." He heaved a breath. "Can you believe that?" he shouted. "She was my mother, and she murdered my father and was going to take my girl away from me."

"So you flew into a rage and stabbed her," the cop said.

"I had to stop her," he said. "With Daddy gone, Brittany was all I had left. I couldn't let her take her away." The memory of his mother's screams and his father's severed bloody hands tormented him as if it was just yesterday. The cop's face blurred and he closed his eyes—and suddenly it was his mother's face and her voice.

"I won't let you do to that girl what he did to me," she cried. "He's a monster and he's turned you into one, too."

He raised his hands and stabbed at her, striking her chest and driving the knife into her cold heart. He wanted to rip it out with his bare hands just the way she'd ripped his out by killing his father.

The blood flew everywhere, spattering the floor and walls, his clothes, his hands, his face. He tasted it and wiped it from his eyes and jabbed the knife in again and again until she fell limp in the blood, her mouth parted in a silent scream, her eyes open in horror.

"You murdered her in cold blood and now you're going to pay for all of it," the detective said.

When he opened his eyes, he stared at the white walls. He could hear the clang of metal in the prison, the voices of the men who acted like animals. Smell the rancid odor of the slop they called food and the smell of body wastes and sweat. No more hunting. No more venison stew.

"You can't lock me up forever," he growled as he looked into her eyes. "I'm a man of the woods. It'll kill me."

A smile curved the detective's mouth, then she stood. "Yes, I know. You're finally getting what you deserve. And just like you enjoyed watching those girls suffer, I'm going to enjoy watching you suffer."

ONE HUNDRED THIRTY-FOUR

CROOKED CREEK

The next day, Ellie called Mandy to check in on her, but the girl said she didn't want to talk on the phone. She wanted to see Ellie in person.

Ellie agreed, although she was hesitant. The last thing she wanted was to frighten Mandy by showing up bruised and battered. She'd also held off hoping Bryce would connect with his daughter.

"Can I come in?" Mandy asked as Ellie opened the door.

"Of course. It's good to see you."

Mandy threw her arms around Ellie and hugged her tight. When she pulled away, tears glistened in the young girl's eyes. "I heard what happened. I was so scared you were going to die, too."

Emotions clogged Ellie's throat but she swallowed. "Oh, honey, I'm sorry. I... I'm okay now."

"But you almost got killed like Mama did."

Sympathy filled Ellie and she cradled Mandy's hands between hers and led her to the living room. "But I didn't," she said softly. "I'm here and I'm fine."

Mandy bit her bottom lip then swiped at a tear that escaped. Her breathing echoed with emotions.

"Is that why you wanted to come over?" Ellie asked.

Mandy shrugged. "Yeah. And..."

"And what, honey?" Ellie brushed the girl's hair back from her cheek.

"Sheriff Waters came by," she said, her voice shaky. "He's my father, but he said he didn't know it until now."

Ellie clasped Mandy's hands again. "That's true, Mandy. He came to see me when he found out. He was upset that no one had told him."

"If he'd known, do you think he would have married Mama?" Mandy looked up at her with questioning eyes.

Ellie sighed. "I don't know, honey. I really don't. Maybe though. At least he might have been in your life."

Mandy sniffed. "He says he wants to be now." Her voice cracked. "But I don't know."

Ellie contemplated that. Maybe Bryce would turn himself around.

"What do you think I should do?" Mandy asked softly.

Ellie thought about her own family and how angry and disappointed she'd been with them. Then how she'd felt when she'd almost lost them. They'd smothered her with love the last few days and she'd decided that everyone deserved a second chance.

"I think he must care if he says he wants a chance," she said softly. "I know it won't be easy, but you'll never know unless you try."

Mandy nodded then threw her arms around Ellie again and Ellie hugged her tight. She just prayed that Bryce didn't let the young girl down.

ONE HUNDRED THIRTY-FIVE

Two hours later, Ellie met Angelica at the police station for a press conference. A weariness had settled over her now the adrenaline of the case had dissipated.

Angelica and her cameraman were waiting, along with Shondra and her captain. Even Bryce was there and greeted her with a tentative smile. She'd never understand why he was so difficult to work with, what made him tick, but she now understood why his behavior was so erratic recently.

Suddenly nervous at the thought of facing the camera, she ducked into the restroom and splashed cold water on her face. Knowing she had to face the town sometime, she stared at her reflection. The woman in the mirror looked haunted with the grisly truths she'd seen. Blinking the ugly thoughts away, she patted her face dry, adjusted her ponytail and pinched her cheeks to add some color, then walked back to the briefing room.

Her breath stalled in her chest when she saw Derrick waiting, Governor Weston by his side. Derrick gave her an odd look when she entered, and she sucked in a breath, straightened and walked toward the governor. Angelica offered a tiny smile of encouragement, but Ellie squared her shoulders. She'd take whatever the governor dished out.

Of course, he might want her badge. Maybe that was the

reason Bryce had given her that little smile. Then again, he had Derrick's complaint against him to deal with.

Jaw clenched, she pasted on a professional look and greeted Derrick and the governor.

Derrick was wearing a shirt and tie today with jeans. The governor, in his gray suit, still looked grief-stricken and somber, which made her heart tug.

Angelica started toward her, but the governor waved a hand and Derrick gestured for her to hold off on filming.

"Detective Reeves," the governor began, his voice filled with emotions. "I wanted to talk to you in person and apologize."

Ellie raised a brow, too stunned to disguise her rection. "Excuse me?"

He fiddled with the buttons of his suit jacket. "When I'm wrong, I admit it. And I was wrong about you."

Ellie blinked in surprise. "I'm the one who's sorry, Governor." Her voice warbled. "So sorry we didn't find your daughter in time."

Pain flickered on his face. "I know I blamed you, but I was just terrified and angry that maniac took her from us."

"I understand—"

He cut her off by holding up a hand. "Let me finish, please."

She nodded, her chest aching with guilt and grief.

"I know now how hard you worked to find that man, that you suffered and put yourself through hell to catch him. That he wouldn't have been caught if not for you." His voice trailed off for a second, then he collected himself. "I know he tried to kill you, but you fought for my daughter and all those other poor girls..." He swallowed hard. "You got justice for them and made sure he won't ever take another family's child from them. I want to thank you by honoring you with a badge of courage and bravery for your heroism—"

"No," Ellie said, uneasy with his praise. "I'm no hero, Governor. Just a detective who wants to protect her town."

An awkward second passed as he studied her, then he offered

his hand. "Then I thank you personally. And you have my support whenever you need it."

Ellie's throat thickened with emotion as they shook hands. Then she moved behind the podium and gave the signal to Angelica that she was ready to begin.

ONE HUNDRED THIRTY-SIX

Thirty minutes later, she wrapped up the press conference, with Derrick and the governor both backing her up. The sheriff, Shondra, Captain Hale, Deputy Landrum—the entire team was there, all exhausted but grateful they could finally put this case to rest.

As they dispersed, Derrick lingered, a sheepish look on his handsome face. "I know it's been a long day, but how about dinner?"

Ellie thought about the press conference and how the town would react. "Thank you, but I don't think I'm up for going out. After today, everyone will be watching us."

His expression softened, a hint of some other emotion flashing in his dark eyes. "I was thinking I'd cook for you."

Ellie quirked a brow. "You want to cook for me?"

He shrugged. "I figured if I was going to work with you on a task force, I'd be around a little more. So I rented a place here, a cabin on the river."

Surprise fluttered through her. "You're staying in Crooked Creek?"

"We'll see," he murmured. "So how about dinner tonight? And..." he brushed his fingers down her cheek. "No work talk either. We both need a break."

She sighed, her heart stuttering, then she murmured agreement.

A few minutes later, she drove home to change while he went to the cabin to set things up. As she passed through town, a feeling of hope burst through the dark clouds hovering over her mind.

Halloween had come and gone while she was in the hospital. She hoped the monsters were all gone, too.

The Halloween decorations, ghosts and spooky creatures had all been taken down. The spider webs and owls that had adorned the big tree in the center of town had been removed, and the Porch Sitters had replaced them with prayer cards in preparation for Thanksgiving in a few weeks.

Tradition held that people could take one and pray for whoever had written their personal needs and struggles on the card, or they could add one if they needed prayer. There were also cards of gratitude where folks wrote their thanks and appreciation for the good things in their lives.

She slowed as she passed, then stopped, parked and got out. She walked up to the tree. Blank cards filled a wooden box in front of the massive oak, and she took one out, and pulled a pen from her pocket.

There was so much she was troubled about. The crimes that had preyed on innocent victims of Crooked Creek. The children and women who'd gone to Heaven before their time.

But the snow had melted and the storm clouds had moved on. The air breathed of sunshine and life and the turning of the seasons with the vibrant colors of fall.

She gazed at the stars glittering in the cloudless sky and was thankful that another predator had been stopped and put away for life.

That the residents and children and women in the town could rest now.

At least for tonight.

A LETTER FROM RITA

Thank you so much for coming back to read more about Detective Ellie Reeves! And if you're new to the series, don't worry—each book continues her journey but is a standalone novel so I'm happy you've found her. If you'd like to keep up with all of my latest releases, you can sign up at the following link. Your email address will never be shared, and you can unsubscribe at any time.

www.bookouture.com/rita-herron

Frozen Souls is the fourth installment in the series and challenges Ellie in new ways, both personally and professionally.

Recently, both children and adults faced the challenge of isolation during a pandemic, which led me to contemplate what it would be like if someone was totally isolated from society and raised in fear their entire lives. The killer you met in *Frozen Souls*, while extreme, was one of those. His skewed thinking led him to prey on innocent young women.

I hope you enjoyed Ellie's determination to stop him from his own madness as much as I enjoyed writing her. If you did, I'd appreciate it if you left a review and share your feedback with others.

I love to hear from readers so you can find me on Facebook, my website and Twitter.

Thanks so much for joining me in cheering Ellie Reeves on!

Happy Reading!

Rita

www.ritaherron.com

 facebook.com/ritaherron

twitter.com/ritaherron

ACKNOWLEDGMENTS

Thanks so much to my fabulous editors Christina Demosthenous and Vicky Blunden for their great advice and editing, which helped make this story better. Also, to Fraser Crichton for copy-editing wisdom and catching the blunders with the dreaded timeline.

Much appreciation also goes to Attorney Aaron Rives for always answering my questions about the law.

And thanks to the Bookouture team for another great cover and title. I'm so proud to have Ellie Reeves in your hands!

Printed in Great Britain
by Amazon